The Mating

Nicky Charles

Edited by Jan Gordon
Line edits by Moody Edits

Cover Design by Jazer Designs
Cover images used under license from Shutterstock.com
Paw print and wolf logo Copyright © Doron Goldstein, Designer

ISBN: 978-1-989058-14-5

Acknowledgements

Many thanks to Ermintrude, the original Beta for this tale, and to Jan Gordon who subsequently helped me edit and revise this story. Also, thank you to all of the 'Gutter Girls' who have offered their support and have allowed me to practise my writing skills on them.

The Mating

Lycans were not made to be alone. They require a mate to share their life, to procreate and to build a pack. Mates must be loyal, supportive, understanding and honest, committed to the union that makes them one.

While all matings are a serious matter, that of an Alpha requires extra consideration. The dual role of Alpha and mate are both equally demanding. Too much emphasis on either position can create an imbalance that is detrimental to either the pack or the mated couple. For this reason, an Alpha must choose wisely, factoring in both the needs of the heart and pack, lest the choice cause dissension.

Source: The Book of the Law

Chapter 1

She lay beside him staring blankly at the ceiling. The deed was done. They were mated. It didn't matter that she had no love for him nor he for her. Political alliances were more important than feelings, or so she had been told. That fact was cold comfort right now as her heart broke within her.

Beside her, he stirred and she sensed him rolling over, his amber eyes staring at her. She made no move to look at him and instead tried to steady her breathing. It was no use. As she inhaled, her breath quivered betraying her emotional state. Despite blinking rapidly, a stray tear trailed down her cheek.

The covers rustled beside her and then she felt his finger move across her face catching the droplet. "I'm sorry, Elise." Kane's voice was deep yet gentle.

"It doesn't matter." She answered quietly, still staring at the ceiling. What he was apologizing for she was unsure. The situation was as beyond his control as it was hers. She swallowed hard. "It couldn't be helped."

"No, it couldn't," he agreed, sighing heavily. His arm slipped around her waist and drew her closer. She let her cheek rest against his muscular chest, too spent to protest; the sound of his steady heartbeat was faintly comforting. "I wish I could have given you more time to get to know me first, but the Elders wanted our union sealed immediately."

She nodded, her mind agreeing even though her heart cried in protest. The good of the pack won out over that tender organ; the fact she loved another—Bryan—a moot point.

Closing her eyes, scenes from the past day flashed through her mind...

~~~

She'd just returned from a run with Bryan where they'd frolicked and played in the cool shaded woods that surrounded her home. He'd been her best friend since they were pups and recently the friendship had grown into something more. Bryan had hinted that he would ask her father for permission to become her mate and she'd been thrilled at the idea. Many of her friends were already mated and, as her nineteenth birthday approached, she was becoming restless, eager to experience bonding with another, but her father had held off choosing her a partner. Naively, she'd thought he was waiting for her to find someone who suited her.

Now she acknowledged that was never the case. While her father loved her, he was first and foremost their Alpha and had to put the well-being of the pack ahead of all else. Her older brother and sister had mated with packs to the north and south. With the sea at their back, it was only to the east that an alliance was needed. When Kane became the new Alpha of that territory, the Elders determined that a union between the packs was needed to ensure continued stability.

That day, as she returned laughing at something Bryan had said, Jake, her father's Beta, had greeted her at the door. "Elise, you're needed in the assembly room."

Something in his tone of voice warned her that all was not well. With a wave to her friend, she followed Jake curious as to what could possibly require her presence. The assembly room was used on occasion for general pack meetings, but usually her father and the council of Elders dealt with all important issues.

As she pushed the door open, a cacophony of emotions hit her; excitement, worry, curiosity. She puzzled over the strange mixture of moods while scanning to see who was present. In the far corner, the Elders appeared pleased as they conversed with another group of older persons, all of whom were strangers to her. Her father, near the middle of the room, had a serious expression on his face and was talking to a man who looked to be in his mid-twenties. She hadn't encountered him before so, rather than approaching her father, took some time to study this new arrival.

The man was taller than her father, at least six foot four, and powerfully built. His shoulders were broad, muscles rippling beneath his shirt as he gestured to make some point. Dark hair topped a pleasing face, with sculpted cheeks and a full bottom lip.

Possibly sensing her inspection of him, he glanced towards the door and his amber eyes locked on hers. There was a hard edge about him, a commanding presence that made her feel as if she were pinned in place. Slowly he studied her from head to foot, his gaze lingering on her body, before returning to her face. She felt herself flush under his scrutiny. As he flashed a brief smile at her, she thought she caught a glimpse of softness in his eyes, but it was quickly gone and he returned his attention to her father.

She sulked. For some reason his apparent dismissal of her rankled.

Her father glanced her way, sighed, and ended his discussion with the stranger. He walked towards her with a scowl on his face. "Elise, you've been running again, I see."

Her reflection in a nearby mirror showed her long brown hair was messy and a faint sheen of sweat gave her sun-kissed skin a dewy look. Noting a smudge of dirt on her nose, she scrubbed it off. Turning towards her parent, she gave a sheepish grin aimed at cajoling him out of his mood. "It was too nice a day to stay indoors."

"But what did I tell you? It isn't safe to be out alone in wolf form. It's hunting season and even though our property is posted, the humans don't always heed—"

"I was with Bryan and we didn't go near the edge of the property. We aren't fools, you know."

"Ah...Bryan..." Her father frowned, and then sighed again. "Elise, I have something to tell you. As you might know, the pack to the east has a new Alpha. His name is Kane." He nodded towards the man standing across the room and Elise shot him a glance again before smiling with polite interest at her father's news.

"He's come to meet you?" She wondered why she was being summoned. The politics between the packs had never been of concern to her. Her father didn't involve her in council meetings, yet clearly, she could only assume that the gentlemen in the corner talking to the Elders of her pack must be representatives from the eastern group.

"Yes, Kane is here to meet me...and you."

"Me?" She couldn't contain her surprise and a strange quivering feeling began to develop within her.

"Yes, you. It has been decided by the Elders that with a new Alpha in charge, a fresh alliance should be created. Kane is willing. He will be mated to you and our packs will continue to live in peace."

"Mated? To me?" She knew her mouth was hanging open in shock. Darting a glance across the room, she saw Kane staring at her blandly, his hands behind his back. If her expression offended him, he didn't show it. She looked at her father, blinking to hold back the tears that threatened to fall. "But... What about Bryan?"

"I'm aware you've had your eye on him, but this is for the good of the pack. We need strong alliances so that we can guard against the human threat. And, allied packs allow access between territories and increase the area in which we have to roam." He stopped speaking and placed a comforting hand on her shoulder. "I know this is a surprise, but don't worry. Kane is a good man. He'll make you a fine mate."

Her mouth had suddenly gone dry and she clenched her fists her sides. Was this how her sister had felt when she had found out she'd been betrothed to a male from the north? At the time, Elise had only been twelve and had been more excited about the festivities than concerned for her sister's feelings. Now the shoe was on the other foot and she found the fit to be decidedly uncomfortable.

4

Finding her voice, she began to protest. "But that's the old way of thinking! Alliances aren't needed anymore. We've gone beyond pack wars, and as for the human threat, most don't even know we exist!" In desperation, she began to toss out facts and opinions to counter the decree that had been delivered to her.

"Packs co-exist peacefully because of the long-standing tradition of alliances. Unions between packs join us together and ensure respect of territories." Her father kept his tone even, but she sensed he didn't enjoy having to explain this to her. He was from the old tradition, as were many in her pack, and expected unquestioning obedience. As the youngest in the family, she'd been treated more leniently than the others; less had been expected of her. Now she could hear the implicit lecture: she should have paid more attention to pack politics, taken an interest in what was going on; if she had, she would already know these things.

He continued to speak. "And the human threat is still real. Not so much that they know we exist, but that they continually try to encroach on our territories. We need to be united and stand firm against selling our land to developers."

She opened her mouth to protest again, but her father's stern look had her shutting it, leaving the words unspoken. It was useless to protest. The Elders had decided and the Alpha had concurred with their decision. To go against the edicts of the pack would result in being cast out. She'd lived her whole life in a pack. The concept of being alone was unthinkable, yet the idea of mating with a total stranger was also abhorrent.

"When?" She managed to pronounce one word.

"Tonight. There is no use in waiting. Kane and his council are here. A dinner is being prepared and the rest of the pack is being notified. We'll conduct the ceremony as the moon rises."

Three hours.

Three hours and she would be bonded for life to a man she'd never met before today. She could hardly process the thought. Suddenly she realized that someone was speaking to her. Looking up, she saw Kane had moved forward and was standing beside her father.

"I'm pleased to meet you, Elise." His voice was deep and low, his eyes steady on hers.

Somehow, she managed to croak out a hello. Kane appeared even larger up close and she wished she had more inches to her height. At five foot six inches, she was an average size, but next to the new Alpha, she felt positively petite. Her father nudged her with his elbow and she noticed that Kane had extended his hand towards her. Tentatively, she reached out and took it. The warmth of his skin immediately enveloped her and shot up her arm. Startled, she craned her neck to look up at his face and noted a smile pass over his mouth.

"I think we will suit each other." He nodded to her father and then gave her hand a squeeze. "I'll see you later at the ceremony." Kane looked her up and down again before taking his leave and heading over to where the councils were meeting.

"Elise, I must go. There's other business to attend to today before the ceremony." Her father kissed her on the forehead and gave her a gentle push towards the door, effectively dismissing her. "Go and find Sarah. She's been instructed to help you get ready." Sarah was Jake's wife and in some ways like a surrogate mother to her. Hunters had killed Elise's own mother years ago and her father had never taken another mate.

She considered running away and going into hiding but knew that wasn't possible. There was nowhere to hide that she couldn't be found, short of taking a car and driving off, yet even if she did then what? She had no money to speak of, nowhere to go...

The rest of the day passed in a blur. She tried to tell Sarah of her reservations but was shushed. It was for the good of the pack. Being mated to an Alpha would give her status. He would take good care of her. The well-meant words swirled around her.

She wanted to find Bryan, to cry on his shoulder and feel his arms around her offering comfort one last time, but that too had been denied her. It wouldn't be proper. There was no time. Were these actual reasons or just excuses? Either way, the result was the same. Three hours later, she was seated at a table beside a man she didn't know.

As she looked around, her heart thudding heavily in her chest, she noted that the hall had been decorated with fall flowers and the best china set out. Linen cloths adorned the tables and various dishes of meat and vegetables, rolls and salads appeared. It always amazed her how Sarah could pull a meal together for a small army on a moment's notice.

No doubt, the food was delicious, but she merely moved it about on her plate, unable to manage even a bite. Well wishes from her pack members were given followed by speeches from the Elders, and then the bonding ceremony began. Kane escorted her to the front of the room and words were spoken which she didn't even hear, let alone comprehend. Worst of all were the agonized looks exchanged with Bryan who stood across the room as the final vows were spoken and her wrist was bound with Kane's by a ceremonial leather rope.

Tied together, Kane led her from the hall to one of the guest cabins that were located not far from the main house where the Alpha resided. He hadn't spoken directly to her since their initial meeting and she cast sidelong glances up at him as they walked across the moonlit lawn. Should she say something to break the silence? Her thoughts raced for an appropriate comment, but none came to mind. Banal talk about the weather seemed ridiculous under the current circumstances and she was too nervous to come up with anything else.

It was not in the nature of an Alpha to be unkind to a member of the pack unless they openly flaunted his authority, and she hoped Kane would be considerate of her. If it was Bryan, it would be different. She had feelings for him. The thought of being with Bryan excited her creating a warmth low in her belly, while the idea of being with Kane only made her stomach muscles clench.

The cabin loomed in front of them. Situated at the edge of the forest with trees all around, it gave the impression of seclusion. It was made of logs and had a weathered look from years of exposure to the elements but was still well maintained with a solid stone chimney, shuttered windows, and a small porch. Kane pushed the door open and gestured for her to enter, following close behind since their wrists were still tied. He shut the door and flicked on the lights, illuminating the room that featured a small kitchenette, eating area and a sofa in front of a fireplace. There was a door to the left that led to a bedroom and a small bathroom.

"Well." Kane spoke, causing her to jump. "First order of business would be to remove this, wouldn't you say?" He held up their joined wrists and she nodded in agreement. Pulling a jackknife from his pocket, he cut the rope letting it fall to the ground. Immediately, she pulled her arm away and rubbed her wrist. It wasn't really sore—the tie hadn't been tight—but the leather had still chafed and the enforced proximity had been uncomfortable.

Kane was also rubbing his wrist. "We have a similar reaction to being imprisoned, I see." He nodded towards the action of her hands.

"Yes." She wasn't sure what else to say.

Silence stretched between them.

Kane rubbed his neck and stared around the room. Did he find the situation as unnerving as she did? Had he really wanted to be her mate, or was he turning his back on someone he loved for the good of his pack, as well? Did she dare ask? Before she had time to decide the wisdom of such a question, he addressed her again. "It's getting late. Would you like to use the bathroom first?"

"All right." She could feel his gaze boring into her back as she walked away, and she forced herself to keep her pace at a normal speed despite wanting to run from the room. As she passed through the bedroom, she noted that someone had made up the bed and her nightgown was lying near the foot. Snagging it in her hand, she entered the bathroom and closed the door.

Relief washed over her and she slumped against the panel. For a few minutes, at least, she would have some privacy and be free of Kane's presence. It wasn't that he was displeasing to look at; in other circumstances, she would have admired his physique. And his manner towards her had been polite, if a bit distant, so there was nothing she could complain about in that regard. The problem was that Kane wasn't Bryan.

Her stomach clenched again and once more she thought of escaping, but where? She couldn't survive without a pack. Wolves were social animals. To be an outcast was an unthinkable fate.

Besides, she'd have nowhere to live, no means of support, and then there was always the fear of detection. It hadn't happened in years, but that wasn't to say that if a Lycan became careless someone couldn't put the clues together. Caution was drilled into a Lycan's head from the moment of birth, and all had a fear of being hunted down. No, she couldn't leave.

Staring at her reflection in the mirror, she undid the simple French braid Sarah had fashioned for the ceremony. Her green eyes seemed wider and a deeper shade than normal, contrasting with her unusually pale complexion. Faint lines of tension showed on either side of her mouth and her jaw ached from being tightly clenched. As a matter of fact, her whole person was tense. Hoping a hot shower would help, she turned on the taps, stripped and stepped into the stall.

The pounding water beat down on her body, the white noise and rising steam creating a temporary cocoon. She closed her eyes and forced herself to relax, letting her mind drift back to the afternoon when she and Bryan had been running together.

A smile drifted across her face at the memory. It had been so much fun running like the wind; feeling her muscles stretched to the limit as she sought to out-distance her companion. Bryan had tackled her to the ground and they'd rolled about, nipping at each other before bounding away, only to jump and tumble again. She'd nuzzled him and he'd licked her face, then they'd run back to the pack house transforming into human form just inside the edge of the woods. Her hair had still had grass stuck in it. Bryan had picked it out before resting his hands on her shoulders and hinting at speaking to her father.

It hadn't happened of course and never would. Her youthful hopes and dreams had been dashed, pushed aside by the political planning of Elders. Did they even remember what it was like to be young? To feel the day brighten at the sight of the one you love? To feel your heart race at the sound of that special person's voice and your skin tingle at the softest touch of their hand?

Not likely.

She shivered and realized the water was growing cold. Reaching out, she shut off the faucet with a shaking hand. She'd delayed as long as she could. Kane would be waiting for her.

Donning her nightgown, she went to meet her fate.

~~~

Her thoughts had brought her full circle and now she was pressed against Kane's chest, his arm around her waist. She felt trapped both by his limb and the fact that her life was now bound to his. The future loomed ahead.

What would it be like to spend the rest of her life with this man? To share his bed? Bear his young? Grow old beside him? Did he like to run in the forest or would he be too busy with his duties as Alpha to spend time with her? And who were the members of his pack? She'd have to leave her friends and family behind. Her new position as his mate would guarantee her respect, but would anyone be her friend or was she destined for a lonely existence?

Fear and doubt tumbled through her mind as she fell into a restless sleep.

Chapter 2

In the morning Elise awoke to find herself alone in bed. There was dent in the pillow beside her, the covers rumpled confirming the previous night hadn't been a dream. She and Kane were mated despite the fact there was no love between them.

If it had been Bryan, they would have made a blood-bond, biting each other's necks to mark the fact that they belonged together. It would have forged a mental connection that would grow throughout their lifetime. Kane had made no move to do this and while she was relieved not to bear his mark, she also was unaccountably miffed by the fact. She would have liked the opportunity to refuse and earn a small victory, proving she was still loyal to Bryan.

With a soft sigh she raised her head and looked around. There was no sign of Kane so she listened carefully, wondering if he was in the next room. All was silent. Well, at least she didn't have to face him right away, though in some ways getting that first awkward greeting over with might have been nice. Rolling out of bed she made her way across to the bathroom, her feet silent on the soft carpeting.

The previous night she'd been too keyed-up to take in her surroundings, but now she looked around with interest. She seldom visited the cabins but knew her father had recently had them renovated. The decor was natural wood and colonial furnishings with splashes of colour found in the draperies and cushions; it was simple but pleasantly welcoming. The bathroom, while small, contained all the needed amenities. She made use of them then dressed in pants and a t-shirt.

She wasn't sure what the day would hold and was musing about the fact when the door opened and Kane entered the room.

"Good morning, Elise. I heard you in the shower when I came in, so I made some breakfast for us."

"Oh. Thanks." She glanced at him, then looked away feeling awkward in his presence.

He extended his arm, ushering her into the kitchenette. The table was set, bacon and eggs, juice and toast waiting. "I wasn't sure what you liked to eat, but this is what I can cook. I hope it's suitable."

"You cooked this?" She looked at him in surprise. Her father had never set foot in the kitchen, always too busy with his work as Alpha.

"I am capable of fending for myself, you know." He chuckled at her expression and helped her into a chair. "And, I can't have you undernourished. People might think I don't know how to take care of you." This final remark was accompanied by a kiss on her cheek and a casual caress.

She froze at the unexpected gesture, but Kane sat down opposite her as if nothing had happened and began serving.

"We'll need to take a few days to get used to each other, to become acquainted with various likes and dislikes. Is there anything you aren't fond of eating?" He paused in the middle of scooping up some egg and looked at her enquiringly.

"Um...not really."

"Good. I'll eat almost anything myself. Do you like to read? Watch movies?"

The meal progressed with Kane asking her questions and her supplying answers. When she didn't question him in return, he would fill in his own preferences. She had to admire him for the effort he was making. He was being friendly and polite, showing an interest in her. Apparently, he was committed to making their union work.

The Mating

After a while, she began to relax and found herself expanding on her answers. Kane smiled at her, obviously pleased that she was making an effort.

"Our territories adjoin to the east, and with our packs under an alliance, we technically have miles and miles of forest to roam in now," he explained, leaning back and sipping his coffee. "Personally, I love a good run over rugged terrain. How about you? When I first saw you, it was apparent that you'd just come in from exercising."

"Yes, I'd been out with...a friend." The smile that had been on her face faded at the memory. If only she'd known it was to be the last time she would ever be with Bryan, she would have savoured the time even more, storing every sight and sound and scent.

"And this...friend...would he be the young male who was looking daggers at me yesterday? Tall with sandy hair, and about twenty years of age?"

She hesitated but knew Kane could find out from anyone in her pack. Her friendship with Bryan had been no secret. "Yes. That was Bryan. He'd hoped to speak to my father about being my...mate." She looked away, her eyes misting over.

"And you?" Kane prodded softly. "How did you feel about that?"

Staring at her hands, she whispered her answer. "I... I was hoping for the same thing."

"I see." He was silent and then sighed heavily. "I'm not surprised. You're a beautiful female and it would be strange if no one in your pack had wanted you." He continued, seeming to choose his words carefully. "You know, Elise, sometimes our lives have moments of great disappointment. It's difficult at the time, but we have to move beyond." He reached across the table and put a finger under her chin, forcing her to look at him. "Our union was of great importance to the well-being of both our packs. It's our duty to them to make this work, agreed?"

His amber eyes bore into hers, the authority of his position evident and, after a moment, she nodded in agreement. He was right. Duty to her pack, and duty to his, necessitated making their relationship work.

He stood and extended his hand to her. Hesitantly she reached out, placing hers in his. Warmth enveloped her hand and slowly worked its way up her arm. Smiling encouragingly, he pulled her to her feet.

An hour later, Elise stood at the edge of the forest waiting for Kane. After cleaning up from their morning meal, he'd headed to the pack house to deal with a few pressing matters, saying he'd meet her in half an hour. She wasn't sure if she wanted to run with him—it had been an activity that she and Bryan had enjoyed together—but knew that she needed to make their union work. Running could turn out to be one of the few things they had in common.

It was another lovely fall day. The trees were painted with orange, red, and gold while the sky was a bright clear blue. Heat from the rising sun was burning off the morning mist but wisps still swirled low to the ground giving everything a faintly magical appearance.

She loved this land and knew every square inch by heart. Closing her eyes, she visualized running down the twisting paths, leaping over fallen logs, splashing through streams. It really was the best place in the world and she couldn't imagine ever being this comfortable or at peace anywhere else.

Inhaling deeply, she let the fresh, crisp air invade her lungs and energize her body. Kane was later than he had thought he'd be and she began to move around restlessly, bending to touch her toes, stretching her arms over her head then twisting side to side.

She glanced towards the house. How much longer would he be? As Alpha, she knew his time would not always be his own, but did that mean that her time must be spent waiting, doing nothing? She stared deep into the woods. The land was calling to her. Did she dare go ahead without him?

Her father had expressly forbidden any pack member to go out by themselves. Hunters sometimes laid illegal leg traps and a wolf could be caught and shot before anyone in the pack was aware. That was how her mother had died.

"Good morning." A voice spoke behind her and she jumped. Spinning around, she saw Bryan standing a few feet away. The sun was shining on his sandy brown hair, giving it a golden glow.

"Bryan!" Her heart leapt with joy and she rushed over to hug him, only to have her friend step away when she was but a foot away. His movement brought her headlong rush to an immediate stop. "Bryan? What's the matter?"

"What do you mean, what's the matter? You know what the problem is."

"No, I don't." She shook her head puzzled at the change in her friend. Bryan was usually so happy and easy going. Now he sounded bitter, a scowl marring his normally handsome face.

"You're mated to Kane. I can smell his scent on you."

His words cut like a knife into her heart. How could he be so cruel? "You know that wasn't my choice! The Elders decided on the need for the union. You were at the ceremony yesterday and heard the speeches just as I did."

Bryan looked away, his mouth tightly compressed. "I know. It's just..." He seemed to be waging some type of internal struggle, his fists clenching and unclenching. Finally, he sighed deeply, the scowl fading away leaving sorrow in its wake. "I had hoped to be your mate."

"I know." She took a step closer and laid her hand on his arm. "I'd hoped for the same thing." She took his hand in hers. "This union was for the good of the packs, but it doesn't mean that I've stopped caring for you."

He turned and looked at her, his gaze drifting over her features. "And I still care for you." He reached out and stroked her cheek, his focus settling on her lips.

Silence stretched between them and she realized that he was leaning closer to her, his intention of kissing her evident. Her conscience pricked and she knew she should step away. Bryan wasn't her mate. Kane was.

A twig snapped behind her but, before she could act, Bryan jumped away, pulling his hand from hers. They both turned to see Kane standing nearby, his eyes narrowing into a glare as he took in the two of them.

"Elise, I'm glad you found a way to keep yourself occupied while I was finishing off pack business." There was an angry edge to his voice which made her skin prickle with anxiety.

"I... I was talking to Bryan," she stammered. His expression frightened her and she stepped back.

"So I see." Kane shot her a brief glance, and then focused his attention on Bryan, a look of disdain on his face. "This is the...friend...you spoke of this morning?"

"Yes, this is Bryan. We've been friends since we were young."

Kane gave Bryan an almost imperceptible nod. "I'm glad you had someone to keep you company while you were waiting. However, it would do your 'friend' well to remember that you are now *my* mate and off limits to all others."

Feeling her face burn at his innuendo, she tried to defend her actions. "We were just talking, nothing else!"

"I don't appreciate other males standing quite so close when...talking...to my mate." The words rumbled from his throat and Bryan retreated, instinctively acknowledging Kane's dominance.

"Elise, I'd better go. I... I'll see you around." Regret laced his voice.

"Yes, I'll see you around." Sadness filled her, knowing that it was unlikely Bryan would approach her again. Their friendship was over. Anger bubbled up inside her and she kept her eyes fixed on the retreating figure, while addressing Kane. "You didn't need to chase him off like that."

"I didn't chase him off. I merely let him know that you are my mate now and a proper distance needs to be maintained."

"He was just—"

"I know what he was *just* doing," Kane interrupted sharply. "I could scent his desire for you and I do not share my mate with anyone. We are bonded and you are mine. No other male is allowed to sniff around you."

"Sniff around me?" She turned to stare at him in outrage.

"Yes. That boy needs to remember you are off-limits before he makes a grave mistake."

She huffed indignantly. "Kane, you—"

"Elise, this conversation is over." His tone was firm, implacable. "You are my mate. Bryan will stay away. End of topic. Now, are we going for a run or not?"

She considered leaving in a snit, but she'd be cutting off her nose to spite her face. She loved to run and Kane was right. As much as she hated to admit it, she couldn't encourage a relationship with Bryan any more. It wasn't fair to him. With a brief nod to Kane, she shifted into her wolf form and ran into the forest.

The leaves crunched beneath her feet, trees and shrubs a mere blur as she raced past. Leaping over logs, skirting around trunks, she ran for the sheer love of it. Her eyes constantly scanned the horizon as she quickly adjusted her path and pace to suit the terrain. At the same time, she was aware of Kane running behind her. He made no attempt to pass her, but she sensed he was holding back. His breathing was slow and steady, no hint of exertion coming from him.

She quickened her pace, curious to see the limits of the wolf behind her. Within seconds, he had matched his pace to hers, the distance between them remaining constant. Again and again she tested him, running faster and faster yet he never once fell behind nor attempted to overtake her.

He was toying with her.

Vexed, she veered off the path heading for rougher terrain. Barrelling over a crest, she headed down a slope, her claws digging into the soil as she sought to gain traction on the slippery, leaf covered ground. At the bottom, a stream meandered along, and she splashed across it, before charging up the bank. Her breathing was ragged now, but she wasn't about to give in. Intent on jumping over a pile of brush ahead of her, she put on a final burst of speed.

Without warning, she found herself knocked to the ground and began to fight the assailant. Snapping and rolling, she kept trying to evade her attacker but to no avail. In a flash Kane had pinned her to the ground, his teeth lightly gripping her throat. Instinctively, she froze and whimpered in submission. Kane held on for a second longer then let go and sat back.

As one, they phased into human form. Kane was breathing faster than normal, but he didn't appear spent. On the other hand, her own chest was heaving as she pulled oxygen in to nourish her starving lungs and protesting muscles.

"Why did you do that?" She panted.

"There's a leg trap directly ahead of you. A few more yards and you would have stepped in it."

She turned and scanned the area ahead of her. Sure enough, barely visible in the carpet of leaves was a glint of steel. A shudder passed over her as she thought of her mother, shot to death with her leg caught in such a device.

"Just this morning, scouts reported more poachers had been seen in the area. We're near the edge of the property so I was on the lookout. Rest here for a minute. I'm going to spring that one and then see what else I can find."

"I'm coming with you." She stood, lifting her chin defiantly when it appeared that he'd have her remain where she was.

"Fine but stay behind me." Kane gave her a warning look before searching for a sturdy stick and carefully pressing it against the trigger of the trap. It was an older model, with sharp metal teeth designed to dig into the flesh of any creature unfortunate enough to step in it. She jumped as the trap sprang shut, snapping the stick in two. Swallowing hard, she thought of how painful it would have been to have her leg caught in such a device.

For another half hour they scoured the edge of the property, discovering four more traps before Kane was satisfied that none remained. "We'll report this to your father when we return, and he can send another set of scouts out to check." He had gathered the traps into a pile and marked the location so that they could be collected later. Traps were never sprung and then left behind. The hunters would just reset them. At least this way the humans would be out money and time since they'd have to purchase new ones.

"Thank you." She touched Kane's arm as he stood up after hiding the traps under some brush.

"For what?"

"For stopping me. I could have snapped a bone if I'd stepped in one of those."

"I'm your Alpha now. It's my job to watch out for everyone in the pack, but especially you. As my mate, you're the most important member to me." He stared at her intently and she flushed.

"Yes, but I should have been more careful. I know these woods. I... I wasn't paying attention."

"What were you thinking about instead?"

She hesitated before answering. "You, or to be more precise, I guess I was testing you to see if you'd keep up."

A crooked smile appeared on his face and he reached out, cupping the back of her head and drawing her in for a quick kiss. "Rest assured, Elise, no matter what you dish out, I will keep up with you."

Somehow, she knew he was speaking the truth.

21

They shifted back into wolf form and this time she followed as Kane led the way to the edge of the woods. When they arrived at the cabin, she headed for the bathroom while he went to the house to tell her father about the traps.

The run had left her hot and sweaty and she couldn't wait to be clean. Leaving her clothes on the bedroom floor, she padded into the bathroom and turned on the water, adjusting the flow and temperature. As the water cascaded down on her, she pondered the morning's events. Kane had been polite to her, even kind. He'd saved her from severe injury in a leg trap and while he'd been bossy, telling her to follow behind, she couldn't really fault him. As Alpha, he needed a take charge attitude.

His reaction to Bryan had been interesting as well. While he hadn't been outwardly aggressive, he hadn't been encouraging of her relationship with the other male either. Was Kane just being instinctively territorial; she was his mate and no one else was allowed near her? Most likely that was the answer. It was too much to expect that he had any feelings toward her beyond a sense of responsibility and ownership.

Would it always be this way; Kane showing polite interest in her but spending most of his time working? Would he ever come to care for her, or was she destined for a lukewarm relationship for the rest of her life? If she'd been mated to Bryan, it would have been so different.

A wave of sadness washed over her and she turned off the water and wrapped herself in a terrycloth robe. Returning to the bedroom, she flopped down on the bed and curled up into a ball, sniffling as she contemplated her future.

Chapter 3

Elise woke with a start from a deep sleep and blinked in confusion at her unfamiliar surroundings. This wasn't her bedroom. Where was she?

A noise from the foot of the bed drew her attention and she was greeted with the rear view of a very well-built and very naked male. The sight stunned her before she remembered recent events. She was in a cabin with her new mate, Kane. The past twenty-four hours hadn't been a bad dream.

She let her head sink back onto the pillow and silently studied the man who was getting dressed before her. Muscles rippled across his back and his taut buttocks. His legs were long and sturdy, also giving evidence of his strength. As his lower anatomy disappeared from view under a pair of briefs, he glanced her way and caught her watching him.

"I see you're awake."

"Uh-huh. What time is it?" Her voice was raspy, her throat still tight from her earlier emotions.

"Almost noon. You must have been tired after our run." He turned to grab a shirt and she noticed a long scar on his side, its pink colour indicating that it was still fairly new. She vaguely recalled seeing it last night.

"What happened to your side?"

Kane barely glanced down at the mark. "Nothing. Just a scratch from a fight."

"That's more than a scratch. Who was the fight with?"

"Another Lycan named Ryne." Kane shrugged as if to dismiss the matter and stepped into his pants.

The scar appeared to have come from a serious injury, not the result of a minor scuffle. Not sure why it suddenly mattered to her, she hitched herself up against the headboard and pressed for more information. "Why were you fighting?"

Kane sighed and finished doing up his zipper before turning and facing her, his arms crossed in resignation. "You aren't going to leave this alone, are you?"

"No. I have an inquiring mind." She gave him a smirk that indicated she wasn't planning on backing down. He might be her Alpha, but she wasn't going to let him walk all over her—she'd come to that decision earlier in the morning—and there was no time like the present to start showing that she had a backbone, especially since she still had home turf advantage.

"Well, in that case, I suppose I should tell you. Otherwise you might ask questions of the wrong people and end up with some incorrect information." He rubbed his hands over his face then walked to the window and stared outside while speaking. "As you know, I'm the new Alpha of my pack. Our previous leader, Zack, was killed in an accident. Ryne and I were both Betas. Half of the Elders favoured me as the new Alpha and half wanted Ryne."

"So, it went to a pack vote?"

"Usually that's what would have happened, but Ryne pulled out the old rules and declared a challenge."

"A challenge?" She sat up straight and shuddered. "That's not done anymore. It's ridiculous! We've evolved beyond that." Two wolves fighting to the death for the leadership was barbaric.

"I agree, but he was within his rights."

"So...what happened?"

"We fought. I won."

"Did you...kill him?" She almost hated to ask the question. The idea that her mate could kill a fellow Lycan was sickening.

"No. It was a long drawn out fight and both of us were pretty beaten up by time it was over. He made an impulsive move. I pinned him down and could have crushed his windpipe, but instead let him go."

The Mating

"And where is he now? Did he stay in the pack?"

Kane shook his head. "Ryne chose to leave. I told him he could stay—we'd been packmates for years—but he said he wasn't going to grovel in front of me. He was bitter and said some crazy things." He paused and shrugged, but the tone of his voice when he spoke again belied his outward lack of concern. "In the long run, it's probably best he's gone. There would have been too much division in the pack if he'd stayed."

"And is the pack united behind you now? Even Ryne's supporters?"

"Yes. The pack mentality still runs through all our blood. The strongest member is the leader and we instinctively accept that." He raised his chin as he spoke, an Alpha's confidence showing in his stance. "I proved myself and the others are at peace with the results."

She considered what he'd told her. It must have been an awful position for him to find himself in; forced to fight someone who, quite likely, had been a friend for years. She was glad he'd shown mercy to the challenger. It spoke well for the kind of mate he would be.

Kane was watching her, one brow cocked, perhaps wondering what her reaction was to his tale.

She gave him a nod. "I'm glad you won and that you healed well from your fight."

"Thanks. It was a few weeks ago; all water under the bridge now." Flashing a smile at her, he seemed to relax, almost as if her reaction had mattered to him. He wandered back to the dresser and picked up his watch. "You need to get up and get dressed. We'll be leaving in an hour."

"Leaving?" She couldn't keep the surprise from her voice.

"Uh-huh. I need to return to my pack. It's only about an hour's drive but I want to get back in good time so that you can see your new home before it's dark." Grabbing his jacket, he left.

She wrapped her arms tightly around herself. In an hour she'd be leaving the only home she'd ever known, leaving all the people she'd grown up with. She'd be joining a new pack, be surrounded by new faces. The only person she'd know would be Kane, and he was still the next best thing to a stranger to her.

Once again, her stomach clenched as she slowly climbed out of bed and prepared to follow him.

A short while later, Elise stood in the doorway of her old bedroom. All her possessions had been packed for her and the room was now bare, almost as if she'd never lived there.

Slowly, she entered, her steps echoing in the nearly empty space. She touched the mattress, smoothed the pillow, then ran her hand over the white dresser and pulled open a few random drawers, checking if anything had been left behind. They were empty. The packers had been efficient it seemed. Peeking into the closet, only one lonely hanger remained on the rod, forgotten and forlorn in the flurry of activity that had no doubt overtaken the room.

How could her whole life be gathered up and stuffed into a few boxes in such a short period of time?

Wandering over to the window, she looked out at the familiar view of the yard and the forest beyond. A reminiscent smile played over her lips as she recalled all the times she'd stared out at the scene below dreaming of the future, planning her life around this small world that she'd grown up in. Leaving had never entered her mind. Instead, she'd envisioned herself blood-bonded to a packmate, raising her pups here, teaching them all the special, secret places in the woods.

Tears threatened and she turned away from the beloved view. Those had been nothing but foolish childhood dreams. She was an adult now with responsibilities that must be faced.

Swallowing hard, she walked to her bed, carefully tugging it away from the wall so that she could feel along the baseboards. There was a loose section and she moved it away, feeling inside the hidden space behind. Was it still there? Surely no one had found it.

The Mating

She reached in further until finally her fingers encountered a soft surface. Pulling it out, she shook the dust off the leather-bound book. It was an old diary; one that she'd kept on and off for years. Lately she hadn't been writing in it, but she couldn't leave it behind. Someone else might take over this room in the future and she didn't want a stranger reading her private thoughts.

Tucking the book into the large purse she had slung over her shoulder, she walked to the door. About to leave, she turned and gave the room one last glance before flipping the light switch and quietly closing the door on her childhood.

Her chin quivered as she stood in the hallway, but she forced her emotions down. Taking a deep breath, she descended the stairs and went to meet Kane where he was waiting to take her to her new home.

The drive was completed mostly in silence. Kane made a few idle comments along the way but seemed content to listen to the radio, his fingers drumming on the steering wheel as he kept time with the music. Elise didn't feel inclined towards conversation either and was grateful for the songs that filled the quietness of the cab. With her head leaning against the window, she stared unseeing at the passing landscape, lost in thought...

~~~

Leaving the house had been hard. Sarah, usually a no-nonsense type of person, had uncharacteristically fussed over her, making her promise to come and visit soon.

"Now remember, just because you're moving away doesn't mean we have to lose contact." Sarah tucked a stray lock of hair behind Elise's ear. "You can call anytime and I'm sure we'll find opportunities to visit."

"I'm sure we will too." She hugged her tightly knowing she'd miss the woman. While Sarah wasn't exactly the warm, cuddly type, she'd still done her best to help raise Elise and her brother and sister, providing some of the attention that they missed once their mother was gone.

Jake gave her a one-armed hug, before ruffling her hair. "I'm going to miss you, kiddo. Who will drive me crazy with their non-stop talking now?"

She leaned her head against Jake's chest, breathing in his comforting scent one last time. She'd always had a fun, relaxed relationship with the easy-going Beta; he was like a favourite uncle who tolerated her questions and teased her unmercifully yet was always there when needed. In many ways, he took the place of her father who always seemed too busy to have time for his youngest child.

When she'd been little, her father had played with her or taken her into the woods but that had been years ago when her mother was still alive. With the death of his mate, the Alpha had seemed to withdraw from his children, perhaps too caught up in his own grief to deal with them. Whatever the reason, she had found herself looking more and more to Jake for fatherly attention and, as a result, felt closer to him than her own biological father. She harboured no bitterness about the fact; it was just the way things were.

"I'll miss you, Jake." The simple statement was all she could get out due to the sudden thickness of her throat.

He nodded at her in understanding and kissed the top of her head. Taking a deep breath, she stepped away and turned to her father. She loved him, but it was a much more formal relationship. He was always the Alpha first and being a father came second. They'd studied each other and then he'd pulled her into an awkward embrace.

"You'll be fine with Kane," he whispered in her ear. "He's a good man."

She nodded, knowing her father had done what he thought was best, and would never have consented to her going with someone totally unsuitable. Being the Alpha wasn't an easy position and the needs of the pack had to be considered first;

she just wished it hadn't come at the expense of her own dreams.

Since there was no going back, she'd plastered a fake smile on her face and climbed into Kane's truck, waving at the other pack members who had gathered outside. Searching the group, she noted Bryan was absent and regretted not seeing him one last time but perhaps it was for the best.

As they pulled out of the driveway, she stared straight ahead. If she had to watch the house slowly disappearing from sight, she knew she'd burst into tears and she didn't want to show such weakness in front of Kane. It wasn't that she thought he'd say anything about it, but she had her pride. She wouldn't be a snivelling, weak mate. There might not be any love between them but at least she'd ensure that he respected her.

~~~

As she came out of her reverie, she began to take note of the passing scenery. They'd left her father's territory about half an hour ago and were now in Kane's. Would his home be similar to her own? Each pack owned large parcels of land that consisted mainly of wilderness, clearly marked as private property. Within a territory, there was always one main Alpha house where meetings were held and the Alpha and Beta's families resided. Surrounding the main home were several small cabins where other pack members could live when needed. Many had their own homes located within the territory and a few chose to live in nearby towns with the human population.

Packs were generally stable. Occasionally new members would join, but they tended to be close-knit societies and spent a great deal of time at each other's homes, though the Alpha house was the centre of most activity. At any given time, members could be found lounging about the living room, preparing food in the kitchen or roaming the property. There was never a chance to be lonely.

"How large is your pack?" She broke the silence between them.

Kane flicked a look her way. "About the same size as the one you grew up in. Our Alpha house has six bedrooms and four baths, office space, a living room, a large dining area and a kitchen. The basement was recently renovated into a multi-purpose room for meetings with a media centre, pool table, and play area for the young ones."

"It sounds nice. Who shares the house with you?"

"Besides yourself?" He grinned over at her before returning his attention to the road. "My Beta is John and his mate's name is Carrie. They're expecting their first in a few months. And then there's Zack's widow—he was the previous Alpha—she's continued to stay on as well. Her name is Helen."

Nodding, she decided having three other people in the house should make things easier. She wouldn't be alone with Kane all the time—she still wasn't that comfortable around him—and having two other women to talk to would be good. Hopefully, they'd like her. If Carrie was having her first pup, she'd be about the same age, so maybe they'd have something in common. "There are always people in and out of our house—I mean my father's house. Is yours similar?"

"Yeah, sometimes it's a three-ring circus. With you arriving, it will probably be especially busy as everyone stops by to meet you."

She bit her lip, not looking forward to meeting so many new people. Names, and scents and hierarchy placements to remember. It sounded overwhelming. Possibly sensing her trepidation, Kane reached over and clasped her knee. "It will be fine. We're not as...traditional...as your old pack. They're a friendly bunch and will be happy to meet you."

As they got closer to Kane's home, he offered further explanations as to who the pack members were as well as pointing out areas of interest. There was a medium-sized town nearby that they went to for supplies, though for the most part the pack stayed within their territory. It was heavily wooded and at the farthest point touched her father's land. Several streams fed a small lake and there was even a waterfall due to ancient, glacier-cut ravines.

They stopped once along the way to get gas and then Kane pulled into a small strip mall, explaining that he needed to pick up a few things. She opted to wait in the truck and watched Kane sauntering down the sidewalk. The few people he encountered nodded at him, but none stopped to talk. What was the pack's relationship with the townsfolk? Were they friendly or did they secretly whisper about the strange group of people who lived outside of town?

From her own experience with her pack, she knew that most people were wrapped up in their own lives and didn't give a great deal of thought to the close-knit group that lived nearby. People thought they were odd, but that was it. No one suspected that a pack of werewolves lived next door.

That hadn't always been the case. She'd heard tales of packs that had been persecuted by the human population, not because they were werewolves, but because their close-knit society was somehow deemed unnatural. Some packs had even been forced to leave their territory for fear of being discovered. All it took was one or two curious humans to start questioning their lifestyle. She hoped that wasn't the case here.

Soon Kane returned and stowed his purchases in the back. He climbed into the cab of the truck and smiled over at her, seeming happier and more relaxed now they were closer to his home. It was only natural, of course. No wolf was comfortable if it was away from its pack for too long.

By the time they pulled into the driveway that led to Kane's house, she was a bundle of nerves. She did her best to mask the fact; it wouldn't do for the others to smell fear on her. As the Alpha's mate, she had a status to maintain. In ancient times, a weak mate might have been challenged by one of the other females who wanted to usurp her, but that wasn't done now, and she was thankful for the fact. Being a new pack member would be hard enough without someone wanting to bump her position.

The truck came to a stop in front of a sprawling two storey home that featured a wrap-around porch. Situated in the middle of a large treed lot, there were woods on three sides. As Kane climbed out, the front door opened and people spilled out, calling his name and enveloping him in hugs. She watched the activity from inside the truck, and when it became apparent that it would be a while before Kane could free himself from the crowd, she stepped out of the cab on her own.

Hesitantly, she stood by the vehicle, unsure of what to do. Kane looked up and, catching her eye, made his way over to her, wrapping his arm around her shoulders. "Everyone, this is Elise, my mate."

His announcement caused everyone to stop talking and stare at her. The silence was uncomfortable and she had to force herself not to cower against his side. Tentatively, she smiled at the small crowd and finally a petite, red-haired woman about her age stepped forward with her hand extended. From the size of her belly, she had to be Carrie, the Beta's wife.

"Hello, Elise. I'm Carrie. Welcome to our pack." Her voice was calm and friendly, making Elise immediately feel welcomed. Some of the tension in her body began to relax.

"And I'm John, her mate, and Kane's Beta." The man was about the same height as Kane, with blond hair and friendly blue eyes.

"I'm pleased to meet you." She tried to sound confident and shook their hands firmly. After that, everyone started talking at once, stepping forward with greetings until her head was swirling with names.

The group moved towards the house and Kane grabbed two of her bags from the vehicle. "Come on inside. The others will bring the rest of your things." A few of the men immediately headed towards the truck, grabbing the remaining boxes. Kane hadn't issued a command, but they knew implicitly what he expected and obeyed unquestioningly.

She followed behind Kane until they got to the door. As she was about to walk in, someone hip-checked her and cut in front.

"Excuse me." A tall, blonde woman threw the comment over her shoulder, blocking the doorway and separating her from Kane.

From the woman's tone, Elise knew there was no real regret for the action. She searched her mind for a name but then realized that this female hadn't stepped forward to introduce herself outside.

"Marla." John growled a low warning to the blonde who was still blocking the doorway.

"Oh. Am I in your way? Sorry, John." The woman—Marla—flashed John a smile and sauntered into the house as if nothing had happened.

Elise looked at John, but the man shrugged and gave her a tight smile. "That's Marla. Just ignore her. She has...issues."

Watching the woman slide up to Kane and rest her hand on his arm while smiling brightly, Elise wondered what the 'issues' might be. Somehow, she knew that Marla was not going to be welcoming her to the pack.

Chapter 4

Elise sat on the edge of Kane's king-sized bed and surveyed her surroundings. The black and white colour scheme was definitely masculine and matched Kane perfectly, but it left her feeling cold and out of place. The idea of her under-things draped here and there, or her makeup scattered on the dresser seemed wrong. A shiver ran through her; would she ever be able to feel at home here?

She spent a few minutes considering how she could make the space more appealing then checked her watch again. It was four-thirty. After showing her to their room, Kane had left, promising to return and give her a tour of the house once he dealt with some pressing business. That was two hours ago. Since then, she'd explored the three rooms of their suite, finished unpacking her things, and familiarized herself with Kane's collection of music, movies and books. Now what should she do? Kane had said he'd be back, but she was beginning to think he must have forgotten he now had a mate. He seemed to vacillate between careful attentiveness to her feelings and blatantly ignoring her.

Right now she was feeling ignored, just as she had upon arriving. Her mind drifted back to a few hours previously...

~~~

Once Marla stopped blocking the doorway, Elise made her way inside and looked around with interest. She could see into several rooms from her position in the main foyer. A living room was to her left, a staircase with an oak banister was in front of her, and a dining room could be seen down the hallway. A few rooms were to her right, but their closed doors gave no indication as to what might be inside.

Her first impression was that the house was simply decorated in a homey, traditional way with comfortable looking stuffed chairs and small occasional tables scattered about. Gleaming hardwood floors and neutral walls were a perfect foil for the dark green curtains that hung from the expansive windows. Light shone in from all sides and the impressive view of the outdoors, combined with the earth-toned decor, gave her a feeling of being one with nature.

Not sure if she should follow the men carrying her boxes upstairs, or wait for Kane, she stood in the middle of the foyer, debating the best course of action. When she hesitantly stepped towards the stairs, Kane quickly called out her name.

"Elise, wait! I'll only be a minute."

How had he known what she was doing when his attention was so focused on Marla? The other woman was speaking intently to him and Kane nodded several times before ending the conversation with a one-armed hug. After watching Marla walk away, he moved to stand by Elise. "Sorry about that. Marla needed a bit of reassurance."

Glancing over to where the woman stood near a window, she noted that Marla was shooting daggers at her with her eyes. Why had the woman taken an instant dislike to her? About to question Kane on the matter, he took her hand and led her upstairs. As she trailed her hand on the wooden rail, she could feel eyes watching her and had to resist the urge to turn around and see who it was.

At the top of the stairs, a hallway led in two directions. Kane turned to the left and guided her to a set of doors at the end of the corridor.

"Our rooms are up here. Since the house is usually busy, I have my own retreat. There's a bedroom, bath and a sitting room that are strictly off-limits to the rest of the pack. Sometimes, even social animals like wolves need their own space." He offered this explanation with a crooked smile, while opening the door and ushering her inside.

The room was large and bright with sunlight streaming in from three sets of windows that spanned the outer walls. A king-sized bed dominated one side of the room and a large closet took up most of the other. Through an open doorway, she could see a sitting area with a fireplace and couch, while a second door appeared to lead into a bathroom. It was much grander than she'd expected. Apparently, Kane's pack was well-set financially.

"This is nice." She wandered about the room, peering into the closet and then into the sitting room.

"Carrie moved some of my stuff over, so there'll be room for your things. She'll help you unpack or rearrange anything that you want."

"Thanks, but I can do it myself. With a baby on the way, I'm sure she's tired and doesn't need the extra work."

"That's considerate of you." Kane came up behind her and squeezed her shoulders, then guided her to the window. He pointed over her shoulder and explained the view. "See over to the west? That's the direction of your father's land. Of course, you can't see it, but possibly it will make your old pack seem not quite so far away."

She looked up at him in surprise. It was a nice thing for him to say. She hadn't supposed he'd understand how she felt. Kane guided her around so she was facing him and cupped her face.

"I know this has been hard on you, Elise. Leaving behind everything you know on such short notice has to feel overwhelming, but I'm proud of how you're handling things; no whining, no temper tantrums, no angry accusations. I was expecting all of that and more."

His words filled her with warmth but also made her stop and reflect. "I think I'm in shock." She furrowed her brow trying to sort out her thoughts and feelings in her own mind. "Everything happened so fast, that I didn't have time to think or react. I instinctively followed the Alpha's orders." She shrugged and sighed. "Besides, there really wasn't much choice. I could fall in with the plan or leave the pack."

"You're right. A wolf that refuses to comply with the Alpha doesn't stay in the pack long, though I doubt your father would have immediately thrown you out."

"Maybe not right away, but he's traditional and expects obedience..." Her voice trailed off. What would have happened if she had kicked up a fuss? She couldn't remember her brother or sister complaining when they'd mated to form alliances, but then again, she hadn't paid that much attention, having been considerably younger than her siblings. Searching her memory, she tried to recall an instance when her father hadn't been obeyed and what he'd done as a result, but no such occasion came to mind.

With a start, she realized that Kane was still talking.

"—and after supper, I'll take you for a walk around the immediate grounds. Tomorrow morning, we can go for another run."

"I'd like that. It looks to be a nice territory." She twisted around and focused her attention on the view again, noting the trees stretching as far as the eye could see. It was nice, she said to herself, just not as nice as her father's land.

Not aware of her thoughts, Kane spoke with pride. "It's a beautiful place, especially down by the lake. I think you'll enjoy it here, but don't go too close to the edge of the property. We have the same problem with hunters and trappers that your old pack has."

She murmured her agreement, his comment about her old home causing her to shift slightly and study the view to the west; that was where her pack was. Pressing her hand against the window pane, a wave of homesickness wash over her. Kane turned her in his arms once again, running his hands down her back, before pulling her body flush against his. "It will take some time to adjust, but soon this will feel like home. Don't worry. I'll be here to help you."

The Mating

She studied his eyes, curious as to how he knew what had been running through her mind. At this moment, he seemed so kind and understanding. Heat from his body seeped into hers, causing a funny flutter in her stomach. Before she could examine what the feeling meant, Kane pressed a kiss to her forehead, then let her go.

"I have a few things I need to do. You stay here and get settled. Check out the sitting room; feel free to move my stuff about, I'm not fussy. I'll be back in about an hour to give you a tour of the house."

~~~

Well, she'd unpacked, and explored, and shifted things about—now what? Wandering around the home of a new pack by herself was intimidating. Wolves were territorial and her unknown scent might cause some ruffled fur; she'd much rather be escorted by her mate the first time she ventured out. However, sitting and waiting endlessly for Kane to return wasn't that palatable either. If she stayed up here much longer, the others might think she was hiding from them. That would really be a black mark against developing any status and rank.

A newcomer to a pack was immediately checked out for how dominant they were, and where they would fit within the hierarchy. As the Alpha's mate, she would automatically be given a certain degree of respect and status, but if she showed herself to be weak and submissive then her position would start to crumble.

Deciding she'd had enough of waiting, she set her chin, put on a brave front and exited the bedroom suite. For whatever reason, Kane seemed to have abandoned her, so it would be up to her to establish herself in the house.

The hallway was quiet, but she could hear the sound of voices below, and the scent of cooking was drifting enticingly through the house. Well, the kitchen was as good a place to start as any. Following the mouth-watering aroma of roast beef and fresh-baked cookies, she made her way down the stairs. Even though she thought she could pick Kane's voice out of the general murmuring, the idea of food was more intriguing; her stomach was rumbling, reminding her she hadn't eaten lunch. Sniffing the air, she followed the delicious scents down the hallway. It was only as she was about to open the door that nerves began to surface, and she took a deep steadying breath before stepping into the kitchen.

Her first impression, as it had been with most of the rooms in the house, was one of brightness. Whoever had designed the home had ensured the outdoors was allowed inside. An impressive view of the backyard and the woods beyond could easily be seen from almost anywhere in the room. Sunlight streamed in through gleaming windows and sparkled off copper and stainless-steel pots, gleaming marble counter tops, and polished appliances. It might have been too bright if not for the homey touches of herbs growing on the window ledge and bits of folk art adorning the walls.

Two women were standing at the counter and immediately looked up at the sound of the door swinging open. One was Carrie, the Beta's mate, who she'd met earlier. The other woman was older with greying hair and a rounded figure. She was probably in her late fifties or early sixties.

"Elise! Good to see you. I was just saying to Helen that I wondered when you'd appear." Carrie smiled over at her and she began to relax. The tiny redhead had a soothing quality about her, and Elise speculated whether she was always that way or if it was impending motherhood that was making her so mellow.

"I was unpacking and waiting for Kane. He said he had some business to attend to and then he'd be back, but I guess he was delayed so I'm exploring on my own." She shrugged, not wanting to let on that she was upset by Kane's abandonment.

"Welcome, Elise. I'm Helen." The older woman eyed her up and down before smiling.

The Mating

"Hi, Helen, I'm pleased to meet you."

Carrie gestured towards the table. "Why don't you sit down and we can talk while we finish making dinner."

"Isn't there something I could do?" She looked around, thinking she should offer to set the table or prepare vegetables.

"Not today, Sweetie." Helen pulled out a chair and indicated that Elise was to take it. "It's your first day here and we already have everything under control. You sit here and let us talk your ear off. Would you like some coffee and cookies? They're fresh."

She smiled and nodded, sitting down as she'd been told. The two women seemed genuinely pleased to meet her. As Helen handed her a plate of cookies and a cup of coffee, Elise felt she should offer condolences to the old Alpha's widow. "Kane told me that your mate died recently. I'm sorry to hear of your loss."

Helen paused, a sad expression washing over her face before she gave her head a shake. "Thank you. It was a shock, to say the least." She walked to the sink as she spoke and began to peel some carrots. "Some days I still can't believe Zack's gone, but we're lucky that Kane was here to take over. He's doing a fine job. You can be very proud of how he stepped up to the plate."

Purposely sipping her coffee to negate the need to respond, she murmured in what she hoped was an appropriate manner. She barely knew the man. It was hard to be proud of someone you'd just met.

Helen continued chatting, oblivious to Elise's thoughts. "I can tell you from personal experience that an Alpha's work is never done. I had to force my Zack to set 'office hours' so that we could have some semblance of a normal life together. You'll likely have to do the same if you ever want to see him outside the bedroom."

Carrie giggled. "They were just bonded yesterday, Helen. I imagine Kane's going to be more interested in something else besides work for the next while." She ended the comment with a meaningful wink.

Not quite comfortable with the direction the conversation seemed to be heading, Elise tried to change the topic. "So, Carrie, when are you due?"

The pregnant woman rubbed her belly. "I've only got six weeks to go and I can tell you, it won't be a minute too soon. My ankles and I haven't seen each other in months and this one kicks up a storm at night. I can't wait until I can get a good night's sleep again."

"Believe me, once that pup is here, you won't be getting any sleep. This is the voice of experience speaking." Helen finished with the carrots and set them in a dish.

"Do you have a large family, Helen?" Elise wondered how old they might be and if they still lived here.

"I have four girls. Two are mated and part of this pack. One moved away to work out west and joined another pack. My baby, Chloe, is in university right now. She's studying Environmental Science."

"Chloe is one smart girl." Carrie added as she peered at the roast, checking its temperature. "Kane's hoping she can give him some advice on what to do about the northern acreage." Glancing over at Elise, Carrie explained further. "There's been a big push by an oil company to allow them to do some exploratory drilling in the northern part of our territory. They want to buy a large tract or lease it. Of course, we're all against the idea, but they've been lobbying the local government. Kane, and Zack before him, have been busy keeping them away."

"But if it's your territory and you say no, they can't come in, can they?" Elise furrowed her brow trying to understand the situation.

"You'd think." Helen scowled as she dried her hands and then leaned against the kitchen counter. "But the humans want oil and feel that it's their right to get it, even if it means destroying some of our property. Kane's probably going over the company's latest proposal right now. They seem to think that if they offer us enough money we'll give in, which is ridiculous. Lycans don't need money; we need space to roam."

Elise was nodding in agreement when Carrie spoke. "Unfortunately, not everyone feels that way. A few in the pack like the idea of the money."

Helen snorted. "Yes and we all know who they are." The two women exchanged knowing looks.

Chapter 5

By the time dinner was ready, Kane still hadn't appeared and Elise was definitely feeling abandoned.

Carrie shook her head in exasperation. "Elise, can you go fetch the men from the office? Knowing them, they're so involved in what they're doing, they'll never come out on their own."

"Okay. Can you point me in the right direction?" She wasn't too keen on searching out the group—more wandering around on her own in 'foreign' territory—but she didn't want to refuse and seem weak.

Helen gasped. "You mean Kane hasn't even shown you around the house yet?"

Embarrassed, she shrugged and shoved her hands in her pockets. "He planned to but..."

"That man! It's ridiculous how tied up in his work he gets. I'll have to have a word or two with him about how to treat a mate!" Helen pursed her lips and shook her head.

"It's all right." Elise tried to smooth things over. The freedom with which Helen was expressing her feelings about Kane seemed strange; her father would never have tolerated that. Of course, Kane wasn't around to hear, so perhaps that explained things.

"No, it's not. He's mated now and has obligations to you. Come on, I'll give you a quick tour and then we'll collect the men." Helen took her by the arm and led her from the kitchen. Glancing back over her shoulder, Elise looked at Carrie who shrugged and rolled her eyes obviously used to Helen's ways. As she followed the grey-haired woman down the hall, Elise supposed that, having been the Alpha's mate, Helen was used to taking charge. After all, it had been her home for quite a few years and suddenly being demoted would be a difficult mental shift to make.

Elise saw the laundry room, spare bath, living room, dining room, recreation area and the guest rooms. John and Carrie's quarters were pointed out, as were Helen's own suite of rooms. The whole house reflected the pride that Helen took in her role. Every room was immaculate, cheery, and welcoming. Too bad it didn't smell right. The scent of foreign wolves assaulted Elise's nostrils as she went from room to room and it made her feel edgy, as if danger was lurking just around the corner. How long it would be before her scent mixed with theirs and she would finally be able to relax?

Eventually they reached the offices, which turned out to be behind the closed doors she had seen from the front foyer. Helen knocked and then entered without waiting for an invitation, shooing the men out with threats of no dinner if they didn't hustle. Kane was the last to exit and Helen grabbed him by the arm and began to scold him for his neglect. Surprisingly, Kane listened respectfully and then thanked Helen for her opinion. Elise watched the exchange, barely holding back a gasp when he winked at her over Helen's head, then grinned and made a face.

As they turned to walk down the hallway to the dining area, Kane whispered in her ear. "Helen thinks she's everyone's mother and can't resist pointing out the error of our ways. She means well, and she was right. I was caught up in something, but it was no excuse for ignoring you on your first day. I'm sorry. Do you forgive me?"

She nodded, taken aback at his admission. Her father never would have done that.

Kane gave her a quick kiss, grabbed her hand, and hurried her down the hall. "Carrie and Helen are great cooks. I can't wait to see what they've concocted for us tonight."

The Mating

The meal was pleasant, with general conversation. Elise mostly listened, trying to absorb as much information about her new pack as possible. It was just the five of them at the table tonight. Had the others stayed away because of her? At her old home, there'd always been extra people for dinner. She couldn't remember how many times she'd been sent to count noses so they'd know how many plates to set out. Was this pack not as close-knit?

As if reading her mind, John explained. "I told everyone to stay away tonight. Since it's your first day, I thought you might find it overwhelming to have everyone here. With only four new faces, you can ease into things."

"That was nice of you." She smiled at him, thinking everyone was certainly trying to be considerate of her. Maybe it was time to explain some of her own feelings. These people were supposed to be her new family and no doubt could sense the unease coming off of her. "I... I must admit that I'm finding it unsettling to be the new wolf in the pack. I feel like I'm violating your territory by being here. It's old instincts kicking in I suppose, but there's this underlying idea that it's dangerous to be walking around and that I should retreat as fast as possible." She scanned their faces hoping she hadn't made a tactical error.

Helen nodded in understanding. "This doesn't feel like your home yet. You'll be edgy and nervous for a while and then one day, you'll find that your scent has blended with ours and you'll wonder why you ever wanted to be anywhere else."

"Changing packs is still a new concept," John added. "A hundred years ago it was almost unheard of. With few exceptions, Lycans lived and died within the same pack. But the world's changing and we have to change with it. People go away to school, get jobs in new cities; packs have to adapt if we're to survive. Some want to cling to the ancient traditions, but our very existence depends on our ability to integrate undetected with the rest of the world."

"And it's even healthy for the packs to have new members." Carrie chimed in. "New members bring new blood. There was too much inbreeding in the past."

Elise was pleasantly surprised with how forward thinking these people seemed to be. Her old pack wasn't exactly in the Dark Ages, but they did tend towards the traditional. "Thanks, that makes me feel better. I hope everyone else in the pack feels as you do."

"It will be fine. You'll find your feet soon enough." Kane hadn't said much yet. Now he reached over and squeezed her hand. She was surprised at the comfort the gesture seemed to bring.

"She'll find her feet a lot faster if her mate spends some time with her." Helen pointedly looked at Kane and he grimaced.

"Yes, mother," he replied with mocking subservience. Helen threw a roll at him, which he promptly caught and bit into. "Thank you. How did you know I wanted more?"

Helen scowled at him and the others burst out laughing.

The rest of the meal progressed in an easy, affable way and Elise began to feel at ease around her new packmates. Even Kane seemed approachable, gently teasing her and laughing as she boldly replied with snappy come-backs. She found herself enjoying his company and had hope for the future. Maybe she and Kane could eventually become friends, at least.

Dessert was being served when the phone rang. John excused himself to get it but returned quickly, his face grave. "Kane, we have a problem. Thomas was out patrolling the far edge of the property today. Julia just called to say he never came home and she can't make a mental connection with him."

The table fell silent. Kane set his cup down with a definite thud and stood up, concern etched on his features. "Call Franz and Michael. We'll set up a grid and go searching. I'll meet you at the edge of the woods." He turned to go then paused, looking back at Elise. "Can I talk to you for a minute?"

The Mating

Nodding, she got up and followed him out of the room. Once they were by themselves, he placed his hands on her shoulders. "I'm sorry, Elise. It's your first day here and all I've done is ignore you. I have to go, but I'll be back as soon as I can."

"I understand. Do you think something serious has happened?"

"Thomas has only recently mated and there's no way he'd be late getting home. Last week we found a whole line of traps in the area he'd have been patrolling. I'm worried the traps were reset and he stepped in one."

Elise paled, thinking of her mother. "I hope he's all right."

"Me too." Kane stared off into the distance, squeezing her shoulders tightly. She winced at the pressure.

John popped his head in. "Franz and Michael will be here in five minutes. I'm heading out to the tree line."

Kane nodded then looked down at Elise. "Carrie and Helen will take care of you. Ask them if you need anything." He pulled her in for a quick kiss and then left.

She made her way back to the dining room and joined the other two ladies in clearing the table and putting away the leftovers. It had been a pleasant meal and she was sorry it had ended so abruptly and on such a down note.

She'd never thought about how busy her father was as Alpha but now she was seeing a whole different side to the job. Maybe Helen was right and Kane would have to set up 'office hours'—not that she was sure how much time she wanted to spend with him—but they needed to develop some sort of relationship.

After cleaning the kitchen and doing the dishes, the three women sat down to watch TV in the new recreation room. Large overstuffed chairs circled the high-tech flat screen and a fire was burning cheerily in the corner taking the chill off the room. Elise declined the honour of controlling the remote and Carrie flicked through the channels before finding a favourite show.

At first, Elise tried to concentrate on the drama unfolding on the screen but found her gaze drifting more and more towards the other two women. Helen and Carrie kept shooting each other glances and seemed to be exceptionally tense. Finally, she gave up the pretence of not noticing and when the next commercial came on, turned to confront them.

"I've noticed you two looking at each other. Is there something else going on besides Thomas being missing?"

"It's probably nothing." Carrie stared down at her belly, stroking the child within.

"That's right. We're being foolish. Thomas is simply late." Helen bounced to her feet. "Why don't I make us some popcorn?"

"No, thank you." She bit back the desire to growl. They were hiding something from her and she didn't like it. "If this is to be my new home, I need to know what's going on, don't you think?"

"Well, yes..." Carrie twisted her fingers and looked towards Helen.

Sitting back down, Helen sighed. "We aren't trying to hide things from you, Elise. It's just that Kane indicated that he wanted to explain the situation to you himself."

"What situation? And why does Kane have to be the one to tell me?"

"Because it involves Kane on a personal level and he wants you to understand where he's coming from."

She frowned. "How does Thomas not coming home, involve Kane?"

"Well, it might not..." Carrie let her voice trail off and shifted in her seat. "We're just not sure. As I said, it could be nothing."

Throwing up her hands in despair, she flopped back in the chair. "You're talking in circles. Kane said it was possible that Thomas stepped in a trap left by hunters. How could that personally involve Kane beyond the fact that he's the Alpha?"

The Mating

"Well, if it really was set by human hunters, then it wouldn't involve Kane and we certainly hope that's the case." Helen nodded as if her positive thoughts could make the situation true.

"If it involves *human* hunters?" she tried to wrap her brain around this new puzzle. What was there besides human hunters? Surely not... The very idea made her gasp. "Another Lycan setting traps? But why? That's absurd!"

The two women exchanged more anxious glances again and then Helen spoke. "It's complicated. Suffice to say that there's been some controversy and division in the pack. We'd hoped it was over, but recent events are leading us to believe otherwise."

"Recent events? Like what?" She queried.

Helen opened her mouth and seemed about to speak, then shook her head. "We really can't say much else. It's Kane's place to tell you."

Sighing in frustration, she realized she'd get nothing more out of her two new friends. If the Alpha had forbidden them to speak, they wouldn't. "All right. I'll ask Kane when he gets back." Checking the time, she stood up. "I think I'll head up to bed. It's been a busy day."

Carrie stood as well. "I'm going to turn in, too. The little guy inside me is quiet right now and maybe I can get a few hours of sleep before the gymnastics start again."

"I'll rest down here for a while. The men should be back soon and might want a cup of coffee or a snack after being out in the cold." Helen picked up the remote and settled back in her chair.

Bidding each other a good night, Carrie and Elise each turned toward their own wing of the house. Opening the bedroom door, Elise didn't bother to turn on the lights. Moonbeams streamed into the room through the bank of windows and she wandered over to them, staring out at the night.

51

Her old pack was out there, miles away. What were they doing right now? Was her father sitting in his office, working late into the night as he often did? Had Sarah finished the apple pies that she always made and then stored in the freezer for the winter months? And what was Bryan doing? She'd been so busy trying to settle into her new home that she hadn't thought of him all afternoon. Mentally, she scolded herself for forgetting the man she loved.

The sound of a wolf howling drew her attention to the shadowy outline of the surrounding forest. Somewhere out there, Kane and the others were searching for the lost pack member. She hoped everyone was safe. Carrie and Helen's cryptic comments had her worried. If there was a problem and Kane was leading the search, would he be the first to stumble into danger? True, he'd noticed the trap this morning, but in the dark he might not be so lucky. Her stomach gave a nervous flutter at the idea of him being injured.

Reluctantly, she turned from the window, changed into her nightgown and climbed into the bed which now seemed even larger than ever. The sheets were cool and she curled into a ball, hugging her knees to her chest as she tried to warm up. It was her first night in her new pack and she was spending it alone. Was this how the rest of her life was going to be spent?

Rolling over so she faced the windows, she stared out at the moon and tried to convince herself everything would be all right.

Chapter 6

Elise awoke with a start, blinking in confusion at the sunlight that bathed her bed. How could that be? Her bedroom window was... Oh. She wasn't in her old bedroom. This was Kane's room. Well, technically it was her bedroom too, but it would take a while before she felt any ownership of the space.

Surprisingly, she'd slept quite well in her new bed. Rolling onto her back, she stretched her arms and legs until they were fully extended, before releasing them and sinking back down in pleasant relaxation. Turning her head to the side, she noted that the other half of the bed was completely undisturbed.

Kane hadn't slept with her last night. Had he come home late and bedded down somewhere else so he wouldn't disturb her, or had he not come home at all? Possibly he and the other men were still out searching for the missing man. If that was the case, then something was seriously wrong.

Getting out of bed, she tried to recall where she'd placed her clothing the previous day. A quick search of the drawers refreshed her memory and she soon found what she needed. Donning a pair of track pants, a t-shirt, and a hoodie, she combed her hair, pulling it back in a clip, and then scampered downstairs in search of someone who could update her on what had happened.

Helen was in the kitchen, preparing bacon and eggs. "Morning, Elise. How did you sleep?"

"Not bad. Is Kane back? Did they find the missing man?"

"Yes, they got in around three in the morning. Kane stayed with him at the infirmary but sent John back home with the news. Thomas was shot. He lost a lot of blood, but he'll be okay."

"Shot?" A chill run through her as memories of her own mother's death came rushing back. All too often, her vivid imagination recreated what must have happened; her mother in wolf form with her leg in a trap, poachers approaching as she frantically tried to free herself. Had her mother tried to transform to save herself, but been unable to due to her injury, or had she feared for the rest of the pack and remained an animal, sacrificing her life so that her family would not be discovered? Her mother would have been terrified; her heart pounding as she desperately called out to her mate for help.

She knew the story well. Her father had felt his mate's terror through the mental connection that all bonded pairs shared. He'd raced as fast as possible to her side, but it had been too late. The sound of the fatal gunshot had echoed through the woods as he came charging up the crest to where his mate was trapped. He'd been too late. They'd never found the hunters; her father had stayed with his mate as she breathed her last, rather than giving chase...

A pan clattered on the stove, causing her to jump and bringing her out of her reverie. She smoothed her sweaty palms on her pant legs and banked down the fear that had been rising inside her.

Helen had her back turned and was busily flipping the bacon, not noticing anything was amiss. "Yes, Thomas was shot; possibly seasonal hunters who wandered onto our property either not seeing the 'No Trespassing' signs or deciding to ignore them."

"So, what will Kane do about someone hunting on his land? Tell the sheriff?" She kept her voice calm, not revealing the inner panic she'd been feeling mere moments earlier.

"It's tricky. We can't let on that anyone was shot. They'd want to see Thomas and it would be hard to explain how the wound was healing so quickly. Kane will probably report that he heard shots fired or that there was a near miss. Nothing will be done though. There might be a few more patrol cars for a day or two, but the local police don't have the manpower to watch this large an area. Nor do we want them around all the time. Like all packs, we try to keep a low profile."

She digested the information. It was just like home. A pack was basically on its own when problems arose. Involving the local police was always too risky. As Helen grabbed some paper towels to lay the bacon on, she realized that she was standing there watching the other woman work. "Can I help with something?"

"How are you at making toast and coffee?"

"I think I can handle it." She found the needed items under Helen's directions and went to take out the plates. "How many do you think will be here for breakfast?"

"Breakfast tends to be pretty quiet around here, so probably just the four of us. Kane's staying at the infirmary and called to say he won't be back until mid-morning. Thomas is still unconscious, and Kane wants to talk to him as soon as he wakes up."

The two women worked companionably as they finished the meal preparations. As the sun streamed in the numerous windows, it warmed the large homey kitchen taking off the morning chill. Elise mused that it was very evident Helen took pride in her culinary domain. The wood cabinets gleamed, as did the various pots and utensils that hung over the large marble topped workstation, and the floors were immaculate. It was intimidating to think that someday she'd be called on to fill Helen's shoes.

Alpha females were in charge of the house as well as organizing social gatherings and dealing with minor problems. It also meant providing leadership and advice to others in the pack yet what words of wisdom did she have to share at her young age? Truth be told, she'd pretty much floated through life thus far, never applying herself overly much to anything in particular. It was disconcerting to realize that at almost nineteen years of age, her life had no goal or focus. She'd have to do something about that now, though exactly what she wasn't sure.

By the time the meal was ready, John and Carrie appeared. John looked tired from his late night and sat down heavily in his chair. Carrie fussed over him, bringing him coffee and putting jam on his toast. Elise watched them while she ate, wondering if she'd ever feel the need to do that for Kane. Was that what was expected of her now? A sigh escaped her. So far, the morning had left her feeling more than a bit inadequate.

Breakfast was partially over when the back door opened and a tall blonde woman entered wearing a skin-tight dress of shocking pink. Elise remembered her from the previous day as the woman who'd cut in front of her and blocked the door before hanging all over Kane and trying to monopolize his attention. What was her name again?

"Marla, this is a surprise." John's greeting supplied the answer. His voice was neutral, but Elise had the general impression that the Beta wasn't overly pleased to see the newcomer. The look in his eyes was icy rather than the usual friendly blue she'd come to expect. Neither of the other two women were overjoyed either, if their suddenly stiff postures were any indication.

"I heard about Thomas and rushed right over to see if there was anything I could do." Marla flipped her long, blond hair over her shoulder seemingly oblivious to her cool reception.

"Since he's in the infirmary, and we all know how you can't stand to be around anyone who is hurt, I fail to see how you'd be of any help." Helen bluntly addressed the beautiful she-wolf.

Marla bared her teeth at Helen in what loosely could be taken as a smile, if one wasn't too fussy. "I meant that with Kane being up all night, he might be tired and need some help in the office. My shift doesn't start until noon and I have done office work before."

The Mating

"Thanks for the offer, Marla," John nodded solemnly, "but I think I'll be able to handle things until Kane gets back. If it does get busy, Elise can help."

"Elise?" Marla raised her perfectly shaped eyebrows and looked puzzled. "Who is...? Oh, I'd forgotten. The new little mate." She acted as if she was searching the room before letting her eyes focus on the newest pack member. "So you're Kane's mate. I must say, you are a tiny thing." Studying Elise from head to toe, she shook her head and made a little moue. "Hmm, you're not very strong-looking. I hope you can stand up to the strain of the position. I know from personal experience how...demanding...Kane can be."

Flushing at the insult and implied meaning of Marla's statement, Elise wanted to sink into the floor, but knew she had to put the other woman in her place, if she wanted to maintain her status. Standing, she circled around the table and advanced on the woman, speaking with a trace of a growl in her voice. "I'm perfectly capable of being Kane's mate and I don't appreciate your comments. If you have a problem with me, say it directly to my face rather than making snide innuendos."

Marla stepped back in surprise. "Why, Elise! I assure you I meant nothing at all. It's just that Kane and I are old friends..." Her voice trailed off and she looked at the table. The others were studiously eating their eggs. A power struggle between two packmates didn't involve them. It was up to the two wolves to work it out.

Elise took one more step towards her and for a moment Marla held her ground, but then retreated. "I'm sorry I interrupted your breakfast. I'll leave you alone, but if you need anything at all..." When no one responded, the woman left, slamming the door behind her.

Exhaling loudly, Elise turned back towards the table. The others were looking at her. "That was...unpleasant."

"Actually, it was quite entertaining." Carrie started to laugh.

Helen snorted. "It's about time someone put her in her place. Good work, Elise."

John sipped his coffee, but Elise was sure he was smiling. She felt a grin breaking out on her own face as well and happily sat down to finish her breakfast. She'd survived her first encounter with a member of the pack—Carrie, John and Helen didn't count—and she'd come out on top. It was a good feeling and erased some of her earlier insecurities.

After breakfast, Carrie and John left for town to pick up some supplies for their soon-to-arrive pup. Helen accepted Elise's help with the cleanup and then shooed her on her way with instructions to go exploring outside. Elise walked into the backyard and looked around with interest.

The early morning air was cool, but the brightness of the sun promised to bring a warmer day once the dampness burned off. Small white clouds dotted the otherwise clear blue sky and the air had the fresh, clean scent that always appeared after a rain. Noting the puddles on the ground, she vaguely recalled hearing some rain hitting against the windowpane sometime during the night. Had it been before, or after Thomas had been found? She hoped it was after the fact, not liking the image of the wounded man lying on the ground, blood and rain soaking his clothes as he awaited rescue.

Shaking the grim image from her mind, she concentrated on her surroundings again. Numerous large trees dotted the lawn, their majestic branches stretching outward to create a canopy overhead. She imagined that in the summer the yard would be pleasantly shaded by their leaves. In the far corner, a substantial vegetable garden could be seen, and a variety of flower beds were placed strategically around the house and outbuildings. Due to it being fall, the gardens weren't looking their best, but evidence of the summer splendour could still be seen in the few hardy flowers that refused to quit blooming despite the cooler nights.

Circling to the front of the house, she carefully skirted a large puddle and then stood on the edge of the driveway. How far did she dare travel on her own? Looking down the drive, she could make out some houses beyond the bend. They were probably the homes of other pack members, she decided. Helen had spoken of an infirmary and she pondered where it might be located and if Kane would still be there. It wasn't that she really *wanted* to see him, she told herself. It was just that she didn't know anyone else or have anything in particular to do.

If she was with Kane, he'd introduce her to some more people and she'd feel braver about exploring. While the members she'd met upon arriving yesterday had all seemed friendly, her encounter with Marla had left her apprehensive. Would she have to stand up to each and every member in order to prove herself, or would they just accept her? Had they only seemed friendly yesterday because Kane had been there? How would they react to meeting her without his protection? At dinner last night, she felt more confident when the others spoke of embracing new ways and new members, but now... She worried her lip as she pondered the questions rolling about in her mind. Joining a new pack was tricky; she'd never appreciated that fact before. Now that she had her own personal insight into the situation, she resolved to be a lot more supportive of new members in the future.

In the distance, she could hear a vehicle approaching. Squinting she noted that it was a red sports car and was travelling rather quickly for such a narrow, twisty driveway. Clouds of dust swirled up around it, obscuring the view of the driver. Something about the vehicle was making her uneasy and she stepped onto the grass as it drew closer. Just as it was almost even with her, the driver jerked the wheel. The car fishtailed and loose bits of gravel flew up in the air. Elise jerked backwards as small pebbles pelted her. Unfortunately, there was a large puddle right behind her and she slipped, landing on her rear in the muddy water.

Gasping in outrage, she looked towards the driveway, prepared to give the driver a piece of her mind, but the vehicle was gone. Muttering vile threats under her breath, she wiped her stinging cheek, not surprised when a trace of blood appeared on her hand. At least one of the sharp, stony projectiles had hit its mark. Thoroughly disgruntled, she clambered to her feet and tried unsuccessfully to wipe the mud off herself but only succeeded in smearing it around. Giving up, she stomped towards the house.

Chapter 7

Elise was thankful the kitchen was empty. Someone had humiliated her on purpose, and advertising the fact was the last thing she wanted. Removing her socks and shoes so as not to leave a muddy trail, she padded barefoot up to her room and then finished stripping off her filthy garments. Setting them in a pile on the floor, she went to clean up.

After turning on the shower, she peered in the mirror while waiting for the water to heat up. The stones had stung as they hit her face and she wanted to check the extent of the damage. Sure enough, there was dried blood on her cheek. Carefully, she probed the cut, judging its severity. Opening the medicine cabinet, she found some antiseptic and dabbed the punctured skin, grimacing as the liquid stung the damaged flesh. A quick perusal found no other injuries beyond her bruised pride. Checking her appearance once more, she decided a casual observer wouldn't notice the wound, which in her mind was a good thing. She didn't want a lot of people questioning what had happened. Once she found out who the driver was, she'd deal with him herself.

Grabbing a clip, she twisted her pony tail up on top of her head so it wouldn't get wet and then turned away from the mirror, only to bump into a solid wall of muscle. Strong hands caught hold of her shoulders as she rocked backwards.

"Oh! You're back." Quite taken by surprise, she stated the obvious. Her breath caught in her throat as she observed Kane was as naked as herself.

"Yep, I just walked in. I heard you moving about in here and, since I need a shower too, I thought we could share."

Skimming her eyes down his form, she took in his sculpted pecs and abs before realizing what she was doing. Her face grew hot and she looked away.

Kane chuckled and caught her by the chin, forcing her to meet his gaze. "Don't be shy. We're mated. You're allowed to look at me. I enjoy it almost as much as I enjoy looking at you." He accompanied his words with actions, sweeping his hand down her body. "You're beautiful, Elise."

The sensation created made her hum with pleasure. Without even meaning to, she found herself leaning towards him, rising up on her toes to encourage him to kiss her. As he complied, memories of their night together flooded her mind and suddenly she couldn't wait for him to once more transport her to that magical place filled with the most exquisite of sensations.

"Do you want me, mate?" Kane eased back and studied her face

"Yes." She whispered the word against his lips.

Growling in approval, he led her into the hot mist of the shower...

When they were both satiated, Kane had carried her to bed. He was exhausted from being up all night and had said he wanted to rest for a while. Within moments of his head hitting the pillow, he was asleep.

Presently, he was spooned to her back. His breath was warm on her neck, and his arm was wrapped around her waist effectively trapping her in place. She'd dozed a bit herself, feeling pleasantly relaxed from their earlier activity. Now half awake, she idly stroked Kane's arm, thinking that she could become addicted to experiences like that.

Sounds from outside drifted in the partially open window. Somewhere a car door slammed, reminding her of her encounter with the red sports car and the puddle. When she found out who owned that vehicle, she'd give them a piece of her mind for the idiotic stunt they'd pulled.

The Mating

The memory reminded her that she had a pile of muddy clothes on the floor. She sighed, not wanting to get up but the clothes weren't going to get washed if she continued to stay in bed.

Carefully, she eased out from under Kane's arm, trying not to wake him. He muttered slightly and rolled over before settling back down, his breathing deep and even. For a moment she stared at him. His face was relaxed and the controlled edge that always seemed to be a part of him was temporarily erased.

He was certainly good-looking; strong and dominant, much more so than Bryan had ever been. She scowled at her thoughts. It was instinct for a wolf to be drawn to a dominant mate, but she felt guilty for comparing the two men. Of course, Kane would seem appealing. He was older, an Alpha. But, she retorted, who knew what Bryan might become in the next few years? Not that it mattered anymore, the voice of reason ruefully acknowledged. She was mated to Kane and nothing could change the fact. It was best to put her old friend out of her mind and look to the future.

With a determined nod, she quickly dressed, grabbed the laundry and headed downstairs, leaving her mate to catch up on his rest.

Elise had just finished the laundry when she heard a sound behind her. Glancing over her shoulder, she saw Kane leaning in the doorway, his shirt hanging open and his hair mussed from sleep. Her heart beat faster at the sight of him. Sliding her eyes over his body, she noted his toned stomach and long denim-encased legs. The jeans rode low on his hips and she forced herself not to blush as she recalled those same hips moving against her. A wave of desire unexpectedly rolled through her. Was she turning into some sort of sex-maniac? How could simply looking at the man have that effect on her?

Did he find her attractive too? He'd said she was beautiful, but did that really mean anything or were they just words? She wasn't quite sure why it mattered to her, except that it would make for a level playing field if they both had an equal physical attraction to the other.

Trying to sound unaffected by his presence, she casually addressed him. "You must have been tired after being out so late last night." She busied herself with folding her towels, keeping her eyes firmly averted and her body angled away from him.

"Yeah. We didn't find Thomas until almost two-thirty, and by the time we got him to the infirmary it must have been after three. I stayed with Julia, his mate, until he woke up. He was pretty groggy, so I need to head back there in a bit and, if he's awake, question him about what exactly happened."

"Did he need a doctor?"

"No. He was lucky. The bullet went straight through, missing any vital organs, so it only needed cleaning and a few stitches. Blood loss was the biggest problem, but thanks to his Lycan genetics, he'll be fine. Nadia, our nurse-practitioner, was waiting for us when we got back. She gave him a transfusion, cleaned the wound, and stitched him up."

"Is she one of us?"

"Uh-huh. We're fortunate to have her, and if something really serious is wrong there's a local doctor who knows about us and can be trusted."

"We have a similar set-up at home." She nodded in understanding as she tidied up the laundry area, still avoiding looking at him. Her heart rate had returned to normal and she wanted to keep it that way. Grabbing the box of soap and the fabric softener, she put them on the shelf and started to clean the lint trap in the dryer. "I'm glad your man is going to be okay and that he's receiving good care."

"Would you like to come along when I go to see him?"

"Sure. I'm almost done here. It will be good to meet some more of the pack." She rinsed her hands while staring blankly at the wall, wondering if she'd see the red sports car parked somewhere. If so, she could pretend a casual interest in the make or model and that might lead Kane into revealing who owned it. He wouldn't have to know the real reason she wanted the information.

Kane straightened up from his position against the door jamb and walking over to her. Placing his finger under her chin, he guided her around until she was facing him. "You seem to be avoiding looking at me. Why?"

"No reason." She looked everywhere around the room except towards him. "I'm busy with the laundry, that's all."

Kane considered her answer then reached up to stroke her cheek with his finger. "There's a cut on your face."

"Oh!" She quickly moved her hand upwards, knocking his aside, and covering the cut. She'd forgotten it was there.

"I didn't notice it earlier. What did you do?" He brushed her hand out of the way and examined the mark, his breath warm against her face. Her heartbeat quickened in response to his proximity.

"I... I must have scratched it on a branch or something when I was out earlier, looking around the yard."

"Hmm... It doesn't look like a scratch to me; it's deeper than that, more like a puncture wound. Are you sure you just got too close to a branch?" The weight of his stare forced her to look at him. He gazed down at her, his face passive, his eyes unblinking.

She wavered under his intense scrutiny. The wolf inside her screamed for her to confess, but she didn't want to. Gathering her courage, she boldly pushed past him, grabbing the pile of folded laundry and walking towards the door.

"Of course I'm sure. It's nothing to fuss over." Inwardly, she trembled. Turning your back on the Alpha and walking away when he'd asked you a question wasn't done without some form of retribution, but she needed to get away. Kane was too close, too compelling, and she wanted to keep her thinking clear.

"Elise!" He growled a warning and she stopped, slowly turning around. Her mouth had gone dry and a frisson of fear formed in her belly. So far, he'd only been kind to her but now, she was getting a taste of what made him the leader of the pack. His eyes were cold and stony, seeming to bore a hole right through her and leaving her in no doubt as to his displeasure. She clutched the laundry to her chest as if it were a shield and raised her chin slightly, exposing her throat in an age-old sign of submission.

Licking her lips, she replied shakily. "Kane, it's nothing. Why don't you get something to eat? I'm sure you're famished. I'll put these away and be back in a few minutes. Then you can show me where the infirmary is and introduce me to Thomas..." As she babbled, her eyes pleaded with him not to make a federal case out of it. She didn't want him to know about the sports car. It was her problem to solve. She had to be able to hold her head up around these people and not always be taking refuge behind her mate.

After what felt like ages he seemed to rein in his temper and sighed loudly. "Fine. I'll meet you at the backdoor in fifteen minutes."

Her tense shoulders relaxed and she started to leave but he spoke again, his words causing her to freeze in her tracks.

"Elise? Don't make it a habit of pushing me too far. You might not like the results."

She gave a quick nod and ran upstairs, thankful for the reprieve she'd been granted.

Chapter 8

Once she was in the bedroom, Elise dropped the laundry on the bed and flopped down beside it, staring at the ceiling. It had been a foolish move on her part, refusing to tell Kane about the sports car, but at the same time, it was such a minor thing. She needed to show him that she wasn't a complete pushover before he took it into his head to walk all over her.

Taking a calming breath, she tried to figure her mate out. As she'd just witnessed, he was definitely in control and not one to put up with insubordination. He was strong, dominant, and cool; he hadn't raised his voice at all, but his message had been as clear as a bell. On the other hand, he hadn't forced her into submission either, giving in to her silent plea that he drop the matter. That must indicate he had some consideration for her and was willing to allow his pack members some autonomy.

Yesterday, as he'd shown her their suite of rooms, he'd actually been quite kind. He acknowledged that she was probably feeling homesick and unsettled. Even when they'd first mated, hadn't he tried to ease the situation for her? And the morning after, he'd seemed to understand that losing her dream of a relationship with Bryan was difficult. How had he put it? 'Sometimes our lives have moments of great disappointment. It's difficult at the time, but we have to move beyond.' Yes, Kane definitely had a more sensitive side.

But then he'd talked about making their bonding work because it was their *duty* to the pack. She, of all people, knew that theirs was not a love match but her young heart still hoped for some tender sentiments and affection from her mate. Of course, as Alpha, his first duty *was* to the pack. She knew that from her own father, and if she'd had any doubt on the matter, the fact that Kane had all but abandoned her on her first day in order to deal with pack business would have straightened out her thinking. Looking back on last night, she recalled how he'd left the supper table and stayed out all night, searching for Thomas. Yes, Kane really did seem to have his pack's best interests at heart. The pack was devoted to him too, though. She only had to look at how everyone had gathered to greet him yesterday afternoon when he'd arrived home.

Rolling over, she propped her chin on her hands. How did she feel about him? Physically, she was drawn to him and, based on his earlier actions, he had some small liking for her, she was sure. After all, he had sought her out and asked her to go see Thomas with him...

Yikes! She'd forgotten that she said she'd meet him in a few minutes. Jumping up, she quickly put away the laundry. Kane hadn't been overly pleased with her when she'd left. There was no point in trying his patience any further today by making him wait! Tossing her clothes in her bureau and the towels in the linen closet, she clattered downstairs in search of her mate.

By the time she met him at the backdoor, Kane seemed in a better mood and didn't mention their confrontation, for which she was extremely grateful. By pack standards, he would have been justified in ripping a strip off her and she still wasn't sure why he'd let her go, however, she wasn't going to question her good luck. At least her mate didn't seem to be one to carry a grudge, she decided.

They walked to the infirmary since the building was only a short distance from the main house. She learned that the driveway wound in a long, narrow oval that started at the highway, came around by the Alpha house, and then worked its way through the front edge of the woods with various houses and buildings located along the way. After that, there were numerous paths that ran through the territory—some well-travelled and others barely visible—leading to the more remote corners of their land. These were often partially overgrown and seldom used except by the most adventurous pack members.

The particular path they were on now was basically a short cut between the Alpha house and the infirmary. As they walked along, she was very aware of the fact that Kane was almost a foot taller than her. Yet for all his size he moved gracefully, his steps barely making a sound.

Sunlight was streaming down through the trees and the gentlest of breezes caused leaves to drift lazily downward, carpeting the ground in gold and orange. She could smell the mustiness that wafted up from the decaying foliage as it was crushed underfoot, and she thought she could detect the scent of water. She questioned Kane about its location.

"Just over that rise, there's a small stream that feeds into the river. If you follow it along for a few miles, you'll come to our lake. It's not overly large but sufficient for us do to some swimming and a bit of fishing in the summer. There's also a waterfall—I think I mentioned it to you yesterday—but it's hard to get at due to the ravines. I'd advise you to go there only when accompanied by myself or one of the more experienced runners. It can be quite dangerous. Wolves have fallen and died there."

The challenge of climbing through the ravines sounded rather appealing, and she made a mental note to ensure that Kane took her there in the near future.

"I can't wait to go exploring." She grinned up at him, her joy at being near the wilderness eclipsing any awkwardness that might have remained from their earlier conflict. Like all wolves, the call of nature was simmering just below the surface and being outdoors in a wooded area gave her a feeling of excitement and home-coming.

"Yes, I'm sure you're eager for a good run." He paused and seemed about to add to his statement when someone called his name.

"Kane! You're back already. I thought I told you to go home and get some sleep." An efficient looking woman in her forties stood outside a simple, white vinyl-clad building. Her brown hair was drawn into a long braid and she was wearing a lab coat.

"I did go home, Nadia, and now I'm back." Kane nodded at the woman and then put his hand around Elise's waist, drawing her forward. "Elise, this is Nadia, our nurse-practitioner. Nadia, this is Elise, my mate."

Nadia looked her up and down as if she was trying to decide whether or not this new wolf passed inspection. She must have met the nurse's standard because she gave the briefest of nods before turning and addressing Kane with a smile. "Thomas is awake now and doing well. He's fortunate that he'd shifted into human form just before getting hit. The extra chemicals in his blood helped minimize the damage."

Elise followed Kane and Nadia as they discussed the healing properties of transformation chemicals. In ancient times, shifting forms had been considered magick but modern science had proven it to be a case of harnessing energy to rearrange one's molecular form, a process that could occur due to certain chemicals shape shifters produced. Elise tuned out, the science behind it of little interest, and, as a result was surprised to find they were at the door, Nadia holding it open for her. She murmured her thanks as she passed by the stern woman who merely raised an eyebrow and then moved off to a desk in the corner where she immediately became immersed in paperwork and files.

As Elise looked around, her nostrils flared in response to the medical smells. She hated hospitals and doctors, and this space was definitely a medical facility. Several beds lined one wall, separated by the regulation curtains. Chairs for visitors were strategically placed near each bed and a TV was mounted on the wall for patients to view. Across the room, there were locked cabinets containing medical supplies, while a partially

70

opened door allowed her a glimpse of what appeared to be an examining table or possibly a small surgery area.

Kane led the way over to the lone occupied bed and introduced her to Thomas. It was hard to judge his appearance since he was lying down and pale, yet he seemed pleasant enough, nodding at her and smiling weakly. His mate, Julia, was standing beside him and trailing her fingers through his blond hair in a comforting gesture. Elise recalled they were newly mated and imagined the separation was especially hard on them.

After exchanging a few pleasantries, Kane indicated that he wanted to talk to Thomas alone and the two women stepped outside onto the small porch that skirted the front of the building. Julia stretched her lean athletic figure and turned her face towards the sun, her warm honey-blond hair streaming down her back. "Gosh, it feels good to be outside. I'm stiff from sitting beside that bed all night but I didn't dare go home, not even once he was patched up."

"It must have been awful for you, not knowing what was going on while they were searching for him." Elise smiled sympathetically at the other girl.

Nodding, Julia wrapped her arms around herself. "Yeah. As soon as he was injured, I knew something was wrong even though he immediately blocked our bond. Crazy fool said he didn't want me to worry." She snorted. "As if being kept in the dark and not knowing what was happening would make me feel better. Men, they just don't get it sometimes, do they?"

She gave a half smile and shrugged. "I couldn't really say. We—Kane and I—haven't known each other that long."

"Oh, I'm sorry, I forgot." Julia clapped her hand to her mouth. "I guess I'm so caught up in Thomas that I'm not thinking. Yesterday was your first day and—"

"Relax. You had more important things to worry about." She hastened to reassure her.

"I'm still sorry I wasn't there yesterday when you arrived. I really wanted to be. We were all so excited when we got the news that Kane was finally bringing home a mate. Everyone has been secretly hoping he'd find someone suitable before Mar—" Julia stopped herself mid-sentence.

Elise wondered what she'd been going to say. Before what? Had the word been 'Marla?' From what she'd seen so far, it was definitely a possibility that Marla had been in the running for the position of Kane's future mate. Yet, if that was the case, why hadn't Kane bonded with the woman already? Why had he agreed to this political joining if he cared for someone else?

Julia continued talking, disturbing her train of thought. "Anyway, I really had planned on greeting you. I was waiting for Thomas to come home, thinking we'd go over to meet you together but then..." She broke off as her voice cracked and she blinked rapidly obviously trying to hold back tears.

"Julia, it's okay. Thomas is fine and neither Kane nor I mind that you didn't make it over. To be honest, there were so many new faces swirling around me that you could lie and say that you were there. I wouldn't even know the difference." She tried to lighten the mood, feeling sorry for the other girl who was worried sick about her mate.

Julia gave her a watery smile. "Thanks. I'm good now. It's silly of me to be feeling teary now that I know he's going to be okay. Delayed reaction, I guess." She dug a tissue out of her pocket to wipe her eyes, then pasted a smile on. "So... Tell me about yourself."

The two of them sat on a bench outside the infirmary and started talking, soon discovering that they had several things in common. Elise began to feel more at ease and Julia seemed to be forgetting the drama of the past day, at least for a while. They were so engrossed in discussing a recent book they'd both read that the sound of the door opening behind them caused them both to give a start.

It was Nadia announcing that she was going to get something to eat but would return in half an hour. Julia agreed to watch Thomas and page her if there was any problem.

The Mating

Nadia seemed to be a no-nonsense sort of individual who didn't have time for idle chatter. As she briskly strode away, Elise hoped she wouldn't need the woman's services any time soon. While she was probably good at her job, Nadia didn't seem that friendly towards her.

Julia leaned over and whispered conspiratorially in Elise's ear, while keeping one eye on the retreating figure of the nurse. "I've never seen Nadia smile at anyone except Kane. Everyone else is afraid of her and I think she likes it that way."

Elise looked at her new friend with relief. "So it's not just me?"

Julia couldn't suppress a giggle. "Nope, she treats everyone that way. I think it's actually all part of a secret plan. If she's grumpy enough, we'll all stay away, and she'll have less work to do."

Stifling a chuckle, Elise decided that Julia had a fun, quirky personality.

By the time Kane was ready to leave, she had agreed to meet Julia for lunch the next day. Happy to have made a new friend, Elise hummed to herself as she and Kane walked back to the Alpha house.

"You and Julia seemed to hit it off." Kane commented as they walked down the driveway.

"Uh-huh. She's about my age, says she likes to shop, and has a great stash of books that I can borrow."

"She's a runner as well; out every day rain or shine."

"Really? Great! Maybe she'll let me go with her." She bounced at the prospect. Things were definitely looking up.

"It's all right with me, as long as you keep to the areas we have marked off as safe. After Thomas' accident, we'll be patrolling the pathways daily, but we can't do the whole territory. I'll be giving everyone in the pack the same message. No free roaming for the next while."

His decree brought another conversation to mind. "Kane, last night Helen and Carrie mentioned something about traps that were being set, but not by humans. They wouldn't explain and said you'd told them not to tell me."

Kane was silent, seeming to consider his words. Eventually, he gave a heavy sigh. "They're right. It's a complicated situation and I want to make sure you have the facts, not some part truths." He looked around and spotted a log near the edge of the woods. "Come on. We'll sit over here and talk. There's less chance of being interrupted outside than there is at the house."

She followed him to the place he'd indicated curious as to what he'd have to tell her. Whatever it was, he looked grim. Sitting down beside him, she waited for him to speak, studying his profile out of the corner of her eye. His jaw was set and his brows were lowered but the dark hair that fell across his forehead softened what might otherwise have been a stern face. When he finally spoke, it wasn't about Thomas, but about an incident that had happened several months earlier.

"Remember how I told you that Zack had been killed in a car accident? He was coming home, took a curve too fast, and ended up going over the edge of the cliff. The strange thing was that Zack wasn't a fast driver and had driven that road all of his life. Negotiating the curve was something he should have been able to do in his sleep. When we checked the vehicle afterwards, we found that there were no brakes. There was a hole in the line and the fluid had all leaked out."

"Were the hoses old and worn out?"

"No. It was a brand-new truck. Helen had given it to him on his fifty-fifth birthday, two months previous."

"Then...?"

"It could have been a flaw in the material, but we suspect that someone actually tampered with the brakes."

She gasped. "That's awful! Did you call the police?"

"No. We left it as driver error. The police would have asked too many questions. The risk of being discovered was too great and outweighed the need for a formal investigation. Nothing could bring Zack back."

"But who would do such a thing? And why? Surely you need to find out."

"At the time we didn't really have any leads. John and I have some suspicions, but no proof. Actually, only a few of us even know about the brake line. We didn't want to upset the whole pack. I'll expect you to keep this to yourself." Kane looked at her for acquiescence and she nodded.

"Who does know?"

"Myself, John, the Elders and Helen. Not even Carrie is aware of all the facts."

"This was all recent, wasn't it?"

"Yeah, two months ago."

"And then you took over."

Kane nodded. "Right after Zack's accident, the Elders met to decide the leadership, but the decision was split. It caused a big controversy, which was unfortunate given that everyone was still upset over losing Zack."

"You mentioned that both you and the other Beta were up for the job. His name was Ryne, wasn't it?"

"Yes." Kane rubbed his hands over his face, obviously upset by the memory. "We were co-Betas and it should have come down to a pack vote, but for some reason Ryne was adamant that the position be decided by a challenge. Several people tried to talk him out of it, but he wouldn't listen. It was so unlike him, too. Anyway, as I told you, we fought and it was pretty nasty. Ryne and I are pretty evenly matched. My advantage is I know how to wait and choose my moment. In the end, I won."

"Do you have any idea where he is now?"

"Originally, we'd heard that he planned to leave the area, but a few of the pack think they've seen him in the distance."

"Maybe he's cooled down and wants to come back?"

"If he does he's never approached any of us, and even if he does ask... Well, let's say it's complicated." Kane sighed. "You see, we suspect Ryne had something to do with the faulty brakes, though hard proof is missing."

"And you still let him live?" She was shocked.

"We didn't come to that conclusion until after the fight. That's when things started to add up."

"How so?"

"Well, after Zack's accident, there were a lot of things going wrong around here. Our electricity was turned off for non-payment, even though the bill had been paid. The Fire Marshall was out, wanting to inspect all of the buildings because of an anonymous tip. We've had traps set on the property, hunters spotted on our land, an oil slick near the mouth of the river that killed off some of the wildlife. It feels like someone is trying to undermine us. Now we have Thomas being shot last night." He shook his head and looked as if the weight of the world was settling on his shoulders. "Once word spreads through the pack about that, there'll be a lot of questions to answer."

"But all of the things you mentioned are coincidences, a string of bad luck, right? I mean, I'm sorry Thomas was shot but accidents do happen, especially in the fall when it's hunting season. The humans aren't always as careful as they should be."

Kane looked at her steadily. "Thomas told me that he scented Ryne immediately before the gun went off."

Her mouth opened in surprise. "Ryne shot a member of his own pack?"

"Quite likely. We thought his scent was around the traps too. It was vague, but detectable. And the oil spill? Boot prints left behind looked like the kind that Ryne used to wear."

"So are you trying to catch him?"

"We have patrols looking, but he's too clever a wolf to stay out in the open. He's holed up someplace, we just can't figure out where that might be."

"So why did you need to tell me all of this? Helen and Carrie said there was something personal involved."

A curious blend of sadness mixed with anger seemed to wash over Kane's face. He picked up a stone and tested the weight in his hand before hurling it into the brush. The dull thud of it hitting the ground broke the silence. Looking at her out of the corner of his eye, Kane answered her question. "There is something very personal involved. Ryne's my half-brother."

She couldn't keep the shock out of her voice. "Your own brother wanted to kill you in a challenge? And now he's out there sabotaging the pack?"

"All signs seem to point that way. And as I said earlier, some even think he's responsible for Zack's accident."

"Did he really want to be Alpha that badly?"

Shaking his head, Kane picked up a stick and snapped it in half. "I didn't think so. He never questioned Zack over anything and seemed content as Beta. We both were. Zack was a good leader and a power struggle was the farthest thing from anyone's mind. Ryne was even talking about settling down. This flared up out of nowhere."

Not sure what to say, she reached over and laid her hand on Kane's shoulder. "I'm sorry."

"Thanks. I might as well tell you all the bad news at once. There's one other problem facing the pack. An oil company called Northern Oil wants to do some test drilling on our land."

"I've heard about that. Helen or Carrie mentioned it."

"Of course we won't allow it, but the company is trying to pull some legal strings to get their way. At one time, a few of the pack members were leaning towards allowing them in—there's a lot of money on the table—but in the end, it's not worth it. Letting the company in would diminish our territory, cause environmental damage, and increase the chances of exposure. Originally, it caused some dissension in the pack, but I've had a few meetings and everyone realizes keeping them out is for the best."

"But will the oil company listen?"

"They're going to have to. Helen has a daughter, Chloe. She's in university now studying Environmental Science. I've had her do a study of the acreage in question and we have a pretty good case for keeping them out. The area is home to several endangered plants and animals. Chloe's working with some of her professors to get the northern corner of our territory listed as environmentally sensitive and a protected habitat."

"Well, that sounds promising."

"It is and thankfully it's good news for a change." Silence fell between them and she noted how tired Kane looked. Stress lines bracketed his mouth and the muscle in his jaw continued to work. She wished she could ease some of his worry and instinctively began rubbing her hand in comforting circles on his back.

Kane looked at her appreciatively. "Just between you and me, being Alpha is giving me a huge headache." He chuckled and stood up, tossing the stick he'd been worrying aside. "Come on, we'd better get back. Who knows what calamity might have occurred in the past hour." Taking her hand, they headed towards the house.

Chapter 9

Back at the house, Kane went off in search of John, and Elise found Helen in the kitchen once again. She was busily making sandwiches and chatting to three other women who were also helping prepare lunch. They all moved about the kitchen with the ease of familiarity, obviously having spent a lot of time here. Looking up, Helen smiled.

"There you are! Elise, I want you to meet two of my daughters, Zoe and Phoebe." Helen nodded at two young women who looked to be in their early to mid-twenties. Both bore a strong resemblance to Helen except that their hair was still dark brown, rather than liberally streaked with grey and their figures hadn't rounded out yet. "And this is Zoe's friend, Rose. She lives near the edge of the territory with her parents and works at the local bank." Rose gave Elise a shy smile and then leaned over the sink so that her hair hid her face. The girl was non-descript with pale blue eyes, brown hair, average height, and weight. She wasn't unattractive, but neither was there anything striking about her that made her overly memorable. Instinctively, Elise knew that Rose was probably one of the lower ranking members of the pack—not that it was a bad thing—but the girl would follow the lead of others and not cause any waves. There'd be no challenges coming from that quarter.

After greetings were exchanged, Elise pitched in with preparations for the late lunch. She found out that both Zoe and Phoebe were married with two children each. The young ones were off with their fathers to pick out pumpkins for Halloween, and the ladies were having a girls' day out with plans to go shopping once lunch was over.

"You should come with us," Phoebe invited. "Since you're new here, we can show you where the best stores are and maybe stop at the teahouse for a mid-afternoon break."

"Well... It does sound like fun." Elise hesitated, wondering what Kane would say but then shrugged. He'd likely be busy and not even miss her. "All right, I'll go."

"Great! Now let's get this food on the table and feed the men so we can be off."

Zoe went to fetch the males, and the other women carried the platters of food into the dining area. Elise noticed that the table had been stretched out to accommodate about a dozen people and sure enough, several men came traipsing in with Kane and John. The meal was noisy with everyone talking at once. Elise sat back watching the interaction, making mental notes of the relationships that she saw unfolding around her. Kane mostly sat and ate quietly while listening to the others, but she noted that the other men kept glancing at him for approval. When he did speak, the others listened without interrupting and seemed to take his comments seriously. Even if being Alpha did give him a headache, she could easily see that he had the needed qualities for the job.

Helen and her daughters were close and chatted about the children. Rose only occasionally chimed in to the conversation. Elise noticed that the shy young woman kept glancing towards a blond-haired young man named Daniel, but always looked away if he turned towards her. A smile played over Elise's lips. Rose had a crush on the fellow but was too timid to do anything about it. After studying the male in question, Elise decided he was equally interested, since he paid more attention to what Rose was doing than to the conversation the men were having.

Glancing towards Kane, she saw that he too was aware of the undercurrent between Rose and Daniel. Their eyes met, and Kane gave a slight nod towards the soon-to-be-lovebirds, a smile ghosting over his lips before he rolled his eyes. She gave him a reproachful look before smiling back. It was good to have that connection with him; a silent communication just between the two of them. The smile slowly faded from her face as she studied her mate, taking in his features one by one. She loved his thick black hair, recalling how it felt as she ran her fingers through it. His nose was straight, his jaw firm and his eyes were the most amazing amber colour that seemed to see right into her. Her mate. It was still hard to believe at times. With a start, she realized that Kane was studying her too and had a softer look about his eyes. Her heart caught in her chest and she hoped he'd make eye contact with her again. For some reason, it felt vital that she see that look directly, but then John called his name and the moment was lost.

Annoyed at the interruption, she returned to her meal and idly listened in on the ladies' conversation while puzzling over her exchange with Kane. It had been companionable, causing a pleasant feeling of belonging and warmth inside her. Was it possible that they were becoming friends? She hoped so; it would be good to have more than physical attraction in common. While they might not ever love each other, a friendship between them would make life much more comfortable.

Soon the simple meal was over, and the men went off to do whatever they were doing; she had never quite grasped what the conversation had been about. Oh well, she and the other women had their own plans for the afternoon. Looking forward to exploring the shops that the local town had to offer, she grabbed her purse and climbed into the waiting van.

Zoe and Phoebe were teasing Rose about her crush on Daniel while Helen chided them. "Now girls, leave Rose alone. If she and Daniel end up together or not, it's none of your business."

"Aww, Mom." The girls moaned in unison then looked at each other and burst out laughing.

Helen shook her head. "Honestly, sometimes I wonder if you two are still pups rather than grown women with your own families! Don't pay them any mind, Rose. When they were dating, they mooned about the house worse than you do."

Rose blushed and murmured something indistinguishable, then stared resolutely out the window.

Relenting, Zoe left her friend alone and turned to Elise. "So, now that we're away from the house and no one can walk in on our conversation, tell us what Kane is really like."

"Kane?" She felt like a deer caught in the headlights. She didn't really know anything about him. Why would they be asking her? They were the ones that had lived with him all their lives.

"Yeah. He's gorgeous and we've all had crushes on him at one time or another. That strong, silent thing he does is so hot." Zoe rolled her eyes and looked rather dreamy as if envisioning Kane giving her a smouldering, lust-filled look.

Phoebe reached over and smacked her sister. "Quit drooling. You've got Bob and you know you love him."

"Of course I do, but a girl can't help being curious. And don't you get all high and mighty with me. You think Kane is eye-candy, too." Both of the young women giggled as they watched Elise expectantly.

"Well..." She hesitated, unsure of what to say. "I don't really know him that well, yet. It... It was a political arrangement." She was embarrassed to admit to that, as if it made her less worthy than those who had been allowed to choose their own mates. It was ridiculous to feel that way— arrangements such as hers weren't that uncommon and she had done it for the good of the pack—but still, it gave her a strange feeling inside. However, the others didn't even bat an eye at her pronouncement so maybe it was all just her.

"We know that, but what's he like? In bed, I mean." Zoe grinned, devilment dancing in her eyes, and Elise heard Helen gasp from her position in the driver's seat.

"Zoe! I can't believe you'd ask Elise such a thing." Helen glared at her daughter through the rear-view mirror.

The Mating

"Mom, don't be such a prude. You've said yourself that Kane was a stud." Phoebe spoke up in her sister's defence.

Helen blushed and looked apologetically at Elise. "Well, yes, I did—I mean you can't help but notice—but I'd never..." She sputtered and then stared fixedly at the road.

She reached over and patted her arm. "It's okay, Helen."

"So?" Zoe wasn't about to let the subject of Kane's bedroom prowess drop and Elise tried to think of what to say. She'd teased her friends in a similar way before, but it was different when the shoe was on the other foot, especially since theirs wasn't a love match. After all, she couldn't really say how romantic he was, or talk about the sweet nothings he whispered in her ear. And Kane was their Alpha, for heaven's sake! It wasn't proper to talk about his performance in the bedroom; it seemed disloyal.

"He's...er..."

Phoebe jumped in with some suggestions. "Hot? Talented? Well-endowed? He makes your teeth rattle and the earth move?"

"Uh...yeah, I guess that pretty well sums it up." Elise felt her face growing red, but the others didn't mention it. They sighed contentedly and sank back in their seats.

"I knew it." Zoe had a satisfied smile on her face.

Phoebe giggled and nudged Rose in the ribs. "See, Rose. You get Daniel to make a move and soon you'll be as happy as Elise is."

Elise inwardly frowned. Was she happy? She wasn't exactly sad, and her homesickness wasn't nearly as bad as she thought it might be. But happy? Well, that might not be the right word, though she really didn't know what would be the correct one to describe her present state of being. Kane pleased her physically and she *did* like him as a person. A future where they co-existed peacefully as friends was a definite possibility. Maybe she wasn't *exactly* happy yet, but she wasn't miserable either and the future was definitely looking brighter than it had a few days ago.

This realization seemed to settle something inside her, and she looked around at the passing scenery with a much lighter heart and a more positive outlook than she'd had yesterday afternoon. Had it only been two days since she'd mated Kane? Somehow it seemed longer. So many things had already happened: the bonding ceremony, meeting the new pack, Thomas being injured, encountering Marla and the 'attack' by the red car. Well, she thought philosophically, at least her new life wasn't dull!

Her new friends had a great time showing Elise all that the town had to offer. They checked out the clothing shops and the shoe stores, trying on the winter fashions that were just arriving. Both Zoe and Rose bought new winter coats while Phoebe lingered over a matching purse and dress boots. Elise tried a few things on but didn't make any purchases. First of all, she didn't need anything, and secondly, she wasn't sure what her financial situation might be.

At home, she'd helped her father with some minor office work and assisted Sarah with the house. For that, she'd been paid a small wage out of the pack's general operating budget. Now, she was basically unemployed with only her small savings to fall back on. She'd have to talk to Kane about the situation. Maybe she could find a job in town waitressing.

Thankfully, no one pressed her as to why she wasn't buying anything. She knew they'd all noticed how much she'd admired a certain green V-necked sweater that matched her eyes. Its soft angora knit had draped over her curves in a flattering way, the low-cut neckline giving a tantalising hint of cleavage. Reluctantly, she'd placed it back on the rack, not wanting to squander her money on something so frivolous until she had her own source of income.

Helen had gone to get her hair done and the four younger women were going to meet her at the Grey Goose Tea Room at three o'clock. Since they still had half an hour to spare, they wandered down the mall idly commenting on various window displays. Elise paused by a small art gallery to look at an exceptionally fine mounted photo of a wolf standing in the middle of the woods. It had a natural wood frame and a deep burgundy mat that added warmth to the blues and greys of the actual picture. "This is nice," she commented to her companions. The others nudged each other and giggled. "What? Don't you like it?"

"Oh, we like it all right. Don't you recognise the subject?"

Puzzled, she studied the picture again. The background looked vaguely familiar. She said as much to them. "But I can't really say where I've seen it before."

Phoebe leaned over and whispered in her ear. "That's a picture of Kane."

"What?" She spoke louder than she'd intended and several shoppers gave her strange looks as they passed by. Ducking her head, she tried to make herself inconspicuous. "That's Kane? I've only seen him as a wolf once before..." Her voice trailed off. How embarrassing, not to even recognise your own mate! As she peered more carefully at the picture, she noticed the wolf's eyes were definitely Kane's. "Who took it?"

The three ladies fell silent and then, unexpectedly Rose spoke. "It was Ryne. He liked photography and was actually pretty good. Quite a few of his pictures have been sold both here and in other galleries around the area, though I think this is the only one I've ever seen with Kane in it."

"You've heard about Ryne, haven't you?" Zoe tentatively asked.

Elise nodded. "Kane told me. It's hard to reconcile someone who can take such a wonderful picture with the person I've heard about. I can't believe any Lycan would endanger its own pack."

"No one understands why Ryne issued that challenge." Phoebe shook her head. "He's lucky Kane didn't kill him."

"Uh-oh. Bitch at twelve o'clock." Zoe hissed a warning, and everyone looked in the direction she indicated. Marla was walking across the gallery and heading their way, an obviously fake smile pasted on her face.

"Oh great," Phoebe groaned. "And it's too late to escape. She's seen us."

Elise tensed and hoped the other woman wouldn't be as snarky now as she'd been first thing in the morning. One confrontation a day was usually her limit, thank you.

"Well, look who's here." Marla's voice was condescending and she smirked at Elise, obviously having recovered from their earlier skirmish and ready to do battle again.

"Hello, Marla." Rose spoke very quietly, meeting the other woman's eyes before staring at the floor, her hands shoved into her pockets. Elise could almost see Marla puff herself up, pleased that at least one of the people present recognized her superior status.

"Marla." Zoe and Phoebe each gave curt nods of acknowledgement.

After considering the situation, Elise decided to stay silent, not wanting to create a scene. Something about the blonde set her teeth on edge. Apparently though, Marla wasn't one to let an opportunity pass by. "Elise, I see you're admiring the picture of your mate. You know, I was there when it was taken. We'd just finished the most...invigorating...exercise and—"

"Oh, give it a break, Marla." Zoe snorted in disgust. "You were out with Ryne and came across Kane by accident. Don't try to make it sound like more than it was. And before you even start, we all know that it was Ryne who managed to talk him into having his picture taken, not as a special favour to you."

Her face flushing, Marla glowered at them. "Better be careful what you say, Zoe, because one of these days you might find that I'm the one with the power. And just like an elephant, I don't forget." With that, Marla spun on her heels and stalked away.

"Her memory isn't the only thing like an elephant," Zoe said in a not so quiet voice, while staring pointedly at the woman's retreating hips.

Marla must have heard for she turned and shot the most evil look their way.

Not finished, Zoe added another stinging comment. "She really shouldn't wear such skin-tight clothing. It shows every bulge and bump."

Elise couldn't believe how rude Zoe was being and simply stared speechless, as Marla spun around and began to walk towards them again.

Phoebe placed a warning hand on Zoe's arm, but Zoe shook it off, hot angry emotions flashing in her eyes as a low growl started to emit from her throat. Marla appeared as if she was about to lose control and Elise began to wonder if she'd end up in a werewolf version of a catfight.

At the last moment, a man wearing a suit coat and a nametag proclaiming him as the gallery manager, called Marla's name. She paused, shot one last hateful look at Zoe, and then turned to talk to the man.

Phoebe and Rose both grabbed Zoe's arms and dragged her out of the mall. Gesturing towards a stately, turn of the century home that was located about a block away, the sisters began to walk briskly down the street.

"What was that all about?" Elise asked, hurrying along behind. Sure, she'd stood up to Marla that morning, but she'd been a wreck inside. Zoe didn't even seem fazed and had, in fact, deliberately provoked the other woman.

With a toss of her head, Zoe began explaining. "Marla and I go way back, but not as friends. She's always been jealous that our father was chosen as Alpha over hers. Now she keeps trying to climb the ladder within the pack by latching onto whoever seems to be next in line. Right now, she's mad because she chose to back the wrong brother. She was sure Ryne was next in line and got her claws into him, changing him from a nice guy into this power-hungry Alpha-wannabe."

"So she and Ryne...?" Elise queried.

"Rumour was that Ryne was planning on making her his mate." Phoebe explained. "But when Ryne lost the challenge and left, she was out of the running again for working her way into the big house. Not that any of us think she ever really gave up. With Ryne out of the picture, she simply changed her target."

"Oh..." Elise let the information sink in. "So that means—"

"Yep." Zoe pulled open the door to the Grey Goose Tea Room. "She had her sights set on Kane. When we got the call that Kane was coming home with his new mate, Marla looked like she was about to burst a blood vessel."

Phoebe giggled. "I wish I'd had a camera handy. I've never seen anyone's face turn that red before."

The sisters quieted down as they waited to be shown to a table, and Elise took the opportunity to check out her surroundings. At one point in time, the Grey Goose had been a private home but was now a combination tea room and gift shop. Crafts, jewellery, scarves, and unique wall hangings were tastefully displayed in small side rooms and alcoves, while tables were arranged in the centre part of the building. The plaster and woodwork had been restored to its original splendour, while period furniture was used throughout. Soft music drifted from speakers strategically hidden in the numerous potted plants, providing cover for the various conversations that came from the patrons.

Impressed with the atmosphere of casual elegance, she wondered what the chances were of getting a part-time job in such an establishment. The waitresses seemed busy enough, so maybe the owner would consider adding one more to his staff. Tucking the idea into the back of her mind, she followed the others as a server led them to their table.

Once seated, Zoe immediately launched into a whispered commentary about someone she knew who was seated across the room. Elise glanced at the person in question, catching a glimpse of Rose out of the corner of her eye. The girl was so quiet, keeping her head down and studying the menu. Rose and Zoe appeared to be total opposites and it seemed a strange friendship. While Zoe had basically been picking a fight with Marla, Rose had almost crawled inside herself and become invisible.

When Rose left to use the ladies' room, Elise broached the subject and Zoe happily explained. "Rose is my 'project'. I've noticed lately that Daniel seems interested in her—Daniel's my brother-in-law—and so I've sort of befriended Rose in the hopes that I can get the two of them together."

"She likes to think she's the world's greatest matchmaker." Phoebe chimed in.

"Well, I got you and Alex together." Zoe pointed out.

"One success and it goes to your head." Phoebe rolled her eyes.

"Well, what about Kane and Marla? I knew they weren't suited." Leaning back in her chair, Zoe crossed her arms and looked smug.

"Knowing they aren't suited isn't the same as matchmaking and besides, everyone knew that Marla wasn't what Kane needed." Phoebe glanced over at Elise. "He needs someone nice, like Elise."

Elise gave a half smile and ducked her head, embarrassed at how the two women were chattering away about her mate. She was sure they didn't mean anything by it. Letting their banter wash over her, she pondered the whole Kane-Marla-Ryne triangle.

Marla had been paired with Ryne, but when Ryne left she'd switched allegiance to Kane. How had Kane felt about that? Had he been interested in Marla even knowing that she'd been with his brother? From what Julia had said earlier, it sounded like others had believed Kane and Marla were a couple. Or did it only seem that way because Marla forced herself into Kane's company? The woman was certainly pushy, but Kane could discourage her if he wanted to. The question was, did he want to? He had spent quite a bit of time talking to her yesterday.

A strange feeling quivered through her stomach. While she wasn't in love with Kane, it still made her uneasy to think another woman had her sights set on him. Somehow, she knew that Marla hadn't given up on the pack's Alpha.

Chapter 10

Elise and the other ladies arrived at the house to discover that the men were planning a barbeque. The weather was unseasonably warm for this late in October and a final outdoor meal had been deemed just the thing. Potatoes were already on the grill baking and the steaks marinating. Helen immediately switched into her super-hostess mode and began pulling the salad fixings out of the fridge. Phoebe headed home to get some pies for dessert, while Zoe and Rose began gathering plates, cutlery, and napkins.

Having been sent to count how many were actually there, Elise stood in the doorway and began to number off the people who would be partaking of the meal. There was Kane and herself, Helen, Zoe, Phoebe, their two spouses and four children, Rose, Daniel, John and Carrie, and two other couples whose names she couldn't recall. In total that made nineteen people; she hoped there were lots of lawn chairs!

It turned out that there was no need to worry. The Alpha house was well-stocked with chairs, and Helen was more than capable of dealing with an impromptu meal for nearly twenty. Elise doubted she could ever be as organized as the older woman, and sincerely hoped that Helen would stay around for years to come.

The meal was a success and Kane had inquired politely how her day was. Elise skimmed over the meeting with Marla, instead commenting on how much she'd enjoyed their tea at the Grey Goose. Phoebe had chimed in, telling about the boots and handbag she'd purchased, and Zoe described the new coats she and Rose had purchased.

"But Elise didn't buy anything, Kane; you won't have to worry about her overspending." Zoe had nudged Elise playfully to show the comment was a joke.

"You didn't see anything that you liked?" Kane queried while serving himself some more salad.

"Not really." She took the bowl from him and passed it over to Zoe.

"Oh, come on, Elise. You were almost drooling over that green sweater at Carter's Casuals." Phoebe chided.

"I didn't really need it." She murmured, glancing at Kane out of the corner of her eye. She'd really have to talk to him about getting a job.

Kane looked as if he was about to comment, but then Zoe's youngest knocked over her glass of milk and in the confusion, the topic was dropped.

After dinner, a small bonfire was lit for roasting marshmallows. Everyone gathered round, couples naturally drifting together, while Helen benevolently watched her grandchildren running about the yard chasing the bubbles she was blowing for them. In the flickering fire light, Elise scanned the assembled group. Carrie was sitting between John's legs with her back resting against his chest. John's arms were wrapped around her swollen body, gently caressing her belly. Zoe was snuggled up to her husband and giggling at whatever he was whispering in her ear, while Phoebe sat beside her mate, contentedly holding his hand.

Elise had learned that the other two couples were Michael and his mate Susan, and Franz with his fiancée, Giselle. The two men had helped look for Thomas the night before. They were sitting nearby, quietly talking about a movie they had seen recently. Near the edge of the circle of light cast by the fire, Elise could just make out Rose and Daniel holding hands, the sight bringing a smile to her face. From what she had seen, they were a good match, and she hoped things turned out well for them.

The Mating

When everyone had first sat down, Kane had pulled Elise to his side, wrapping his arm around her waist. Now he was moving his hand across her thigh, tracing lazy patterns on the sensitive skin. Frissons of awareness shot through her body. It was decidedly unsettling how his touch could affect her, and she wasn't sure she liked him having such power over her. Surreptitiously, she observed him, noting he seemed to be mesmerized by the dancing flames and totally unaware of what his hand was doing.

She traced his features with her eyes, taking in his straight nose and strong jaw. A strand of dark hair fell across his forehead; she had to clench her fists to keep from reaching up and brushing it back into place. Forcing herself to look away, she stared at the fire. Flames danced in the darkness, causing shadows to flicker across the ground and waves of heat to shimmer in the air. Occasionally a log would shift, sending sparks into the night sky.

The other couples could barely be seen as darkness descended. Encased in their own little pool of light, it was as if she and Kane were alone in the night. His scent drifted around her, invading her senses and clouding her mind. She found herself leaning towards him. With a start, she pulled herself back and sought a means of distraction.

Reaching for a marshmallow and stabbing it onto a stick, she nonchalantly worked herself away from him. The slight distance made her feel better, more in control, and she breathed a sigh of relief. Concentrating on toasting her marshmallow to perfection, she withdrew it at just the right moment; the skin a warm toasted brown with the promise of a sweet, melted interior. Her mouth watered in anticipation and she sat back, blowing gently to cool the treat in preparation for consuming it. Just when it was ready, a large hand reached around and pulled the stick from her grasp.

Indignantly, she turned around just in time to see her marshmallow disappearing into Kane's mouth.

"Hey! I toasted that!"

Kane grinned at her. "I know, and I thank you for preparing it just the way I like it."

She opened her mouth to protest, but Kane swooped forward and covered her mouth with his. She could taste traces of the sweet confection on his lips and hummed in appreciation. Slowly, they withdrew and she found herself staring into his face, his amber eyes seeming to search hers for the answer to some unspoken question. Something tugged within her, as if she was being pulled into him and she struggled to read his enigmatic expression, wondering if he too felt a sense of connectedness.

Whatever Kane was looking for he must have found it, for he smiled and lifted her up so she was cradled between his knees, her rear end firmly in contact with him. He pulled her back so that she was leaning against his chest, similar to Carrie and John. Reaching around her, he put another marshmallow on a stick and prepared it, while his chin rested on her head. At first, she was self-conscious, but soon realized that no one was paying them any attention. Slowly, she relaxed within the warm circle of his arms and Kane, obviously sensing the change in her, growled his approval.

Over the next half hour, they fed each other marshmallows, each one accompanied by a kiss to clean the sticky sweet off their lips. Her breathing grew increasingly ragged. Kane wrapped an arm around her waist and gently rocked his hips against her. A heavy, aching warmth was growing within her and she pushed back against him in response. He muttered something indecipherable then threw the marshmallow sticks into the fire.

In one swift motion, he scooped her up into his arms and stood. "We're turning in now," he announced to the others as he began striding towards the house.

She hid her face in his shoulder, embarrassed. "Kane! What will they think?"

"That we're newly bonded and I can't keep my hands off my lovely mate." And sure enough, the good-natured calls that accompanied them across the yard left her in no doubt that the others were thinking exactly that.

At some time during the night, she awoke to the sound of ringing. Beside her, Kane grumbled and kissed her cheek apologetically before rolling out of bed. Fumbling around on the floor, he searched for his pants and the cell phone that he'd left in his pocket. Through her bleary eyes, she watched him check the number, then pad into the sitting room and partially close the door.

Who would be calling in the middle of the night? Hopefully it wasn't another pack emergency like last night. Straining her ears, she listened to Kane's deep voice as he answered the phone.

"Marla? ... No, no, of course you're not interrupting anything ... Shh ... Don't cry. What's wrong? ... No, don't hang up! ... You could never be a bother. You know you can call me anytime." The door to the sitting room clicked shut, effectively blocking out the rest of the conversation.

Searching her mind, she tried to think of what could be so important, that Marla had to call in the middle of the night. And Kane hadn't sounded at all upset. Hmm... What exactly *was* Kane's relationship with the woman? Zoe and Phoebe had said that Marla had been chasing after Kane. Was she still trying to catch him, even though he was now bonded to another? And did Kane have any interest in her? He certainly didn't seem to mind that she was bothering him right in the middle of—

Well, no. That wasn't true. They weren't in the middle of anything right now. Of course, a short while ago they *had* been in the middle of something. She smiled recalling how she'd daringly traced the scar on Kane's side with her lips and his enthusiastic response to her bold gesture... She exhaled softly at the memory.

But now, now they'd just been sleeping. It had been a companionable sleep though, with Kane's arms holding her tight, her head cushioned on his chest. Her mouth shifted into a pout.

She tried to stay awake until Kane returned to bed, but the hands on the clock kept moving and moving without him reappearing. Soon the ticking of the clock and the indistinct murmur of his voice began to lull her to sleep. Pulling the bed sheets up around her neck, she curled into a ball and closed her eyes, wondering when her mate would return to her.

Chapter 11

The next morning, Elise woke to the feel of Kane sliding his hand up and down her stomach. For a few moments, she pretended to be sleeping. Memories of the previous night drifted through her mind, and she couldn't keep a smile from appearing on her lips. Never had she imagined that her body was capable of such feelings. Being with Kane was definitely a special experience. She stretched and then snuggled in closer to him, inhaling the male scent of him.

"I know you're awake." His voice was gravelly, revealing that he hadn't been awake that long either.

"No, I'm not." She kept her eyes closed, wanting to prolong this companionable moment.

"I beg to differ."

"Well, you're wrong. I'm sleeping and I'm in the middle of a very pleasant dream, so don't bother me."

"I could make reality even more pleasant." His hand drifted upward.

"Mmm... Maybe I am awake." She opened her eyes, her lashes brushing against Kane's cheek as he nuzzled her neck.

"Good morning." His breath feathered over her ear and she giggled in response.

"That tickles."

"Really? How about this?" He ran his fingers lightly up and down her sides and she bubbled with laughter, squirming away from him.

"Hey! I'm just waking up. No fair!"

"Who said I play fair?" He reached out and pulled her closer, tickling her one more time.

"You're the Alpha; you're supposed to set a good example." She pressed her hands to his chest, involuntarily caressing the muscled surface as she tried to move away, but he was too strong for her.

"True, but no one's here to see except you."

"And I don't count?" She tried to look affronted.

"You..." he leaned in to kiss her forehead, "count very much." He kissed the tip of her nose, then pulled her close and tucked her under his chin. "You're my mate."

She smiled at the possessive way he said that. It was strange, but even after such a short time together, she found herself inexplicably comfortable with the idea of belonging to him. Maybe it was some ancient, instinctual thing that made her feel connected. She supposed in the olden days such a bond would have been nature's way of ensuring that two wolves stayed together to raise their young... Oh well, analyzing it wouldn't affect how she felt, and at this moment she was happy to be with Kane, in his bed, knowing that he was happy with her.

When they were snuggled in bed, she was more at ease with him than she was during the rest of the day. Possibly it was because at least here she knew what to expect. In the bedroom, at least they had a physical relationship. The rest of the time, she wasn't so sure.

She was his mate, but exactly what did that mean? What was she supposed to be doing? How should she be acting? Whether it was true or not, she had a feeling that the others were watching and judging how she interacted with Kane. Was she being too bold or too submissive? Too affectionate? Too distant? She really wasn't sure of her role in his life, or even within the pack for that matter. Too bad there wasn't an instruction manual!

Suddenly a recollection from last night popped into her head. "Kane, in the middle of the night the phone rang, didn't it?"

The Mating

His hand, which had been drawing lazy circles on her hip, stilled before continuing its movement. "Did that wake you? Sorry. I tried to be quiet."

For some reason that she didn't even understand herself, she didn't want him to know that she'd overheard him talking. She wanted him to tell her himself. "Was it an emergency?"

He sighed. "Kind of. It was Marla."

She inwardly smiled. He'd told her the truth. That must mean he wasn't harbouring any secret feelings for the woman. "Oh. I met her yesterday, twice in fact."

Kane shifted beside her and his voice subtly changed from one of teasing indulgence to a quieter, sterner Alpha tone. "Well, that's one of the things she called about. Apparently, you were rather rude to her yesterday morning."

"What?" She sat up and stared down at him, incredulous. "*I* was rude to *her*?"

"Marla said that you took whatever she said right out of context and were very aggressive towards her. Now—" He raised his eyebrows when she opened her mouth to protest and she subsided. "I know yesterday was your first full day, and you might have been stressed, wondering where you fit in, but asserting your authority as my mate in that manner won't win you many friends."

Totally flabbergasted, she stared at him. What exactly had Marla said to him?

Kane continued before she had a chance to enquire. "Then at the mall, when she tried to approach you, you wouldn't even talk to her, instead falling in with Zoe, who—before you say anything—I will be speaking to later on."

"I didn't say anything inappropriate to Marla!" She finally got her wits about her and started to protest.

"Possibly not. She was a bit unclear about that part, but you were aggressive towards her, weren't you?"

"Well, maybe a little at breakfast, but I was only standing up to her—"

Kane interrupted her again, "And at the mall, you didn't try to stop Zoe's verbal attack, did you?"

"Well no, but Phoebe and Rose..."

"Yes, I know they were there too. Frankly, I'm surprised at all of you. You're behaving like a bunch of nasty schoolgirls. Marla's had a hard time of it lately and really needs a friend."

"Well, she sure has a strange way of showing it," she muttered.

Of course, Kane heard what she said, "Elise, Marla isn't like you, and she willingly admits it. She's more comfortable around men and has trouble getting along with her own sex, but that doesn't mean that she doesn't want friends." He reached for her hand and laced his fingers with hers, his tone becoming gentler. "Elise, you managed to make friends with several of the pack within one day of being here. Marla's just like you. She wants to fit in, but the difference is, she doesn't know how. Over the years, she's been pretty good about it, never complaining about how the females treat her, but it's been hard on her always feeling like she's on the outside. Did you know that she was the next thing to engaged to Ryne? When he left, she was devastated and she's still trying to come to grips with the loss. She doesn't have the energy right now to deal with women being catty to her."

He put a finger under her chin and tipped her head so that she was looking him in the eye. "I'd really appreciate it, if you'd cut her some slack. Maybe even try to befriend her. If the others see that you like her, they might be willing to reach out to her as well."

"Me? Befriend Marla?" She knew her voice betrayed her shock, but she felt she was justified. After all, according to Zoe and Phoebe, the woman had purportedly been after her mate less than a week ago.

"It won't be so bad. Once you get to know her, you'll see." He squeezed her hand gently and gave her a tender kiss. "Please? As a favour to me? Knowing that someone is watching out for her would really ease my mind, and it would be one less thing I have to worry about."

She sighed heavily, knowing she was already defeated. "All right. I'll give it a try."

"Good. She's coming over for lunch today." He stood and started to walk towards the bathroom.

"Lunch today? But I'm meeting Julia for lunch!"

Apparently not noticing her tone of voice, he casually answered her over his shoulder. "Well, that's perfect. Marla can go with you." With that, he shut the bathroom door.

Huffing indignantly, she got up and began picking up last night's discarded clothing from the floor. Great. Now she had to spend time with a woman who most likely wanted to steal her mate. All her happiness from her early morning cuddle with Kane rapidly disappeared at the prospect of the coming day.

The hiss of the shower filled the room and she pictured Kane stepping under the hot spray. Dammit, he was her mate and belonged to her. No way was she going to let Marla take him away. So what if Marla had a relationship with him before? Kane had chosen her...

She paused in the middle of picking up her shirt. Well, really, he hadn't *chosen* her. He'd simply gone along with the idea. But, she assured herself, he hadn't protested...at least not that she knew of, anyway. She pondered the situation as she dropped her clothing into the hamper. What if he hadn't really wanted to bond with her, but had done it for the good of his pack, pushing his personal wants and needs aside? What had he said? "Sometimes our lives are filled with moments of great disappointment." At the time, she'd thought he was referring to her feelings for Bryan, but what if he'd been referring to himself?

No! It couldn't be, not after last night. Kane had been so kind and thoughtful, putting her pleasure first. He couldn't be harbouring feelings for Marla, just as she was no longer harbouring feelings for Bryan...

Her thoughts skidded to a halt. Where had that come from? Of course she still cared for Bryan! Didn't she? Yes, but...it wasn't in the same way as she cared for Kane. Bryan was...well...a dear friend, someone she'd known her whole life.

Hmm... Could that be how Kane felt about Marla? Perhaps she should just ask him.

She played the scene out in her head. 'Kane, what exactly is your relationship with Marla?' He'd answer that they were simply friends and then she'd feel much better. She gave a satisfied nod and started to make the bed.

'But,' a nasty little voice asked, 'what if he says they used to be lovers?' She paused, the pillow clutched to her chest. What would she do then?

Well, she'd straighten her shoulders and ask if it was definitely in the past. He'd say it was all over, and that would solve the problem. She fluffed the pillow and then dealt with its twin.

The nasty voice returned. 'How will you know if he's telling the truth? What man is going to admit to his mate that he's having an affair with someone else?'

Growling in frustration, she pulled up the bedspread with more vigour than strictly needed. This was getting her nowhere. She needed to tell Kane her side of the story. How Marla had insinuated that she knew Kane intimately and that she, Elise, wouldn't be able to handle him. Oh, that would be a fun conversation! Her face burned in anticipated embarrassment as she pictured that talk going in all sorts of uncomfortable directions.

By the time Kane exited the bathroom, she was still trying to sort things out. His hair was slicked to his head and little drops of water decorated his back where the towel hadn't reached. She decided to start a conversation about Marla and see where it went. As he walked past her to the closet, he pressed a quick kiss to her forehead. "I'm done in the bathroom, if you want to use it."

Nodding, she took a deep breath. Kane was a good man. He wouldn't be cheating on her, even if he had, at one time, harboured feelings for Marla. Gathering her resolve, she decided to explain her side of what happened. Then Kane would understand why she didn't want to spend time with Marla and he'd realize that the woman had twisted everything around to her own advantage.

"Kane?"

"Hmm?" His voice drifted out of the closet, where he was gathering a shirt and pants.

"I wanted to explain to you—" The phone rang, interrupting her.

Kane tossed a smile her way, raised a finger to indicate she should wait a minute, and answered the phone. "Kane here ... Yes? ... Uh, huh ... I see ... Well, if you feel that's necessary ... All right ... I'll meet you there in about half an hour ... Right, I'll see you then." He hung up and stood pinching the bridge of his nose, stress radiating from his very pores.

"Kane? What's wrong?" She stepped closer and laid her hand on his arm.

"What?" He looked at her as if he'd forgotten she was even there. "Oh, that was the lab that tested our water after the oil spill. They want to take another sample and also do testing on the surrounding soil for possible contaminants. If it leached very deep into the ground, we'll have to do a major clean up that would involve digging down deep enough until we reach 'clean' dirt, removing all the contaminated soil and taking it to a toxic waste facility, then replacing the soil and plants... It would be a massive undertaking and extremely costly, not to mention having people traipsing all over our land." He rubbed his hands over his face. "This is *not* the news I wanted to hear this morning." He sighed heavily before looking over at her. "You wanted to tell me something?"

"Uh—nothing important." Her problem with Marla was insignificant in comparison to what Kane already had on his plate. She squeezed his arm and kissed his shoulder. "I'll just go take a shower. I hope your day doesn't go too badly."

"Thanks. And thanks for helping out with Marla, too. I really do appreciate it."

Chapter 12

Over breakfast preparations, Elise confided to Helen that Kane thought Marla needed a friend. Helen snorted and shook her head.

"That girl can put on the best act around the males and they buy it every time, hook, line and sinker! I can only imagine the tale she spun for Kane. 'I was just trying to be friendly. Everyone misunderstands me. And I'm still so broken up over Ryne.' Bull! She's mad because Ryne lost the challenge and now, she isn't lady of the house." Helen was getting worked up and beating the eggs faster and faster as she spoke, the sticky mixture threatening to fly over the edge of the bowl. "Kane, of course, won't hear anything against her. He's still too caught up in misplaced guilt over her father, which was not his fault, no matter what he says! And then, when you throw in the incident with Ryne; well, we all know how that messed with his head!"

As Helen paused for breath, Elise interrupted, not understanding one of Helen's earlier comments. "Wait. Back up. What happened with Marla's father?"

"Dietrich? He died in a freak accident about eight or ten years ago. Kane was, oh, about fifteen or sixteen at the time, I think—barely out of being a pup, in my mind—but he wanted to learn how to do patrols." Helen set down the whisk she'd been using to beat the eggs and gave Elise her full attention. "Even back then, Kane was showing leadership potential. While all the other boys were sniffing around the females, he was trying to learn pack business. He was such a serious little fellow." She smiled reminiscently. "Anyway, Dietrich said he'd take Kane with him and show him the ropes. It should have been a basic patrol, especially with a young one along, but Dietrich was showing off, at least that's my opinion. He took Kane over some of the roughest territory we own, down by the cliffs and ravines—there was absolutely no need to go there." Helen shook her head. "Dietrich was running full out, which was just plain craziness on that type of terrain, probably trying to show up Kane and prove that he couldn't keep up with the adult males."

Giving a heavy sigh, Helen concluded the tale. "To make a long story short, Dietrich missed his step and fell down a ravine, breaking his neck. He died instantly, but, at the time, Kane didn't know that. Kane tried to reach him and when he realized he couldn't, he ran back for help. Of course, it was too late." She paused and pursed her lips.

Elise recalled Kane's early warnings. "That was one of the first things Kane warned me about, not to go near the ravines by myself. Now I know why. He probably relives the horror of the experience every time someone is in that area."

Helen nodded. "The accident affected Kane deeply. Everyone told him he wasn't responsible, that Dietrich knew the area and should have been watching, but Kane wouldn't listen. He felt it was his fault for wanting to go along, for not getting help fast enough. That boy beat himself up for months over the accident. Then, he pulled himself together and decided that he should be Marla's protector. Kane said that with her father gone, it was his job to watch out for her."

"But what about Marla's mother?"

"Jeannie left a few months after the accident. She'd married into the pack and decided to go back home." Helen shrugged. "I don't think she ever really felt comfortable away from them. Some wolves are like that; they can't make the transition no matter how long they're with another pack. Marla didn't want to leave; she'd been born here, after all. So Kane promised to keep an eye on her. He got her an apartment, helped her get her driver's license and even tried to screen her boyfriends."

The Mating

She smiled at the image of a young Kane trying to vet who Marla dated. That probably hadn't gone over well!

"Marla, being Marla, lapped up all the attention and put on her 'poor little me' act whenever she wanted something. Kane never could see through it. I suppose guilt blinded him. For a while, I thought Marla would talk Kane into being mates. They dated a bit, but then she switched over to Ryne." Helen resumed preparing the eggs, adding a dash of salt and pepper. "I think Kane was confused at first. After being responsible for her for so long, he didn't know what to do. About that same time though, he became Zack's Beta and threw himself into the job wholeheartedly. Zack and I used to worry about him." A frown marred the woman's brow as she slowly stirred the eggs again. "The poor boy always tried too hard, worrying about everyone else before himself. That was one of the reasons Zack had Ryne become co-Beta. He was trying to get Kane to ease up and start living his own life. It only worked for a while though. And now with Zack gone, well...it's all back on Kane's shoulders again."

Elise spoke softly. "I guess that explains why Kane wants me to be nice to Marla. He still feels responsible for her."

Helen snapped out of her reverie. "Yes, but he should be more concerned about you. You're his mate, after all, not Marla. Mind you, Marla's playing all her cards right. She knows exactly what buttons to push to get Kane to do what she wants. Right now, she's got Kane thinking it's his fault she's by herself. He feels guilty about being the reason Ryne left, even though the challenge was Ryne's own idea. And Marla could have gone with Ryne if she chose—I'm sure he asked her—but the idea of living on the road and trying to find a new pack, or forming one of their own, would have seemed like too much work for her. Oh, no. She wanted to stay right here in the lap of luxury, with a well-established pack and a hefty bank balance." Helen had once again picked up a head of steam while talking about Marla and resumed vigorously beating the already thoroughly whisked eggs.

"Um, Helen?" She decided she should try to save the eggs, surprised they hadn't turned into meringue! "I think the eggs are ready now." She raised her eyebrows and looked meaningfully at the frothing bowl.

"Oh!" Helen stared nonplussed at the dish and gave a guilty chuckle. "Sorry, but I've never liked nor trusted that girl, and the idea that Kane is trying to make you befriend her just makes my blood boil. Why, I've a good mind to go and tell him—"

She laid her hand on Helen's arm. "It's okay, Helen. Kane is really stressed from all of the problems the pack seems to be having right now. If befriending Marla for a while takes one worry away from him, then I guess I can do it. I might not like it, but I'll do it."

Helen studied Elise's face for a minute, then smiled. "Elise, I know your mating was arranged but...are you falling for our Alpha?"

Shrugging, she turned and busied herself buttering the toast. "I honestly don't know. Before I was mated to him, I had a boyfriend named Bryan. We'd been friends all our lives and I thought I was in love with him, but now...I don't know. I mean, if I really loved Bryan, how could I be drawn to Kane? I haven't known Kane for that long, but I do like him as a person. He's been very considerate, and when we're together, there's this feeling, a connection, that just seems so right."

Leaning against the counter, Helen spoke hesitantly. "Elise, I'm used to 'mothering' everyone in the pack, so don't take this the wrong way—I'm not being nosey like my girls, inquiring into your personal life—but I can't help noticing that there's no mark on your neck. You and Kane haven't blood-bonded yet, have you?"

Flushing, she shook her head.

"Can I ask why? Did you refuse or are you nervous? I know the idea of someone sinking their teeth into your neck can be scary, but I can tell you, amazingly enough, the bite doesn't really hurt. At that point, you've lost all rational thought anyway and the wolf takes over. You're too caught up in the moment to even know—"

She interrupted before Helen went into even more details. "No, I'm not scared, and I didn't refuse. It's...well... Kane hasn't suggested it, or even tried. I think he's wants to give me time to settle and get to know him better." She wasn't sure this was the case or not, but it was preferable to the alternative which was Kane wasn't sufficiently attracted to her to want to blood-bond. Not that she was ready for that yet, but pride had her wanting to at least be asked!

"Hmm... Well, I suppose that's considerate of him, but from the sounds of it you already are bonding on some level. You simply don't have the mark to prove it." Helen carried the egg mixture to the stove. "You know I hold Kane in great esteem. He's a fine man and a good Alpha, but like any male, he can be plain stupid. This whole thing with Marla, and not blood-bonding with you, is a perfect example. You know, you should just tell him you want to do it. It's an incredible experience. And once it's done, you'll feel that connection even more strongly, and so will he."

Feeling her face growing warm once again, she sought to change the topic. "I'll think about it, Helen. Thanks for your advice. Oh, look! This toast is ready. I'll go set it on the table." She grabbed the plate and hurried from the room.

Helen meant well, but she was pushing for something Elise was still ambivalent about. A bonding ceremony joined a couple but there were occasions where it could be broken. A blood-bond was for life. Some said it was akin to being telepathically connected, and while she wasn't sure if that was an overstatement or not, she didn't want to chance it until she was sure how she felt about Kane, and how he felt about her.

Marla arrived around eleven o'clock and Elise met her at the door, gritting her teeth but trying to be welcoming, even though spending time with the woman was the last thing she wanted to do. For her part, Marla smiled and offered a polite, civilized greeting even bringing her a present. "Our first meeting didn't go too smoothly, so I thought we should start again. Here's a little something to welcome you to our pack."

Removing the tissue from the brightly coloured gift bag Marla handed her, she found a bottle of fragrance. Sniffing it cautiously, she found that it was surprisingly pleasant. The scent was light and delicate, floral rather than musky, and quite in keeping with her own preferences. She'd have thought Marla would choose something heavier and cloying, but apparently was one of those people who instinctively read others correctly. It was probably quite a useful skill when it came to her work at the gallery. Knowing what a client might prefer would certainly help in guiding them towards the right sort of art and boost chances of a sale.

Murmuring polite thanks, she glanced over Marla's shoulder to see Kane leaning against the doorframe of his office. He still had an aura of stress, but at that moment he was beaming approval her way and she felt a warm glow within at having been the cause of his happiness. Giving her a wink and a nod, he disappeared back into his work space.

Leading the way into the living room that was across from the office, she tried to make some small talk. "So, do you always have Sundays off or is this a special occasion?"

"I only work part-time at the gallery and my hours are pretty flexible. Most clients are quite wealthy and have very discerning taste. They call me when they want something in particular and if Bastian's Gallery doesn't have what they need, I go looking for it. It gives me a chance to do some travelling, and I get to write it all off as a business expense."

"It sounds like nice work, if you can get it."

"I've found that if you want something badly enough in this world, you have to make the circumstances work for you." Marla shrugged delicately as she looked around the room. "You haven't made any changes yet, I see. If this were my house, I'd waste no time in starting to redecorate. This 'old homestead' decor is so outdated. When you're ready, let me know and I'll help you transform this place into something suitable for the current century."

"I'll keep that in mind." She smiled while seething inwardly. She'd just arrived, for heaven's sake. Redecorating was the last thing on her mind. Besides, while it wasn't exactly up to date, the house wasn't shabby; it was comfortable and homey. Helen had probably decorated it years ago and, while the older woman wasn't technically lady of the house any more, Elise couldn't imagine taking over and redoing everything. This had been Helen's home for years and would continue to be for quite a while to come. Any changes that were made should be agreed upon jointly by her, Helen and Carrie. After all, they all shared the house.

Deciding to change the topic, she tried to sound perky and pleased at the woman's presence. I'm doing this for Kane, she reminded herself. "Marla, Kane didn't know when he invited you to lunch, that I'd already made plans with Julia, but you're more than welcome to come along."

"Oh. Julia isn't overly fond of me. Perhaps I should just stay here. I can help Kane in the office and keep him company while you're gone." Marla glanced across the hall towards the open office door. Kane could be seen bending over the lower drawer of the filing cabinet, his pants pulled taut, showing off his muscular thighs and tight rear-end to their best advantage. Both women paused and admired the view.

Forcing her gaze from her mate's butt, Elise countered Marla's suggestion. "Oh, Julia doesn't mind at all. I've already explained the situation and she's looking forward to seeing you." Crossing her fingers behind her back, she made a mental note to buy Julia something really nice as soon as she had some money of her own. Julia had sympathized with her over the phone, telling her to bring Marla along so that they could share the misery.

Marla looked as if she'd continue to refuse, and while Elise really didn't want to have lunch with Marla, she didn't want Marla spending time alone with Kane. Deciding that keeping the woman in sight was the better option, she pressed her case. "Kane knows about the planned lunch with Julia and even said how good it would be for you to come along, since you're trying to expand your circle of female friends."

Barring her teeth in an insincere smile, Marla finally acquiesced, and they set out towards Julia's house.

Lunch at Julia's wasn't a complete disaster. All three women made an effort to get along and chatted about Thomas' condition—it was rapidly improving—the state of the weather—unseasonably warm—and recent movies in the theatre. Julia had made a delicious quiche and tossed salad and when Marla complimented her on the meal, Julia offered to share the recipe. After clearing the table, Julia hesitantly mentioned her plans for the afternoon.

"I thought I'd give Elise a tour of the woods. We found out yesterday that we both like to go for a good run, and she hasn't had a chance to explore yet. I know you're not really that in touch with your wolf side, Marla. If you'd rather not—"

"Oh, no! Don't change your plans for me. I haven't been out for a while and I can use the exercise. I can even show Elise some of the spots where Kane, Ryne, and I used to go when we were all pups together."

Elise and Julia exchanged looks but made no comment. It had been over an hour without any snide remarks coming from Marla. The reprieve had already lasted longer than either of them thought possible. Was this the start? Hopefully not.

Julia gave a little bounce and clapped her hands in what was probably feigned excitement over Marla's participation. "All right then. Marla and I will act as your tour guides, Elise. Follow me!"

They walked across the lawn and ensured they were actually into the woods where the trees started to thicken, before shifting into wolf form. It was private land and while the chance of someone from the outside seeing them transforming was negligible, it was better to be safe than sorry. Elise noted that Julia had become a dark grey wolf, while

The Mating

Marla's animal was a rather dull, mousy brown, which was totally in contrast to her flamboyant blonde human physique. Was that why Marla wasn't as fond of her wolf side and hadn't been in the woods recently? Being a plain, ordinary animal probably vexed the other woman no end.

Elise had always been pleased with her own wolf's appearance. Her fur was thick and silvery with touches of black near the tips of her ears and tail. Idly, she thought that she and Kane made a handsome couple, his solid black contrasting nicely with her silver.

Julia was prancing, eager to begin her run and Elise quickly followed her, carefully noting all that she encountered. The air was crisp and clear, carrying on it intriguing scents while the ground was slightly damp and spongy underfoot, providing a good grip as they raced along. Elise darted her eyes from side to side, taking in all the sights, her ears pricked with curiosity. It had been several days since she'd been out in wolf form and it felt incredibly good to be back in the wild.

Understanding that Elise would want time to absorb her surroundings, Julia politely stopped at a number of spots along the way. Elise yipped her appreciation and sniffed the ground, trees, and bushes, her wolf's brain sorting and storing the various scents while making a mental picture of the land and the animal life that inhabited it. Deer, rabbits, squirrel and even skunks occupied the woods, and she anticipated going hunting in the near future. While she seldom killed her prey, she loved the thrill of the chase.

For her part, Marla trailed behind them and flopped down disinterestedly whenever they stopped. It was only when the scent of water indicated that they were nearing the river that she seemed to perk up. Marla began trying to take the lead and head south while Julia kept cutting in front and herding her in another direction. In frustration, Marla snapped and snarled but Julia stood firm, growling and lowering her head in warning. Eventually, Marla backed down and Julia phased into human form. As soon as she could talk, she verbally began to rip into Marla.

"Will you stop being such a bitch? You know Kane's forbidden anyone to go near that area unless accompanied by himself or one of the more experienced patrollers."

Marla returned to her human form and immediately countered Julia's claim. "We're not that close and besides, Elise is new here and wants to see more of the territory."

Elise had changed while Marla spoke and knew something was up by the way the two women snarled at each other. She tried break the tense atmosphere that was developing.

"I do want to explore more, but it doesn't have to be today. I can wait until Kane takes me. What's so special about that part of the river anyway?"

Julia glared at Marla while explaining. "Well, first of all, it's where the oil spill was. We haven't had conclusive results back yet to prove the area is safe, and until he knows all the contaminants are gone, Kane doesn't want anyone there. Secondly, it's very rocky and dangerous, which is one of the reasons the oil spill grew as bad as it did; a lot had leaked out of the containers before anyone came by and noticed."

Elise nodded. "Kane mentioned there was a particularly treacherous area, but I didn't know exactly where it was. Oh!" She remembered the phone call earlier that morning. "And he got a call about the oil spill this morning. The lab wants to do further testing. There was something about the oil having leached into the ground and the possibility of having to do a major environmental cleanup in order to prevent further damage." Elise noted the worried expression on Julia's face and tried to offer some reassurance. "It wasn't definite though; they were just checking."

"See?" Julia looked smugly at Marla. "Yet another reason to stay away. The ground could be contaminated as well as the water. If we went that way, we could end up getting sick."

Marla seemed to cool down and returned to the pleasant persona she'd been assuming. "You know, Julia, you're right.

The Mating

I'd totally forgotten about that. We are supposed to keep clear. See what happens when you stay away from the woods for too long?" The apology almost sounded sincere, but Elise had her doubts. Still, she was curious as to the other woman's motives.

"Why did you want to go to that particular spot, anyway?"

"Like I said, it would be interesting for you to see, and Ryne and I used to spend a lot of time there as well. He loved taking pictures around here." She shrugged. "I really miss him sometimes and revisiting places that we shared helps me deal with the loneliness. Ryne and I were very close. We'd actually discussed becoming mates, rather than just lovers, and now that he's gone... Well...I feel that a part of me is missing, too." Marla's eyes began to fill with tears and Elise awkwardly patted her shoulder.

Julia looked at Marla and shook her head. "If you miss him so much, then why didn't you go with him when he left?"

"Umm, I..." Obviously searching for an answer, Marla shifted uncomfortably. She looked around the woods and shrugged. "This is my home. I couldn't just leave it."

"Yeah, that's what I thought." Julia snorted in disbelief. "Well, it's time we were heading back anyway. I want to visit Thomas again and it gets dark early this time of year. While we might be able to see quite well, those stupid hunters can't. After Thomas' close call, I'm not taking any chances." With that, Julia shifted form. The other two followed suit and they began loping home.

Chapter 13

Marla managed to get herself invited to dinner and ended up sitting on one side of Kane, while Elise was on the other. As he entered the dining room, Kane gave Elise a peck on the cheek and it was only when Marla stood looking at him expectantly, that he absentmindedly helped her into the chair. Rolling her eyes, Elise sat down moving her chair in by herself. She wasn't helpless and could manage her own chair just fine, thank you very much!

For his part, Kane seemed oblivious to any undercurrents between the two women, merely inquiring how their day went. Marla happily reported that she and Julia had shown Elise some of the woods. Elise wanted to point out that Marla had basically tagged along, but Kane seemed so pleased that their day had gone well that she didn't want to burst his bubble. His face seemed exceptionally drawn and he kept rolling his shoulders and turning his neck as if his muscles were too tight. She wondered what had happened that day to make him so tense and made a mental note to offer him a shoulder massage later on.

Despite his obvious stress, Kane thought to apologize to her for not conducting a personal tour of the territory. "I'd really meant to take you out myself, Elise. I'm sorry. My intentions were good, but with one thing and another the time slipped by."

"That's okay. Julia did a fine job of showing me the most popular trails. Maybe one day you can take me to some of the less well-known spots." Under the cover of the table, Kane give her thigh a squeeze. Her heart did a quick flip flop when he didn't immediately remove his hand, and the look he gave her seemed to hold interesting promises for later in the evening. Who knew where that shoulder massage might lead?

Marla chose that moment to lay her hand on Kane's arm, drawing his attention away from Elise. As Marla opened her mouth to speak, Carrie suddenly shoved a bowl of mashed potatoes in front of her face. "Here, Marla, you have to have some more of these. They're Helen's special recipe, you know." Forced to take the bowl that was practically touching her nose, Marla removed her hand from Kane. Immediately, John got Kane's attention by asking about a pack meeting that had been called for that evening.

Elise chuckled inwardly at how her friends were putting up road blocks to keep Marla away from Kane. Looking across the table, she met Helen's eye and received a slow wink from her. Smirking, she knew the older woman had clued the other two in on the situation. Elise stared at her plate and ate quietly, concentrating on the men's conversation to keep from laughing out loud at Marla's sour expression.

"I've called everyone about the meeting tonight at seven o'clock. Even our members that live in town are coming here for it. Only Julia and Thomas won't be there." John summarized his afternoon efforts. "I told Thomas you'd probably stop by tomorrow and give them a personal update."

Kane nodded in approval. "That will work; I didn't get a chance to check on him today. I have the outline for the meeting run off and the chairs are set up downstairs, so everything is ready."

"Helen and I made some cookies and muffins for refreshments." Carrie added. "And John carried the coffee urn downstairs so it's ready to go."

Elise marvelled at how efficient a team they all seemed to be and wondered when she'd find her own niche in this group. She hadn't even known that there was a meeting tonight! Was it a regularly scheduled event or something special? And why hadn't they told her? Of course, she'd only been here a few days, and she'd been out of the house all afternoon, but surely someone might have mentioned it in passing. Trying to be positive, she decided that it had likely slipped their mind that she wouldn't know and at least this gathering might give her some more insight into how this particular pack functioned. She didn't like feeling that she was out of the loop and was coming to realize that Kane's pack wasn't nearly as traditional as her father's.

"So what's on the agenda?" Marla asked, flipping her hair and leaning towards Kane, obviously trying to draw his attention.

"Just an update on recent events. I'd rather not go into it right now. You'll get all the details the same time as everyone else." Kane calmly ate his meal, not really looking at Marla so he missed the frustrated glare that quickly passed over her face. Apparently, Marla wasn't used to having to wait for what she wanted.

"I wasn't aware that there was a meeting tonight," Elise tentatively stated.

"Really?" Kane looked surprised. "I thought Helen said she'd tell you."

"Me? Now, Kane, why would you expect me to tell your mate about the meeting?" Helen looked at Kane in puzzlement.

"Well...I suppose I thought you'd see her during the day while you were working around the kitchen since I was in and out all the time..." Kane's voice trailed off as Helen shook her head at him.

"Kane, you really need some lessons on being a mate." John good-naturedly teased him. "Rule number one is never assume your mate spends all her time in the kitchen. Rule number two is never spring a surprise on her because then she'll fuss and fume about her hair and her clothes. I mean, look at poor Elise right now. There's a meeting in less than an hour and she hasn't had a chance to comb her hair from her run or even change her clothes and she'll be meeting the rest of the pack..." Suddenly John quit speaking and gave a grunt of pain as if someone had kicked him.

Indeed, someone had kicked him. Carrie was glaring at him and he gulped in anticipation of her ire. "John, you have the biggest mouth in the world! Don't worry, Elise. You look perfectly fine." Carrie smiled encouragingly at her.

Marla smirked.

Elise felt herself flushing. She hadn't really looked in the mirror when she came home. Did she have twigs in her hair or dirt on her face? If it was bad enough that John had noticed... Pushing away from the table, she excused herself. "Maybe I should go and get cleaned up. John's right. I was out running and I'm probably a mess. Do I have time for a quick shower?"

"Well, yes. But you really do look okay to me." Kane caught her hand.

"Right. You look fine. I didn't mean—" John began.

"No, no. It's okay. I want to look presentable..." She pulled her hand free and backed out of the room, before turning and hurrying up the stairs.

After taking the quickest shower on record, she and then stood in front of the closet trying to decide what to wear. What was the appropriate attire for a pack meeting when you were the Alpha's mate? The meetings at home were usually rather stuffy and she'd avoided them like the plague, but were they the same here? She didn't want to dress too casually and look as if she didn't care. On the other hand, too formal of an outfit would make her seem stuck up, as if she thought she was better than the rest.

Finally, she decided on an almost new pair of black jeans and a cotton sweater. Slipping in a pair of gold earrings and a bracelet, she studied herself in the mirror, hoping she'd hit the right note. Her hair fell softly around her face and she used a touch of eye shadow to bring out the green in her eyes. After adding a bit of lip-gloss, she decided the look was about as 'middle of the road' as she could hope for. Yet again she wished there was a manual that explained the ins and outs of being an Alpha's mate. To be sure, her father was Alpha, but he'd been a widower for many years, and as a child, she'd never paid attention to what her mother did or wore.

The bedroom door swung open and Kane walked in. She was still standing in front of the mirror, adjusting her clothes. He swept his eyes over her and an approving smile appeared on his face. "I see you're ready for the meeting."

She nodded nervously. "Do I look all right? Not too casual or too dressy?"

Kane pulled her into his arms and gave her a comforting hug, then kissed the tip of her nose. "You look perfect, but then again, you did before as far as I was concerned. I thought you might be nervous and wouldn't want to walk into the room by yourself, so I came to get you."

"Thanks. I wasn't looking forward to that. It's nerve wracking to think that I'm the Alpha's mate. Everyone will be expecting me to be like Helen."

"No they won't. They expect you to be you." Kane gave her another hug, then taking her hand, he led her down the stairs to the meeting room. She concentrated on steadying her breathing and composing her nerves. Wolves could smell fear and that wasn't the first impression she wanted to make.

The buzz of voices could be heard coming from the other side of the door. "It sounds like everyone is there already. I thought the meeting didn't start until seven?" She checked her watch. It was still only six forty-five.

"I guess they're all early for some reason." Kane shrugged and pushed the door open.

She peeked inside and gasped.

Kane grinned and tugged her into the room as everyone called out, "Surprise!" Two large banners were strung across the far wall. One said "Welcome Elise!" and the other had "Congratulations Kane and Elise" printed across it.

She scanned the room, taking in the sea of smiling faces, not knowing what to say. Kane squeezed her hand and led her to a table where a slab cake was decorated with a little plastic bride and groom. Someone had made little furry tails and taped them to the figures. Kane picked one up and examined it with raised brows.

Carrie burst out laughing. "They don't make Lycan bride and groom cake decorations, so I improvised."

"Hmm..." Kane looked at Elise. "If my tail ever sticks out of my suit coat like this, you will tell me, won't you?"

She chuckled and nodded before being enveloped in a bear hug by a repentant looking John. "I'm sorry for what I said about how you looked at supper, but I was told to do it. We wanted you upstairs so everyone could sneak in, and figured if you were in the shower and changing your clothes, you wouldn't hear them arriving."

"Well, it certainly worked." She pretended to scold him. "I figured I must be a real mess, and that Carrie and Kane were simply trying to be nice when they said I looked fine."

Smirking, Carrie explained further. "I know how we woman think. The more we tried to reassure you, the more you'd believe something was wrong. It was a foolproof plan."

"Enough chit chat! Open the presents!" Helen urged her towards a large table covered in gifts.

Elise took in all the boxes and bags then looked at Helen and the assembled crowd in shock. "You didn't have to bring presents. The cake, and the banner, and... Well, everyone being here was more than enough!"

"We weren't able to give you two a shower or attend the bonding, so we're having our own celebration." Helen said smugly.

"Besides," Marla added, appearing beside Kane. "We usually do a large birthday and anniversary party at these meetings for anyone in the pack who had a special day that month. October was empty and we had nothing better to do." She smirked at Elise and leaned against Kane. "Just teasing, of course."

Carrie's eyes flashed with temper that matched the red of her hair. She grabbed Marla's arm and gave it a firm tug.

"Marla, come help serve the coffee and tea." Before Marla could protest, she was whisked away.

Kane and Elise spent the next half hour opening presents and thanking everyone who had gathered around them. Elise felt overwhelmed by everyone's generosity and was happy Kane was at her side to speak to all the well-wishers. Just as on her first day there, most people seemed pleasant, a few were curious, but everyone seemed genuinely welcoming. Well, except for Marla, but that was a different story.

As she stood by Kane's side nodding and smiling, she allowed her eyes to drift over the room. Had Marla managed to escape Carrie?

After a few moments of searching, she found her near the beverage table. While she wasn't serving coffee or tea as Carrie had asked, at least she was still in the general vicinity of her post. Why hadn't Marla abandoned the job as soon as no one was looking? It would have been in character. A shift in the crowd allowed her to see that Rose was standing with Marla as well.

Hmm... She hadn't thought of those two as being friends, though Rose had greeted Marla in the mall on Saturday, even if it had been in a rather subdued manner. Watching the interaction between the two, it was hard to determine if they were enjoying each other's company or not. They barely looked at each other and to the casual observer, it probably wouldn't even be apparent that they were speaking. Rose's face was impassive but her fists were clenched at her side. What had Marla said to upset the girl?

A group of people momentarily obscured the view and by the time they had passed by, Marla was by herself again appearing exceptionally smug while Rose was across the room standing near Phoebe and Zoe. Daniel, Zoe's brother-in-law was there, and seemed to be talking earnestly to her. At least if Marla had said something cutting, Rose had Daniel there to help pick up the pieces.

Chapter 14

Once the presents were opened and the cake served, Kane cleared his throat. "As much as I hate to interrupt the festivities, we do have a monthly meeting to hold, so if everyone would take a seat, we can begin."

The general rumble of conversation slowly dissipated as people settled into their seats. Helen, Carrie, and Elise sat to the side near the front, while Kane and John took their places at a central table and podium. After smiling over at Elise, Kane began.

"Before we start, I'd like to thank all of you once again for your good wishes and the warm welcome you've given Elise. I know we both appreciate it. Your support means a lot to us, especially in these difficult times." A polite round of applause cut him off, and he waited for it to die down before continuing. "I have a number of important points to bring up tonight and then we'll open the floor to discussion.

"First, as I'm sure you all know, Thomas was shot two nights ago while out on patrol. I'd like to assure you that he is recuperating at the infirmary and will be fine. At this time, we're not sure who was responsible. It could have been human hunters from town trespassing on our property—it's been known to happen before—but..." Kane paused before dropping the bombshell. "Thomas thought he scented Ryne just before the gun was fired."

Gasps filled the room and then conversations burst out all over. Elise's eyes widened as she took in the bits and pieces of dialogue that flowed through the room.

"Shocking."

"I don't believe it."

"It can't be true. Not Ryne!"

"Kane should have killed him when he had the chance. That's how a challenge works."

"That's what you get for being too easy on upstarts."

"There has to be a mistake!"

Some seemed to be angry that Ryne would do such a thing. Others denied it could even be true. A few voices were advocating killing the offender; Elise found that to be the most disturbing. Wisely, Kane allowed a few moments for the assembly to express their feelings, before trying to proceed.

"I know it's unthinkable that someone who was once a member of our pack could do such a thing, but we don't have hard evidence against him so there's still the possibility—"

A voice from the back interrupted. "Thomas wouldn't make something like that up. If he scented Ryne, then Ryne was there!" The crowd murmured in agreement.

Kane nodded. "True. No one is saying Ryne wasn't there. Obviously at some point in time he was in the area, though 'when' we can't say, nor do we know if he pulled the trigger or not."

Another voice called out. "You don't want to admit Ryne is guilty because he's your brother."

A hush fell over the room and Kane's nostrils flared. Elise watched as he gripped the podium with his fingers and she was surprised the wood didn't break under the pressure. With steely eyes, Kane responded to the accusation, his voice a low, deep rumble that sent shivers up her spine. "Are you suggesting that I put personal feelings ahead of my duties to the pack?"

The speaker shook his head and seemed to sink into his chair, realizing that in the heat of the moment, he had spoken out of turn.

Kane continued. "Rest assured, that since I've become Alpha, I have put the needs of each and every one of you above all else."

The Mating

"I can't believe anyone would doubt Kane's loyalty." Marla was sitting a few rows away and spoke in a sotto whisper. Elise could clearly hear what she was saying, though she didn't think Kane could. "After all, he agreed to be mated to Elise, just to ensure political stability. Now that has to say something about his dedication to our well-being." Looking towards Elise, Marla leaned her way and smiled condescendingly. "Don't take that personally, Elise."

Feeling her face growing red, Elise stared at the floor and seethed, forcing herself not to cause a scene. That woman was such a bitch! She knew what buttons to push. Elise tried to reassure herself that an arranged bonding was nothing to be ashamed of; it wasn't like no one had wanted her and a political arrangement was the only way her father could get rid of her!

Carrie must have sensed her distress and grabbed her hand, squeezing it comfortingly. Once she had herself under control, Elise peeked at the audience to see who else had heard the comment. A few people were looking at her speculatively while others were glaring at Marla. It gave her some small comfort to know that most of those within hearing range considered the remark inappropriate. She could only hope that they didn't secretly agree with the comment despite its lack of good taste.

Kane, unfortunately, hadn't caught the exchange as he was listening to an elderly man who had stood up. "May I address you, Alpha?"

Nodding, a ghost of a smile passed over Kane's lips at the old man's formality.

Helen leaned over and whispered in Elise's ear. "That's William. He was Alpha over thirty years ago and is now part of the Council of Elders. William is very wise and a great supporter of Kane."

Elise nodded and listened intently, pushing Marla's comment aside. She would not let that woman get to her!

"Ryne was your brother, yet he challenged you for the leadership of this pack. Such a challenge, according to the ancient laws, could have only one conclusion. The death of one wolf and the victory of the other."

Again, Kane nodded.

"Kane, you were the victor. Why was Ryne allowed to live and cause such havoc among us? If he were dead, we would all be happier, and Thomas would not have been shot." Unlike the previous speaker, this man didn't falter under Kane's gaze, instead standing with his head slightly tilted to the side in inquiry.

The room went deadly silent watching Kane and waiting for his reply. Elise clasped her hands tightly together. If this man was one of Kane's supporters, she'd hate to think what those who weren't as fond of him might be like. This Elder was basically saying that Kane had broken pack law, messed up as leader, and endangered them all! Nervously, she wondered how her mate would refute such a claim.

Kane stood impassively surveying the crowd before speaking. "The council of Elders agreed to allow the challenge to proceed so that the most capable leader could be determined. The minute I won the challenge, I became Alpha. By virtue of that fact, everyone who lives in this pack is subject to my rules and my decisions. It was my decision to allow Ryne to live, and it was not based on brotherly love; there was little, if any, of that left. The needs of the pack were foremost in my mind, even during that first moment of victory. Ryne had many friends within our pack and his death would have served no purpose except to cause grief, division, and discord at a time when we need to be unified.

"As for the law, as Alpha, I know them better than most. Even before the challenge began, I had carefully studied the ancient rules as part of my Beta duties. While it does state that the victor will become Alpha, it does not say his opponent must die." Kane opened up a very old leather-bound volume and began to read. "The challenge shall proceed with no interference until only one stands victorious as the Alpha. All who dwell in the pack shall bow before him and be subject to his decrees. His dictates shall be abided by, upon the fear of death."

Slowly Kane closed the book. "The death, or life, of any pack member has always been in the hands of the Alpha. Our ancestors were not as civilized as we are, and often chose to kill their opponents. We, however, have evolved beyond that. To revert to killing out of fear, or to maintain power, would be to turn our backs on all the advances we've made and to become little more than creatures governed solely by ancient instincts.

"Ryne may or may not be responsible for Thomas' injury. We are searching for him and when he is found, he will be questioned about this incident and the others. Once his innocence or guilt is determined, suitable consequences will follow."

The Elder slowly nodded. "Wisely spoken, Alpha. You not only know our laws, but rule with justice and fairness. We are fortunate to have one as enlightened and dedicated as you to lead us." William turned and surveyed the room calmly before sitting down. Elise was sure you could have heard a pin drop.

Helen poked her in the ribs and whispered in her ear. "See? William was playing devil's advocate; he knew what the law was. He wanted to give Kane a chance to say his bit."

Kane waited before talking again, giving any further dissenters time to speak, but no one came forward. Returning the Book of the Law to the table, he picked up the agenda and addressed the next point. "Due to Thomas' accident, I'm declaring much of the woods out of bounds. The primary pathways will remain open for your use and I've doubled our patrols in those areas, but we can't cover every acre of the entire property every day. Patrols will still be dispatched throughout the territory, but we're focusing most of our energy on those places closest to home in order to ensure your safety. Any questions?"

When no one spoke up, Kane nodded to John who began to hand out what appeared to be a map of the pack's territory. Two areas were marked off in colour. Elise studied it with interest. What was the significance of the coloured regions? After the maps had been distributed, John began to explain.

"The next point on this evenings agenda has to do with Northern Oil. I've given each of you a map so you can see the exact areas in question. The section outlined in red indicates where Northern Oil wants to do its exploratory drilling. It's close to several underground streams and could possibly result in the contamination of our ground water and thus our wells. In addition, in order to bring in the needed equipment, several large tracts of land would have to be cleared and temporary roads constructed. As you can see, it's a significant area, despite their claims otherwise.

"They've offered us a very large sum of money as compensation if we sell outright. Alternatively, they've proposed leasing the land, and if no oil is found, they would assist us in replanting. However, should oil be discovered, we'd be bound by the lease for a specified number of years or until the wells ran dry. During that time, there would be inspectors and trucks visiting the area regularly and it would be out of bounds to all of us. I know this isn't new information, but I wanted to bring it to your attention again, since they've upped their offer substantially—it's noted at the bottom of the page, in footnote number three."

As people read the amount, gasps could be heard around the room. Elise had difficulty not exclaiming herself. It *was* a significant amount of money. Again, conversation erupted around the room.

"We'd be rich."

"Look at all the land they'd be clearing."

"Well, we really don't use the northern corner that much."

"I wonder if they'll raise the offer even more."

The Mating

"If we don't take this, and the courts order us to allow them in, I wonder how much the amount will drop."

"It's ridiculous. We're wolves. Money means nothing. Territory is everything!"

John called for quiet and as they settled, he looked over the crowd. "Yes, it is a sizeable sum, but at our last meeting we decided that our privacy and the need for space were more important. Both Kane and I still feel that these factors take precedence over monetary gain. However, another issue has come to light and it might require us to reassess our stance on Northern Oil. It's the third item on our agenda."

Kane took to the podium once again. "On your map, you'll see an area outlined in yellow near the mouth of the river and around the north side of the lake by the roadway that cuts through our property. As you know, earlier this month we found several large barrels of oil had been left at the base of the bridge and had been slowly leaking into the water for an unknown length of time. We immediately cordoned off that section of land and called in environmental experts to help us assess the damage and coordinate the cleanup. Oil booms were used to contain the spill and most of the oil was skimmed up. Chemical dispersants also helped to break the oil down, to make it less harmful to plant and wild life. Unfortunately, there was a significant loss of fish and water fowl. Tests are being continuously run on the water to ensure it is free of contaminants; hopefully, we'll soon receive an all-clear so that we can start using it for drinking again. But even as that problem starts to fade, we're now faced with cleaning the shore line.

"People from the lab were here today, gathering samples and outlining possible steps we might have to take. It was initially thought that it was a surface problem and we could just remove a thin layer of the contaminated topsoil. However, the lab now thinks the oil might have been there much longer than we suspected. It's possible that it's leached deeper into the ground than we originally thought. If this is the case, we're looking at yet another very big, very expensive cleanup project.

"On the other side of the map, I've outlined some of the steps that have already been taken as well as what still needs to be done. We'll have to hire trucks and backhoes, then remove a significant layer of soil and gravel and send it away to be cleaned or taken to a toxic dump. Many of the plants are severely damaged and will have to be destroyed and removed. Sorbents will be spread in the final stages, to pick up the remaining oil and then we'll have to retest to ensure that we've got it all. Finally, we'll have to replace all the soil that was removed and replant the shoreline. If the testing comes back positive for oil having seeped into the ground, the cleanup will require a lot of time, money, and effort."

Someone with black, spiky hair raised his hand. "Do we have the money for this?"

John answered. "Yes, but between what we've already spent on containing the spill in the water, combined with the expense of the land clean up, it will severely deplete our reserves."

"So we might be forced to take Northern Oil up on their offer, just to clean up this mess and keep our accounts out of the red." The spiky haired man summarized.

"Not necessarily, but we are planning for a worst-case scenario. While the lab tests might have better results than we expect, we need to be realistic."

Marla snorted. "With everything that's been happening around here lately, I sometimes think we should cut our losses, sell everything to Northern Oil and buy some land elsewhere. With what they're offering, we'd certainly have enough money to afford it." The assembled crowd reacted noisily to Marla's statement.

"How could she even say such a thing?"

"Marla has a point."

"I could never live anywhere else. This is my home!"

The Mating

Elise noted that the muscle in Kane's jaw was working and she knew he was extremely irritated by Marla's comment. Surprisingly though, his voice was calm when he called the crowd to order yet again. "That is also an option. This land is our heritage. It's belonged to our pack for hundreds of years and, as Alpha, I'm charged with caring for it. However, if the pack as a whole feels the need to move on, then we would do what we must do."

"I was playing devil's advocate, Kane." Marla smiled at Kane. He gave the briefest of nods, but his brow was still furrowed. Elise noted that Marla's expression sobered in the face of the Alpha's disapproval.

"Uh-oh. Now she's done it. Marla's pissed off Kane," Carrie whispered gleefully in Elise's ear. Pressing her lips tightly together to keep from smiling, she gave the briefest of nods, still focused on her mate. Kane was listening to someone from the far side of the room now.

"Do you think the oil company is deliberately poisoning our land in the hope of forcing our hand?"

"It's a possibility that we've been looking into, but we'd need hard evidence to make such a claim stick." Kane agreed. "It could also be that someone unthinkingly dumped the oil by our river or maybe it fell off a delivery truck. There is a bridge there where the highway crosses that corner of our land."

"Ryne's footprints were found in that area, weren't they?" One of the Elders stood and addressed Kane.

"Yes, they were. His scent was also near the traps we found. That's common knowledge. Whether any of these events are related or if they are coincidences, we don't know. But rest assured we're looking at every possible angle." Kane checked his watch. "It's getting late, if no one has any other business that needs to be brought to the floor, we'll adjourn. John and I are both willing to stay and answer any questions you still might have. And, of course, my office door is always open if you have any issues that need to be discussed in private."

When no one spoke up, Kane closed the meeting. A buzz filled the room as everyone stood and started to talk. Small crowds began to gather around both Kane and John. It was easy to see that the evening was far from over for the Alpha and his Beta.

Chapter 15

Elise and Helen worked together to clean up the meeting room, having sent Carrie off to bed. With her pregnancy so far advanced, she tired easily and her ankles were swollen. As Elise gathered paper plates and napkins, she glanced towards the front of the room. A few people still remained talking to Kane and John. Marla was standing near the edge of the group and seemed to be trying to catch Kane's attention, but the Alpha was too busy to notice.

Helen walked by with the remains of the slab cake and paused, taking in the scene. "Marla made a strategic error tonight when she mentioned selling the land. Now she's trying to backpedal. Kane loves this place and he's been worried sick about losing even a corner of it. Her 'playing devil's advocate' line didn't go over well. William could get away with it—Kane knows he's a crafty old coot and was setting things up so the facts could be stated; but Marla was simply planting seeds of doubt. It's going to take something pretty big to get her back into Kane's good graces." Smiling smugly, Helen went on her way.

Elise finished collecting the garbage, keeping one eye on the group at the front. Eventually, it was down to Kane, John, Marla, and Franz. Marla was looking distinctly irritated that Kane was basically ignoring her, and Elise wondered how the woman couldn't get the message. Shrugging, she began to gather the chairs, stacking them in the corner.

"Elise, I can do that." Kane began to walk away from the group, but Marla grabbed his arm.

"Kane, I need to talk to you—" The curvaceous blonde pressed herself closer to Kane, but he stepped away.

"Marla, I'm tired. Whatever you need to say, you can tell John."

"Oh, but I was hoping you'd be able to drive me home tonight. One of my headlights isn't working and..."

Kane cut her off. "Franz is heading into town, aren't you Franz?" The man nodded. "I'm sure he'd be willing to give you a lift, or follow behind your car, to make sure you get home in one piece." Pulling his arm free, Kane walked away and started to fold up chairs, failing to see the astonished look on Marla's face, which then turned into a pout. Abruptly, the woman turned and stomped out of the room. John and Franz shrugged and continued their conversation.

Elise had watched the whole incident with interest. Helen was right. Kane was upset, and Marla would have to do some fancy footwork to get on his good side again. The thought pleased her, and she was barely able to stifle her smile. Kane was her mate, and while she wasn't sure exactly how she felt about him, she did know that she couldn't tolerate the idea of Marla getting her claws into him.

Between the two of them, they soon had the chairs put away. John carried the coffee urn upstairs and Helen declared that the room was 'good enough' for the night.

"We can vacuum, wipe the tables, and deal with the presents tomorrow. I don't know about you young people, but my old body doesn't appreciate being up until midnight anymore." With that, Helen took her leave and John headed upstairs as well.

Turning off the lights, Kane put his arm around Elise's waist and led her to their suite. Once upstairs, he wearily pulled his shirt off, stretching his neck as his tense muscles twinged. "What a day. I'm exhausted." He dropped to the edge of the bed and took off his shoes and socks then rested his forearms on his knees. "I don't know how it was for you, but the unease of the pack during that meeting was really noticeable to me. I'm not sure if John and I managed to

136

reassure them sufficiently or not." He exhaled gustily and rubbed the back of his neck.

Remembering her thoughts during dinner, she sat down beside him and began to rub his shoulders. "I think you did the best that you could, given the circumstances. It seems to me that with so much happening all at once, there's really no way to completely soothe everyone's concerns. You presented the facts, stated what you were doing to deal with the issues, and now they have to have faith that their Alpha will do his job."

"Thanks. I know that the pack is behind me and some needed to air their concerns, but it's really wearing trying to remain calm and reasonable. The Alphas of old would have ripped the throat out of anyone who questioned them or gave them a hard time. It wasn't the right way to do things, but in some ways it was easier." Kane gave a rueful chuckle and smiled gratefully at her. "Mmm, that shoulder massage feels good." He leaned appreciatively into her hands.

"Here, lie down." She gave him a gentle push and Kane rolled onto his stomach. Straddling his hips, she began to work on the stiff muscles of his shoulders, neck, and back. "My goodness, I've felt concrete with more give than your back."

"That's where my stress always goes; right into my shoulders." Kane closed his eyes and gave a moan of pleasure as her efforts began to meet with some success. "I can't believe the mess I'm facing. When I was Beta, there were never this many problems, but since Zack's death it's been one thing after another."

"You do seem to have more than your fair share to deal with." She shifted to apply more pressure to a particularly nasty knot in his shoulder.

"Problems with hunters and trappers are common every fall, but this business with Ryne is really getting me down. I never would have thought he'd turn on his pack like this, and despite what I'm saying to the others, I'm beginning to have my doubts as to his innocence. There are too many coincidences."

"What was Ryne like?"

"Well, he was always more impulsive than me. Quick to fly off the handle or jump to conclusions, but he was equally quick to apologize and admit he'd made a mistake. Ryne was hard-working and loyal to the pack, but he fit into the human world quite well, too. He had a promising career as a nature photographer and actually had a few exhibits of his work. They weren't economically profitable, but there was quite a bit of critical praise for his pictures."

She suddenly remembered the picture she'd seen and admired in the mall. It had been one of Ryne's. Opening her mouth to comment on it, Kane sighed and began talking again before she could speak.

"In the weeks before Zack's death and the challenge, Ryne seemed to change. He'd usually been upbeat and sociable, but suddenly he was like a bear with a sore paw, keeping to himself and miserable with everyone. Something was bothering him, but he would never tell me what it was. Even so, it was a complete surprise when he issued the challenge for the leadership. He'd seemed happy as a co-Beta and more interested in pursuing photography than seeking more responsibility. Being Alpha wouldn't have left him with much time for taking pictures."

"Did you ever consider not accepting the challenge?"

"No. There was something inside me that wouldn't let me back down. Call it instinct or ego, but I knew that I had to step forward, that the pack needed me and I was the best man for the job. That's not to say that on days like this, I don't wish that I had remained a Beta." He chuckled into the pillow.

"So what do you think Ryne's doing right now? Is he really going around trying to hurt members of the pack as some sort of twisted revenge against you?"

"It's the only reason I can think of, though any vendetta should be against me, not the whole pack." Kane shifted under her and rolled over, folding his hands behind his head. Her palms rested against his chest and their eyes locked. "I've had enough work for one day. Let's talk about something more pleasant." Reaching up, he twirled a lock of her hair around his finger. "Did you enjoy the party?"

"It was certainly a surprise—I honestly had no idea—and it was very nice of everyone to be so welcoming."

"Helen and Carrie approached me with the idea the first day you were here. Initially, I thought it was a welcoming party for you, but somewhere along the line it became the next best thing to a bonding party. Both of them felt a public acknowledgement of our union was needed." He shrugged then tugged gently on her hair, pulling her down so that she was lying on top of him. The steady beat of his heart thudded under her ear and he wrapped an arm around her waist while trailing his other hand up and down her spine.

"Are you happy here, Elise? I know it's only been a few days, and I've been so caught up in business that I haven't given you the attention you deserve but... Is it okay? Is this working for you?"

Feeling the warmth of his body spreading through hers and the play of his muscles beneath her, she could only think of how right it felt to be pressed against him, to feel such closeness. She nodded. "Yeah, so far it's been okay."

"Good." He rubbed his hand leisurely up and down her back. "You know, I was nervous about this whole being mated business. I've never really had a family—a long boring story that I'll tell you some day—but it's something I've always wanted. I'll give you fair warning, I'm not sure exactly how to be part of a small family unit. I know how to belong to a pack but being close to just one person is foreign to me. I promise I will do my best by you, though."

She lifted her head and looked down at him. He seemed vulnerable at that moment, not the self-assured Alpha that had faced a large crowd a few hours earlier. "I know you will," she whispered softly, pressing a gentle kiss to his lips.

"I think I'm going to like this." He replied half teasing, but she could see the sincerity in his eyes. "It will be nice to be myself around someone and not always the stern, oh-so-wise Alpha."

"Somehow, I think the Alpha part isn't going to disappear simply because we're alone." She chuckled softly as she tried to picture Kane being an ordinary, run of the mill person.

He considered the point. "You're probably right. When I became Alpha, I could sense a change within myself, like a set of extra dominant chemicals or genes were suddenly set free within me. I'm trying to remain calm and impartial, but I find myself having to rein in my temper when someone opposes me." He gave a rueful smile. "I guess the old instincts will always be there."

"It's who we are. Yes, we've evolved and become more civilized over the years, but on some level the wolf mentality will always be a part of us; it's our heritage."

"You're pretty wise for one so young." He kissed the tip of her nose.

"I've always thought so!" Smiling smugly, she rested her head on his chest again, gently tracing patterns on his upper arm with her fingertips. This was nice, being together, just talking. There was a level of comfort developing between them and it made her feel good inside.

Kane's breathing was slowing and his arms around her waist were loosening their hold. Lifting her head, she saw that his eyes had shut and he was sound asleep. Carefully, she climbed off him and he murmured in protest but didn't wake up. She changed into her nightgown, removed Kane's belt and pulled off his pants so he'd be more comfortable. Settling a blanket over him, she crawled into bed beside him.

"Good night, Kane," she whispered as she turned out the lights, quickly falling into a deep sleep with her head against the shoulder of her mate.

Chapter 16

Kane was gone when Elise woke up the next morning. She stretched luxuriously and smiled. Last night had been nice. They'd just talked and then slept beside each other, yet she felt so much closer to him. Knowing that he really wanted to build a future with her made her feel more confident. Let the Marlas of the world do what they will!

Rolling out of bed, she showered and wandered downstairs. Kane didn't show up for breakfast, but he'd left a her a note stating that he had a meeting with the pack's lawyers concerning the Northern Oil issue and would be back for lunch. She was pleased he'd informed her himself rather than having someone else pass the word along, feeling it showed he was really trying to build a relationship with her.

After breakfast, she went downstairs to the recreation room where they'd had the meeting and party the previous night and began the task of taking the bonding presents up to their suite. There were picture frames and vases, gift certificates and even an intricate carving of a wolf guarding his mate. She wasn't sure where to put everything but thought maybe she and Kane could decide that together. Her morning was busy running up and down the stairs and by noon she was ready to sit and rest for a while.

Kane was back for lunch as he'd promised, and afterwards they went to visit with Julia and Thomas, Kane holding her hand as they strolled along. Thomas was chafing at having been confined inside for so long and Julia rolled her eyes as he expressed his frustration. Grabbing Elise's hand, she pulled her out the door, calling over her shoulder to Kane. "You listen to him complain for a while. I'm going for a walk with Elise while I still have my sanity!"

Once they were outside, Julia stopped and rubbed her temples. "I know being stuck inside for an extended period is hard on any wolf, but to listen to Thomas tell it, he's the only man to have ever been subjected to such inhumane treatment. Let me tell you, Elise, I love him dearly, but if he complains one more time today I won't be responsible for my actions!"

"It can't be that bad, can it?" Elise looked doubtfully at her friend.

"Just you wait. One of these days, Kane will get a head cold or something and he'll turn into the biggest baby you've ever seen. I swear, the tougher they are when they're healthy, the worse they are when they get sick!"

"Gee, I can hardly wait."

They looked at each other and laughed then headed into the woods for a run. By the time they returned, Thomas was napping and Nadia informed them Kane had left to inspect the site of the oil spill.

With the remainder of the afternoon looming ahead of her, she wandered upstairs to their sitting room. She searched through the stack of books that Julia had lent her, and finding one that looked suitably interesting, settled back to become lost in a romantic suspense set a number of centuries earlier.

Kane found her sleeping there several hours later and after a rather satisfactory interlude, they went down for dinner. As usual, it was a good meal with friendly conversation, but Carrie and John got up immediately afterwards explaining that they were meeting Franz and Gisele at the local theatre. Helen also headed off to her room, insisting there was a marathon of old TV shows on that she didn't want to miss. As the room suddenly emptied, she and Kane looked at each other.

"Alone at last?" He cocked one brow.

"So it would appear."

"Hmm—I wonder if they purposely cleared out so we'd have some alone time."

The Mating

She blushed at the idea but wouldn't put it past Carrie and Helen. Those two were unrepentant matchmakers who wouldn't let up until she and Kane blood-bonded!

That day established a pattern for the rest of the week. Elise would get up, poke about the house, have lunch with Kane, visit Julia, read, and eat dinner. The others seemed to find various reasons to leave them alone each evening and she found that becoming her favourite time of the day. She would read while Kane finished up any urgent business or they'd watch TV together until bedtime. Some nights they just cuddled while others…well, there was no doubt her mate was a skilled lover and she was becoming addicted to his touch.

Helen pointedly looked at her neck each morning but never mentioned the blood-bond again, though Elise could sense the woman was getting impatient with them. Elise paid her no mind. It was between her and Kane and since he hadn't brought it up, she wouldn't either.

At times, she did watch John and Carrie with envy. They often slipped an "I love you" into their greetings or departures and seemed to seek each other out, holding hands or brushing against each other. Would she and Kane ever become that close? A hollow feeling would appear inside her when she thought too much about it, so she firmly pushed the idea away.

Thoughts of Bryan also passed through her mind, especially in the mornings since she'd taken to writing in her diary again. She was trying to analyze her feelings for him and Kane and found that writing them down seemed to help. To be sure, she missed Bryan and the good times they'd had together but was coming to suspect that her feelings for him had been more that of deep friendship based on years of togetherness, rather than an all-consuming, passionate love.

Her new existence was pleasant and on the one-week anniversary of her arrival, she found herself in Kane's office again, reading as he worked. It was a companionable way to spend the evening; the scratching of Kane's pen and the

143

occasional rustle caused by the turning of a page kept the room from being totally silent.

Despite her claims that her book was engrossing, she found her gaze wandering from the text and staring at Kane's back as he bent over his work. The time spent with him this week had been nice, but she knew that he wouldn't always be home for lunch nor have time for late afternoon romps. At this point in time they were experiencing an unusual lull in pack business; the oil company negotiations were in the hands of the lawyers, they were still waiting for lab results on the oil spill, and no further problems with Ryne had occurred. Somehow, she knew that a rush of activity must be just around the corner.

Yes, it had been a good week, but long as well with nothing in particular to do. She couldn't begin to imagine how she'd occupy herself once Kane became really busy again. Spending the rest of her life wandering around the house and reading held little appeal. Helen had the house under control, and while Elise had helped with the various meals and cleanup afterwards, she knew her assistance wasn't crucial.

Thinking she'd have to find something to keep herself occupied, she recalled her half-formed plan from the day she'd gone shopping with Zoe and Phoebe; getting a part-time job. How would Kane feel about the idea? Did Alpha females ever work outside the home? She suspected it wasn't done but maybe she'd be able to talk Kane around to her way of thinking. Studying him for a moment longer, she decided when he was finished with his report she'd broach the subject.

Satisfied with her plan, she went back to reading her book.

It was some time later when Kane interrupted her reading. "Elise?"

"Hmm?" Looking up, she was surprised to find their roles reversed and now Kane was watching her. "Oh! Are you done with your report already?"

"Already? I've spent almost two hours on the damn thing! But yes, it's done." He stretched his arms out and then leaned back in his chair. "Listen, I was thinking that maybe tomorrow

144

when I drop this paperwork off, you'd like to come with me and we could pick out a car for you."

"A car? For me?"

"Yes. A car. For you." He chuckled at her surprised expression. "We're quite a ways out and you'll want to get about on your own sometime."

"Kane, I don't know what to say. That's a great idea, but I really can't afford a car right now."

"What do you mean you can't afford a car? You're my mate. I'll buy you a car. As a matter of fact, I was going to set up an account in your name tomorrow, too. You'll want to go shopping and get your hair done and... Well... Whatever else you ladies do."

She frowned at his condescending view of how *ladies* spent their time but, to be fair, she hadn't done anything yet that showed great initiative. Now was the time to change that.

"That's very generous of you, Kane. Actually, I was going to talk to you about something. I was thinking that I'd like to get a part-time job." He opened his mouth to speak but she ploughed on, giving him no chance to interrupt. "Back home, I helped out a bit in the office and around the house, and I earned a small wage from the pack's general operating budget. I know you probably don't need that kind of help here, so I was thinking I'd apply for a job waitressing in town."

"Elise, you don't need to work. Despite the possible financial problems, the oil spill will cause us, the pack isn't destitute yet." Kane folded his arms across his chest. Inwardly, she winced. That wasn't a good sign.

"I know, but I like the idea of having my own money and being independent."

"Well, the Alpha female has an allowance because of her position. You'll be 'earning your keep' by hosting visitors, cooking and helping with meetings."

"Not really." She pulled a face. "Those are Helen's jobs."

"Because she was the Alpha female. Now, as my mate, it's your job."

Nicky Charles

She had been afraid of this but continued on, putting forth her defence. "Helen's done those jobs for years and she loves it. We can't take that from her. She looks so happy when she's organizing and cooking. I'm sure she'd step aside if I said I wanted to take over, but I wouldn't be nearly as good at it and she'd probably feel hurt, even lost."

His expression seemed to be wavering, so she pressed her advantage.

"Don't get me wrong, I'm not trying to avoid my responsibilities. Someday, when she wants to retire, I'll take over but until then I'd rather stay on the sidelines and help out now and then, sort of like being an understudy or an Alpha-female-in-training."

"Hmm, I see your point about Helen. But you still don't have to work. I have more than enough for the two of us."

"But what will I do with my time? It was nice to wander around this week, visiting and reading and napping but I can't do that all the time. I'll get bored with nothing to do. I'm not talking about anything full-time, just a few hours a day."

Kane looked at her for a minute, and then sighed. "All right. It's highly irregular, but I can see your point. However, I'm still getting you a car though and setting up an account. A part-time job waitressing won't earn you that much."

"Okay." She conceded deciding it wasn't worth arguing over and he was right about the car, she'd need one, especially if she got a job. As for the bank account, he could open one for her but whether or not she ever used it remained to be seen. Kane was her mate and if it made him feel good to think he was providing for her, then that was fine.

"Do you have any idea where you might apply for a job?"

"There's a place in town called the Grey Goose. I was there with Helen and her girls the other day. It seemed like the sort of place where I'd feel comfortable working."

Kane nodded. "I know exactly where it is, and yes, it would be a good choice. I can drop you off there tomorrow

146

morning; you can talk to the manager while I take care of my business. Then we can go hit the dealerships."

The next morning, they drove into town and Kane let her off outside the Grey Goose. "I'll only be about half an hour. Wait for me here when you're finished and then we'll go find you a car."

She hopped out, waved as he left, then turned to face the entrance of the building. Biting her lip, she began to question the wisdom of trying to get a job. She'd helped serve large meals at home when the whole pack got together, but her actual work experience was sadly lacking. It would be embarrassing if no one would hire her, especially after she'd insisted to Kane that she needed to work. Wiping her suddenly sweaty palms on her pants, she took a deep breath and entered the Grey Goose Tea House determined to put her best foot forward. Hopefully a cheerful, willing attitude would compensate for her lack of formal training.

Half an hour later she met Kane in the parking lot, beaming with excitement. "I've got a job! It's only a few hours a week, until he sees how I work out, but at least that's a start. At first, I didn't think he'd hire me given that I had no experience, but then he got called away to answer the phone and when he came back, he said he'd thought it over and would give me a try. Isn't that great?"

Taking in her glowing face, Kane nodded. "If it makes you this happy, then it is. When do you start?"

"Tomorrow I go in for some training, and after that, he'll put me on the schedule."

Kane pulled her close and kissed her brow. "Well, I guess we'd better get you some transportation then, hadn't we?"

The car lot was just down the road and soon Elise was walking up and down the rows of vehicles, her head spinning as Kane and the salesman engaged in deep conversation about engine size and fuel consumption. As long as it was an automatic, not too big, and a decent colour, she really didn't care what she drove. They finally selected a burgundy four door with a sporty grill and automatic everything.

"You can pick it up tomorrow." Kane told her as they climbed into his vehicle. "I'm having my mechanic go over it and check all the fluid levels, belts, tires, and brakes. Once he gives the go ahead, we'll come back and get it."

Impulsively, she leaned over and kissed him on the cheek. "Thanks. I really appreciate you getting me that car."

"I want you to be happy here." He put his hand behind her head and drew her close for a deeper kiss, then started the engine and headed for home.

That evening, the others disappeared as usual, so the newlyweds would have some time alone. Helen was going to a friend's for a card party while John and Carrie were meeting with another couple to see a production put on by the local theatre group. Elise and Kane watched a movie together, Kane complaining because it was a 'chick flick' while she defended the story. When it was over, Kane stood and put the DVD back in its case, then set it on the table so they'd remember to return it in the morning.

Stretching and yawning, he looked at her expectantly. "I think I might make an early night of it. Want to join me?"

"Well, I'm really not that tired; I did have a nap this afternoon."

Kane walked over and pulled her up out of the chair. "That's not exactly what I meant." He nibbled on her throat and ran his hands up and down her back.

"Oh! Well, in that case, you might be able to persuade me to head upstairs."

"Persuade? In the old days, an Alpha simply chose his mate and carried her off." He leered down at her.

"Well, this isn't the old days." She replied smugly.

"Possibly not, but as you pointed out the other night, on some level the wolf mentality is always there." With that, he picked her up and threw her over his shoulder, carrying her out

148

of the room. She gave a shriek and tried to struggle, but not too hard. It was rather exciting to be carried off!

They'd almost reached the stairs, when the phone rang. Kane hesitated then shook his head. "Nope, I'll let the answering machine get it." Shifting her in his grip, he reached over to turn the answering machine on before continuing on his way but accidentally turned the phone onto speaker instead. Suddenly Marla's panic-stricken voice filled the room.

"Kane? Elise? Oh please, let someone be there! I need help. It's—" A scream filled the room, then the sound of wood cracking as if a door was being broken down. Footsteps and angry voices could be heard.

Kane froze, one foot on the bottom step, digging his fingers into Elise's body before letting her slide from his arms. They both took a step towards the phone, only to still when Marla's voice could be heard again. "Please, please, Ryne! Don't hurt me! I—" The sound of flesh hitting flesh and Marla's cry of pain had Kane leaping into action.

He grabbed the phone and growled down the receiver. "Marla? Marla! Don't worry, I'm coming. Ryne, if you can hear this, you keep your fucking hands off her or this time, I *will* kill you!" He turned to Elise, the look on his face causing her to step back in fear. "I've got to go to her! Elise, do you have a cell phone?"

She nodded.

"Good, keep listening on this line so we have an idea of what's going on. Call John on your cell, here's his number." Kane shoved a hastily scribbled number into her hand. "He's in town and can probably get there before I do."

As he turned to go, she caught his arm to stop him from leaving. Quickly she kissed him. "Good luck and be careful. I'll be waiting here."

With the briefest of nods, Kane ran out the door.

Chapter 17

Elise called John several times before she finally got a response. Apparently, he'd been in the theatre and his cell phone was set on vibrate, so he hadn't noticed it right away. As succinctly as possible, she explained the situation and he said he'd head right over to Marla's.

Twisting her fingers, she listened to the sounds of the argument going on at Marla's apartment. There'd been no more screams, just yelling and angry voices, but she couldn't make out what was being said except once she was sure she'd heard Kane's name. At that her stomach had clenched in fear. What if Ryne was trying to lure Kane over to Marla's so he could attack him? After tense moments, a door slammed and glass broke, then all was silent. Tentatively, she called into the receiver. "Marla? Marla? Can you hear me? It's Elise. Kane's on his way. Marla?"

There was a scuttling sound and then Marla spoke, sniffling and obviously crying. "Elise? Is that you?"

"Yes, it's me. Marla, are you all right? What happened?"

"It...it was Ryne. He broke in and...and... He was going crazy, yelling at me and hitting me." Marla's voice cracked and she started to sob.

"Marla, shh, it's okay. John and Kane should be there any minute." Elise's eyes filled with tears at the sound of the other woman's grief. While Marla wasn't her favourite person, she didn't deserve to be treated that way. Eventually, she heard Marla's doorbell ring and then John's voice was on the phone.

"Elise? I'm here. Marla's pretty upset and it looks like Ryne slapped her, but I think she'll be okay. I'm staying with her until Kane arrives, then I'll go look around to see if Ryne left a trail. If you don't mind, I think we'll be bringing Marla back with us. She's in no state to be left by herself."

"Of course! She can't stay there. I'll make sure the guest room is ready."

"Good, we'll see you in a while."

"Okay— and John?"

"Yes?"

"Make sure Kane doesn't do something crazy like going after Ryne on his own tonight. He was really upset when he left here and—"

"Don't worry, Elise. I'll keep our Alpha in line."

"Thanks." She hung up the phone and leaned against the wall, slowly sinking to the floor.

She hadn't realized how tense she'd been holding herself until now. Her arms and legs felt rubbery and she was light-headed. Thank heavens Ryne had left before Kane arrived. While she knew Kane could take care of himself—he'd defeated the other man before, hadn't he?—she didn't want the two meeting.

What if Ryne had a gun or a knife? Kane could be seriously hurt, and the very idea of that happening caused an ache in the centre of her chest. Forcing her mind away from that possibility, she switched her thoughts to Marla. The poor thing; Ryne had been her lover. How could he turn on her like that? What real or imagined action on Marla's part had sparked the man's fury? There could be no doubt about it now; he was definitely unstable and extremely dangerous.

She shook her head. Just the other night, Kane had been telling everyone that there was no hard evidence against Ryne; that he might not be guilty of shooting at Thomas, but now... Well, there was no doubt in her mind about the man, and she certainly hoped she'd never come face-to-face with him. Frowning, she realized that she had no idea what Ryne even looked like. Possibly there was a picture of him somewhere; she'd have to ask Helen tomorrow. Gathering her energy, she stood and went upstairs to prepare a room for Marla.

The Mating

It was late by the time they got back to the house. Marla's face was bruised on one side where Ryne had hit her, and her wrist sported a bracelet of bruises from being grabbed. Elise got ice and salve to apply to the injuries and then helped Marla into a nightgown. The woman shook with fear and kept bursting into tears. Holding her hand, Elise offered what comfort she could, finally getting her to take a mild sedative so that she could rest.

Once Marla was asleep, Elise convinced Kane that he needed to go to bed as well. He and John had done a cursory look in the area around Marla's apartment building and were planning on a more thorough search in the morning. Ryne had definitely been there—his scent was strong in the immediate vicinity, but he'd travelled by car and the smell of exhaust and fuel obliterated the trail once they reached the main highway.

"I should have listened to Marla the other night," Kane muttered as he prepared for bed. His movements were angry and abrupt. "She told me tonight that Ryne had left a threatening message on her answering machine. That's what she wanted to say after the meeting, but I wouldn't listen. I was too mad at her for even thinking that we should sell out to Northern Oil. If I'd paid attention to her, this wouldn't have happened." He balled up his shirt and threw it in the corner before flopping onto the bed, his dark brows set in a scowl.

Elise hesitated before climbing in beside him, sliding up against his side, and laying her hand on his arm in a comforting gesture. "Hindsight is always twenty-twenty. And from what you've told me about Ryne, this type of behaviour is totally out of character. Even if you'd known about the message, you probably wouldn't have suspected he'd actually carry it out."

"But I should have, especially after the incident with Thomas. Despite what I said at the meeting, Ryne is my half-brother and I wanted to give him the benefit of the doubt. Now, he's obviously becoming increasingly unstable and we have to find a way to catch him before he really hurts someone or does something that could expose the pack to the humans."

He scrubbed his face with his hands. "Tomorrow I'm going to personally head up the hunt for Ryne. We'll put even more men on it and if he's still in the area, we'll find him."

"Just be careful, okay? I'm sort of getting used to you, and I don't want to have to start breaking in a new mate."

Kane smiled at her teasing. "Thanks a lot." He rolled over and faced her. "You did well tonight, Elise. Staying on the phone, then getting hold of John. You were really compassionate to Marla, too." He brushed a strand of hair from her forehead. "That's one of the things I like most about you."

She felt all warm and mushy inside from Kane's praise, but shrugged in response. "I didn't do that much."

"I still appreciate it." A yawn escaped him, even as he brushed the pad of this thumb over her lips. "I guess I'd better get some sleep. Tomorrow looks to be pretty busy." He reached over and turned out the light, then pulled her to his side.

The next few days passed in a blur of activity. Elise picked up her car and started her job, working a three-hour shift to help with the lunch crowd. Marla was now staying at the house, too nervous to return to her apartment and unwilling to go to work until the bruises faded. Kane left early each morning and came home late at night, busy heading up the search for Ryne. Each night he returned looking exhausted and even more frustrated, quickly eating dinner before burying himself in the office to catch up on the day's work. A few nights he even went on patrol, hoping to catch Ryne sneaking about the property, but nothing came of it.

Elise found herself reminiscing about the 'good old days' of the previous week when she and Kane had had time to themselves. Kane was so tired at night that he fell into bed and was sleeping before his head even hit the pillow. And while he did put his arm around her if she snuggled up close, she doubted he was aware of what he was doing. Even when he was awake, he seemed preoccupied and spent what little free time he had chatting with Marla. The topics ranged from reliving childhood memories, to trying to think of where Ryne might be holed up, to offering the woman comfort and assurance that he wouldn't allow her to be hurt again.

At first Elise had sat in on these conversations trying to contribute, but soon concluded that her presence was superfluous. It irritated her, but since the attack Marla was being so pleasant that Elise felt she could at least let the woman have an hour of Kane's company each night. While it did mean he had less time with her, Marla had experienced something traumatic and needed extra attention for a while. Also, Elise didn't want Kane to think of her as a nagging, jealous mate. She trusted him and—she crossed her fingers—she supposed she could trust Marla too.

While being attacked was never a good thing, it certainly seemed to have had a positive effect on Marla's personality. She was quieter, withdrawn, and hadn't said anything snarky since arriving. In fact, she went out of her way to be polite, offering to do various chores around the house. Even when talking to Kane, she was keeping a respectful distance rather than hanging on his arm. Elise began to relax around the woman and even Helen had to admit that Marla wasn't being her usual nasty self.

With Kane working so much, Elise was more than happy to have her new job to keep her busy. Being out talking to people was fun and the work wasn't too hard; her biggest challenge was keeping the orders straight. She admired the other waitresses who rarely had to write down anything.

After her shift ended, she usually wandered the mall for a while, always stopping at Bastian's Art Gallery to admire the picture of Kane that she'd seen that first day. It was still on display in the window, the astronomical price making a quick sale unlikely. She didn't mind that no one bought the photograph, though. It was like her own little secret. While everyone around her saw a wolf, she saw her mate and since he was working so much lately, it was one of the few times she did get to see him.

When the picture went missing near the end of the week, she was more than a little surprised. At first, she wondered if they had rearranged the displays, but a quick inquiry told her that it had been sold to a collector who focused on art featuring wolves. She left the gallery disappointed and wishing she could have afforded to purchase the picture herself. Maybe Marla, having been close to Ryne at the time, might have a small copy of the original that could be scanned. Making a mental note to ask Marla at dinner that night, she headed home.

The meal was almost over when Elise remembered the photo and introduced the topic. Since Marla hadn't returned to work yet, Elise thought she'd be pleasantly surprised to learn of the sale. There'd likely be a commission in it for her, as she was probably acting as Ryne's sales agent.

"Guess what, Marla? That wonderful picture of Kane finally sold at the gallery. I was by there today after work and it wasn't in the window, so I asked inside and they said someone who collects art featuring wolves bought it yesterday."

The whole table suddenly went silent and she looked around wondering what was wrong. Everyone was frozen in place. Helen, Carrie, and John appeared surprised while Marla's face had turned white as a sheet and her hands were clutching the edge of the table tightly. Turning to Kane, Elise discovered why. Kane was glaring at Marla, and without a doubt, he was absolutely furious.

Helen was the first to speak. "I'd forgotten all about that picture. I'm surprised that you allowed it to be displayed, let alone put up for sale, Kane. It's not like you at all."

Carrie and John nodded in agreement.

"And what picture would that be?" Kane's voice was a deep, low growl.

The Mating

Elise swallowed nervously. She'd obviously introduced a touchy topic. "It... It was a picture of you in your wolf form, down by the lake." She glanced at Marla, who looked ready to leap and run at any moment. "Um...Marla said Ryne had taken it a while back. It was very good. I really liked it," she ended weakly.

"Marla, how could you?" Kane's fist hit the table, rattling the dishes and causing everyone to jump.

"N-n-now, Kane, calm down. It's not what you think," Marla stuttered, pushing her chair back.

"How can it not be what I think? As a favour to you and Ryne, I let him take that picture with the express understanding that it was a practice shot, never to be shown. Now I find that it's been on display in a public mall for several weeks and you never thought to tell me? That is directly disobeying my orders!" Kane stood up and towered over Marla, who seemed to be trying to disappear into the floor.

Gathering her nerve, Elise stood up and stepped between the two, placing her hand on Kane's arm. "Kane, calm down. It really was a great picture. You'd be proud of it and there's no harm done. No one will ever know it's you."

Kane shook her hand off and glared. "No harm done? Didn't you say the picture went to a collector? A collector of *wolf* art, who no doubt has other similarly minded collectors examining his purchases. What's going to happen if one of those people notices that there's something unusual about that wolf? That the proportions are off, the slant of the forehead is different, and the set of the ears isn't quite right? And don't you think someone might question where such a *large* wolf might have come from? To the average observer a wolf and a Lycan are identical, but we know differently. One of the collectors might decide that there's a new undiscovered species in the area and start poking around here, looking for tracks and dens, maybe setting up time-lapse cameras or traps. What's going to happen then? Hmm? I'll tell you what. We'll be constantly looking over our shoulders, worried about being

157

discovered." Kane whipped his head around and snarled at Marla. "We've spent years in this community, trying to stay below the radar. Your little stunt here might very well have jeopardized the well-being of every member of this pack!"

Marla started to cry. "Kane, don't be angry with me. I... I didn't want to do it. I know how you feel but..." She took a deep breath and swallowed hard. "I have a confession to make. About a week after the challenge, Ryne came back to see me. He needed money to leave the area and start fresh somewhere else, and he wanted me to sell off all his remaining pictures. I said I could find buyers for all of them, but not the picture of you—I remembered what you'd said—but he was desperate for money and I... I loved him, and I wanted to help. I never thought that the picture could endanger the pack. I... I'm so sorry." With that, Marla ran from the room. A minute later, her bedroom door could be heard slamming shut.

Kane stood with his fists clenched, a muscle working in his jaw, then he shoved Marla's chair against the wall and stormed out.

Elise woke the next morning and saw that Kane's side of the bed was undisturbed. Had he been so angry that he'd not come home at all or had he been out on a patrol? What if he'd come across Ryne and there'd been a fight! Anxiety filled her as she imagined him lying injured somewhere with no one even aware he was missing.

Hurriedly she threw on her clothes and ran downstairs to look for him. He wasn't in his office or in the kitchen and there was no note on the fridge. Worrying her lip, she wondered who might know what was going on. As she stood there wondering what to do, John walked in.

Grabbing the Beta's arm, she spoke in a rush. "John, Kane never came to bed last night and I'm worried. He was so angry when he left. Do you know where he might be?"

The Mating

"It's all right, Elise. I talked to him about half an hour ago. He went on patrol since he didn't think he should be anywhere near Marla."

Relieved, she released her death grip on John's arm. "Was selling the picture really as bad as Kane made it out to be?"

"Yes and no." John wandered over to the stove and poured them both a cup of coffee. Handing one to her, he continued. "There's always a chance that someone will notice something unusual about the photograph, and the fact that it went to a collector who specializes in wolves makes it even riskier. Kane is extremely protective of the pack and the idea of someone endangering it is really hard for him to handle. Then there's the whole obedience and trust thing. Marla not only broke his trust, but disobeyed a direct command, basically flaunting his authority. On top of all that, he's stressed to the max and working way too hard. It's not a good combination."

"I didn't think he could get that angry."

"I've seen him worse, and believe me, it's not something you want to see. Our Alpha keeps himself under a pretty tight rein. He tries very hard to be civilized and not let the wolf take over, but sometimes it still slips out. When it does, it's usually justified like last night. Marla was lucky. A few generations back, the Alpha might have killed her."

She shivered at the thought. While she was proud of her heritage, there were some aspects of it that she wasn't as fond of. "So what's going to happen?"

"He's decided that part of Marla's punishment is that she has to get that picture back. I don't know what kind of a tale she's going to have to spin or what it will cost, but that's her concern. Beyond that, if she's smart she'll lay low for a while. Kane doesn't carry a grudge. He blows up and then cools down. He'll be fine by tomorrow."

Kane didn't come home for lunch, but Marla—just to be on the safe side—stayed in her room most of the time. Since it wasn't her day to work, Elise found herself with nothing in particular to do and decided to make a call back home to help fill in the time. Sarah answered the phone and Elise was surprised to feel tears welling in her eyes. She hadn't realized how much she missed the woman.

They chatted for over half an hour, catching up on the news from home. Elise wanted to ask how Bryan was, but the conversation hadn't worked around to him yet. Finally, Sarah mentioned his name in passing and she jumped on the chance to inquire about him, unconsciously squeezing the handset tighter.

"How is he? ... Really? ... He'll be coming this way tomorrow? ... Well, yes of course I'd love to see him ... Maybe he could meet me in town. My shift is done at one o'clock ... Uh-huh ... Well, pass the information on to him and if it works for him, he can call me and make it definite ... Okay ... I miss all of you too ... Yes, I promise to call again soon, but you can call me too, you know! Right ... I'm looking forward to it. Bye. I love you!"

She hung up the phone and gave a little twirl of happiness only to come face to face with Marla. "Oh! Hi, Marla. How are you doing today?"

Marla had a strange look on her face, but it quickly disappeared as she answered Elise's question. "I'm fine I guess. Still feeling like a whipped puppy over that incident with Kane last night, though."

"I'm really sorry I brought it up. Like you, I never thought it would be such a big deal." She gave Marla a sympathetic smile.

"I know. And I shouldn't have given in to Ryne, but he can be so persuasive and I was in love." Marla studied her for a moment. "Have you ever been in love?"

Shifting uncomfortably, her face grew warm as she tried to think of a diplomatic answer. She didn't mind Marla that much anymore, but she didn't want to discuss personal matters with her either. "Well...I..."

The Mating

"It's okay, Elise. We all know that you and Kane didn't make a love match, but it will work out in the end, you'll see." Changing topics, Marla asked about her phone call. "I wasn't eavesdropping, but I couldn't help overhear part of your conversation. You sounded pretty enthusiastic about meeting someone tomorrow."

"Just an old friend from back home. We grew up together."

Marla nodded. "That should be fun. Well, I'd better get moving. I'm going to grab a bite to eat and then hide upstairs again. I figure by tomorrow Kane will have calmed down enough that I can try to make some apologies."

Marla left, humming under her breath which, for some reason, made Elise feel uneasy. Looking back on the conversation, she couldn't think of anything in particular that would have caused it though, and finally shrugged it off.

Chapter 18

Marla and Kane had a long conversation in his office before dinner and she left the meeting looking rather subdued, her face tear stained. Elise wondered what had been said but wasn't sure she should ask. She tiptoed past the office, peeking in the open door and saw Kane sitting in his chair. He had his fingers steepled and his eyes closed. A troubled look was on his face, almost as if he were sad. What was he thinking? How was he feeling? There could be no doubt that recent events were weighing heavily on him, and she speculated that he probably felt everything was falling to pieces around him.

Hesitating by the door, she waged an internal battle. Part of her wanted to go in and offer comfort, or at least a listening ear, yet she wasn't sure if it would be welcome. Perhaps he wanted to be left alone for a while without anyone making demands on him. Then again, maybe he was wishing he had someone to share with... Did he ever feel lonely? She realized how very little she knew about her mate. Kane had allowed her small glimpses inside himself—she knew a few of his likes and dislikes with regard to food or music—but for the most part he seemed to be a very private man.

Feeling guilty, she reflected on their time together. They'd developed a physical relationship and she was comfortable with Kane on that level, however their relationship outside the bedroom was superficial. She knew next to nothing about his background and hadn't really made a great deal of effort to find out much about him. So far, she'd been worried about herself—her own feelings, her own insecurities—and hadn't spent much time thinking about the inner workings of his mind, beyond the fact that as Alpha he felt responsible for the pack.

He did want some form of relationship with her—he'd said as much the other night—but she hadn't pursued that conversation, which really wasn't very fair of her. She needed to try to find out more about him, ask him some questions about himself…unless he didn't want to have a heart-to-heart talk. Lots of men weren't into that. Her father certainly never opened up about anything, at least not since her mother had died.

Nervously, she hovered outside the office door. Should she go in or should she leave him be? The ringing of the phone, took the decision from her. Kane reached for it and she walked away, relieved, yet also disappointed the moment was lost.

Kane was in a better mood at supper that night, though it was hardly possible that he could have been in a worse frame of mind than the previous evening. He announced a call had come in saying the soil testing looked promising, and it seemed the environmental cleanup costs wouldn't be as extensive as first predicted. Not only would this save the pack a lot of money, but they'd have even less reason to accept the offer from Northern Oil.

Everyone was happy about the news until Marla came in and the atmosphere tensed again. No one was quite sure how she and Kane would interact, but Kane addressed her civilly a few times, nothing special, just a 'pass the rolls' and 'I've called about getting your apartment door fixed' and the tension in the room began to ease as everyone realized that the two had reached a tentative peace.

"I'm going for a long, relaxing run after dinner to celebrate the good news about the oil spill," Kane announced at the end of the meal. "Anyone want to join me?"

Carrie patted her rounded tummy. "I think Junior and I will pass. I'm barely waddling as it is these days."

The Mating

"I'll stay in and keep you company." Helen chimed in. "I'm getting too old for late night runs."

"And I'm on patrol tonight," John said glumly. "I'll be out already, but it won't be for fun."

"That just leaves you girls." Kane looked at Marla and Elise expectantly.

Marla stared at her hands and responded quietly. "You and Elise haven't had much time together lately. I've been monopolizing you quite a bit. Why don't you two go by yourselves?"

"You're more than welcome to come, you know." Kane seemed to be trying to let Marla know that all was forgiven.

"No, that's okay. You two have fun."

"All right." He shrugged and stood, extending his hand to Elise. "Are you ready?"

"Well, I should help with the cleanup first..." She hesitated, looking at the table laden with dishes.

"Elise, go and spend time with your mate! I'll help with this." Marla made a shooing motion at the couple.

"Thanks, Marla. I appreciate it." She smiled at Marla, while trying to figure out if an alien had somehow abducted the other woman. Maybe the incident with Ryne had brought her to her senses.

"No problem. That's what friends are for and besides, I know how much you enjoy being out in the woods."

Kane ruffled Marla's hair by way of thanks and tugged at Elise's arm, leading her outside.

A blue-black dome arched overhead dotted with twinkling white lights and the occasional grey shadow of a cloud as it drifted slowly across the night sky. There was still enough illumination from the crescent moon to allow Kane and Elise to see easily as they crossed the lawn towards the woods. Good night vision was one of the bonuses of being a werewolf, Elise thought as she easily stepped over a large stick that would have likely tripped anyone with less acute eyesight.

The night was extremely quiet. Frost had killed off all the insect life, so there were no comforting chirps or fluttering wings to fill the silence, only the soft sound of their feet moving across the ground. She felt the familiar frisson of unease as she walked beside her mate. It was just the two of them and silence lay heavily between them. She darted a glance at Kane curious if he felt it too, but he seemed lost in thought. Should she start a conversation? A number of trivial topics crossed her mind and were quickly dismissed as too cliché. Once again, it was being brought home to her that she only had a physical relationship with Kane. Tightening her lips, she resolved to try and build some depth into their life together.

Pausing at the edge of the tree line, Kane cocked his head and listened carefully, then sniffed, testing the scents that drifted by. As she waited for Kane to finish checking the area, she acknowledged the crispness of the air. It bit at her nose, cooling her cheeks and ears. She didn't mind the temperature however. It was yet another perk of her wolf-like genetics.

"The patrols have been here recently." Kane announced. "The area is secure, so we can safely run." With that he shifted into the form of a sleek black wolf and she quickly followed suit.

The change to wolf form always made her feel exhilarated. Her senses were heightened and she could feel the latent strength of her muscles. Stretching first her front legs and then her back, she raised her muzzle to the sky, squinting up at the moon and sniffing the air. An exciting blend of scents assaulted her brain: other wolves, plant life, rabbits and squirrels, but most importantly, Kane.

There was something about being in wolf form that made their bond seem stronger and hope fluttered inside her. Maybe this was what they needed, the chance to do things together just for fun, to let their inner wolves get to know each other. Already instinct was kicking in and she couldn't resist rubbing against Kane and licking at his face.

166

The Mating

For his part, Kane seemed equally affected. He nuzzled her then began sniffing at her from head to toe. When he finished his inspection, he yipped at her to follow and soon they were off, loping through the woods. Unlike the previous time they had run together, she let him take the lead. This was his territory and for all that she had explored some of it with Julia, she knew her mental map of the land was not yet sufficient to lead a midnight run.

Kane kept a leisurely pace at first but once they reached a well-beaten path, picked up speed. Joyfully, she followed, happily stretching her muscles and pushing the limits of her speed. This was what she needed; the thrill of running with her mate, of being with him and experiencing nature together. Trees and shrubs flashed past as they gracefully moved in tandem, matching each other stride for stride. The sound of their paws hitting the ground, combined with their panting, created a rhythmic overture that echoed through the otherwise quiet woods.

With his greater strength and speed, Kane finally began to out-distance her, drawing farther and farther ahead. He rounded a bend in the path, temporarily disappearing from sight. She raced around the corner, and then skidded to an abrupt halt. The path stretched out straight in front of her, but Kane was nowhere in sight. She stood frozen, her eyes narrowed, searching the woods on either side while her ears strained for the sound of his running paws. Where had he gone? He couldn't have disappeared that quickly. Her heart pounded as she envisioned all sorts of calamities befalling him. Had he stepped off the path and into a trap? The patrols had cleared the area, but possibly they'd missed something.

A twig snapped behind her and she whirled around, only to be knocked to the ground by a large, black mass of fur and muscle. Her breath whooshed from her lungs and she struggled to inhale while her brain tried to process what had happened.

Rolling to the side, she sprang to her feet growling only to bite back the sound as she saw who stood before her. With a shake of her head, she glared at Kane, her expression conveying exasperation at the trick he'd played on her.

Obviously enjoying himself, Kane bent his front-end down low, indicating his playful mood. Then, without warning, he pounced on her again. Soon they were tumbling across the forest floor, snarling and nipping in a mock battle. In no time, Kane had her pinned to the ground.

As he loomed over her, their eyes met, and in one accord they phased into human form. Kane was on top of her and he brushed her hair away from her face, studying her intently.

"You look so beautiful lying on the ground beneath me." A low growl emitted from his throat before he leaned down and kissed her roughly.

She kissed him back with equal fervour, raking her fingers through his hair, holding his head firmly in place.

The kiss seemed to go on forever until they were both gasping for breath. Burying his face in her neck, Kane inhaled deeply, as if trying to absorb her scent into his body. "Mmm, Elise, you smell so good." He gently ran his teeth over her neck and she threw her head back, exposing her throat to him.

"It's my heat cycle, no doubt." Through a haze of desire, she offered up an explanation for how he was feeling.

"Maybe..." He sniffed again and she felt him quirk his lips against her skin. "I love how you smell all the time; your cycle just makes it even more intoxicating to me."

Her heart gave a leap. He'd said 'love.' Mind you, it was her scent, not her, but the idea still thrilled her.

Kane was nibbling at her ear now, his breath tickling and sending delicious shivers through her body. She moved restlessly against him, revelling in the weight of him pressing down upon her. He gently rubbed himself against her in response.

"Elise, do you think...?" He paused, sounding uncharacteristically unsure of himself.

The Mating

"What?" She shifted so she could see his face.

He hesitated, but then seemed to gather his nerve. "Do you think...? I mean... Would you be willing...?" Stopping again, he rolled away from her and stared up at the night sky. He took a deep breath and proceeded in a detached voice. "With your cycle so near, I was wondering if you'd given any thought to what you were going to do. Our infirmary has the usual drugs to curb it, if you're opposed to having a pup. I know we've only been mated a few weeks, so you might not be ready..." He let his voice trail off and looked at her out of the corner of his eye.

She knew her face was probably expressionless at that point, giving him no indication of how she was reacting to his message, but she was completely thrown off balance by his question.

When she said nothing, he continued in a rush. "It might not even happen, though, even if you let the cycle follow its natural course, but I think we should talk about it. I... I hope you'd consider it, having my pups someday, that is."

She detected something different in his voice. Hope? Wistfulness? She rolled to her side and propped herself up with her elbow, staring down at him. At first his question had shocked her; they'd only been together a short while and she was only now starting to feel more comfortable about their relationship. The idea of pups hadn't even entered her mind. She gave herself a mental kick. Lycan biology wasn't a mystery to her, and she should have realized there was a chance she could become pregnant the following week. Truth be told though, it had slipped her mind.

As an unmated female, she'd taken drugs to curb her previous heats, though she didn't react well to them. The side effects were unpleasant and almost flu-like—headaches, nausea, a slight fever, and general irritability—but that was preferable to having all the unattached males following her around, trying to mount her. Now she had a choice, but what to do? They'd barely been mated two weeks and didn't even have a blood-bond yet, though she knew it wasn't a requirement for procreation.

On the other hand, Kane was her mate and their lives were now inextricably entwined. Did it matter if they started a family sooner, rather than later? The idea of being impregnated by Kane—his seed growing within her—was strangely erotic. And it wasn't even a sure thing that she'd conceive.

She suddenly noticed that Kane was looking expectantly at her and she decided to speak plainly. "Kane, I have to admit that I hadn't even considered this. I don't like taking the medication—I usually react badly to it—and I'm not opposed to the idea of a family, but we've only been together a short time. I... I don't know if I'm ready to be a mother yet. I would like to have a family someday but..." She shrugged and smiled at him shyly. "I'm waffling here, aren't I?"

"Yes, but it's understandable." He reached up and cupped her cheek, his thumb stroking gently over her skin. "It means a lot to me, to hear that you do want a family eventually. I don't want to pressure you if you aren't ready. How about I take care of protection next week? It won't be one hundred percent, but it will minimize the odds, and then maybe next cycle you'll feel ready."

"And if it does happen—if I end up pregnant this time—I'd be okay with it. A miniature Kane wouldn't be all bad. His father's sort of growing on me." She brushed his hair from his forehead.

Kane grinned up at her, his eyes shining with delight and she couldn't help but grin back. They were having a real conversation about something important, and she'd learned something meaningful about him. He wanted a family. It wasn't earth shattering news—most wolves did—but it gave her a sliver of information that she didn't have before.

Leaning over him, she placed a lingering kiss on his lips. "Maybe we should start practising for next week."

The Mating

"I like how you think." He stood, pulling her to her feet and hugged her close.

Back at the Alpha house, Kane and Elise headed upstairs, their arms wrapped around each other's waists. The house was quiet and dark, only the lamp in the entryway left on. As they reached the upper landing, Marla's bedroom door popped open, spilling a wedge of light across the darkness. She peered out at them and smiled. "Looks like you two had a good time."

"It's about to get even better." Kane nuzzled Elise's neck, not even looking in Marla's direction.

Marla giggled as Elise playfully smacked Kane's arm while giving him a dirty look. "Elise, I promise I won't keep you away from your mate for long, but can I see you for a minute?"

Elise looked at Kane. He shrugged and then nodded. "Make sure it's only a minute."

"I promise. I just have a phone message that I said I'd deliver personally." Marla explained.

Kane gave Elise a quick peck on the cheek and went down the hall to the bedroom. Once the door was shut, Marla turned to Elise, speaking in hushed tones. "Someone named Bryan kept calling for you tonight. At first, I let the answering machine pick it up, but after the third time I thought I'd better see what he wanted since he sounded so anxious in his messages. Apparently, you're supposed to meet him outside the Grey Goose tomorrow at one o'clock."

"Really? Wonderful! He's an old friend from back home. I heard he was going to be in town and was hoping we could get together for a while." A bubble of excitement rose up inside her.

"He sounded pretty pleased about the prospect, too." Marla winked at her. "Well, that's all I wanted to tell you. You better get going before Kane comes looking for you. I think he has some very definite plans for the rest of your evening." Giving her another friendly smile, Marla turned and went back into her bedroom, closing the door softly behind her.

As Elise walked down the darkened hall, she wondered what it would be like to see Bryan again. They'd had such good times together while they were growing up; he'd been her best friend for years. Pausing outside her bedroom door, a nasty revelation hit her. What kind of a person was she? She'd just been excitedly contemplating a meeting with Bryan tomorrow afternoon, and now she was going to bed with Kane! There was something wrong with this picture, wasn't there?

She knew she loved Bryan. They'd been together for years but... There was something about Kane that made her feel all warm and fuzzy inside. Bryan's tentative kisses never made her feel the way Kane's did. She'd never ached for Bryan's touch like she did for Kane's. The love she had for Bryan seemed totally different than the love she had for—

She stopped mid-thought. Had she just been thinking that she loved Kane? No! It wasn't possible... Was it? Kane was strong, good-looking and sexy. He was also kind and considerate, loyal to his pack, intelligent and sensitive, though she suspected he'd deny that last point if asked. Yes, he had lots of great qualities, but did she really love him?

The bedroom door swung open and the object of her thoughts stood before her, naked except for the pyjama pants that hung low on his lean hips, barely disguising his desire for her. Her gaze traced the six-pack of muscles that comprised his abdomen and the long, faintly pink scar that ran up his side. Moving higher still, she noted his strong arms and broad chest, the firm set of his jaw and the dark shaggy hair that fell across his forehead. His amber eyes seemed to be glowing as he looked upon her. A crooked smile adorned his face.

"There you are! I was going to come looking for you. What did Marla want?"

"Oh, she had a phone message for me from a friend back home who's going to be in town tomorrow. We're meeting at the tea house after work."

The Mating

"Mmm, that'll be nice for you." Kane answered distractedly as he swept her up into his arms. As the door shut behind them, she felt the waves of desire building again. She didn't know if she loved Kane or not, but at the moment the need growing within her blocked out all other logical thought.

Chapter 19

Elise sat in the kitchen idly nibbling on a bagel while watching Helen mix up a batch of muffins. Sunshine was streaming through the white lace curtains into the homey room. It beamed across the marble counter top, highlighting little specks of flour that drifted lazily through the air. The grey-haired woman hummed under her breath as she stirred flour, raisins and spices into the thick, rich batter. Helen never seemed happier than when she was preparing food for the endless stream of visitors through the Alpha house. Sometimes Elise suspected the pack members came more for a sample of Helen's cooking than they did to talk with John or Kane.

This morning, half a dozen men were gathered in the office to discuss a recent financial report. Since the pack was old and well established—well over a century—they'd amassed a tidy sum through the pooling of resources and sound investments. The current economy and the oil spill cleanup were having some minor negative impacts on their capital, or so Kane had explained to her that morning. Not having a head for finances, she'd merely nodded politely at the gathering before heading to the kitchen where the topics of conversation where likely to be more to her taste.

Carrie was also avoiding the drone of voices embroiled in financial mumbo-jumbo. She sat across the table from Elise, her feet propped on a chair. Her ankles already showed signs of swelling, despite the fact that it was still early in the day. A cup of herbal tea rested on her bulging stomach and she idly rubbed her abdomen as she grumbled. "I am going to be so glad when this is over."

Helen raised an eyebrow. "It seems to me just a month or two ago, you were raving about the wonders of expectant motherhood."

"Yeah, well that was before, when I could still see my feet and get a decent night's sleep." Carrie shifted in her chair. "Now I want this pup out of me and in my arms so that my body is my own again."

"Being pregnant is pretty taxing it seems." Elise eyed Carrie with a frown. When she'd decided last night to let nature take its course with regards to starting a family, she'd only been thinking about the two ends of the project. She'd conveniently ignored the middle part.

"It has its moments," Carrie sighed but then a smile crept over her face. "But for the most part, it's been an amazing experience. Are you and Kane already thinking of having a family?"

She shrugged. "We talked about it. My cycle will start next week, and I think I'll go drug free and see what happens, especially since I don't react well to the medication."

Carrie giggled. "I'll tell you what will happen. Your pheromones will turn Kane into the most passionate, possessive mate you've ever seen, while you'll be this out of control maniac."

"No, I won't! Er...will I?" She bit her lip in trepidation, Carrie's description creating visions of her chasing after Kane and ripping their clothes off regardless of where they were or who was about.

Helen snorted and then offered some reassurance. "Carrie's teasing you, Elise. Your first un-medicated heat will seem more intense, because you've never unleashed that side of yourself before and you're not sure what to expect, but it's not a constant state. It's more like waves or the tide. It builds up to a peak, and then ebbs for a while before building up again."

"Oh! That's good. How many...er...tides should I expect?" It was embarrassing to admit that she didn't know these things, but she'd grown up without a mother. Sarah had stepped in as a surrogate, but this topic had never come up. And the giggling, teenage conversations with her friends probably hadn't contained the most reliable information.

"You can expect two or maybe three a day, depending on your emotional state." Helen supplied the answer while popping the muffins into the oven.

"You better hope they aren't tidal waves!" Carrie quipped before reaching over and patting Elise's arm. "I'm sorry. I shouldn't tease you. It wasn't that long ago that John and I were newly mated. I remember all the uncertainty that went with it."

"That's okay. I'm happy for any advice or insight you have to offer." She traced a pattern on the table. Should she broach the subject that had been weighing on her mind since last night? If she didn't ask, she'd never find out, so... "As a matter of fact, I was wondering if I could ask you something about Kane."

"Sure. We might not know the answer but ask away." Carrie glanced at Helen who nodded in agreement. Grabbing a cup of coffee, Helen sat down at the table and they both looked expectantly at her.

"Well..." She began slowly. "Last night, when Kane and I were discussing having a family, he seemed sort of sad or wistful. And a while back, he mentioned not really having much of a family life while growing up, so I started wondering about his background. Where are Kane's parents? He's not that old; I would have thought they'd still be here."

"Well, it's not really a secret." Carrie paused and sipped her herbal tea thoughtfully.

"No." Helen agreed. "I suppose Kane won't mind us telling you. His mother, Mindy, was originally mated to Ryne's father who belonged to another pack. No one knows why, but the relationship didn't last, and she came back here when Ryne was only a baby. Not long after that, a rogue wolf passed through. She hooked up with him—despite everyone warning her— and left, taking Ryne with her. Then about two years later she was back again, but this time she had Kane as well as Ryne. They stayed for another year, then Carter— that's Kane's father—came around again. He tried to live with the pack but could never seem to fit in. When he left, Kane's mother took the boys and went with him again, only to return after a few months on the road."

"That set the pattern for several years until finally the Alpha at the time put his foot down. They had to either stay or leave because the constant coming and going wasn't good for the pack. Every time he arrived, Carter upset the balance of the hierarchy. He wasn't interested in being a team player and was only concerned about himself, rather than the good of the pack. Carter's personality was too dominant to accept someone as his Alpha; he was meant to be a lone wolf. He didn't have the temperament to be around others; too quick to fly off the handle, if you ask me. Anyway, after the ultimatum, Carter left and Mindy went along, only this time she left the boys behind with me and Zack. Ryne was thirteen and Kane was almost twelve. I think Mindy knew the moving around wasn't good for them, but she loved Carter too much to give him up, so she did what she thought was best."

"We haven't seen Mindy or Carter since. Someone once said they'd gone to Europe while another rumour had them in South America." Carrie shrugged. "No one knows for sure."

"That must have been really hard on Kane and Ryne, always moving about, constantly joining the pack, then leaving again. And then to be abandoned by their mother..." Elise felt an ache in her heart. She'd lost her own mother at a young age but at least her parent hadn't chosen to leave her. Had Kane and Ryne felt hurt and betrayed? Wolves were pack animals, and with a few exceptions, needed the stability and structure of a group. Even if the pack was a family unit with only four members, to have that taken away must have been devastating.

Helen's next words confirmed her suspicions. "The boys were pretty shook up at first, but after a while they came to accept that we were giving them a permanent home. Kane especially seemed happy to be settled finally. Both boys were so grateful for anything we did for them. Neither of them ever said anything, but I'm sure they'd had very little to live on for most of their lives, what with following Carter around all over the country. The man never kept a job for long. And personally, I suspect that he wasn't the best role model. His temper was short and nasty, and he had a roving eye, too. I can only imagine what the boys experienced. Neither Kane nor Ryne ever really talked about it, but we all had our suspicions."

Carrie spoke, a distant look in her eye. "Growing up, we all played together. I remember how Kane and Ryne kept appearing and then leaving. All the other kids thought it was strange because our pack was so stable. Sure, someone new came along now and then, but it was a revolving door with those two. They'd be there one day, then gone the next, and half a year later they'd reappear once more. Sometimes, when they first arrived back, they'd be so distant, as if they were afraid and didn't dare join in. Both of them seemed thin, too, like they hadn't eaten enough. Even as pups we noticed it."

"It wouldn't surprise me." Helen pursed her lips. "I talked to Mindy about how Carter treated her and the boys, but she always said nothing was wrong. If I saw a bruise or a mark, she had a story to go with it. She'd fallen, or the boys had been playing too rough. Zack even tried to make her talk but she never would admit anything. It was sad and a bit strange that she felt such loyalty to Carter when he obviously didn't deserve it."

Elise could easily imagine Kane as a child, underfed and dragged from one place to the next, subjected to the whims of a domineering, ill-tempered man who didn't care enough about his family to provide them with a stable home life. She wasn't sure how she felt about his mother, but at least by leaving them behind she'd given her sons a chance at a normal life with Helen and Zack.

Absentmindedly, Carrie stirred her tea as she continued to talk. "Ryne and Kane were really close, like they'd formed their own little pack to compensate for not having one of their own. There was always a reserve about them, as if they didn't dare get too close to anyone for fear they'd leave. Once, we were all talking about how great it would be to see the world—you know how you get itchy feet in your mid-teens—anyway, someone complained about how boring life in the pack was. Kane got really mad. He said it was awful never knowing where your home was, or to have close friends because of always moving from place to place. He felt that belonging somewhere and having a family was the most important thing in the world."

"You could see it in the boys' eyes, especially Kane's, when they finally realized this was home and they belonged here." Helen reminisced. "Such a change came over them. The two of them scoured over every nook and cranny of the whole territory, learning every feature and immersing themselves in pack history. It was like we'd given them the best gift in the whole world. I think that's why Kane is so passionate about the land and protective of the pack. He knows what it's like to be an outsider and now that he has a home, he'll do anything for it."

Just then the timer for the oven rang and Helen jumped up to check on her muffins.

Elise glanced at the clock and gasped. "Oh no! Look at the time! I'm going to be late for work if I don't get a move on." Dashing from the kitchen, she raced upstairs intent on grabbing her purse and a coat. Thankfully she was already dressed in her waitressing uniform. Opening the bedroom door, she slammed into Marla who was just leaving the room.

"Oh!" Marla was clutching a book in her hand and looked flustered. "I... I was getting a book to read. I remembered that Kane had a great collection in his sitting room."

Surprised to find Marla in her room, Elise brought up a point Kane had mentioned to her the very first day. "I thought

180

Kane said our rooms were out of bounds to the rest of the pack."

Something—possibly irritation—flashed across Marla's eyes but it was gone before Elise was sure. "Kane meant the rest of the pack. I'm such old friends with him; he doesn't mind me popping in now and then."

"Oh... Sure." Elise paused. Something seemed off about the story but unfortunately, she didn't have time to question Marla about it. And really, what harm was there in borrowing a book, anyway? Dismissing the whole situation, she brushed past the other woman. "Sorry, I have to run; I don't want to be late for work."

"That's okay. I'll talk to you later." Marla stepped into the hallway.

As Elise grabbed her purse and coat, she took a quick glance around the room but saw nothing amiss. Giving a shrug she left the room, carefully closing the door behind her.

Marla was still standing in the hallway. "Don't forget I told that fellow you'd meet him at the Grey Goose after your shift was over."

"I know. I haven't forgotten, but thanks anyway," Elise waved in acknowledgement as she ran down the stairs and rushed out of the house.

Chapter 20

Elise spent most of her drive to work thinking about Kane. His childhood explained a lot about him now as an adult. As Helen had pointed out, not having a stable home or a real pack while growing up, made him fiercely protective and loyal of what he had now. And his consideration of her as a new member of the pack made sense too. How many times had he experienced that awkwardness, moving somewhere new and trying to fit in? Then there was his speech about 'moments of great disappointment'. She kept coming back to that, but it could have any number of meanings. At one time, she thought it might have referred to Marla, or it could be about his brother turning on him, but now she wondered if it was his mother leaving him behind, or possibly even his whole childhood.

The more she thought about it, the more she realized that Kane was a very complex person, with one foot in the past—dealing with the ancient traditions and animal instincts of a male werewolf and pack Alpha—and the other in the future—trying to follow modern cultural norms and expectations. She imagined that the two extremes often fought for dominance inside him, requiring a great deal of self-control. On top of that, he had experienced more than his fair share of difficulties growing up, yet despite it all he was still one of the nicest men she'd ever met.

Did Kane take after his mother or his father? Probably the former, if Helen and Carrie's recollections of Carter were to be believed. Kane's father reportedly had a nasty, uncontrolled temper and while Kane had shown his anger on a few occasions, it seemed to be kept on a leash. Carter also had—how had they put it—a 'roving-eye'. Had Kane and Ryne been aware of that? And if so, had they followed the man's example?

Her arrival downtown ended her train of thought. A quick glance at her watch showed she only had a few minutes to park the car and get to the Grey Goose for the start of her shift. Pulling into a parking spot, she moved to turn off the engine only to pause when she noticed a warning light was lit up on the dash.

Darn!

Supposedly a mechanic had checked the car over thoroughly, but something must have been missed. Well, she didn't have time to worry about it now. After work, she'd stop by a garage she'd noticed the other day and get it checked out. Locking the car, she ran across the street and hurried into the restaurant.

When one o'clock finally rolled around, Elise breathed a sigh of relief; her shift had been a busy one. Taking off her apron, she hung it on her hook and grabbed her coat, thinking longingly of sitting somewhere quiet and putting her feet up. As she rounded the corner towards the door, the sight of a tall, sandy-haired man brought her up short.

"Bryan!" Joyfully, she launched herself across the remaining few feet and jumped into the open arms of her childhood friend.

"Elise!" He spun her around and then kissed her cheek. "It's so good to see you." He smiled down at her, his hazel eyes warm and welcoming.

"Same here." She slid down from his arms and stood gazing up at him with what she knew must be a ridiculously happy grin on her face. Impulsively, she gave him another bear hug. Behind her, someone cleared their throat and she suddenly remembered she was still in the restaurant, no doubt making a spectacle of herself.

The Mating

Stepping back, she glanced over her shoulder and saw her boss frowning at her. "Sorry, Mr. Mancini. This is an old friend of mine, Bryan. I haven't seen him in a while."

Mr. Mancini raised one brow and her grin faltered. Apparently, her boss didn't appreciate his employees hugging friends in the entryway.

"Er... We'll go somewhere else to talk."

Mr. Mancini folded his arms and nodded.

Elise grabbed Bryan's arm and led him outside. There was another restaurant down the road, where they could sit and talk. Turning to the left, she started to lead the way.

"Who was the grump?" Bryan asked as he casually put an arm around her shoulders.

"Mr. Mancini? He's my boss. Usually, he's really nice. When I applied for the job, I didn't think he'd hire me, but after he thought it over, he did. Since then, he's helped me learn the ropes, given me good shifts, and generally been really great. I'm not sure what was wrong just now." She considered the incident, then gave a shrug. "We were really busy today, so maybe he's tired. I know I am."

They arrived at the restaurant and sat down. Under the cover of the table, she slipped her shoes off and wiggled her toes, sighing in relief. Bryan noticed and playfully reached down, grabbing her ankle. She gave a squeak and jerked her foot back while Bryan grinned, looking entirely too pleased with himself. She couldn't help but laugh. Gosh, but she'd missed him.

"So, how have you been?" Bryan reached across the table and took her hand. His expression sobered. "Has that Alpha been treating you okay?"

"His name is Kane," she gently reminded. "And yes, he treats me very well."

Bryan looked disappointed. "Yeah, I supposed he would. Much as I'd like to hate the guy for taking you away, everything I've heard about him tells me he's all right. I think a part of me wanted him to be a rotten thug so I'd have a reason to beat him up." He shrugged and smiled sheepishly. "Male ego, I guess."

Thinking that Kane would likely wipe the floor with the younger man, she made no comment. Instead, she turned the initial question back on him. "And how are you? And I mean really, not the politically correct 'fine' that people always give." She studied his face carefully. The last time she'd seen him, he'd been bitter and angry, almost slinking away after Kane had warned him off.

Silence stretched between them. Bryan was staring intently at their entwined fingers, his thumb tenderly caressing the back of her hand. She waited, letting him gather his thoughts.

Finally, he looked up. "I'm all right. I spent the first few days in an angry funk and then another couple wandering around feeling sad and lost. But now I'm okay. I've actually been doing some thinking—"

The waitress arrived to take their orders, interrupting whatever Bryan had been going to say. He chose a burger and fries while she picked the soup and salad luncheon special. As they placed their orders, Bryan started searching in his pocket for something. When the waitress moved away from their table, he pulled out a crumpled piece of paper and held it up triumphantly for her to see. "Here, before I forget. Sarah sent her recipe for squash soup. She said you'd been talking about it." He made a face. "Who calls to talk about soup?"

She laughed. "We do. I was telling her about Helen, one of the members of my new pack, and how she likes to cook. Sarah said that she was making squash soup when I called and then I said that Helen told me she'd never made it before and..." Catching the look on Bryan's face, she giggled and snatched the paper from his hand. "Never mind. Just tell Sarah thanks."

"Sure." Bryan stared at her, a smile on his face. "You know, Elise, when you laugh like that you have to be one of the prettiest girls I've ever seen." He tucked a strand of her hair behind her ear with the ease of familiarity and let his fingers trail down her cheek before allowing his hand to return to the table top where he fiddled with the cutlery.

Feeling inexplicably uncomfortable with the gesture, she picked up her napkin and arranged it in her lap, keeping her eyes down. "Thanks, Bryan. That was a nice thing to say."

"No, it wasn't a nice thing to say. It's the truth. I've always thought you were pretty and when you laugh, your eyes get all sparkly. Plus, you're sweet and always trying to see the positive side of things."

She shifted in her chair, suddenly nervous. What was Bryan getting at? He'd never gone around spouting her virtues like that before. Surely, he wasn't still thinking that they—?

The arrival of their meal cut into her line of thought and they both waited silently for the waitress to place the food on the table.

Once the server was gone, she cleared her throat. She had a bad feeling that Bryan was going to ask her to run away with him or some such thing and she wanted to head him off. "You know, Bryan, I am bonded to Kane."

"I know that. I—"

"And it wasn't a normal bonding. It was part of a political alliance to keep peace between the packs and ensure that we all have enough territory to roam. It's binding for life."

"Right. That's why—"

"And Kane is an Alpha, so—"

This time, Bryan interrupted her. "Elise, are you happy with Kane?"

Was she happy? Two weeks ago, she'd thought her world was coming to an end but now... It didn't take her long to come up with an answer. "Yes, Bryan. I... I like him very much and I'm happy." She reached out a hand in anticipation of comforting him but paused in surprise when she heard his response.

"Good. That takes a lot off my mind. As I was saying earlier, after you left I did a lot of thinking and... Well..." He hesitated and then spoke in a rush. "After seeing you again today, I've come to realize that while I still love you, I think it's more of a brother-sister kind of love. We've known each other all our lives and we drifted into a relationship but after you left, I found that I wasn't as devastated as I thought I'd be." Bryan seemed to be apologetic and was holding his breath, waiting for her response.

She blinked. That wasn't what she'd been expecting at all and yet it mirrored what she'd been coming to suspect. A self-deprecating laugh escaped her. Here she'd been thinking he wanted them to run away together and instead he was letting her down easy!

"So you're basically 'breaking up' with me?" She smiled at him so he'd know she was teasing but even still, he squirmed looking uncomfortable.

"Yeah, I guess I am. Have I hurt your feelings?"

"No. I was coming to the same conclusion myself. We shared some great times but now we've grown up and moved beyond the 'puppy love' stage."

Bryan groaned. "Puppy love? Oh, Elise that's a really bad joke."

"Well, what else would you call it? We were puppies and we thought we were in love." She defended herself with mock indignation. This was what she'd always enjoyed about their relationship, the friendly camaraderie, the teasing and bad jokes. They grinned at each other then Bryan's stomach growled, sending them both into a fit of laughter again.

As they ate, they talked about old times and Bryan questioned her further about her relationship with Kane. Strangely enough, she found it helpful to talk to someone from outside her new pack. Helen, Carrie, and Julia saw Kane not only as their Alpha but also as a much beloved friend. Bryan had very few preconceived notions and she felt he'd be able to interpret things in an unbiased fashion. By the time they had finished eating, they'd reached the conclusion that she was definitely falling in love with her mate.

The Mating

"After all," Bryan said as he walked her to her car. "What's not to love about the man? He's done everything he can to make you happy and except for sticking you with Marla, he hasn't made a wrong move, has he?"

"No, and even Marla isn't that bad any more. I think Kane and I will have a good future together. He seems to like me and maybe one day he'll... Well, who knows?" She turned to look at Bryan, placing her hands on his chest. "Thanks so much for listening to me ramble on about Kane. It was really good to see you again." She paused, realizing something. "You never did say why you were in town."

"No, I guess I never did. I..." He shifted uncomfortably. "Don't take this wrong—it's nothing against your father, I swear—but I'm thinking of heading out and seeing a bit of the world, maybe even forming my own pack one day."

"Really? Your own pack?"

"Yeah. I... I think I have it in me to be an Alpha or at least a Beta someday, though not for a few years to come. There's this feeling that's been growing in me for a while now, but I always ignored it because I knew, or at least I thought I knew, that my future was with you. Now that you're gone, I'm starting to realize that I want more out of life and the chances of advancing in our pack are really limited. It's too big, with too many other wolves in line."

"But your own pack? You don't have the money to buy land or even a house. What will you do?"

"I've heard rumours that there's another wolf who also wants to strike out on his own. I'm in town to see him and maybe we can work a deal." Bryan shrugged nonchalantly but there was an excitement about him that she hadn't seen before, as if he couldn't wait to start a grand new adventure.

She stared at him then reached up and brushed his sandy brown hair from his eyes. "I hope it works out for you, Bryan." Standing on tiptoe, she pressed a gentle kiss to his lips then took a step back. The boy she'd known was turning into a man and she was proud of him.

"Thanks. If this meeting goes the way I hope, I'll be on my way before the week is out. There are a few things I have to wrap up and naturally I won't leave the pack without saying goodbye to everyone. And of course I have to explain to your father." He made a face and she laughed.

"Good luck with that."

"Yeah." He rubbed the back of his neck likely anticipating the awkward exchange. "Listen, if I'm heading back this way, could we meet again?"

"Sure. I'd really like that."

Bryan gave her a quick hug before opening the car door for her. "Okay, I'll give you a call in a day or two."

"Great. I'll be waiting." She started the car and pulled away. As she left, she rolled down her window and waved.

"Bye, Elise. Take care. Love ya!" Bryan called after her.

"I love you, too!"

Chapter 21

Elise hummed to herself, thinking of how nice it had been to see Bryan again and to have things worked out between them. The confusing feelings she'd harboured for him over the past few weeks were finally straight in her mind, allowing her to focus on Kane without any guilt or ambiguity. Kane was her future and she was pretty sure she was beginning to love him. Yes, she'd thought she'd loved Bryan, but this was totally different. Hugging Bryan had been familiar and comfortable, while being with Kane gave her a sense of security and completeness along with an interesting, tingly excitement that just felt…right.

Stopping at a traffic light, she glanced down at the dashboard and grimaced. That warning light was on again. Rolling her eyes in exasperation, she altered her course and headed towards the nearest garage. Thankfully, it wasn't too late, and the mechanic was still on duty. He took the car back into the service area to check it, while she sat waiting in the front office.

It wasn't the cleanest place she'd ever been; the smell of old oil and gasoline assaulted her nose. A coffee maker was in one corner on an old Formica counter, while the cash register beside it sported a sign offering a complimentary cup of coffee while you wait. She poured herself some and took a sip, then grimaced at the taste. It was several hours old and as thick as tar. Setting the coffee aside, she perched uncomfortably on the edge of one of the old vinyl chairs. Its plastic surface was cracked and sadly in need of cleaning. A dog-eared magazine was lying on the chair beside her and she flipped through it. Unfortunately, it was several years old and focused mostly on sports cars and motorcycles that were draped with scantily clad, buxom beauties. Dropping the magazine in disgust, she stood and looked out the window.

There wasn't much to see. The sky had darkened to a dull grey that threatened rain or possibly even snow. Cars zoomed by on the highway that ran in front of the garage, a billboard advertising insulation was to the right, and a parking lot with cars for sale occupied the space to the left. Idly, she studied the cars, her gaze skimming over the shades of brown, blue, and grey until coming to a stop on the lone flash of red. It was a sports car, bright red in colour and strangely familiar.

Drawn like a magnet, she pushed open the outer door, the bell above jingling merrily to signal her exit. Walking over to where the car was parked, she circled it, studying the vehicle from all angles. She'd be the first to admit that she knew nothing about cars, but she'd bet her last dollar this was the one that had sprayed gravel at her two weeks ago. It wasn't a common make, possibly an import.

Tugging at the door handle, she was surprised when it opened. Didn't people usually keep their cars locked? Leaning over, she examined the interior. It was clean, with no papers or garbage lying around. She wondered who the owner was and sniffed but didn't detect any recent scents.

Thoughtfully, she closed the door and made her way back to the customer waiting area. Once inside, she glanced towards the door that led to the service bays. It was ajar, and she could see the mechanic was still working on her car; the noise from the engine obviously had kept him from noticing her brief departure. Casually she strolled over to the counter and leaned against it. Ostensibly pouring herself more coffee, she peered at the labelled binders that were stacked on the other side of the counter.

Keeping one eye on the door, she picked up a binder entitled 'Auto Sales' and began to flip through the listings. About half-way through, she came to a snapshot of the red car. There was a write up about its age, engine size, and number of miles. The date on the page indicated that it had been brought in about a week and a half ago and the owner was listed as Ryne Taylor!

She snapped the book shut and pressed it to her chest. Ryne must have been at the house just two weeks ago! He was the one who had peppered her with gravel. But it had only been her second day, she hadn't even been there forty-eight hours yet. How had he known who she was? And why had he shown such disrespect to her? Was it because he hated Kane and she was guilty by association? Or perhaps he was a maniac when driving and thought the stunt he'd pulled was funny.

She'd have to tell Kane what she'd discovered. It might prove to be a lead that helped them locate the rogue wolf. Carefully, she slipped the binder back where it belonged and sat down again to wait for her car, all the while thinking how pleased Kane would be with her news.

It was almost five o'clock by the time she finally got home. The problem with the car had been a malfunctioning sensor light, rather than an actual fault with the engine or brakes. A new sensor was on order and the mechanic said he'd call when the part came in.

After kicking off her shoes, she padded towards the stairs, thinking longingly of putting on some comfortable sweats and having a cup of tea. She'd just started her ascent when Marla popped out of Kane's office.

"Hey, Elise! You're late getting back. How was your day?" Marla was grinning as if she knew something Elise didn't.

"Fine, just long and tiring." She paused at the bottom of the stairs.

Marla's face fell. "Nothing 'exciting' happened?"

"No, not really. Well, I did meet my friend for lunch." She smiled at the memory.

"That's right. I remember now. His name was Bryan, wasn't it? Your meeting went well?"

She nodded and began to climb the stairs, thinking that Marla almost seemed disappointed.

"You didn't see anyone else? Just this fellow?"

"Just Bryan," She reiterated wondering why she cared.

The other woman followed her up the stairs. "I thought you might have bumped into Kane. He was supposed to pick up a package at the Gallery for me this afternoon."

"No, I haven't seen him since early this morning... Oh, wait!" She snapped her fingers as the memory popped into her head. "Kane told me about that this morning, but he was still in a financial meeting when I left for work. Maybe he forgot, or he had someone else do it. I'm sorry, I was right there. I should have offered to get it for you. Was it important?"

"No, it wasn't that crucial, I guess." Marla frowned. "So... Are you going to see this Bryan guy again?"

"Well, maybe. He might be coming back this way in a few days, but I don't know for sure."

"Hmm..." Marla was silent, her brow furrowed, as if deep in thought.

When they reached the top of the stairs, she leaned close and gave a sniff. "Don't take offence, girl, but you smell funny. Sort of like oil and gas."

Groaning, she explained how she'd spent the later part of her afternoon. "I think it's mostly on my coat."

"Here, give me the coat." Marla took the garment from her and first sniffed it, then Elise. "Well, the coat smells like a garage, but you..." She paused as if trying to decide whether or not to say something, then a smile appeared on her face. "You, my dear Elise, smell like a male werewolf." Marla smirked and winked. "So tell me again, just how friendly was this meeting?"

The Mating

Elise felt herself flushing. "It was nothing like that, Marla. Bryan's an old friend. We grew up together."

"Uh-huh. That's your story, but will Kane believe it? He has some jealousy issues, you know. It's because of his parents." Marla leaned closer and whispered conspiratorially. "His father ran around all the time and now Kane has this thing about honesty and fidelity." Marla straightened and looked her square in the eye. "Did you tell him who you were meeting?"

"Well, no." She bit her lip. Why hadn't she told Kane about seeing Bryan? Probably because the only time the two men had met, it hadn't gone well. "But I'll just explain to him—"

"Elise, let me give you some advice. I know this is sort of personal but hey, it can't totally be hidden. I can tell that you're almost in heat, and the smell of your pheromones will be upping Kane's sense of possessiveness. You know how territorial male Lycans get about their mates at a time like this. He's not going to be overly receptive to hearing about you meeting this Bryan guy."

"Oh, I don't think—"

"Listen. I've known Kane longer than you have. We were even an item for a while, so you have to trust me on this one. I know how he'll react and it won't be pretty. When I realized that I loved Ryne rather than him, Kane almost went berserk; it was totally out of character for him, but that's what he did."

She paled at the idea of Kane getting really angry at her. For the most part, he was so calm and level-headed, but she'd seen flashes of his temper. Helen had commented on how Kane had been confused and lost when Marla broke up with him, but there'd been no mention of violence. Then again, maybe Helen didn't know everything. What would he do? Probably he'd start by growling or yelling, which was pretty frightening. Then he'd do that cold staring thing that made the recipient want to sink into the ground. If he truly thought she'd been with another male, she wasn't sure what he might be capable of doing. As Marla said, male werewolves were very territorial, but she hadn't been thinking of that when she'd agreed to meet Bryan.

"So, how are we going to keep Kane from finding out about this guy?" Marla's question jolted her back from her imagined encounter with an enraged Kane.

"Umm... I'll grab a quick shower."

"No time for that. Kane will be home any minute, and besides what about your clothes? Even stuffed in the laundry basket he might notice. I suppose you might have time to get them down to the laundry before he gets here, but what if you meet him on the stairs?"

"Then I'll just..."

"Elise, you are so lucky that I'm here to help you out. Here's what we'll do. Do you remember how I gave you some perfume about a week ago? Have you used it yet?"

She shook her head. "No. Why?"

"Okay, well put some on—quite a lot actually. It will help mask that scent. If you use it, Kane will have no idea that you've been near anyone else. And if you see Bryan again, use it then too. What Kane doesn't know won't hurt him and it will save you from his temper.'

"I'm not sure this is such a good idea, Marla. If I explain—"

"Elise, do you remember how angry Kane was over that picture of him I had in the Gallery? Well, that will seem like nothing compared to how this will set him off. You've only been around attached males so far, so you really don't know how possessive he can be."

She thought back to how Kane had reacted to Bryan talking to her that first morning. Was it possible Marla was right? Perhaps she should simply avoid mentioning the whole incident. "Well..."

"Good! I don't want Kane to be upset with you, not when he seems so happy right now." Marla grabbed her arm and pulled her into the bedroom. "Now, where's that perfume?" Before Elise could even speak, Marla spotted it on the dresser and began to douse her with the stuff. When she was done, she stepped back, looking exceedingly pleased. "There! All taken care of and not a moment too soon." She checked her watch. "Kane should be here any minute, so I'll scoot on my way." With a friendly wave, Marla hurried out of the room, leaving Elise feeling as if she'd been caught up in a windstorm.

She lifted her arm and sniffed her sleeve. She couldn't scent Bryan at all and the perfume itself didn't actually smell that bad. In fact, it was vaguely familiar though she couldn't quite place it. It was on the fringes of her mind, if she could only remember... From past experience she knew that the harder she tried to recall something, the more elusive the memory became so she put the matter from her mind and returned to thinking about Bryan.

Even if the perfume did work, not telling Kane about the meeting didn't sit right with her. Marla could be wrong. Kane might not be that upset and even if he was, at least it would be all over and done with, rather than hanging over her head while she waited for him to find out through some other obscure source.

Giving a decisive nod, she grabbed a brush and quickly began to fix her hair, only to knock an earring loose. It tumbled to the ground and gave the faintest of tinkles as it rolled across the floor. With an exasperated sigh, she set the brush down, got onto her hands and knees and began crawling along searching for the small bit of jewellery. It wasn't immediately visible, so she lay flat, stretching her arm underneath the dresser and feeling around, but having no luck.

Darn! Where had the silly thing gone? Still on all fours, she surveyed the floor in frustration. She was sure it had rolled towards the dresser but possibly she'd been wrong. Bending her head closer to the floor, she surveyed the surface in front of her.

Suddenly something nudged her butt and she shrieked. Turning quickly, she lost her balance and fell onto her side landing in an undignified heap. Brushing her hair from her face she looked up to see Kane standing over her, in his wolf form. His tongue was hanging from his mouth and she knew without a doubt he was laughing.

"That was not funny!" She spoke slowly and distinctly, letting her irritation show. "You scared me half to death."

He cocked his head to the side showing no remorse, then shoved a cold wet nose against her face.

"Hey! Stop that. What's with you?" Despite herself she giggled, his whiskers tickling, and reached up to run her hands through his fur and scratch his ears. With her arms still around him, Kane suddenly shimmered and became human again. His head dropped down and he kissed her thoroughly until they were both gasping for breath.

"You smell...different...tonight." Kane looked at her in puzzlement.

She froze, a knot of fear forming in her stomach. Trying to sound casual, she responded. "Really? How so?"

Kane sniffed her again. "I don't know. Your own scent is muted and there's this floral smell. It's sort of familiar, but I can't place it."

Okay. This was her chance. Gathering her courage, she began her explanation. "It's that new perfume Marla gave me. You see, she had this silly idea that—"

A hot mouth suddenly cut her off, teasing her lips and driving all thought from her mind. He slowly pulled away and moved to nibbling at her ear. "Oh yeah. I remember that now. It was nice of her, but I like your own scent better. Don't wear this stuff too often, okay?"

Nodding, she tried to focus on the topic of Bryan, but Kane was now nuzzling her neck causing shivers of delight to course through her. All right. Maybe this wasn't the time. But later on tonight, she'd definitely let him know.

She ran her hands across his shoulders and down his back, luxuriating in the feel of his bare skin and solid muscle. A thought occurred to her. "Hey! I think you forgot something when you shifted."

The Mating

"Hmm? What?"

"Your clothes, silly. You forgot to think 'clothes' when you phased back." She giggled. Only an inexperienced young Lycan would forget to magick back their clothes when changing forms.

"No I didn't. I purposely left them off. I have great plans for us." He began to work on the buttons of her shirt and she grabbed his wrists to stop him.

"Appealing as that might sound, it's almost dinner time."

A rumble worked its way up from deep in Kane's throat. "They can eat without us. Food is the last thing on my mind right now." He confirmed the fact by scooping her up and then dropping her on the bed.

As he loomed over her, need flowed through her faster than she'd ever thought possible. Yep, her heat was definitely coming on. This next week might prove to be extremely…interesting.

Chapter 22

When they finally made it downstairs, dinner was over and everyone had gathered in the game room. Elise apologized to Helen for their absence at the table, but the older woman smiled knowingly. "Don't worry about it, Elise. There's some leftover pasta in the fridge, despite the best efforts of those two," she nodded towards the group who were circling the pool table. "Thankfully Daniel and Franz didn't eat us out of house and home this time."

The two young men in question grinned and Franz called out, "We're growing boys. We need our food."

Giselle, who was also there, simply rolled her eyes, and resignedly shook her head.

"Are you sure you want to be bonded to this one, Giselle?" Kane asked from his position leaning against the doorframe.

"I ask myself that question every day." She responded dryly. Franz affected a wounded pose before turning back to his game.

Rose was standing in the corner observing the others and being her characteristically quiet self. When the girl glanced her way, Elise gave her a friendly, encouraging smile. As their eyes met, Rose looked her up and down and then, seeming to find her worthy of contempt, the usually shy girl curled her lip and pointedly turned her back.

Anger combined with shocked disbelief filled her, and it took Elise a moment to push down the desire to march over there and demand an explanation. Glancing around, she saw that no one else had witnessed the exchange. Had it actually happened? She quickly replayed the event. No, she hadn't imagined it but what was the reason? Was Rose attempting to assert herself and move up in the pack? If she was, picking on the Alpha's mate was certainly not the place to start!

Elise considered dealing with the incident immediately then dismissed the idea. There was no need to create a scene by putting Rose in her place in front of everyone. That would only create more animosity. No, she'd wait and speak to the girl privately.

Kane, apparently oblivious to the exchange that had just happened, pushed off from the doorframe. "Well, I'm going in search of food. How about you, Elise?" With another thoughtful look at Rose, she nodded and followed him upstairs into the kitchen.

"It will only take a few minutes to heat up the pasta." She peered into the fridge and pulled out the food while Kane took plates from the cupboard and set them on the table.

"All right. Do you want me to make a salad?" He pulled open the cutlery drawer.

"No, I can do it."

"Okay, then while dinner's heating, I'm going to check on something in the office." Kane headed down the hallway and she nodded absentmindedly as she pressed the appropriate buttons on the microwave. Once it was heating, she pulled out a head of lettuce, cucumbers, and tomatoes in order to make a quick salad.

Marla wandered through while she was working and snatched a cucumber slice out of the bowl. Casually leaning a hip against the counter, she munched on the veggie, then grabbed a piece of tomato. "So, how did it go? Did the perfume work?"

She nervously glanced down the hall to ensure that Kane wasn't within earshot. "It was fine, but I still don't feel right about this. I'm going to tell him the truth as soon as I get a chance."

Marla shook her head. "I don't know if that's a good idea."

The Mating

"If what's a good idea?" Kane walked into the kitchen frowning.

"Er... Elise and I going shopping tomorrow. I think next week would be better." Marla made a quick recovery.

"Oh, that's nice." Kane seemed distracted and Elise asked him what was wrong. "Nothing, really. I've misplaced a report that was on my desk. It was the one from Chloe and her university friends about the negative environmental impact of drilling for oil on our land. I was sending it to our lawyers tomorrow."

"I didn't know you'd had a study done on that." Marla picked up another veggie, only appearing mildly interested.

"It wasn't general knowledge. Only those in the Alpha house really knew about it." Kane ran his hand through his hair. "Was anyone in the office today moving things about? That room is supposed to be off-limits if I'm not there but..."

The microwave signalled their food was ready and Kane, being the closest, stopped mid-sentence and removed the steaming bowl of pasta. While his back was turned, Elise stared at Marla. The blonde woman had been leaving Kane's office when she'd arrived home that afternoon. Did Marla know where the report was? Opening her mouth to ask, she saw Marla making a pleading gesture and shaking her head.

Against her better judgement, Elise pressed her lips together and remained silent. Marla had been trying to be helpful this afternoon, in her own twisted way, so she supposed she could return the favour. Mouthing the words 'you'd better tell me what's going on later', Elise schooled her face into a pleasant expression before Kane turned around.

Marla wandered off, ostensibly to make a phone call, while Kane and Elise ate, but returned before they were finished. She poured herself a cup of coffee and sat down to visit, idly chatting about her day.

Kane was done eating first and started to gather up the dishes, while Elise finished her meal. He spoke over his shoulder as he placed the items in the sink. "Marla. I almost forgot. I didn't make it into town today, but Rose was going in, so I asked her to stop by the Gallery to get that package for you."

"Really? Rose was in town, but you weren't. Hmm, I wonder..." Marla's voice trailed off.

Elise looked up from her plate. "What do you wonder?"

"Nothing. I'm just curious if she got the package or not. She didn't give it to me, so maybe it wasn't even in, after all. I'll have to ask her later." Smiling, Marla glanced at her two companions. "I'll clean up, if you two want to take a walk or something."

Elise raised questioning brows and looked at Kane. It was a nice evening and the idea of a walk appealed to her.

He nodded in agreement. "Sounds good. I'll tell the others we're going in case anyone wants to tag along."

As soon as Kane disappeared from sight, Elise turned to Marla and questioned her sternly. "Why were you in Kane's office this afternoon if it was off-limits? And what did you do with that report?"

"I didn't do anything with the report, at least not on purpose. Kane's computer has the fastest processor in the house, so I was using it to do some research on the collector who bought that photograph. I must have scooped the report up with my stuff by accident."

"Why didn't you tell Kane then?"

"Because I wasn't supposed to be in his office and I didn't want to mention that picture again. He's been in a good mood lately and I don't want to spoil it."

Elise took a deep breath and exhaled slowly, not liking the situation at all. "Okay. But if you're not supposed to be in his office, then stay out of his office. I don't want to have to cover for you again. Find that report and put it back."

"It already is. I snuck back in while you were eating and slipped it under some files. He'll think he missed it somehow."

She nodded but had a funny feeling about the incident.

The Mating

It turned out that everyone except Marla and Carrie wanted to go for a walk. Carrie planned to rest and Marla needed to do her nails so the rest headed towards the woods. They fell into a loose pack formation, the other couples instinctively walking behind Kane. Elise was one step back and to the right of him. John came along next, followed by Helen, then Giselle and Franz, while Rose and Daniel brought up the rear. The arrangement effectively cancelled Elise's hopes of having a private conversation with Rose but she still hoped to deal with the matter before the night was over.

As they entered the tree line, a sound came from the left and in a blur of movement, Kane and John positioned themselves protectively in front of the others, muscles tense and senses alert. It took less than a second for them to identify the source and realize there was no danger. As the two men visibly relaxed their stance, Julia and Thomas emerged from the brush.

"Hi there!" Julia called out. "Great night to be out, isn't it?"

Kane nodded in acknowledgement but looked inquiringly at Thomas. "Your first night back on patrol?"

"Yeah, just the immediate area, nothing too far from home yet." Thomas looked down at Julia who was holding his arm. "And she insisted on coming along."

Julia grinned. "After last time, I don't want you out of my sight." Thomas rolled his eyes, but none the less, looked pleased at the extra attention he was receiving.

"Anything to report?" John inquired.

"Nope. All's quiet. You folks are heading out for a run?" Thomas surveyed the group.

Helen piped up. "Some of them are running, but I, for one, am planning a leisurely stroll."

"Well, have fun. It was a long shift, so we're heading home." As they turned to go, Thomas accidentally brushed against Elise, then froze in his tracks, a rumbling emitting from his throat. His sudden stop tugged on Julia's arm causing her to bounce back against him and in turn he bumped into Elise, who stumbled and half fell to the ground. Thomas spun around, growling low and threatening, his eyes narrowed. In a flash, Kane had him by the throat, his hand like a vice-grip, while the other was swung back, preparing to strike. A low growl ripped from his chest and he looked on the verge of changing forms. Julia screamed and Elise scrambled to her feet, her heart pounding as she took in the scene before her. Unthinkingly, she rushed forward, shoving herself between the two men.

"Kane, no! It was an accident! I'm all right." She grabbed his arm. The others around them stood frozen, possibly from shock or possibly because Kane was the Alpha. It was his right to discipline the members as he saw fit. John took half a step forward, but then stopped as Kane snarled even louder.

Realizing she was the only one who might be able to defuse the situation, Elise reached for Kane's face, trying to force him to look at her. "Kane, listen to me! No harm was done. Let him go!"

He blinked twice and as her message sank in, began to relax, slowly releasing Thomas. The other man stepped back and swallowed hard but continued to sniff the air, shifting his eyes nervously over the crowd and peering into the woods behind them.

Julia hugged Thomas' arm and looked nervously at Kane. Elise placed her hands firmly on Kane's shoulders and took a deep breath to calm her pounding heart. Stepping in front of an angry Alpha was not the smartest move to make, but she'd reacted to the situation as instinctively as Kane had done.

Slowly, she slid her hands down to his chest, rubbing them soothingly over the muscled surface. "It was an accident. You didn't mean to knock me down, did you, Thomas? And you weren't growling at any of us, were you?"

Thomas still appeared disoriented but nodded in agreement. "No. Sorry. It's just that I... I suddenly scented something, and it triggered a memory. For a moment I could have sworn I was back in that clearing where Ryne shot me." He sniffed the air again, searching for the source, before focusing on Elise again. He took a half step forward and sniffed again, a puzzled expression forming on his tanned face. "That's strange. It's coming from you."

"Me?" She squeaked in surprise. "I don't smell like Ryne, do I?" She looked to the others for confirmation.

"No, it's not Ryne's scent but..." Thomas seemed to be searching his memory. "It was there at the same time as Ryne. I'm sure I remember both scents."

"Hmm..." Kane sniffed at Elise. "You're wearing that new perfume that Marla gave you. But why would Ryne have been wearing it?"

Elise wasn't sure what to say. Marla said the perfume disguised scents so that would explain Ryne wearing it, but if she told Kane this, he'd want to know why she was using it. Then she'd have to explain about seeing Bryan... Out of the corner of her eye, she took in the assembled group. Confessing in front of the pack was less than ideal but... She opened her mouth to explain only to realize that no one was expecting an answer from her. They'd all continued to talk while she'd been thinking.

"Maybe Ryne was trying to hide his scent from us by overpowering it with perfume." John suggested.

"Could be," Kane nodded. "But it didn't work, since Thomas still knew he was there." He ran his hands through his hair and huffed in exasperation. "Who knows what Ryne is thinking anymore? None of this makes sense to me."

The others murmured their agreement.

With a sigh, Kane brought the impromptu meeting to a close. "If anyone still wants to go for a run, they should head out now, before it gets much later."

Helen checked her watch. "I think I'll head back to the house. That was enough excitement for me."

The others decided to continue on and, phasing into wolf form, melted into the night, leaving Kane, Elise, Thomas, and Julia standing at the tree line. The two couples looked awkwardly at each other until Kane finally broke the silence.

"Thomas, I'm sorry I overreacted a few minutes ago." Kane gruffly apologized, shoving his hands in his back pockets. "But when I saw Elise on the ground and you growled, well..."

"No need to apologize. Any mate would have done the same; it's your right." Thomas dismissed the incident with a shrug. "I shouldn't have reacted so strongly, but like I said, that scent had me flashing back. I was sure I could even hear the click of the gun. While on some level I knew it wasn't real, I couldn't stop myself. Sorry. It won't happen again."

Kane nodded and Thomas stuck out his hand. With a grin, Kane shook it. There were no hard feelings on either side and the two couples chatted for a while longer before parting amicably.

"Do you still want to go for a run?" Elise asked.

"No, not really. There's a bench over there. Could we just sit and enjoy the moonlight?" Kane indicated a spot a short distance away.

With a nod, she agreed and Kane took her hand, leading her towards the secluded niche. The bench was surrounded by pine trees on three sides and gave the illusion of being in a private little room.

Sitting down, Kane tucked her to his side and sighed. "Elise, there's something I have to say."

Chapter 23

Kane put his arm around her shoulders, his thumb gently rubbing over her upper arm. When he spoke, his voice held both regret and self-reproach. "I can't believe I reacted that strongly to Thomas knocking you down. I acted without even thinking and I never do that. I'm the Alpha, the one that's supposed to be in control. But when I heard that growl, I lost it. My only thought was to protect my mate. I'm sorry if I frightened you."

"I wasn't frightened, at least not exactly. Surprised, worried, wondering what the hell was going on. But frightened of you? No."

"I'd never hurt you."

"I know."

He tightened his arm around her and she turned in towards him, leaning her head against his chest. They sat there in silence, absorbing the warmth and essence of the other.

Elise savoured the moment. This was what she wanted. Time when they were just together as a normal couple. She wanted an actual relationship, where they talked and shared their ideas and feelings. Maybe Kane wanted that, too. The intense emotions of a few minutes ago seemed to have loosened his tight self-control. While she was reluctant to ruin the companionable silence between them, she didn't want to let this opportunity go by. Gathering her courage, she wet her lips, then spoke softly. "Kane, this afternoon—"

At the same time, he started to speak as well. "You know—"

They both stopped and laughed self-consciously. Kane laid a finger on her lips. "Let me, please? I'm not good at sharing stuff and I've finally got my nerve up, okay?"

She nodded. Her news wasn't that earth shattering really. It could wait. This was Kane's time.

"I try to be a leader of the twenty-first century; calm, reasonable, civilized, setting an example for the others to follow. I want my pack to move forward and fit into society, but sometimes, like tonight, my instincts take over and I find that I'm more wolf than man. Don't get me wrong, being a wolf is an important part of who I am; it's just not always easy to keep it under control."

"I think you do a fine job balancing the man and the wolf." She idly traced the pattern on his shirt.

"I'm glad you think so. Me, I'm not so sure." He inhaled deeply then surprised her by seeming to change the subject. "Has anyone told you about my parents?"

"Well, I've heard some stories..." She answered hesitantly, not sure if she was or wasn't supposed to know.

"My father was a rogue wolf; a throwback to days long gone. The kind of rogue who could never settle down or integrate into a pack. He dragged us all over the countryside, spending a month here, a month there. I think my mother was the only one who could tolerate him for any length of time." Kane tipped his head up and stared at the night sky as if a picture of the man was forming in the stars. "He had his good points. He could be spontaneous and fun, always coming up with ideas for a new adventure. Apparently, he was quite a charmer of the ladies and a rather smooth talker too, which was a good thing because it got him out of quite a few scrapes. Unfortunately, even his glib tongue wasn't always sufficient and his temper was what lingered on in everyone's memory. We were kicked out of more places than I care to remember because of him."

"That must have been awfully hard on you."

"It had its moments. We—Ryne and I—became pretty good at reading the signs and staying away when he was in a mood. Mom was great and did what she could to keep us fed and safe, but it didn't always work." He paused and seemed lost in his own memories. She could easily imagine him as a child, undernourished and afraid, his dark hair all tousled, while his amber eyes solemnly assessed the mood in the house, wondering if it was safe or if he should hide. It was so foreign to her own experiences. She wished she'd been there to offer him some comfort. Her father might not have had time for her but she had always had the necessities and felt safe in her home.

Kane came out of his reverie and turned his head so he could look in her eyes. "Sometimes I worry about how much of my father is in me. I don't want to be him, Elise. I don't want his anger to be part of me. I fight to keep that side buried. But sometimes, like tonight, it escapes. I worry about what could happen."

"Nothing happened." She reassured. "You stopped yourself."

"No, I didn't. You stopped me, which, by the way, was a very brave but foolish thing to try and do. I could have accidentally hurt you."

"I wasn't brave. I just reacted. And no, you wouldn't have hurt me. You don't have it in you. You stopped yourself. If you'd really intended to kill Thomas, I couldn't have prevented it. You would have ripped his throat out before I even got to my feet."

Kane looked sceptical but she continued on.

"You're a good man, Kane. You didn't hurt Thomas tonight. You didn't kill Ryne in the challenge. You aren't your father. Yes, you have a temper—every werewolf does, especially the males—but you control it, not the other way around." She paused, trying to clarify her own thinking. "I think we're all walking a tightrope, trying to fit in, to control our wolf and not to be discovered. I'm always amazed at what a good job we do and how few people actually know we exist."

He studied her, his eyes gleaming in the moonlight, before leaning forward and pressing a slow kiss to her forehead. "You're very clever you know."

"I always thought so." She smiled up at him.

"Thank you."

"For what?"

"For being you. For trying to make 'us' work, despite the fact that you were thrown into this." He took her hand and laced their fingers together. "I know I'm not good at expressing myself, but I hope you know how glad I am that you're here with me. The pack is my extended family, but I've never really had anyone that was just mine, until you came along." He brought their entwined hands up to his mouth and kissed hers gently. "You're my mate, Elise." He whispered the words, his soft tone making them even more meaningful.

She felt her eyes getting misty. There was so much feeling evident in Kane's gaze and voice. He might not be saying the exact words that she wanted to hear, but she was sure the emotion was there, just unspoken. With his upbringing, he'd probably learned never to get too attached, to keep a wall of reserve around his heart and never to say how he really felt. But he was trying now, in his own way.

"I want 'us' to work, too." She whispered back, pressing a soft kiss to his hand, before wrapping her other arm around him and resting her cheek on his chest.

Elise skipped down the stairs the next morning. It was a beautiful day, even if the sky was grey and overcast. Last night had been incredible and its afterglow was transferring to her whole day. Kane had made love to her not just had sex. It had been slow and sweet, everything she had ever imagined. He'd worshipped every inch of her, gently stroking and caressing, all the while whispering tender words that had made her heart melt. While he hadn't initiated a blood-bond, she was sure he was close. His teeth had grazed her neck several times and he'd seemed on the verge of saying something, only to draw back. At one point, she'd considered mentioning it, but then he'd used his wickedly talented fingers to distract her.

Never mind, it would be soon she consoled herself. She could tell. A secret smile played over her lips; her cycle would likely start tomorrow or the next day. Surely then Kane would lose his reserve. Already she was feeling so much closer to him. What would it be like to be blood-bonded and to be privileged to have a sense of his actual thoughts and feelings? An excited shiver ran through her at the very idea.

Impulsively, she turned towards his office instead of the kitchen, which had been her original destination. She rapped lightly on the door and popped her head in. He was hanging up the phone and looked more than a little frustrated. The smile left her face and she walked over resting her hands on his shoulders. "You look like you lost your last best friend. What's wrong?"

He leaned back against her and sighed. "You know the environmental report I was telling you about? The one I thought I'd misplaced yesterday? Well, I found it this morning and read it over, but it's not nearly as positive as I'd been led to believe it would be."

"You mean the land isn't environmentally significant?"

"No, the report doesn't negate the fact the area is of interest, but it doesn't say anything about it being endangered if the oil drilling were to occur." Kane rubbed his eyes. "I don't get it. Chloe and the people at the university knew what we needed in the report and had sounded so positive when we'd met, but this reads like a whole section has been left out."

"Could someone have forgotten to print out part of the report?"

"I suppose it's possible. Maybe I'll give Chloe a call and ask her about it." He shrugged his shoulders as if trying to ease the tension and she began to knead the tight muscles. "To top things off, I just finished talking with our lawyers. Apparently,

Northern Oil has already gotten wind of our having a study done. Now they want their own people to do another assessment because they question the validity of our experts."

"But how did they find out so fast?"

"I don't know. Only a few of us in the Alpha house knew about it. Maybe someone at the university let it slip."

"Does it really matter? I mean, won't another assessment show the same thing? It could even help if their own people come up with similar findings."

"That's not how these companies work. Their 'experts' will make sure the report is favourable to the company that hired them. Studies and statistics can always be reworded and twisted around so they seem to support whatever point of view you want."

"So it comes down to our word against theirs."

"Pretty much. The courts will have to look at the qualifications of the 'experts', check previous work done by them, their educational background, even how much they'll profit by the report. It's a long drawn out process and can get really petty." Kane turned in his chair and pulled her down into his lap, nuzzling her neck. "But enough of that. Your incredibly talented fingers have managed to transfer the tension in my shoulders to an entirely different location."

"After last night, I don't know how you could possibly need—"

"Elise, when I'm around you I always need." And with that, he kissed her thoroughly

Eventually, the ringing of the phone had her pulling away.

"We should answer that," she panted.

"Let the machine take it. I'm too busy." He nipped at her ear lobe. The answer machine came on and a crackly male voice spoke. "Hey, this is Marty's Auto calling. The part for the sensor in your car is in. If you can have it here before noon, I can get it installed today."

She groaned and regretfully pulled away from Kane. "As much as I hate to stop, I really should go. I want to get the car taken care of today. The mechanic could be fixing it while I'm at work."

"I suppose you're right." Kane had a slight pout on his face, as he slid his hands out from under her clothing.

Giving him a quick peck, she climbed off his lap. "We can finish this tonight, I promise."

"I'm holding you to that."

Smiling, she started to leave, then paused in the door way. "That voice didn't sound at all like the mechanic I talked to. I think you need to get a new answering machine."

"It's getting old and the tape is probably worn out, too. I'm actually thinking of going with an automated voice mail through the phone company."

"Might be an idea." With a wave, she headed for the stairs to their rooms to gather her coat and purse and then hurried downstairs, intent on getting her car to the shop and still making it to work on time. Opening the back door, she walked right into Marla.

"Oh, sorry, Marla. I wasn't expecting you." Looking at the other woman, Elise frowned at her appearance. She'd never seen Marla dishevelled before; the woman always seemed to have stepped out of a fashion magazine. Today, her hair was windblown and her hands were dirty. Even a few of her manicured nails appeared to be broken. Glancing down, Elise noted that mud still clung to her shoes and pant legs. "What happened to you?"

Brushing at her clothing, Marla gave a nervous laugh. "Oh darn, you caught me. Don't tell the others—I have to keep up my image of being a total sloth, you know—but I was out for a run and went farther than I'd planned. Excuse me." She pushed past Elise and hurried inside, her head down.

That was strange, Elise mused as she walked to her car. From all reports, Marla hardly ever did the wolf thing, being more in touch with her human side. Why had she suddenly changed her habits and where had she been running to have gotten so muddy? There hadn't been any rain for almost a week.

Shrugging, she pushed the matter from her mind and headed to the car, only to come up short as she started to open the door. Darn! She'd forgotten about Bryan. Kane still didn't know. She considered running in to tell him, but then thought about the time. She only had a few minutes to spare and if it took longer at the garage... Well, the fact that she'd met with Bryan wasn't that earth shattering of an event, was it? Last night had shown her that she and Kane were building a good relationship and something as minor as seeing Bryan wasn't really a problem. Yesterday, she'd allowed Marla to get her all worked up over nothing.

Climbing into the car, she pushed the matter aside. Tonight would be soon enough to let Kane know.

Chapter 24

It was ten-thirty when Elise arrived at Marty's Auto Repair. She hoped he had a car he could loan her. It was quite a walk to the Grey Goose and shifting into her wolf form to run down the street really wasn't a good idea. If need be, she'd have to hire a cab. When she asked, Marty looked her up and down and smiled.

"For a pretty girl like you...anything." Expansively he waved his hand towards the rows of cars that were for sale. "Take your pick."

She forced herself not to roll her eyes at the mechanic, who obviously saw himself as something of a ladies' man. He wasn't that bad looking with short brown hair and a pleasant smile, but compared to Kane, he definitely fell into the 'average' category.

Ignoring his flirting, she glanced over the line up then impulsively pointed to the end of the row. "That red one, the sports car."

"Ah! You're a lady of discriminating taste, I can see." Marty nodded at her knowingly. "Marlene, my girlfriend, has a fondness for that one too. Always wants to borrow it rather than a nice conservative grey sedan." Marty stepped closer. "A hot sports car always looks good on a hot lady."

She stepped back and folded her arms. "I have to get to work." She looked pointedly at the rack were the keys hung.

Marty gave her a wink and then strolled over to get the keys.

"Have your girlfriend and you been together long?" She asked idly while waiting for Marty to get the key. Honestly, if the man already had a girlfriend why was he acting this way towards her?

"Oh, we're on and off. She was really keen about six months ago and even wanted to help me around the shop so we could spend more time together. She looks like one of those runway models, but she doesn't mind getting her hands dirty and even asked me to teach her about how the brakes and steering work! I was real disappointed when she dropped me sudden like, but now she's back again and I ain't one to look a gift horse in the mouth. Besides, I'm getting smart. If she can have someone on the side, then so can I." Once again, Marty winked at her.

Marty and Marlene sounded like they deserved each other, and she didn't really want to know any more details about their relationship, but Marty wasn't done. "Marlene thinks I don't know that she's seeing other guys, but I found some men's clothing in the trunk of that car one time. I figure if she's going to pull one over on me, I can do it back."

They'd almost reached the car by that time, when Marty suddenly exclaimed. "Damn! I've got the wrong keys. Just wait by the car and I'll be right back."

Anxious to be on her way, she stood impatiently tapping her foot and checking her watch. She looked around without really noticing anything in particular until her gaze landed on a large truck and two men, who were busily loading a collection of steel drums onto the back of the vehicle. A sign on the side indicated it was a waste disposal company that recycled used motor oil. There were probably a dozen containers sitting there awaiting pickup. The men worked from the front of the clustered containers towards the back, their muscles flexing as they heaved each metal drum up onto the truck.

Studying how the barrels had been arranged, she noticed that there were three empty spots near the rear. Circular marks in the soil, and the compressed weeds, showed where the barrels had sat, while scrape marks on the ground showed how they'd been dragged away. That's unusual, she thought. Why would they load those barrels first or...? Could someone have taken those other barrels? But who would want used motor oil?

She looked up to see Marty approaching with the keys, her interest in the barrels averted by her need to get to work. Mr. Mancini hadn't been too pleased with her when she'd been talking to Bryan yesterday, and she didn't want to give him any cause for complaint today.

As she backed the car out of its parking spot, something niggled her memory. Hadn't the car been facing forward yesterday? She remembered that she'd seen the front fender, not the rear taillights. Not really sure why it should matter, she rolled down the window, calling over to Marty who was now watching the oil drums being loaded. "Hey, Marty! Did anyone take this car for a test drive yesterday?"

"Nope. It hasn't moved this week. Why? Is there a problem?" He leaned on the window and surveyed the interior.

"No, I was just...er...curious as to how long it's been since it was driven."

"Well, like I said, about a week, but it should still be running fine." Marty stood up and tapped the hood of the car. "You have a good day and I'll have your car ready for you by two o'clock at the latest."

With a nod, she rolled up the window and drove off. Turning to the right, she headed towards the Grey Goose, drumming her fingers on the steering wheel. Something was bothering her, but what? Thoughtfully, she sniffed the air that surrounded her. The faint scent of perfume—Marla's perfume—hung in the air and underlying it was the barely detectable scent of another werewolf.

Had Marla been in this car with another Lycan? But when and why? And why had Marty lied about it? Or did Marty not know? Could it be Ryne who'd been in the car, using Marla's perfume to hide his presence? That would explain the clothes that Marty had found in the trunk. Ryne might still have a set of keys for the vehicle, so he could sneak it out, use it, and then return the car with no one being any the wiser.

Stopping for a red light, she glanced around the interior looking for any clues that might prove Ryne had been in the vehicle. Nothing jumped out at her, just some dried mud on the floor. Hmm... Marla had muddy shoes this morning, but would Marla have keys to the car? Possibly, or—it hadn't been locked yesterday—would Marla know how to hotwire a vehicle? It didn't seem like the sort of skill the fashionable she-wolf would cultivate but... Wasn't Marty's girlfriend supposedly interested in cars? And her name was Marlene. Marla, Marlene...? It seemed quite a coincidence. But why would Marla go about moonlighting as someone else?

Marty said he and Marlene had been together six months ago. Would Marla want to date a mechanic while she was still seeing Ryne? If Ryne was anything like Kane for looks, then Marty would come in a poor second and really didn't seem Marla's type. That meant that Marla must have been trying to get something from Marty, but what? And what was Marla doing out at night getting all muddy?

She rubbed her temple, trying to figure this out. Someone had moved the car and Marty claimed he wasn't aware of it. The car smelled like the perfume that Marla used, and there was dirt that could have come from Marla's shoes. There was another unidentified scent in the car, and she made a stab in the dark and decided it could be Ryne's even though she didn't know him. After all, she'd met most of the pack so far, his was one of the few remaining unknown scents. Were Marla and Ryne still together? But what about the fight? She'd treated Marla's injuries; surely the woman wouldn't fall back in with someone who had abused her?

As the light changed to green, she decided she'd have to tell Kane about her suspicions. If Ryne was sneaking around town in this car, then they could lie in wait and capture him when he came for the vehicle next time he felt the need of a ride. And Marla? Well, she'd broach that subject carefully. Kane still had a blind spot when it came to the woman.

Elise made it to work with a few minutes to spare. It was another busy day, so there wasn't much down time, but she did notice Mr. Mancini staring speculatively at her. She smiled at him and he nodded in acknowledgment, but there was no return smile. Surely, he wasn't still upset about Bryan? When she'd been hired there'd been nothing said about not meeting friends on the premises and it had been after her official work hours. Nibbling her lip, she decided to let it pass for today. If he still seemed upset with her tomorrow, she'd ask him what the problem was.

With her shift finished at one o'clock and her car not ready until two, she decided to wander the mall for a while to fill in time. Halloween was over and Christmas decorations were starting to appear. She shook her head in amazement at how the stores seemed to push the season more and more each year. Still and all, the displays were lovely.

As she paused in front of a clothing store, she recalled the green sweater she'd seen there a few weeks ago. Maybe with her next pay check she'd treat herself. There was a substantial balance in an account that Kane had set up for her, but she was still reluctant to use it. Perhaps once they'd been together longer, it wouldn't seem so strange to accept money from him.

Entering the store, she scanned the racks, but couldn't find the sweater anywhere. Humph! Wasn't that always the way? When you finally had money, the item you wanted was gone. A sales lady approached, asking if she wanted any help and she inquired about the green top, just in case there was one in the back. After a few moments, the woman appeared and regretfully explained that there was one in the back, but it was on hold. Making a mental note to return in a few days, in case the sweater made its way back onto the shelves, she turned and began to wander down the mall again.

Two familiar faces could be seen a short distance away and she grinned in anticipation. Zoe and Phoebe were headed towards her. Maybe they could stop somewhere together and have a coffee. Waving, she made her way over to where they were. "Hi! Fancy meeting you here."

The two women looked at her coldly and didn't reply.

Her smile faltered. What was wrong? She tried again, glancing at the bags in their hands. "So, have you bought anything interesting?"

Zoe narrowed her eyes and spoke from between clenched teeth. "I am so mad right now, I could smack you."

Shocked, she stared at her supposed friend. "Smack me? Why? What did I do?"

"Don't try and act so innocent. We know all about it. Rose told us." Phoebe glared and crossed her arms.

"Rose?"

"Yes, Rose. She saw the whole thing and told me this morning. You're lucky she hasn't told Kane yet!" Zoe's voice was getting louder and they were starting to attract attention.

"What did Rose see? What's she going to tell Kane?" Elise was starting to feel panicky. She wasn't sure what the problem was, but it sounded like it would be something that would upset Kane, and after last night, she didn't want anything to mar their budding relationship.

"You know perfectly well what we're talking about." Zoe stepped closer and Elise had to fight the urge to back up.

"How could you? Especially when he obviously worships the ground you walk on! I thought it was so great when Kane brought you here; that you'd be perfect for him. Apparently, I was wrong!" Phoebe looked on the verge of tears. "Come on, Zoe. Let's get out of here!"

As they stalked off, Elise watched them leave feeling as if she'd been run over by a steamroller. What had that been all about? Rose had definitely been acting strangely last night and apparently it was because of something she thought Elise had done, but what? She walked back to the red sports car and slowly climbed in, still puzzling over the strange encounter.

The Mating

An awful thought suddenly popped into her head. Kane had mentioned Rose was in town yesterday to pick something up at the Gallery. What were the chances that Rose had seen her meeting with Bryan? She replayed her time with her old friend and groaned. To an onlooker, it might have seemed really bad. They'd hugged several times and hadn't she called out "I love you" as she drove away? That could easily be misinterpreted as her seeing someone behind Kane's back!

Oh great! What if Rose had already told Kane? How would he react given all she'd heard about his parents' relationship? She could only hope that he'd been busy all day. As soon as she got home, she'd have to find him and tell him the whole story before Rose put her own spin on things. Then she'd have to go to Rose and find out who else she had told the story to... Hitting the steering wheel with her hand, she cursed herself for ever having listened to Marla and her harebrained scheme!

Thoroughly deflated, she turned the key in the ignition and drove to Marty's.

Chapter 25

By the time she arrived home, Elise's stomach was in knots over the prospect of talking to Kane. Even though she hadn't done anything wrong, it still wasn't a conversation she was looking forward to. After all, who knew what Rose might have said? It had been an innocent meeting but apparently Rose was willing to believe the worst of her and jump to conclusions, which was rather upsetting given the fact that she had tried her best to be pleasant to the other girl.

Mentally, she played out what she'd say to Kane and how he'd react. How did she start? 'Did you hear a rumour about me?' No, that probably wasn't a good opening line. Neither was, 'You know that rumour Rose told you about me and another man...?' She shook her head. A straight-out explanation would be best. She would simply tell him she'd had lunch with Bryan but what with one thing and another, it had completely slipped her mind. Not because she was trying to hide anything, but simply because it wasn't that important. Yes, that sounded good and it was the truth. She nodded, satisfied with her plan.

Now all she had to worry about was Kane's reaction. Surely it wouldn't be that bad, her rational side told her. Kane wasn't one to jump to conclusions; he'd listen calmly and understand. Unless, the other side of her brain told her, Rose had got to him first. After all, he really hadn't liked Bryan the one time they'd met. He'd told Bryan to stay away and implicit in that command, she was to stay away from Bryan as well. In a roundabout way, she'd directly disobeyed his orders. Darn but this wasn't going to go over well at all.

Suddenly realizing, she'd been standing on the porch for some time, staring blindly at the door, she swallowed hard, wiped her sweaty palms on her pant leg and stepped inside. The house was unusually quiet, and she strained to hear a sound that might indicate where everyone was. When nothing reached her ears, she gave a sigh of relief. She'd have to face the firing squad eventually, but any reprieve was welcome.

Peeking into Kane's office, she saw that it was empty. A late afternoon sun streamed weakly into the room, leaving the corners in shadow. The smell of leather mixed with the unique scent of Kane permeated the space and drew her inside. Tucking her hands in her pockets, she looked around curious as to where he might be.

The desk held the usual piles of paper and the answering machine was blinking, indicating several messages were waiting for Kane's attention. She wondered if he'd replaced the tape or not—the quality really had been poor this morning. Impulsively, she wrote a reminder on a sticky note and attached it to the machine. While at the desk, she noticed that the computer hadn't even been started yet for the day. Had he even made it into the office? Seeing nothing that would provide an answer to her question, she exited the room, shutting the door behind her.

Next stop was the kitchen. Despite the fact that it was mid-afternoon, there was no sign of Helen or dinner preparations being made. The coffee maker held the dregs of the morning's coffee and the dishes weren't done. Something was definitely up; Helen never left her kitchen in disarray. Heading to the message centre on the fridge, she scanned the notes and found the answers to everyone's whereabouts.

Carrie had gone into early labour and John and Helen were at the infirmary with her. Ah! That explained the state of the kitchen. Well, since first births usually took a considerable time, it wasn't likely she'd be hearing from them anytime soon. Crossing her fingers, she sent positive thoughts towards the infirmary, hoping both mother and baby would be fine.

The Mating

The next message was from Kane. He'd been called away to the lake region. A patrol had found something that needed his attention and he wasn't sure when he'd be back. Relief washed over her as she realized she wouldn't have to tell Kane about Bryan for a while. This was immediately followed by a large dose of worry. What if someone else told him first? The longer he was gone, the greater the risk and the more likely it was that others in the pack would hear the story. It had only been twenty-four hours since she'd met with Bryan, but rumours spread notoriously fast. Putting a stop to it was paramount.

She wished Helen were there. The woman had a level head and would know what to do. Worrying her lip, she searched her mind for someone neutral she could call who might understand her current predicament. Perhaps Sarah...? Grabbing the phone, she dialled the familiar number, twirling the cord around her fingers as she waited for a reply. After a dozen rings, she hung up in frustration. Just when she needed someone to talk to, no one was around. Sighing, she wandered through the large, rambling home wishing that the usual steady stream of visitors would start up. Instead, it seemed as if everyone knew that all the 'important' people were away and there was no need to stop by for a visit.

Throwing herself into a chair by the front window, she scrubbed her face with her hands. Her emotions seemed to be all over the board and she didn't feel like herself at all. Could it be because of her upcoming heat? Possibly, but the knowledge was of little comfort when she felt like her world was falling apart. This thing about Bryan wasn't that big a deal, but for some reason it seemed like it was. She was teary and worried, angry and indecisive. Her stomach kept knotting up and even though she knew it was ridiculous, she was sure her relationship with Kane was in jeopardy. Inelegantly, she sniffled and wiped a lone tear from her eye as she succumbed to self-pity. A nasty rumour was at this very moment probably spreading through the pack, costing her the new friendships she'd formed and no one was around for her to talk to about it.

A car door slammed outside and she sat forward, peering through the curtains to see who it was. Darn! It was Marla. That was another cause for complaint. The woman was up to something, though Elise still wasn't sure exactly what. Maybe instead of thinking about what to tell Kane, she should concentrate her energy on figuring out Marla. At least it would take her mind off one problem.

As Marla came up the walk, Elise debated as to whether or not she should confront her about where she was last night, and why she'd been with Ryne. Or should she say nothing so that the woman didn't warn Ryne? It was only supposition on her part that Marla had been in the car, even though Elise strongly believed it to be true.

Deciding to say nothing, she wiped her face, grabbed a magazine, and arranged herself into a casual position in her chair. When the door opened, she looked up feigning surprise as Marla walked in. "Oh, hi Marla."

"Elise." Marla's greeting was short, her gaze watchful as if expecting a question.

"How was your day?"

"Fine."

"That's good."

It felt like they were both tiptoeing around the other. Marla picked up the mail on the table and flipped through it, which was presumptuous given that the woman didn't officially live there.

Setting the envelopes down, Marla suddenly spoke. "I saw you in town today."

Elise shrugged, "I went in for my shift at the Grey Goose."

Marla nodded. "I was at the Gallery and you drove by. You were in a different car, a red sports coupe."

"That's right. I had to get something fixed on mine and the mechanic let me borrow a car so I could get to work."

Again, Marla nodded. "I never would have pictured you as the sports car type."

"I thought it would be fun to try."

"So, what did you think?"

"It was a nice car. There was nothing special about it though. I guess I prefer my own."

Marla seemed to be studying her, as if weighing each of her answers, looking for hidden meanings. Obviously, she found none, for she suddenly smiled. "Well, it's been nice talking to you; I've got lots to do. Tell the others I won't be here for dinner." Turning quickly, she left, her heels clicking a staccato on the wood floors as she made for the stairs.

Elise could hear the door to Marla's room open and close. Moments later, it opened again, and Marla quickly descended the stairs and left without a word, slamming the front door behind her.

As she watched Marla drive away, Elise wondered if the woman had bought her act or not. Marla was definitely up to something. She was obviously curious if Elise had noticed anything while in the red car, but what was she hiding and why? The answer was there, just waiting for someone to figure it out.

Rubbing her temples, she tried to organize her thoughts but they kept floating about in her head like bits of paper caught in a whirlwind. No one had told her that an unmedicated heat would leave her brain addled! In frustration, she grabbed a piece of paper and began to write down anything she could think of that she'd heard or seen about Ryne or Marla.

After a few minutes she threw down her pen in disgust. It was all rumour and supposition, random facts and events that may or may not be connected. None of it made any sense.

The phone rang then and she picked it up, pleased to hear Helen's excited voice. Carrie and John had a son and while there were a few minor complications, mother and child were doing well. Helen wouldn't be home until late and Elise assured her that was fine. She asked her to pass along best wishes to the new parents and told Helen yet again, that she'd manage to make her own meals. Smiling, she hung up and wandered toward the kitchen all the while thinking about what it would be like to have a pup in the house.

Staring into the fridge, she eyed the various selections. What should she make? It would only be herself and Kane for dinner; maybe an intimate meal would be a good way to start her confession about Bryan. Pleased with the idea that was forming in her mind, she picked up the phone. She'd call Kane on his cell and see what time he expected to return then plan the meal accordingly.

Kane answered almost immediately. "Kane here."

"Hi, Kane! It's Elise. How are things going?"

"Busy. We've been out here all day. What about you?"

She hesitated. She didn't want to tell Kane over the phone, nor worry him. "Not bad. I really want to talk to you though."

"I miss you, too."

Well, he'd misinterpreted that, but now wasn't the time to explain. "Oh, John and Carrie had a baby boy."

"Really? That's great!" She could hear the excitement in his voice. He partially covered the phone and called out the news to the others before turning his attention back to her. "Give them all my best and tell them that I'll stop by to see them as soon as I can."

"When do you think you'll be home?"

He sighed heavily. "I can't say for sure. Probably not until late. Don't wait up for me."

Darn! There went her plans. "What's going on?"

"I don't really have time to explain right now. I'll fill you in when I get back. Listen, I've got to go. Take care."

"Sure. You too." She slowly hung up the phone. So much for a romantic meal followed by a heartfelt discussion. Suddenly eating wasn't overly appealing and she settled for heating up a can of soup instead.

The Mating

The night dragged on, the Alpha house seeming to be overly large and very lonely. She was inexplicably restless and unable to settle down. Half-heartedly she looked at the list she started earlier but couldn't concentrate. Grabbing the remote, she tried to lose herself in a romantic comedy, but found herself becoming too worked up over the love scenes. When the male lead kissed his partner, her own desire skyrocketed and found herself shifting uncomfortably on the couch, her panties becoming damp, her heart racing.

Leaping up, she began to pace the room, desperately looking out the window for any sign that Kane was coming. Running her hands through her hair, she then wiped the sweat from her upper lip and tugged irritably at her clothes. They felt tight, uncomfortable, and the tag at the back was suddenly irritating her endlessly.

Heading upstairs, she stripped off her clothing, threw on a light cotton nightgown, and turned to look out the bedroom window. Kane was somewhere out there, and she needed him *now*. A growl rumbled up from her chest as her frustration mounted. She spun away from the window and paced the room, halting when she caught sight of herself in the mirror. Her pupils were dilated making her eyes seem almost black and her face was flushed.

That's when it dawned on her. Her cycle had started and Kane was nowhere in sight. A sudden pain in her palms had her realizing that her fists were clenched, her nails digging into her flesh. She felt like she was going to crawl out of her skin if she didn't get some relief soon. This was not how it was supposed to be. When she'd decided to go drug free this time, she'd assumed Kane would be around. A growl formed in her throat. How dare he leave her at a time like this!

What to do? What to do? She paced the room, chewing on her thumbnail. Helen had said it was waves not constant, so maybe she could ride it out without going insane. How had females ever survived this before the advent of drugs?

231

Heat—what a great name. It was so apropos. She felt like she was burning up. Maybe the age-old remedy of a cold shower might help. Peeling off her nightgown, she headed for the bathroom.

Half an hour later, she emerged shivering, but more in control. She hoped Kane would be home for the next wave, because that feeling of overwhelming need was definitely not something to experience by oneself. Crawling into bed, she pulled the covers up and closed her eyes willing Kane to return as soon as possible.

Chapter 26

Kane didn't come home that night. Elise's sleep had been restless as she kept waking to check his side of the bed only to find cool sheets and a smooth pillow beside her. As a result, she started the day over-tired and with a sense of impending doom. She hoped another wave of desire wouldn't hit her while she was at work. It would be rather difficult to explain why she was hiding in the meat freezer trying to cool down when it was barely above freezing outside.

She was also worried that she hadn't yet told Kane about her meeting with Bryan, which increased the chances of him finding out from someone else. Nor had she talked to Rose. Checking her watch, she saw that there was still some time before she had to leave for work. She decided to stop by the infirmary to see Carrie and the baby first, then she'd go looking for Rose, Phoebe or Zoe and set them straight as to what had happened.

Just in case Kane came home while she was gone, she wrote him a note and taped it to the mirror where he was sure to see it. 'Dear Kane, I need to see you and talk as soon as possible. It's important.' She hesitated over the signature. Should she just put 'Elise' or 'love Elise' or maybe some x's and o's for hugs and kisses? Deciding to go out on a limb, she penned 'I love you, Elise' and was surprised at how good it felt to write the words. Giving the note a kiss, she taped it to the mirror and went on her way.

The stop at the infirmary was fun. Carrie looked wonderful—if a little tired—and had a definite glow about her. The baby, John Jr. was adorable, and Elise found it hard to set him down. Sniffing, she inhaled the intriguing scent of new baby and marvelled at the strength of his tiny fingers as they clung to her own.

"Oh, Carrie, he's perfect." She smiled as she handed the baby back to his mother. Immediately her arms felt incredibly empty and she knew that if by chance she became pregnant, she would have no regrets.

She stayed and chatted for a while longer, before saying her goodbyes and promising to visit again later in the day. Her next stop was Rose's house but no one was there. Darn, Rose! How dare she not be home? She was probably out there right this minute spreading rumours! Stomping down the steps, she headed to the right in search of Phoebe or Zoe. Hopefully, they'd at least be home and she could nip the rumour mill in at least one spot.

She was so intent on her thoughts that she was surprised to find herself at Phoebe's house so soon. Her quick rap on the door was answered immediately, though gaining entrance was another thing.

"Elise." Phoebe greeted her coldly and made no move to let her in.

Deciding to assert her authority, she stepped forward, pushing the door open. "We need to talk."

Phoebe looked startled and ready to protest, but then acquiesced.

Elise gave herself a mental pat on the back. Score one for her Alpha female authority!

Once inside, she quickly took stock of the house. It was a typical family home. From her position in the entryway, she could see into the kitchen where the children's artwork was on the fridge. A family room to the side had toys and a few newspapers strewn about and a basket of laundry waiting to be folded on the sofa.

Gesturing awkwardly, Phoebe led her into the kitchen. Zoe was there and looked surprised when she realized who had been at the door. The atmosphere in the room immediately became thick and uncomfortable. Elise sat on the edge of the chair and cleared her throat. Deciding not to pussyfoot around the issue, she jumped right in.

"Okay, you two, I'm pretty sure I know why you were acting the way you were yesterday. It's because of Rose, isn't it?" She watched them shoot glances at each other but didn't wait for a reply before continuing. "She told you that she saw me in town with another male and that she saw us hug and—"

"Don't forget the part where you said you loved him." Zoe interrupted spitefully.

"Right. I did say that. It's all true. But what Rose didn't know is that the male was Bryan and he's from my old pack. We grew up together and he's like my brother, not a lover."

"Oh!" The two ladies spoke in unison, an equally stunned look on each of their faces. The expressions then changed to embarrassment as they realized their mistake. It was almost comical how alike the two were. They then began to fall over themselves offering apologies and explanations.

"It's just that we're all so fond of Kane and hate the idea of him being taken advantage of," Phoebe explained.

"That's right," Zoe added. "Kane doesn't show his feelings, but we all wondered how hurt he really was when Marla dumped him for Ryne. We couldn't bear the idea of it happening again. Mind you, it was a lucky escape in my estimation. You're a much more suitable mate for Kane than she ever was."

Phoebe jumped in when Zoe stopped to catch her breath. "So when Rose told us about seeing you with another male, we wondered if you hadn't really wanted to be with Kane and had been putting on an act all along. It seemed possible that you might go back to an old lover. No offense intended, but it was an arranged mating after all."

"I know what you mean. Don't worry." Elise was so relieved to finally be able to tell someone what had happened that she didn't hold any hard feelings. It *had* looked pretty bad; her hugging another man and telling him she loved him. "At one time, Bryan and I thought we had something between us, but then we realized it was just friendship. I'm happy with Kane." She hesitated, and then made herself say the words. "I... I love him."

Both women squealed with delight and hugged her, exclaiming how they knew it was meant to be all along. Elise wasn't so sure about that statement, but let it slide. She was coming to realize that the two sisters were very different from their mother. Both were flighty, but basically harmless. In the future, they'd be fun friends but not the type that she'd want to depend on in an emergency. Julia and Carrie were much more sensible.

Reassured that all was well with their Alpha and his mate, Zoe now wanted to hear the whole story about how Elise had grown up with Bryan, and they spent some time discussing the young man and his future.

"I hope he's making the right choice," Elise confided. "It's a big step, striking out on his own with another wolf he's never met. Establishing a new pack won't be easy."

Phoebe frowned. "I wonder who it could be that he's meeting. It must be someone who's passing through. No one's mentioned a new wolf in the area and we usually know right away."

"It couldn't be Ryne, could it?" Zoe asked.

Elise felt the colour drain from her face. Ryne? He was responsible for shooting Thomas! She didn't want Bryan heading off with him. "I never thought of that. I'm going to try and get hold of Bryan and warn him." Automatically she reached for her cell phone but remembered she'd left it at home. She stood up quickly, almost tipping over her chair. "I've still got a few minutes before I leave for work, I'll call his home and see if he's still there."

She ran home and dialled the number with shaking fingers. "Hello? Sarah? Is Bryan still there? ... He isn't? ... Do you know where I can reach him? ... He's headed here? To Smythston? ... Okay. Thanks." Hanging up before Sarah could ask any questions, she tried Bryan's cell phone only to find that it wasn't on. She checked her watch. Darn! It was time to leave for work. Maybe once her shift finished, she could try to find Bryan, though she had no idea of where she'd look.

Her nerves were on edge the whole time she was working. Usually, the soothing ambiance of the restaurant made her feel calm and at ease throughout her shift. Soft music played in the background and numerous potted plants ensured the air was always fresh, while the burgundy and cream decor created a warm, hospitable atmosphere.

Today it was a totally different story. The smell of the food, the sounds from the kitchen, the murmuring of the patrons; everything seemed heightened and grated on her nerves. For what seemed like the hundredth time that day, she inhaled deeply, pasted a smile on her face, and tried to look patient while her customer dithered over the cream of tomato soup and grilled salmon, or quiche and a roll. It was all she could do not to scream at the woman to hurry and make up her mind. Was this what being in heat was supposed to be like? Or was it a combination of frustrated desire, lack of sleep and nerves about telling Kane and finding Bryan? It was with great relief that she hung up her apron at the end of her shift.

There was a small area near the rear of the restaurant, which housed the employee's washroom, a place to hang coats and a few chairs for sitting. She plopped down and dug through her purse for her phone. First, she called home but Helen said Kane had already left. She wondered if Kane had gotten her message and if he'd noted the 'love' at the end or not. Would he see the significance of it? She hoped so.

Since he wasn't home, she had a few minutes to try and find Bryan and discover who he'd met with. If it was Ryne, she'd warn him about how dangerous the other man was. On the off-chance that Bryan had turned his cell phone on, she tried calling him again. It rang through and she gave a silent cheer. Something was finally going her way!

"Bryan! Thank heaven I finally reached you ... No, everything is fine, but I have to see you right away ... Really? ... Okay, I'll be by my car in five minutes ... It's parked right across the road from the Grey Goose ... Right. Bye." She smiled as she hung up the phone. Bryan was around the corner from her. She'd be able to warn him not to get involved with Ryne, and then be able to concentrate on tracking down Kane so she could talk to him.

As she flipped her phone shut, she noticed that Mr. Mancini was standing in the doorway. From the look on his face, he wasn't happy.

"Er... Hello, Mr. Mancini. I was just talking to a friend."

"So I heard." He nodded towards the phone in her hand. "Might I remind you, Elise, that you are married?"

She forced herself not to roll her eyes and respond calmly. "Yes, I'm fully aware of that fact, Mr. Mancini. The call you heard, it isn't what you think. Bryan and I are old friends. We grew up together." Mr. Mancini gave her a sceptical look and she opened her mouth to explain further, but the man was called to the kitchen and he left before she could say anything.

Exhaling gustily, she pulled on her coat. Why was everyone so quick to believe the worst of her? Just because she was talking to a man didn't mean she was involved with him. What was it with the people in this town? Yes, they were all fond of Kane, but why assume she was cheating? So what if Marla had been two-timing him? That didn't automatically mean that she was! Tomorrow, she'd deal with Mr. Mancini and make sure he understood how wrong he was. Right now, Bryan was waiting for her.

Standing in the parking lot watching the traffic go by, Elise gave a start of surprise when someone's hand landed on her shoulder. Swinging around, her arm automatically rising in a defensive gesture, she laughed when she realized it was Bryan. He'd always enjoyed sneaking up on her, supposedly proving his superiority through his stealth.

The Mating

"Ha! Caught you off guard again, Elise!"

She playfully shoved his shoulder. "Bryan, quit doing that. You know I don't like it."

He grinned at her before enveloping her in a bear hug.

The hug lasted slightly longer than necessary and she extracted herself quickly, all too aware of how things could easily be misconstrued.

"Bryan, I called you for an important reason. That wolf you were meeting with—the one who wants to start a new pack—what was his name?"

"You mean my new Alpha?" Bryan seemed to swell with pride, forgetting the awkward moment that had just occurred. "His name's Ryne. I'm going to be his Beta, and as soon as he finishes some personal business here, we're heading out."

She shut her eyes and groaned. Trust Bryan to get mixed up in something like this. As much as she hated to burst his bubble, she couldn't let him go off with Ryne. It was too dangerous. Taking his hand, she led him to a nearby bench. "Bryan, let's sit down. I have something I have to tell you."

After explaining what she knew about Ryne, Bryan looked at her silently for a few minutes before speaking. "Elise, I know you mean well, but I've met Ryne. You haven't. He wouldn't do anything to hurt his pack. Yeah, I believe you about the challenge, but I think there must be more to it than you know. Something's been left out of the story. And the other stuff—the traps and the shooting—there has to be an explanation. The Ryne I've talked to wouldn't do that."

"Maybe he's putting on a really good act. The people in my new pack wouldn't be attributing these things to Ryne without good cause. His scent was at the scenes, for heaven sake!"

Bryan stared at the ground, slowly shaking his head. "I don't know, Elise. My gut is telling me you're wrong about him."

She leaned towards him, placing her hand on his arm. "Please, Bryan, think this over. I don't want to see you hurt."

He angled his head to look at her and she hoped he could see her sincere concern for his well-being. Finally, he sighed. "I'll think it over, but that's the most I can promise you."

She'd hoped for more but knew from past experience that Bryan wasn't easily swayed. He'd need to mull the situation over on his own and come to his own conclusions. Hopefully, they would be the right ones. With a nod, she stood up and Bryan walked her to her car.

"I hope I get to see you again some day." He took her hands in his.

"You will, Bryan. This isn't goodbye. Our paths will cross again, I know." She desperately hoped she was telling the truth. Bryan had been a big part of her life and she was going to miss him.

He gave her hands another squeeze, but she wasn't really aware of the pressure. A strange feeling was washing over her, as if someone was watching. Slowly she turned to look across the road towards the Grey Goose. Standing on the steps talking to Mr. Mancini, was Kane.

Even from this distance, she could feel the anger radiating from him. It was as if his eyes were boring holes right through her and she gave a shudder of fear. Never had she thought she'd be on the receiving end of such wrath.

Sensing her distraction, Bryan turned to see what had caught her attention. A low whistle escaped his lips. "Hey, Elise, isn't that your Kane?" She was only capable of giving a short nod. "He looks majorly pissed off."

"He is. You'd better leave." Not even looking at Bryan, she shoved him away.

"Will you be all right? Maybe I should stay."

"No!" She forced her gaze away from Kane and looked at Bryan's worried face. "Leave. Please. I'll be okay." She remembered how territorial Kane had been the last time he'd met Bryan. She didn't want the two of them ending up having a fight in the middle of town.

The Mating

Reluctantly, Bryan left. Elise kept half an eye on him to ensure he kept going, while trying to watch Kane at the same time. Mr. Mancini was talking to him, but Kane wasn't listening. A cowardly part of her considered leaving, but she knew she'd have to face Kane and explain at some point in time. She might as well get it over with now.

She didn't have long to wait. Either the conversation ended abruptly, or Kane just walked away for suddenly he was crossing the street towards her. Vaguely she was aware of Mr. Mancini shaking his head as he watched Kane leave, giving a melodramatic shrug before going back inside, but mostly she focused on Kane's approach. His nostrils were flaring, no doubt picking up the scent of her pheromones wafting towards him on the gentle breeze that was meandering down the street. Oh great! That was going to set him off even more.

Her mouth felt dry and she was sure her knees were knocking. Licking her lips, she started to speak as soon as he reached her side. "Kane, I can explain everything."

"Explain? How can you begin to explain meeting with an unattached male?" His voice was so low and filled with anger that she could scarcely get her next words out.

"Bryan's not another male, he's my friend."

Kane snorted. "I remember the kind of 'friendship' the two of you have."

"No! It's not like that anymore."

"No? Then tell me, why have you been secretly contacting him?"

"I haven't been *secretly* contacting him!"

"Of course, forgive me. *He's* been contacting *you*." She tried to protest, but Kane continued speaking, his voice increasing in volume. "Don't try and deny it. I heard him on the answering machine. Three times he's called you!"

"What?" She couldn't believe what she was hearing.

"Next time you remind me to change the tape in the answering machine, make sure you've erased all the old messages first. I suppose you never thought I'd listen to it before throwing it out."

She stared at him open-mouthed as she tried to make sense of what he was saying. Bryan had only called once and Marla had taken the call. Except... Hadn't Marla said that someone had phoned for her several times and she'd let the answering machine take the calls before finally deciding to pick up? It had completely slipped her mind until this very moment. That must be what Kane was talking about.

"Kane, I can—"

"Explain? I'd like to see how." Kane looked around as if suddenly recalling that they were standing in the street and their raised voices were attracting attention. He grabbed her arm, opened her car door, and pushed her inside. "We'll finish this at home and don't try to run off with your friend. I'll be following right behind."

It took her a few tries to get the key in the ignition; she was so upset her hand was shaking. Kane was really angry, and while she could see his point, he should have some faith in her. She'd done nothing to warrant such suspicion.

Glancing in the rearview mirror, she saw that Kane was driving about two car lengths behind her. Hopefully, he'd cool down on the way home and be willing to listen to reason. His background while growing up would make him more sensitive to the idea of infidelity. Marla had dropped him for Ryne, so possibly he was expecting the worst based on past experiences. He'd watched her with Bryan and those phone messages were pretty incriminating, but at least there was nothing else. Unless he'd heard Rose's rumour. But if he had, surely he would have mentioned it.

Unsure of what to think, she found herself becoming increasingly tense the closer she got to home. By the time she pulled into the driveway, she was a mess. Would Kane be reasonable or angry? Had he heard the rumour or not? Would he listen to her explanation or continue to jump to conclusions based on his own past?

The Mating

The more she thought, the more her agitation increased. Suddenly, she realized she was sweating. It was too hot in the car, the air stale, the space feeling claustrophobic. She unzipped her coat, while pushing the door open, welcoming the rush of cool air over her skin. As she went to get out, something jerked her back inside. Damn! She'd forgotten to take off her seatbelt. Fumbling, she worked the clasp, wanting to scream in frustration as the lock resisted her initial efforts. Finally free of the restraint mechanism, she slammed the car door shut and stomped towards the front porch.

The sound of Kane pulling in behind her had her turning to look his way. Through the windshield, their eyes met and she could tell by the set of his face that he was still upset. The injustice of the situation struck her and she shot a glare at him, spun around and, with a flip of her ponytail, stalked inside.

Chapter 27

Elise stormed up the stairs towards the bedroom. The front door slammed behind her as Kane entered, but she didn't look back. Her emotions were vacillating rapidly; at the moment anger was foremost. How dare Kane accuse her of infidelity?

Once in their room, she headed for the bathroom, locking the door behind her. Running cold water, she splashed some on her face, trying desperately to cool down. She was so hot, her nerves were on edge, her skin was crawling... Leaning against the vanity, she looked into the mirror. Oh great! It was last night all over again: eyes dilated, cheeks flushed, rapid breathing. At least this time Kane was here, but jumping her bones probably wasn't his main priority right now, and quite frankly, she was too upset with him to find the idea very appealing either.

The door handle rattled. "Elise, come out of there this instant!"

"Keep your shirt on!" She shouted back. The sound of Kane huffing and stomping away followed her comment.

She considered staying in the bathroom but hiding wouldn't prove anything. As she hesitated, the intoxicating male scent of him drifted under the door and into the small room, teasing her nostrils and elevating her hormones. He was aroused too—she could smell it—and her body yearned for his. Her hand reached for the handle and turned the knob.

As the door swung open, she saw Kane standing by the dresser, a book clutched in his hand. It looked like her missing diary. Temporarily distracted, she stepped forward. "Is that mine?"

"Well, it certainly isn't mine." Sarcasm dripped from his voice.

"That's personal! You shouldn't be reading it!" She stalked towards him, intent on retrieving her book.

"Then don't leave it open on the dresser, especially not to the parts where you're swooning over that pup." Kane fairly snarled at her, throwing the book down in obvious disgust.

"Don't call Bryan a pup! And I'm not swooning over him!"

"Oh no?" Kane snatched up the diary from the floor and read it in a mocking tone. "Bryan's so good-looking. I love watching him move and seeing his muscles ripple. When he touches me, I can hardly think straight, and his kisses drive me insane."

Her mouth dropped open. "I never wrote that!"

"Are you saying this isn't your writing?" Kane shoved the book at her and she took it, studying the entry. It looked like her handwriting, but she never would have written that. Flipping back a few pages, she discovered that someone had forged several entries after the last one in which she'd said she was meeting Bryan. Dismayed, she looked up at Kane, shaking her head in denial.

"Kane, I swear I didn't write that. I don't know who..." Her voice trailed off as she recalled the day that she'd found Marla leaving their room, claiming to have been looking for a book to read. Well, she obviously found something to read and it was *her* diary! "Kane, I'm sure Marla wrote that. My diary went missing the same day I found her in our room—"

"Oh come on, Elise. Quit blaming Marla for your own mistakes. You got careless and left this out."

"No, it's true! She's jealous and wants to break us up."

"Then why has she been encouraging us to spend time together? Explain that."

"Well...I don't know why." She dug her nails into the book's cover, unsure of Marla's motives.

246

"Because there *is* no reason. Face it, Elise. I caught you red-handed. The messages, the diary, I even saw you with him."

"But none of this is what it seems! Before today, we met once to talk, and it was only because he happened to be in town."

"Right, and I'm supposed to believe that?" His mouth twisted in a sneer.

"It's the truth." Her frustration had her raising her voice.

"Then why are there at least three messages from him on the answering machine?"

"We were out for a run. He must have called a few times in one night." The facts suddenly fell into place. "That's it! That's the night Marla told us to go out. She'd heard me on the phone talking to Sarah and knew that Bryan would call to confirm a time. Then she made sure we were out and let the machine pick up his calls so there'd be a record of it. Marla was planning to use the tape all along!"

"That's just wild supposition." Kane turned away and stalked across the room, breathing heavily. He ran his hands through his hair, before turning to face her again. "You know what I can't figure out, why didn't I smell him on you?"

"Because of Marla and her stupid perfume." She answered bitterly. "That's what caused this mess to begin with. If I hadn't let her—"

"How the hell does Marla's perfume work into this?"

"When I met Bryan for the first time—for a platonic meeting, I might add—Marla scented him on me and said you'd be angry, just like you are right now. She put some perfume on me that masks scents."

"Oh, so now it's all Marla's fault that you decided to hide something from me?"

"I never intended *not* to tell you. Things kept getting in the way. But I planned on telling you. Really, I did! That's why I left you that note..." She gestured towards the mirror and then blinked in surprise. The note was gone! Rushing over, she checked the surface of the dresser and even peered onto the floor, but nothing was there.

"Well? Where's this supposed note?"

"It's gone. Marla probably took it when she left the diary here."

Kane rolled his eyes.

Her temper began to override her sense of guilt. "Kane, be reasonable."

"Reasonable? I think I'm being damned reasonable. After discovering those messages, I came into town to find you, but you weren't even at work. You were across the street fawning over Bryan. It was amazingly reasonable of me not to go after him and rip him to shreds today, especially after Edward explained to me how he'd overheard you making the arrangements to meet."

"Edward?"

"My friend, Edward Mancini. Your boss."

"Mr. Mancini is your friend?"

"Of course!" Kane snorted. "How do you think you got the job? You had no qualifications. I pulled a few strings to get you hired so you'd be happy."

She gasped, her pride hurt. "How dare you interfere with me getting a job? I wanted to do that on my own!"

"Well it doesn't matter now anyway because you're done working. You are not leaving this property unsupervised again."

"You can't do that. It's not the Dark Ages anymore!"

"I can do anything I damn well please. I'm the Alpha and you'll do as you're told."

"Well screw you, because I'm not listening." She couldn't believe the rage boiling inside of her. She wasn't acting like herself but couldn't seem to stop the words spilling from her mouth. For some reason, she felt compelled to test Kane to see what he would do. Twirling around, she made for the door.

"Don't you dare walk away from me!" Kane grabbed her arm, yanking her back before she could even touch the handle.

The Mating

He crushed her to him, the look he gave her was hard and she could feel the coiled tension in his body. She'd challenged the Alpha wolf and he was in no mood to be lenient. As his mouth swooped down on hers in a punishing kiss, she knew she'd made a fatal tactical error.

Kane's tongue plunged into her mouth, invading every corner while his free hand swept possessively over her body. When he finally lifted his mouth, she was shaking with both anger and desire.

Picking her up, he tossed her onto the bed. Her back came into contact with a brightly coloured box that was lying on the mattress, and she grunted as the sharp corner dug into her shoulder. Kane grabbed it and threw the package on the floor before crouching over her, his hot gaze pinning her in place.

"I am your Alpha, Elise, *and* your mate. Don't ever forget that."

Despite the fact that her body was screaming with need, her contrary emotions had her shaking her head. "Oh, I wish I could!"

Kane laughed. "No, you don't. You want me. Deny it if you want, but we both know the truth."

He was right, damn him. Pressing her lips together, she tried not to respond when he buried his face in her neck. His warm, calloused hand skimmed up and down her side, stimulating her already heightened nerve endings. While he nibbled and licked the juncture of her neck and shoulder, shivers of delight ran through her as his teeth lightly grazed her skin.

The feel of his torso pressed to hers was arousing. She fought to suppress it, to hang on to her anger but logic was slipping away. Without even realizing it, she was drawing him close, needing what only he could give.

A deep rumble sounded in Kane's chest as he stared down at her, his expression almost feral. His rage, just like hers, had been replaced by a hot, hard wildness that demanded he claim her.

And, when he did, she did nothing to stop him, encouraging him with soft whimpers and gasps, caressing his strong body, breathless yet urging him to ease the ache that clawed at her.

She pulled him closer, demanding more, *needing* more, begging him not to stop. The tension was unbearable. She was on the brink, ready to go over the edge, when the fringes of her mind sensed a change.

Through passion hazed eyes, she saw Kane looming over her. His lips were pulled back, his canines were extending. A frisson of fear shot through her and she tried to focus, tried to make sense of what was happening except an all too familiar tingle was overtaking her. Her body was responding to his change, her own canines growing. She was shifting too, but for once she seemed to have no control over it and panic filled her. What was going on? She couldn't do this, not now! Yet, no sooner had the thought formed, when the whole process stopped, leaving her suspended in a mixed state.

Shifting had always provided her with a split second of ecstasy—some likened it to the feelings associated with a sneeze—but now...now she was caught mid-change. Her body quivered in anticipation of a transformation that never came. It was frightening yet exhilarating; her senses heightened to her wolf level, her hearing preternaturally sharp. She could make out her own heartbeat as well as Kane's, the sound of laboured breathing, and above it all, her attention was caught by the thrum of blood rushing through veins.

She stared at the juncture of Kane's neck and shoulder. A vein throbbed there, its movement holding her fascinated. From somewhere deep inside a voice arose.

Bite him, it commanded. Taste his blood. Mark him as yours. Your provider, your protector, your mate, no one else's.

She raised her head and licked his skin, inhaling deeply.

Yes! The smell, the taste; he is the right one to choose.

She needed to do this, to bind him to her so he would never stray and only be hers. Vaguely, she was aware of Kane mimicking her movements, but she was too intent on her own mission. Opening wide, she bit into Kane's flesh giving a jolt of surprise as she felt Kane's teeth puncturing hers as well.

The momentary pain quickly became pleasure and somewhere in the recesses of her mind, something niggled, an awareness that she was not alone. Kane's mind was touching hers, she was sensing what he was sensing: tension, excitement, passion, need. It blended with her own, growing stronger every second, taking her to unimaginable heights until she couldn't breathe, couldn't think.

She clutched at him, needing to be closer, needing more and yet unsure she could bear it. Their feelings had melded together into a massive ball of anticipation. His thoughts were her thoughts, his pleasure became hers, multiplying exponentially as they soared ever higher.

Her heart was pounding, her mind exploding with images and feelings, with pleasure too great even to comprehend until...until... her entire being shattered into a million shards and then everything went black.

Chapter 28

The cacophony of thoughts swimming around in her brain was the first thing Elise became aware of as she gradually regained consciousness. It was as if someone had a remote control and they were channel surfing through her head. Ideas and feelings flit past before she could focus or make sense of them and she moved her head from side to side in protest.

"Ah!" A soft gasp of pain escaped her lips. Her neck was stiff and sore. She must have fallen asleep in an awkward position. Tentatively, she moved her limbs. They felt tired and heavy. In fact, her whole body was lethargic as if she'd just had a marathon work out.

Furrowing her brow, she considered opening her eyes, but it seemed too much of an effort. Instead, she tried to focus her thoughts again. So many feelings were tumbling about... Hmm... Regret and... Sadness? Was she sad? She hadn't thought so, but maybe she was, otherwise why would the thought be in her head? The more she concentrated on the sadness, the clearer it became, and she felt an ache in her heart. No, it wasn't her, but someone out there was sad and needed comforting. She should try to find them, help them... Forcing herself to open her eyes, she tried to sit up, but moved too quickly. A quick stabbing sensation from her neck had her crying out.

Instantly an intense wave of disgust and loathing washed over her and she tried to recoil from the dark, negative thoughts. What was going on? She felt confused and afraid. Was she losing her mind? She darted her eyes around the room as she searched for an explanation.

There was movement beside her and she saw that it was Kane. Of course! It all came rushing back to her now. Their argument, the angry accusations, her emotions all over the place. She'd pushed Kane too far and he'd snapped and then... They'd blood-bonded!

She quickly moved her hand up to her neck and touched the source of the pain. No wonder it hurt; Kane had had his impressive canines dug into her flesh while they'd wildly mated. She imagined that their frantic movements had resulted in the skin and muscle being more than a bit torn. Well, the hurt wouldn't last, but at the moment it was definitely tender.

Sitting on the far side of the bed, Kane was hunched over. His bare back was to her and he had his head propped in his hands, with his elbows resting on his knees. She shifted so that she was sitting and tentatively reached out a hand to touch him. "Kane?"

He jerked at her touch, hesitated before turning. His face was impassive, but the expression in his eyes couldn't totally hide how he was feeling. His eyes. They were bleak pools of despair and regret.

It suddenly all made sense to her. If they were blood-bonded, their minds now connected. Her confusion was because both of their feelings were rushing through her brain and she didn't know how to sort them out yet. But, she frowned and felt her heart lurch. If these were Kane's feelings, then he was the one who was regretful. He'd blood-bonded with her in the heat of the moment and now wished he hadn't. He didn't want to be bonded to her. She disgusted him!

Tears began to well up. At the same time, Kane groaned, closing his eyes. Another wave of loathing washed over her and she felt her lips tremble as she acknowledged how he felt about her.

Kane wiped his face with his hands, looked back at her and sighed heavily. "Elise, I'm sorry. This—" He dipped his head towards her neck. "It was a mistake. I never should have done it."

The Mating

Unable to stop them, tears began to spill down her face. She'd been hoping Kane would want to blood-bond with her and now that he had, he thought it was a mistake! He didn't love her; she'd misinterpreted his actions completely. While he tolerated her in his home, he didn't want to be bound to her mind, body, and soul. She felt like someone had ripped a chunk out of her heart.

Through a haze of tears, she saw Kane lifting his hand towards her, and she recoiled back. She couldn't bear to have him touch her right now, knowing that it didn't really mean anything. As she moved away, his arm froze mid-air, then fell to his side, fist clenched. She shuddered; now his pain and anger swept through her. He was likely remembering the whole mixed up mess with Bryan and was angry at her. It was all her fault.

She wiped her hands across her face, watching as he got dressed with angry, jerky movements, his face set in stone. He was leaving her. There had to be a way to fix this. In a trembling voice, she started to speak. "Kane, about Bryan. I swear I never did anything—"

"Just forget about it, Elise. It doesn't matter." His mind seemed to be building up some kind of a wall, his feelings becoming harder to read, as if he was able to lock them all away.

Grabbing a pillow, she hugged it to hide her nakedness, feeling exposed and unsure. He would know how she was feeling too, and she was desperate to hide it from him, but didn't know how. She couldn't let him know how hurt she was. Sniffling, she reached for a tissue from the bedside table, turning her back. There was a click behind her and she stilled. The bedroom door had shut, and she was left alone.

That was when she really broke down. Throwing herself across the mattress, she sobbed, heartbroken and mourning the loss of all her dreams. Kane loathed and hated her. She disgusted him. How could she have been so wrong? He'd seemed to genuinely care for her, so what had gone wrong?

There was the mix up over Bryan, but could that be enough to turn him against her? If he'd truly cared, he would have stayed and talked to her. She laughed bitterly at the irony of the situation. Now that they were blood-bonded, they were farther apart than ever.

Rolling over on the bed, she stared at the ceiling and tried to find Kane with her mind. There was an inkling, a sense that he was annoyed. She pulled her mind back. He didn't want her bothering him. Somehow, he was managing to block her from his mind and didn't appreciate her trying to break down his barriers. She blinked and curled up into a ball. Never before had she felt so sad and alone.

She must have been exhausted from the emotional turmoil and her restless sleep the previous night, for when she awoke dawn was breaking; she'd slept through the whole night. Once again, Kane hadn't come home, his side of the bed undisturbed. Melancholy overtook her, and she seriously considered rolling over and pulling the covers over her head. Unfortunately, her bladder had other ideas and she forced herself to sit up. Pushing her hair from her eyes, she clambered out of bed. After taking only two steps, pain shot through her foot eliciting a curse. Glancing down, she realized she'd stepped on the hard corner of a box that was lying on the floor.

Glaring at it, she vaguely recalled that she'd landed on it yesterday when Kane had thrown her on the bed. She kicked it out of the way, and continued to the bathroom, deciding to find out what it was once the call of nature had been dealt with.

After relieving herself, she stared into the mirror. Messy dark brown hair and a tear stained face stared back at her while the deep green of her eyes reflected an inner sadness. Examining her neck, she noted the puncture marks and reddened skin that indicated where Kane had bitten her. Yes, there would definitely be a permanent mark there.

Deciding to take a shower, she adjusted the temperature, and stepped under the spray. Recollections of sharing the shower with Kane caused her to smile faintly. She'd been happy back then, if she had but known it. The future had been filled with endless possibilities; Kane had been eager to be with her. Now, all that was gone. Instead, she had a mate that she was blood-bonded to and he didn't even like her! Feeling tears starting to well up again, she abruptly finished washing and stepped out of the shower.

She spoke sternly to herself as she dried off. She had to get a grip and face reality. This wasn't the first time life had thrown her a curve ball. When her father had suddenly decided to have her mated to Kane and she'd had to leave Bryan, she'd simply stiffened her lip and made the best of the situation. Well, this was no different. Things hadn't worked out as planned with Kane, but she'd have to find a way to handle it.

As she vigorously towel-dried her hair, she ran though the possibilities. She could go home, return to her old pack. Her father wouldn't like it, especially since it would break the alliance, but was the alliance really needed? Their packs weren't at war with each other. The alliance was to keep developers out and from the sound of things, this pack wasn't willing to sell out to anyone, so it was a moot point.

Grabbing a comb, she began to work the knots out of her hair. If she chose to leave she'd have to ask Kane's permission to do so, otherwise he had every right to follow her and drag her back. But would he? Not likely, given how he seemed to have been feeling towards her when he left.

She found an elastic to hold her hair back into a pony tail and efficiently restrained her long tresses. Yes, leaving was a possibility, but then she'd never see Kane again, never feel his arms around her, never feel his kiss. That would be hard. If she stayed, there was still a chance that they would maintain a physical relationship, but would it be enough? She really didn't know.

Wrapping herself in a robe, she padded back into the bedroom intent on getting dressed, lost in thought. Halfway across the room, she stopped short. There was that package, still on the floor. At one point in time, it had been wrapped in colourful paper with a pretty bow. Now, the corner was crushed and the bow was decidedly squished.

She picked it up, turning it over in her hands until she found the tag. It was written in a bold scrawl, but still quite readable. 'Happy Birthday, love Kane.'

It had been her birthday yesterday and she'd totally forgotten about it! Her lips trembled as she stared at the tag. He'd written 'love Kane.' Had he meant it or was it a throwaway term used when signing a card? His feelings a few hours ago led her to believe it was the latter. Kane had no love for her, even if he had remembered it was her birthday and bought her a present. A lone tear rolled down her face and she quickly scrubbed it away.

When had he set the present out? The package had been on the bed when he'd thrown her down, so he must have placed it there at some point after coming home in the morning and before listening to the tape. But why hadn't Marla taken it when she'd come into the room to leave the diary and steal the note? It made no sense.

Should she open it or not. It was addressed to her, though she doubted Kane still wanted to give her anything. After some hesitation, she sat down on the edge of the bed and opened the box, curiosity winning out. Drawing away the layers of tissue paper, she gave a soft cry of delight. It was the green angora sweater she'd looked at on her second day. Gently she picked it up and stroked the soft material against her face. How had Kane remembered her mentioning it?

Confusion filled her. What was going on? Did Kane care or not? The present seemed to indicate yes, but his feelings after blood-bonding were a definite no. Maybe he had felt something, but her deceit over Bryan had ruined it.

Realizing that she was clenching the sweater in her hands, she smoothed the material and refolded it into the box, then threw out the wrecked paper and bow. The card she kept, tucking it into her small jewellery box. Even if it meant

The Mating

nothing, she wanted to remember that at one point, Kane had cared a little bit.

Standing by the dresser, she considered what she should do next. She didn't feel like facing the rest of the pack. Logically, she knew they wouldn't be aware of what had happened, but she didn't feel up to faking happiness. Unfortunately, hiding in the room wasn't a solution either. Eventually, she had to face the world. As she wavered, practicality won over. Her stomach rumbled reminding her that she hadn't eaten since lunch the previous day. Taking this as a sign, she dressed and went in search of something to eat.

Chapter 29

Elise followed the familiar clatter of pots and pans that let her know Helen was back in her domain. As she entered the warm, friendly kitchen, she pasted a smile on her face and tried to sound perky. "Hi, Helen. I missed you yesterday."

Helen was pulling a ham out of the oven and answered over her shoulder. "I indulged myself and slept in since it was around two in the morning when I finally got home, and then I guess our paths never crossed."

"Wow! You really stayed late with Carrie and John."

"Well, it was mostly John. The man was a total wreck after the birth and was convinced he'd never go near Carrie again for fear of making her pregnant."

"I take it he didn't do well during labour?"

Snorting, Helen shook her head and after testing the temperature of the ham, popped it back in the oven. "He's fine now, but at the time it was touch and go with him." She closed the oven door and finally turned to look at Elise. Giving a cry of joy, Helen hurried across the room and embraced her. "Oh, Elise, I'm so happy for you."

Automatically, Elise returned the hug. "Uh...thanks, but why?"

Stepping back, Helen beamed at her. "The blood-bond, you silly goose."

Feeling herself flush, she clamped a hand over the mark on her neck. Darn, she should have worn something with a higher neck.

"So you and Kane finally took the big leap. Was it like I described it?"

"Er... Yeah, it was...amazing." She answered slowly, not sure what to say. Yes, it had been the best, most mind-blowing experience she could imagine, but afterwards things had definitely gone downhill.

"Now don't be shy. I still remember what it was like with my Zack." A dreamy look washed over her eyes for a moment before focusing again. "So, where's Kane? I'm surprised he didn't keep you locked up in the bedroom all day."

"Kane is... Well... I don't really know. He left right afterwards and I haven't seen him since." She shoved her hands in her pockets and stared at the floor.

Helen looked shocked by the news, but quickly composed herself. "Use your connection. Think about him and you should get some sense of where he is or what he's doing."

She shifted uncomfortably. "I... I can't. He seems to be blocking me out."

"What? Blocking you out when you've just bonded! Now, that's strange. I mean, it's possible to learn to keep the other person out sometimes—handy for planning surprises and such—but I've never heard of anyone doing it the first day."

"Well, our Alpha is a private sort of guy, I guess." She darted a glance up at Helen, feeling the need to tell someone about what had really happened. "We didn't part on the best of terms."

Helen's face reflected her disappointment. "You had a fight after blood-bonding! Whatever was it about?"

In the face of Helen's concern, all of the feelings from yesterday came rushing back and her pep talk about being strong fell to pieces. Blinking rapidly, she tried to keep her tears at bay and shook her head, pressing her trembling lips together.

Helen laid her hand on her arm. "You're crying! What's wrong? I was mated for quite a few years. Maybe I can help."

The soft words proved to be her undoing and she started to sob loudly. Helen gathered her close, soothing and clucking while the whole story was related. When she was done, Elise wiped her face with a tissue that Helen handed her.

"So you see, he loathes me. He thinks I was cheating on him and he wishes we'd never blood-bonded. The very idea disgusts him and that's why he's blocking me out."

"Now, Elise, maybe you have it all wrong. When a couple first start to sense each other, it's usually vague emotions and it can be hard to interpret exactly what they mean or what caused them. It takes practice and time for the connection to fully develop."

She shook her head sadly. "No, I felt those emotions and they weren't coming from me. They were Kane's. And if he wasn't loathing me, then why was that feeling there?"

Pursing her lips, Helen shook her head. "I don't know, but I'm sure there's an alternative explanation. That man loves you. Why, he even had a birthday present delivered for you! It came around noon yesterday, but he'd already left, so I set it on your bed. Did you find it?"

She nodded. "It was lovely, but I think he's changed his mind about me now."

"People don't change their mind about who they do and don't love that quickly. I'm not saying he wasn't upset with you earlier, but it wouldn't cause him to fall out of love. It was a misunderstanding and once he thinks about it, he'll see that."

"No he won't. He believes Marla can do no wrong."

Helen sighed heavily. "True. She's his blind spot, but Kane's bound to realize the truth through what he's sensing from you. Has he been reading you at all? Any tingling in your mind, like someone else is there?"

She shook her head. "I don't think so."

"Humph! Stupid man. How is he ever supposed to understand you, if he doesn't make some effort?"

"I really don't think—" The door opened behind her, and she stopped mid-sentence.

John walked in grinning from ear to ear. Immediately, he grabbed her by the waist and spun her around before planting a kiss on her face. "Hey, Elise! Did you hear the news? I'm a daddy!"

His happiness was infectious, and she couldn't help but smile and hug him back. "So I heard. Congratulations, John. I saw Carrie and the baby yesterday."

"Isn't he perfect? And strong too! Takes after me." John boasted as he crossed the room and peeked in the oven. "Mmm, ham and scalloped potatoes for lunch! Helen you're the best. The guys will appreciate that after being out in the cold and wet."

"Wet?" She glanced out the window. It wasn't raining.

"Yeah, down by the mouth of the river. Someone—aka Ryne—left three barrels of oil there. Thankfully, the patrols scared the guy off before he tipped over all three. The clean-up won't be nearly as extensive since we caught it so early. Kane's been out there coordinating the operation almost constantly for the past two days."

Helen looked meaningfully at her. "That explains it, Elise. He's been so busy; he hasn't had time for anything else."

She gave Helen a faint smile, not nearly as hopeful as the other woman was, but at least she now knew where Kane was spending his time. Hmm... Barrels of oil. Oil containers were missing from the back of Marty's garage. It was too much to be a coincidence. Ryne had probably seen the oil there when he left his car, or Marla—posing as Marlene—had noticed it and told Ryne.

Recalling how dishevelled and muddy Marla had been coming in the other morning, it now made sense. She'd been out helping put the barrels in the river, though why she was helping Ryne after he'd threatened her, still made no sense.

The next question was how to convince Kane of what was going on. There was no hard evidence. Marla wouldn't be dumb enough to leave muddy shoes and pants lying around, and obviously she'd masked her scent since no one mentioned scenting her.

The Mating

Furrowing her brow, she wondered how she could prove her suspicions. She considered telling Helen and John but decided to go to Kane with her evidence first. Even if he was mad at her, he was the Alpha and anything concerning the pack on a large scale needed to be brought before him.

Deciding some fresh air might help her think about how to present her case, she took her leave of Helen and John. Helen seemed reluctant to let her go, but she assured her she'd only be gone a short time.

Standing in the back entryway, she looked out the window checking the weather, hesitating about going back to get her cell phone. She didn't plan on being out for long. Did she even need a coat? It was chilly, werewolves were immune to slight fluctuations in the temperature though, like all creatures, prolonged exposure to the cold could have its effects. Finally deciding to grab a light jacket, she stepped outside.

After an extremely warm October, November was proving to be colder than normal. The trees were now bare skeletons, their once colourful foliage long gone. A cool, damp breeze danced across the open spaces, reminding everyone that winter was just around the corner and, on most nights, frost blanketed the land.

As she stared up at the sky, she noted the heavy grey clouds gathering on the horizon and sniffed the air. Snow was likely. For the most part, she enjoyed the wet, white stuff especially in her wolf form. It was great to tumble in, and the white blanket made the whole forest seem like a giant treasure hunt. Interesting smells would rise through the snow, begging her to dig through the fluffy layers in order to discover what was hidden beneath. She wondered if Kane enjoyed a winter romp as well, but the idle thought made the smile leave her face. He probably wouldn't want to go with her anyway.

Shoving her hands in her pockets, she stared at the ground as she walked instinctively heading for the woods and the trail that ran through it. The sound of footsteps caught her attention and she looked up curious as to who else was there. With narrowed eyes, she watched the figure approach. Average size, light brown hair, shoulders hunched. It was Rose. Pausing, she waited for the other girl to catch up to her. To the best of her knowledge, Rose hadn't spread her rumour beyond Zoe and Phoebe, but Elise felt the need to set her straight just in case.

"Morning, Rose." She called out once the girl was close enough to hear her.

"Elise." Rose looked at her warily, as if unsure what to do, then took a deep breath and gave a forced smile. "I was heading out for a walk. Care to come with me?"

Surprised by the offer, she hesitated before nodding. This was a change. Where was the angry attitude of a few days ago? Could Zoe have talked to her and explained the situation? Possibly.

"Uh... Sure. A walk would be great."

They headed into the woods together, each cautiously observing the other. Finally, tension seemed to get to both of them at the same time.

"Elise—"

"Rose—"

They both gave a short laugh and Rose nodded for Elise to go first. Since she was technically the higher-ranking wolf present, Elise decided to take what was her due. "Rose, I know what you think you saw the other day—"

"I didn't *think* anything. I know what I saw."

Elise raised her eyebrows and the other girl fell silent. "Yes. You *saw* me with another male, but your *interpretation* of what you saw was all wrong."

Rose cocked her head obviously not understanding.

"I mean, it looked like I was having a...a romantic meeting with someone, but it wasn't. Bryan is an old friend from my former pack. We grew up together. At one time, we thought there was something between us, but now we both realize we're more like brother and sister than lovers. It's a platonic friendship."

Rose walked along silently for a moment, considering the information. She looked at Elise out of the corner of her eye. "So there's absolutely nothing between you two?"

"Nothing at all. Just friendship."

"And you're in love with Kane, not this other guy?"

She hesitated, but then decided it could do no harm to tell Rose the truth. She did love Kane, even if it wasn't reciprocated. "Yes, I really do love Kane." Impulsively she decided to press the point and pulled her jacket open, revealing her neck. "See? We've even blood-bonded."

Rose stared at the mark, apparently speechless. Finally, she collected herself and smiled with a forced cheerfulness. "Well! If you guys are blood-bonded, then what you're saying must be true. Kane would know if you were cheating on him."

He would if he cared enough to try and find out, she thought sadly to herself, but put on a happy face for appearance sake. "So, are you convinced now?"

Flushing, Rose nodded. "I'm sorry, Elise. When I saw you with that other guy I was so surprised, and then angry for Kane, and mad at you." She shrugged and looked at Elise apologetically. "I guess I've always sort of hero-worshipped Kane and the idea of someone hurting his feelings really had me upset."

Did Kane know how lucky he was to have so many in his pack worried about his well-being? She supposed it was a statement of how much he must care for them, that they would have such devotion towards their leader.

A sound drew Elise's attention and she saw Julia slowly loping towards them, her breath appearing as white puffs as she ran down the woodland path. Once she drew near, Julia phased into her human form. "Hey, Elise. I haven't seen you for a few days."

"I know. I'm sorry. The time seems to fly by now that I'm working more days." Elise apologized.

"It's okay. I understand. Where are you off to?"

"Just taking a walk and talking," Rose supplied.

"Do you want to join us?" Elise noticed that Rose seemed to stiffen at her suggestion and wondered if the two didn't get along, though Rose was usually so soft spoken and demure it would be hard not to get along with her.

Julia checked her watch. "As much as I'd like to, I really don't have time today, but we'll get together soon, okay?"

After promising to call each other and saying their goodbyes, Julia left and Elise glanced at Rose as they continued to stroll along. "Don't you like Julia?"

"Why do you say that?"

"Well, when I asked her to join us, you didn't seem thrilled with the idea."

"Oh. Well, I have a confession to make and I'd prefer not to have an audience. I... I told Zoe and Phoebe what I saw, or what I thought I saw."

"I know. I met them in the mall and they were really mad at me, but since then I've cleared things up with them."

"And you're not angry with me?" Rose looked rather surprised.

"Not now. I was at first, but I can understand how it looked from your point of view."

"But they probably told everyone..."

"No. I was lucky. They decided to keep it to themselves. What about you? Did you tell anyone else?" She braced herself for the answer.

"I... I also talked to Marla about it."

"Marla?"

"Well, actually, she approached me, saying she was suspicious that you were cheating on Kane and asking if I knew anything about it."

Oh really, Elise thought to herself. The conniving bitch knew all along that there was nothing going on, but twisted things around to make it look bad. "When was this?"

The Mating

"Um...the morning after I saw you." That would have been Wednesday.

So Marla had most of Wednesday and Thursday to plan her sabotage. Had the other woman somehow known Bryan would be in town yesterday and manipulated events so they'd have to see each other? If the Marla-Ryne relationship was still intact, then she would have known because Ryne was Bryan's Alpha. Did that mean Bryan was also somehow involved in all of this? She hoped not.

Rose gave a short laugh. "Marla is sure going to be surprised when she learns the truth."

"Why do you say that?"

"Well, she called me this morning, saying how worried she was about Kane and that maybe the two of us could help keep your relationship stable. She wanted us to get together and talk to you; convince you that seeing this Bryan guy was a bad idea. Just wait until she finds out how wrong we both were!"

"Marla said that?" She couldn't keep the shock from her voice. Something was wrong with this picture. What was the woman planning now? And why involve Rose? "Um... So where were we supposed to be getting together?"

"In the woods. She said how you loved being out here, and that you'd be more receptive to what we had to say if you were in a comfortable environment. Actually, we're almost at the meeting spot now. It's just over this rise."

Elise looked around, suddenly taking stock of her unfamiliar surroundings. She'd been so busy thinking that she hadn't really noticed where she was going until now. Tall trees surrounded the place where she stood, and only the faintest evidence of a trail was noticeable through the tangled, dried grass. The sound of rushing water told her she must be near the waterfall Kane had told her about and sure enough, a glimpse of the lake was evident through the trees. Realizing they must be in one of the places that Kane had said was restricted, she moved to walk away. "Rose, I don't think we're supposed to be here. Wasn't most of the area around the lake declared off-limits?"

Rose took Elise's arm in a firm grip, stopping her from leaving. "Technically, yes. But the cleanup is happening a few miles away, almost on the other side, so we're in no danger. Marla thought there'd be less chance that we'd be disturbed here." Rose checked her watch and then sat down on a fallen log, pulling Elise down beside her. "She should be along any minute."

A nervous feeling skittered down Elise's spine. This whole setup didn't seem right. "Rose, I don't think we should stay here. Let's go back."

"But Marla's going to be here soon. It would be rude to leave without letting her know. If we wait, we can both explain the mix-up and then walk back together."

"I don't care if it's rude or not. We need to go." She tugged her companion to her feet then froze when a twig snapped behind her. Closing her eyes, a feeling of dread washed over her. Somehow, she knew who was going to be behind her.

Chapter 30

Elise turned to face the newcomer. As she'd suspected it was Marla, though her attire was decidedly un-Marla-ish. Sturdy boots, jeans, and a winter jacket weren't Marla's usual garb and would almost lead a person to think the woman was planning to do physical labour of some kind. She was smiling too, though it didn't reach her eyes.

Rose stood up and nodded in greeting. "I wondered when you'd get here."

"I knew you'd wait for me. Why should I hurry?" Marla flipped her hair arrogantly and Rose compressed her lips, as if holding back a retort. Instead, she replied in her usual quiet tones.

"Well, we don't want to keep Elise too long. You'll never guess what exciting news she has. Did you know that she and Kane have *blood-bonded*? I'm sure he'll be keeping tabs on her now." She strangely over-emphasized the words 'blood-bonded'.

Frowning, Elise stared at her. What was Rose doing? It seemed a rather unusual way of delivering the news, almost as if she was trying to tell Marla something without actually saying it out loud.

Marla didn't take the news well. She looked at Elise, then at Rose, and back to Elise again. Her mouth was opening and closing, but nothing came out. Finally, words burst from her painted red lips. "That's impossible! Kane's angry. He thinks you've been cheating! He wouldn't blood-bond with you, even if you were the last female on earth!" Storming over, she grabbed the collar of Elise's coat and pulled it down, revealing her neck and the mark from the bond.

Watching the woman's face turn purple with rage, Elise couldn't help but smirk. "That's right, Marla. Your plan backfired. Even after hearing the tapes, and seeing the false diary entries, Kane still wanted to bond with me." While that wasn't quite the truth, Elise didn't feel the least bit guilty about altering the facts. After all that Marla had done, she deserved it.

Growling in rage, Marla tightened her fingers around Elise's collar and pushed her backward. Stumbling, Elise barely kept herself from falling, but she didn't really care. A feeling of triumph was coursing through her. At last, something good was happening on this miserable day. Sure, Kane wasn't even acknowledging her existence, but at least Marla had finally been put in her place. It was with great satisfaction that she watched the other woman storming back and forth across the small clearing, running hands though her perfectly coiffed blond hair, and totally ruining the look.

Eventually, Marla quit pacing and stood with her back to the others, breathing heavily before spinning around and looking at Rose. "Now what do we do?"

Rose spoke calmly and slowly, as if speaking to a child. She was staring straight into Marla's eyes. "We don't have to talk to her now about cheating on Kane. She and Kane are connected. He'll know the truth about what's going on."

Again, Elise frowned. Yes, most would assume that since they had a mental connection, Kane would know the whole story—even though he didn't, she included wryly—but the way Rose was explaining everything made her uneasy. They seemed to have a different agenda than the one Rose had explained.

Marla began to protest. "No!"

"On the way here, we also ran into Julia. She knows I'm with Elise." Again, Rose seemed to be explaining something to Marla. Elise looked from one to the other. It was as if they were having their own coded conversation.

The Mating

"I don't care. We've waited long enough. The original plan stands. I'll think of a way of dealing with Julia." Shoving her hands in her pockets, Marla glared at Rose.

Rose's voice became slightly louder. *"You'll* think of a plan! No way. I've kept a low profile through all of this, and I'm not about to let that change."

"It's too late to worry about that now. We can't pretend that we were going to talk to her and let her go back home as if nothing was wrong. Even someone as dimwitted as Elise must realize something is going on now." Marla gestured derogatorily towards her.

Elise bristled at the comment but held back a retort instead concentrating on what was going on in front of her.

Rose scowled. "As much as I hate to admit it, you're right. Julia knows I'm with Elise, so whatever happens, I'll have to think of an alibi." She turned to look at Elise, "Sorry about this, but you're in the way of our plans." With that, she pulled out a gun.

Elise felt her eyes go wide as she stared at the barrel pointed towards her. Whoever would have thought that sweet, mousey little Rose would be in on this, whatever 'this' was! "What are you planning on doing?" She knew it was a dumb question but couldn't help asking.

"Killing you." Marla grinned. "We're going to drug you, weigh your body down, and dump it in the lake. Kane will think you've run off with your friend Bryan, and the way will be clear for me again."

An icy chill ran through Elise. The two women before her seemed so calm and matter of fact, as if they were talking about getting their hair done rather than killing someone.

"We can't use that plan anymore, Marla." Rose rolled her eyes, as if fed up with her partner in crime. "If Elise and Kane are blood-bonded, he'll be sensing her fear. She wouldn't be afraid if she was running away with Bryan."

"Rose, when are you going to stop being such a wimp? The blood-bonding doesn't change anything. I've got Kane out of the way; he's busy with another oil spill. Even if he and Elise are blood-bonded, his mind is occupied elsewhere. We have to do this. Too much planning has gone into it to turn back now

"But we can't use the runaway bride story anymore. If Kane knows there was no affair, it wouldn't make sense for her to run off." Rose pursed her lips and her fingers flexed on the handle of the gun. Elise tensed, hoping the woman didn't accidentally touch the trigger.

"True." Agitated, Marla chewed her manicured thumbnail.

As Elise eyed the gun in Rose's hand, the most inane thoughts began popping into her head. This was ridiculous. Werewolves didn't carry guns. They changed into wolf form and fought! Hadn't either of these two read any popular literature lately? Of course, Marla wasn't into the whole wolf thing, and possibly Rose wasn't either, so maybe it did make sense. Elise gave herself a mental shake. She was definitely suffering from shock if that's all she could think about at a time like this! Get a grip she chastised herself.

The gun was still aimed in her direction, but Rose wasn't paying attention to her. As the two talked, Elise began to inch away. She couldn't believe that Marla was so desperate for Kane that she'd be willing to kill just to have him. And why was Rose helping? What was in it for her? Well, no matter; she needed to make her escape before they came up with a plan for her demise.

"Maybe we could hold her for ransom, and send a note demanding cash. Once it's paid, I'll transfer the money into the Swiss account I've set up for us, so it will be untouchable. Then we can still get rid of her." Rose glanced at her absentmindedly and Elise froze, but the gun-wielding woman made no comment and returned to her conversation.

Nodding, Marla's eyes lit up. "That's good, really good. You know, Rose, you continually surprise me. It's amazing what you can do with that computer at the bank." Rose blushed at the praise, and Elise rolled her eyes as she continued to distance herself slowly from the women.

"Now where can we keep her until the ransom is paid?" Rose furrowed her brow but quickly brightened. "I know! At your apartment!"

"All right, but how do we get her there?" Marla studied Elise who was hugging her arms around herself and pretending to be passively awaiting her fate.

"We could still drug her, but then you'd have to carry her to your car and get her into your apartment unseen." Rose decided.

The comment drew Marla's attention back towards Rose. "Me? Carry her? Why can't you carry her?"

"I came up with the idea. You have to contribute something." Hands on her hips, Rose glared at Marla, obviously not noticing the gun was no longer pointing at their captive.

Sensing this might be her best chance, Elise shifted into her wolf and began to run. A shout sounded behind her when they realized what she'd done, and several shots rang out. The bullets whizzed past, thankfully missing her and hitting the surrounding trees, causing chunks of bark to fly out like miniature explosions. Glancing over her shoulder, she saw the other two women changing form and taking up the chase.

Having a head start only gave her a minor advantage. She didn't know the terrain in this part of the woods well enough to run at full speed. Keeping herself low to lessen wind resistance, she sped along as fast as she dared, constantly scanning the ground ahead of her for possible trip hazards, while keeping her ears attuned for sounds of pursuit.

A ravine was coming up, and she wasn't sure how big it was. Could she clear it? It seemed awfully wide. Making a split-second decision, she veered to the left, and ran along its edge while frantically searching for a way across it. As she ran, she berated herself for not having paid closer attention while walking earlier. She had no real idea where she was. All she knew was that the Alpha house was north of her present position. If she had the time, she could have simply followed their scent back into familiar territory, but with two wolves on her tail, it wasn't possible.

Glancing over her shoulder, she frowned. Only Marla was in sight. Switching her gaze forward again, Elise strained to hear what was going on behind her but could only detect one pursuer. Where was Rose? There was little time to think about it though. A fallen tree was coming into sight, and it spanned the ravine. If she could only make it that far...

Movement ahead of her had her growling in frustration. Rose had obviously gone cross country and was coming at her from the side. Elise dug deep, calling on all her reserves, and ran as fast as possible. The makeshift bridge was approaching. She could make it. Her lungs were starving for oxygen and she was panting heavily. She was almost there. Gathering all her strength, she prepared to leap, coiling her muscles, and launching herself through the air, just as a large furry object appeared in her peripheral vision. It hit her in the side, knocking her to the ground.

The momentum of their bodies sent Elise and Rose tumbling. The edge of the ravine was approaching and Elise dug her claws in, trying to prevent herself from going over the edge, but it was no use. Clods of dirt flew into the air. Stones and shrubs bruised and abraded as she spun over and over. The air was filled with the sound of breaking twigs and clattering rocks, cries of fright and gasps of pain. Her leg caught in a crevice and she twisted. A bone snapped. She yelped in agony, then slammed to the ground in a sudden stop.

For a moment everything was eerily still and quiet. Then she became aware of her own laboured breathing and cautiously tried to move. Pain shot through her and she bit her lip, holding back a whimper. Opening her eyes, she noted that at some point during the wild tumble down the ravine, she'd phased into her human form. Shifting her glance sideways, she saw Rose's body lying a few feet away in a pool of blood, her neck twisted at an unnatural angle. Bile rose in her throat and she shut her eyes, swallowing hard.

A sound overhead drew her attention. Standing at the top of the ravine was Marla back in human form.

Licking her lips, Elise managed to call out. "Marla, you have to get help. I... I think Rose might be dead and I'm pretty sure my leg is broken."

"Aww, now isn't that a shame." Carefully, Marla picked her way down until she was beside Elise. Looking around, she dusted off a rock and sat down, cocking her head sideways and staring bemusedly at the woman before her. "You know Elise, I'll never understand what Kane sees in you."

"What?" The woman's words were so unexpected that Elise was sure she'd heard wrong. Rose was probably *dead,* and Marla was just sitting there! "Marla, you've got to check on Rose. She might still be alive and if we can get help in time—"

"You're so...so ordinary. Boring. Why he ever agreed to be mated to you is beyond me." Marla continued as if she hadn't heard what Elise had said. "Oh well, you'll be gone soon and then I'll get him back. He always comes back. Guilt can work wonders on a man with a conscience."

Realizing that Marla wasn't going to do anything to help Rose until she'd had her say, Elise tried to focus on the conversation. Even though she had a sinking feeling she knew exactly what Marla was talking about, she decided to ask. "Gone? What do you mean I'll be gone? I'm not going anywhere."

"Oh, I'm afraid you are. Rose and I had it all planned out. She lured you here and, as I said, we were going to drug you, tie you up, and sink your body to the bottom of the lake. Then we were going to convince Kane that you'd run off with Bryan. He'd be upset, but not overly surprised given your recent behaviour. Of course, I'd be there to comfort him."

Marla sighed. "It was all going so well. Even the little glitches weren't a problem. I managed to think of a reason for

Kane to be in town that first day you met Bryan. Of course, in the end Kane didn't go, but he sent Rose instead and that was fine. She would have been able to be an 'eye-witness' when explaining your disappearance later on. And the fact that you were hiding the meeting by using that perfume I gave you would only have increased suspicion that you were guilty." She glared down at Elise. "Yesterday should have been the icing on the cake. Kane actually saw you with Bryan. I know he heard the messages and I set the diary out for him to see. How did he end up blood-bonding to you? What went wrong?"

Elise didn't feel inclined to answer. Marla studied her for a moment shaking her head, then shifted a bit and poked Elise's shoulder with the toe of her boot, pulling her coat down to reveal the mark Kane had left. "I guess Rose was right. The blood-bonding has put a kink in our plan. Eventually, Kane's going to sense something's wrong—the oil spill will only keep his mind busy for so long—and when he realizes it, he'll come looking for you." Marla tapped her finger to her lips as she thought out loud. "The kidnapping and ransom story won't work now, so the question is, what to do with you? I suppose I'll have to arrange it so that it looks like you were killed. Ryne can be blamed again. He's such a good scapegoat."

"Ryne's a scapegoat?"

"Of course, he is! He's hot-headed, but I could never get him to do any real dirty work. He's too full of annoying honour for that. I did manage to convince him to challenge Kane for the position of Alpha, but he left the area after losing and only came back once that I know of." She touched her face as if remembering the bruise Ryne had given her. "Luckily, I had a pair of his old boots and enough of his sweaty gym clothes at my apartment that I was able to convince people he was still around. I covered my own scent with perfume so no one ever knew I was there. Then I wore his boots and clothes, making it seem like he'd been present each time and ensuring he was the one that got blamed for everything that went wrong."

That would explain the perfume and the other scent in the red car; it had been from Ryne's clothes, Elise thought to herself. Still, she couldn't figure out what Marla was going to gain from all of this. Stalling for time, in the vain hope that someone might come to the rescue, she decided to ask. "But why?"

"I need control of the pack." Marla answered as she stood and walked over to look at Rose, then shrugged. "You're right. She's dead."

For all that she'd known Rose was dead, having it proclaimed out loud caused tears to prick Elise's eyes. She hadn't known Rose well, and even though the girl had been working with Marla, the fact that she was dead saddened her.

Marla continued on in a conversational tone, as if she were discussing nothing more important than the weather. "It's a shame in a way that she's dead. Rose was actually quite clever, but no one paid much attention to her or ever suspected her of anything. You know the eagerly awaited environmental report? I gave it to her and she altered the version that Kane saw, making it seem almost worthless while the original went to Northern Oil. They paid us a tidy sum for that. And your gushing diary entries about Bryan? Rose wrote those, too. She did a good job copying your penmanship, don't you think? And some of the cheques she's forged... Well, let's just say that if anyone ever does an in-depth audit of the local bank, it won't be pretty." Shaking her head, Marla turned away from Rose's broken body. "It's too bad that she's gone though. I had a few more jobs for her before I severed our relationship thought it does save me getting rid of her later on. Ryne can be blamed for her death, too."

Elise tried to move into a more comfortable position, but nothing alleviated the pain. Her broken leg throbbed and the various abrasions covering her body stung. Trying to keep Marla talking so the woman held off killing her, Elise brought up more questions. "Why do you need control of the pack? If you want to be an Alpha female, why not go with Ryne and start over?"

Marla laughed sarcastically. "Are you serious? As if I'd ever go off and live like a pauper while Ryne tried to establish a pack somewhere. Being Alpha female is only a means to an end. I want money and this pack is loaded. Northern Oil is offering a fortune for the land, but most of the pack is too stupid to take it. Only Rose, myself and a few of the others see things clearly. If we sell out to Northern Oil, we'll be rich."

"But you said this was your home and you couldn't leave it."

"I lied. Being a wolf isn't that great. Rose hated being the Omega of the pack and wanted out of that stupid hierarchy system. And me, I could happily live as a rich human for the rest of my life, and that's exactly what I intend to do."

"But how?"

"Don't you worry your little head, Elise. I've been planning this for ages. First I got rid of Zack by cutting the brake line—"

"So that's why you pretended to be 'Marlene' and hung out with Marty!"

"Oh, what a clever girl you are." Marla mocked. "You're right. Marty showed me enough about how an engine works that I can hotwire it or sabotage it. Once Zack was dead, I figured Ryne would be the logical replacement since he was older. When it looked undecided, I gave matters a little push. I thought Ryne would win a challenge, so I told him that Kane had sabotaged Zack's brakes. Being the impulsive, hot-headed type that he is, Ryne issued the challenge before he had time to think things through. Unfortunately, he lost and it set my plans back. I'd been working on Ryne for weeks before then, convincing him that selling out was the right choice, and now I had to start all over again."

So that's why everyone thought Ryne was behaving differently before the challenge, Elise realized.

The Mating

Marla stared disinterestedly at the various rocks and trees that decorated the ravine, her lip curling slightly as if she found her surroundings somewhat distasteful. She gave a quiet snort, before continuing. "With Ryne gone, I went to work on Kane, trying to convince him to sell out. I poisoned the water, set traps, had the electricity turned off, called the fire inspectors. Even that picture was part of the plan."

"The picture?"

"Remember how worried Kane was? How he thought someone might notice that the wolf in the picture isn't a real wolf? If someone comes to check it out, the pack could be discovered. I might even hire a few actors to do that, now that I think about it. People poking around town, looking for wolves is a guaranteed way to spook our Alpha. You see, Kane cares too much about his pack and that's his weakness. If I can convince him it isn't safe here, he'll agree to sell out and move elsewhere. Once the cash is in his hands, I can electronically siphon it from his account into my own Swiss one." Marla stopped and looked down at Elise, scowling. "Everything was going great until you showed up."

"Marla, if it's money you want, I can talk to Kane. I'm sure he'd give you some."

"Some!" Marla scoffed. "I don't want some. I want it all." She checked her watch. "Well, as much as I've enjoyed this scintillating conversation, I'd better go get Ryne's clothes on again. If I'm going to kill you, I want his scent all over you." Winking, she kicked Elise's broken leg. "Don't go anywhere while I'm gone."

Elise tasted blood in her mouth from where her teeth were biting into her lip. She wouldn't cry out and give Marla the satisfaction of knowing how much that had hurt, even though her body was screaming with pain. Closing her eyes, she listened to the sound of retreating footsteps until they could be heard no more.

Finally, she could let her aching body relax. Unclenching her hands and her jaw, she took stock of her situation. She was alone at the bottom of a ravine, with a broken leg, a money-hungry she-wolf coming back to kill her at any moment, and a dead body for company. Blinking, she reached up a shaky hand to brush a lone snowflake from her face. Yes, she was alone, and no one knew where she was.

Chapter 31

Surrounded by the quiet stillness of the woods, she sat at the bottom of the ravine, listening to the sound of her own laboured breathing. Every square inch of her body hurt. She'd completed what felt like a herculean task by working herself into a sitting position and sliding her way over to the base of a small tree. Now, as she leaned against the trunk, she fought against the waves of blackness that threatened to overtake her. The move had been excruciating and her immediate plan, to put as much distance between herself and this location before Marla returned, would have to wait until the urge to vomit and faint had passed.

She had no idea how she was going to get out of this mess she'd landed in. Her cell phone was at home and her attempt to contact Kane, seeking him out with her mind, had only resulted in a mere spark of sensation that may or may not have been him. Regardless of what is was, it had quickly fizzled out leaving her feeling empty and alone once again.

Staring up at the sky, she watched as more snowflakes began to fall. They landed on her face and caught in her lashes. It was actually quite pretty, she mused, letting her mind drift away from the pain that shot through her with every breath. If she was back at the Alpha house, she'd be sitting in the kitchen sipping a fresh cup of coffee and watching Helen bake. The mug would be warm in her hands and the smell of fresh baked cookies would fill the air while they chatted about pack life. In her dream world, Kane would come walking in and place his hands on her shoulders. Then he'd nuzzle her neck and trail his warm lips along her jaw until their mouths met in a slow, warm kiss. She smiled at the thought and let her eyes drift shut, cherishing the picture.

She must have drifted off, for the cry of a blue jay had her becoming aware of her surroundings with a start. Grey rocks jutted out of the dark soil that composed the sides and base of the ravine while sickly thin saplings and dried weeds haphazardly popped up here and there. Evidence of what might be a stream in wetter weather could be seen meandering down the centre of the ravine floor, but at present only the tiniest trickle of water was evident.

Looking down towards her injured leg, she saw that a small amount of snow had accumulated around her and she realized that she was shivering. Her warm wolf fur would come in handy right now, but she hesitated to change forms. Her leg was broken, and she wasn't sure how shifting would affect it. Could the reshaping of the bone cause further damage or would it help it to heal faster? And then again, did she even want it to heal faster if it wasn't properly set? Could she end up with a permanently damaged leg or one that needed to be re-broken in order to be corrected? She decided to hold off changing forms as long as possible, but if necessary, she'd risk being lame over being dead.

Glancing at her watch, she saw that it had broken in the fall, so she had no real idea of the time. Squinting up at the sky, a very hazy glow from the sun could be seen through the cloud cover. From its position, she assumed it was almost noon. By now, Mr. Mancini would be having a fit that she hadn't shown up for her shift at the Grey Goose, though Kane had forbidden her to work there anymore. She wondered if he'd meant it, or even remembered having uttered the words; it had been said in the heat of the moment after all. The way Kane had ranted and ordered her around yesterday still rankled underneath the hurt of his rejection. When she saw him again—if she ever saw him again—she'd have to clear that up. She liked her job. It was just waitressing, but she was becoming good at it and enjoyed interacting with people.

The Mating

Working at the Grey Goose was her first taste of independence and she wasn't going to give it up without a fight.

She gave a dry laugh. Why was she getting so worked up about her job at a time like this? Staying alive was a more pressing matter. Her stomach chose that moment to rumble and she recalled that she hadn't eaten breakfast, instead spending her time telling Helen her troubles. She remembered with longing the delicious smells that had been floating around the kitchen earlier. Everyone would be gathering at the Alpha house now and enjoying Helen's lunch of scalloped potatoes and baked ham. Would anyone notice she was missing and wonder where she was? Would Kane try to establish a connection with her in order to locate her? Once again, she tried to contact him, but soon gave up in frustration. If he was receiving her, he wasn't giving any acknowledgement of the fact.

Damn him for being so stubborn and pigheaded! Her anger started to grow. If he had only listened to her, rather than believing all the evidence against her, he'd have left the connection between them open. Then he'd know she was in trouble and get his butt over here. A part of her said she was being unfair. If the tables had been turned and she'd seen him hugging Marla, along with reading love notes and tape-recorded messages, she'd be inclined to see him as guilty too. Still, she'd like to think that she'd have checked up on his well-being now and then, especially if he didn't show up for a meal and had left no explanation.

Running her fingers through her hair, she realized that the temperature must have risen. She wasn't feeling as cold any more. In fact, a thin film of sweat was forming on her brow and she unzipped her jacket, closing her eyes and relishing the feeling of the cool air as it hit her overheated body. Ah, that felt better. Suddenly she popped open her eyes. Oh no! Not now! She was becoming used to reading the signals her body gave out; one of those waves was approaching again. Dammit, heat cycles were supposed to be fun. So far not a single one had lived up to her expectations. Kane had been away for the first, mad at her for the second and now, who knew where the he might be!

Well, she wasn't going to hang around waiting for him. She'd funnel all her frustration into trying to escape the ravine. There were a few sticks nearby that might serve as a crutch and slowly, painfully, pulled herself over to them. After testing several, she took the longest and sturdiest one available and, using the tree for support, heaved herself up into a standing position. Once upright, she swayed precariously until the world quit tilting and then slowly began to hobble in a northerly direction.

After only a few steps, she was bathed in perspiration, the pain shooting up from her leg was almost unbearable, but she forced herself to keep moving. She had to get away. Marla was returning with plans to kill her and no one knew where she was. No one was coming to rescue her; she had only herself to rely on. Focusing solely on walking, she repeated the patterned movement over and over in her head: balance on the good leg, move the stick forward, use it for balance while hopping ahead, swallow hard and ignore the pain each lurching step caused, then repeat.

Her good leg was starting to tremble with fatigue. Reluctantly, she stopped and leaned against a tree, panting for breath. It felt like she'd been travelling for ages. Glancing backward to see how far she'd come, she wanted to scream; she could still see Rose's crumpled body, now partially covered with snow. All her efforts had gained her was a few hundred yards. Tears of frustration and self-pity swam in her eyes and she brushed them away, sniffing inelegantly. She couldn't give in, she had to keep trying. Where was all that anger and frustrated sexual energy when she needed it?

Squaring her shoulders, she made another hopping step forward and then cried out in fear as her makeshift crutch slipped on the snowy ground and she fell forward. Twisting midair, she managed to protect her face by landing on her shoulder. The air left her body in a whoosh as she hit the partially frozen earth and she wheezed, trying to catch her breath. This time she allowed the tears to fall, beating the ground as she vented. She knew it was totally unproductive but didn't care. She was scared. She hurt. Her hormones were raging, and quite frankly, life sucked!

When she was finally done sobbing, she felt only marginally better. While the crying jag seemed to have curbed the heat, she still hurt all over and was more scared than she ever thought possible. Lying on the ground she gave a forlorn hiccup and wiped her nose on the back of her hand. She had to get up and keep trying. No way was she waiting for Marla to come and finish her off. Rolling over, she manoeuvred herself into a sitting position and began to look around for something to use to help lever herself upward.

In the middle of her search, the faintest of sounds reached her ears and she froze, listening intently as she tried to decipher what it might be. Heavy breathing, footsteps—no, make that paws—and a slight snuffling sound. Someone was coming in wolf form and they were sniffing, following a trail.

Was Marla back already? Or maybe Julia had decided to join her and Rose? Could it be Kane finally coming to rescue her? Should she call out, assuming it was a friend? But what if it was Marla? No use in tipping the woman off.

Scooting herself back towards a tangle of shrubs, she attempted to conceal herself. She'd watch and see who appeared. If it was rescue, she'd call out. If it was Marla, well, she'd stay hidden as long as possible, and then fight tooth and nail for her life when the time came.

Minutes passed like hours as she listened to the sounds growing louder. Whoever was coming was approaching with caution, picking their way along, sniffing carefully. She forced herself to breathe slowly and lightly in order not to make a sound, keeping her eyes sharply fixed on the point where she felt the wolf would first appear.

Her vigilance was finally rewarded and she gave a slight gasp of relief. A large black wolf was coming into sight. Kane was looking for her! She began to lean forward, but then paused.

Something was wrong; the way the wolf moved, the set of his ears... It wasn't Kane, nor was it any wolf she'd encountered before. Sniffing, she tried to pick up his scent, but the wind was blowing the wrong direction. Narrowing her gaze, she studied the animal.

It stood poised at the top of the ravine almost exactly where she and Rose had tumbled over the edge. Slowly the wolf scanned the area and she resisted the urge to move backward, aware that any movement on her part would draw the beast's attention. Thankfully, its gaze passed over her and fell upon Rose's body. With a yip, the wolf made its way down the steep slope and nuzzled the corpse.

Biting her lip, she considered her options. She could stay hidden or call out for help, but she didn't know who this person was. Were they a friend, someone just passing through, or possibly even an accomplice of Marla and Rose that she hadn't yet heard of?

The decision became moot when the wolf began to sniff around Rose's body and then, obviously picking up her scent, began to head her way. Reaching around for her walking stick, she held it firmly in her hands. It wasn't much protection, but it was better than nothing.

Closer and closer the wolf came. She could feel her heart beating faster and her palms becoming sweaty. She shifted her grip on the stick and raised it in preparation for swinging as hard as she could. The wolf stopped a few feet from her hiding spot and gave a whine. Licking her lips, she hesitated. It was a friendly, non-threatening greeting. She opened her mouth to speak, and then blinked. The wolf was looking directly at her and had the most incredible blue eyes.

The air shimmered and the wolf disappeared, only to be replaced by the best-looking man she'd ever seen, after Kane.

The Mating

In fact, the man was almost a carbon copy of Kane, except for the eyes and a few subtle variations in the slant of the nose and breadth of shoulder. This had to be the mysterious Ryne!

Chapter 32

The usual clatter of utensils filled the dining room as hungry pack members ate Helen's culinary offering. Most had been outside since early morning, either helping to clean up the oil spill or patrolling the perimeter of the territory looking for signs of trespassers.

Kane sat at the head of the table, poking at his food, unable to eat. Elise was off to work by now and he couldn't help but think of how badly they'd parted. Yesterday morning, he'd had such hopes when he'd come home early, leaving Franz temporarily in charge of the oil clean up. It had been her birthday and he'd been planning the day for quite some time; Ryne and his annoying childish pranks weren't going to be allowed to spoil the day he'd mapped out.

Staring blindly across the room, he reviewed how the day should have gone. He'd arranged for a private room at the Grey Goose where the two of them would have had an intimate meal together. His friend, Edward Mancini, had even had the chef make a special menu for the occasion. When Elise finally finished her shift, Kane had thought he would meet her in the parking lot, blindfold her, and then bring her in through the private side door—Edward having assured him that Elise hadn't yet seen the exclusive suites upstairs. She'd be so surprised by the luxurious surroundings; he could imagine the look on her face when she saw the four-poster bed, complete with a curtained canopy, the hot tub and even the gold faucets in the bath.

After a leisurely meal, he would give her his presents. He smiled thinking how she'd react to the green sweater he'd bought. She'd mentioned it on one of her first days here, but probably never realized how closely he'd been listening to what she said. The sweater had been sitting on hold at the store for the last two weeks, with instructions to deliver it that morning so there was no chance of Elise accidentally finding it. Next, he'd planned on presenting her with a delicate gold bracelet he'd picked out to suit the fine bones of her wrist. It had a small wolf medallion hanging from it, inscribed with their names and the date of their mating.

For his last gift, he was planning on professing his feelings, thus giving her his heart. He'd always been cautious about opening up to anyone, but with Elise it was different. He felt comfortable sharing his inner self with her and wanted to ask if she'd blood-bond with him. Then, if everything went as he'd planned, they'd spend the rest of the afternoon making love and discovering each other's most secret thoughts and feelings.

Of course, that was all a dream. Nothing had happened as he'd planned. Instead of an intimate afternoon of bonding, they'd spent the time arguing. He'd crossed all the lines, leaving her frightened and confused. Would she ever forgive him? The temptation to go poking about in her mind to discover how she was feeling was strong, but he knew he had no right. In ordinary circumstances, blood-bonded mates would think nothing of tiptoeing through each other's thoughts, but he and Elise were hardly ordinary.

He'd forced the bonding on her, and even though in the end she'd actively participated, he still felt as if he'd almost raped her. Self-loathing and disgust consumed him. How could he have done that? Losing control was never an option for him. His father's tainted blood ran through his veins and he knew what he was capable of if he didn't keep constant guard over his emotions. But yesterday... Sighing heavily, he acknowledged the truth. Yesterday, he'd let the famed werewolf possessiveness take over. Reason had been lost and he'd brutally forced himself on his mate. What kind of a monster did that?

The Mating

Absentmindedly, he noted the fork in his hand was bending under the strength of his grip and his jaw clenched as he carefully set the utensil down on the table. What was happening to him? His behaviour was totally unacceptable, as if the wolf side of him was dominating the human. Indeed, when he'd blood-bonded with Elise, his wolf had taken over, driving him to claim his mate so that no one else could ever have her. He'd been too rough, too animalistic; so caught up in the act that by the end he'd dropped exhausted at her side, immediately falling asleep without even checking how she was feeling.

When he awoke afterward, he'd stared horrified at the mark he'd inflicted on Elise's neck. She'd moaned in her sleep and it had been like someone stabbing his heart. He'd hurt his mate, marking her in a fit of possessive rage, doubting her word... True, the evidence against her was substantial, but he should have examined it with calm reason rather than reacting in anger.

When she'd finally stirred, he'd sensed she was scared and confused. Then, as the reality of what had occurred sank in, sadness seemed to consume her. He'd reached out to her, but she'd drawn back in fear and that was when he knew he had to block the connection between them. She didn't want him—she desired him physically—but she couldn't really want him in her life anymore. His actions had destroyed the tentative relationship they'd been building.

It wouldn't surprise him in the least if she asked to leave, to return to her original pack. Such an action would break the alliance and he'd have to fight the Elders on it.

Once again, he sighed heavily, knowing he could never let her go, even if it was allowed. She was *his* mate and the possessiveness of their race would never allow him to set her free, but he'd do his best to leave her alone, to give her the space she needed. It went against every instinct he had, but he'd do it. A wry smile drifted over his face. Even now, his wolf was working against his human resolve, trying to convince him that Elise wanted to contact him. The tingle in the back of his mind had him automatically opening up, but he caught himself in time and firmly shut the door. It was wishful thinking on his part. Elise wouldn't be calling to him. Giving her privacy was the least he could do.

Sensing someone beside him, Kane glanced up. Helen was there with a worried expression on her normally pleasant round face. Raising his brows, he looked at her questioningly.

"I'm sorry to bother you, Kane, but the Grey Goose called. Elise didn't show up for work today and they were wondering if she was ill. I know she went for a walk this morning, but she never came back. Her car's still here..." Helen's voice trailed off and she twisted her hands nervously.

Kane pushed his chair back and stood up, nodding for Helen to follow him. He didn't want the rest of the pack overhearing their conversation. Once in the kitchen, he rubbed the back of his neck and looked at Helen out of the corner of his eye. The woman was almost like his mother and he felt like a little kid confessing to her.

"Helen, Elise and I... Well, we had a...er...disagreement yesterday and I told her she couldn't work at the Grey Goose anymore. I guess she thought I meant it."

"You what?" Helen looked at him incredulously.

"Yeah, I know. I'm an idiot. She's really mad at me, so she's probably waiting until I'm gone before coming home for lunch. I guess she forgot to call Edward to tell him."

Helen paused and frowned before speaking. "Kane, it's really none of my business, but I can't keep this to myself. Elise told me some of what happened yesterday, about the diary and Bryan, how you fought and then bonded. She was really upset—"

He interrupted. "I know. She's scared of me now and sad that I took away her chance to blood-bond with someone she really lov— Hey! What was that for?" Helen had just slapped him across the back of the head! He bit back the snarl that such an action would have earned anyone else.

The Mating

"Standard treatment for stupidity." Her hands were on her hips and she appeared to be shaking her head in despair.

"Stupidity?" In the back of his mind, he acknowledged that only Helen would dare say that to the Alpha.

"Yes. And if Elise was here, I might slap her too, though she's young and in a new pack, so I'm more inclined to forgive her, but you! You're the Alpha, our supposed leader! You, of all people, should be able to read your own mate. Haven't you used your bond to figure out what she's really feeling?"

"I did, right afterwards. She was confused, scared, sad... I blocked her out after that. I'm not a suitable mate for her. Giving her a bit of privacy was the least I could do."

Helen snorted. "What you did was convince her that you didn't care; that you didn't want her near you."

"That's not true!"

"Whether it is or not, that's what she thought. Of course she was confused and scared! All of a sudden she had all your thoughts in her head and she couldn't sort them out. And you—you were feeling pretty down on yourself for the circumstances surrounding the bonding, right?"

He tightened his lips but nodded.

"Well, Elise took that to mean you hated her and regretted bonding with her, not just the circumstances surrounding how it happened. She was crying her eyes out this morning because she loves you, but she's under the impression you don't love her back."

He stared at the floor, wincing as an actual pain attacked his heart. He never meant to hurt Elise. It was the last thing he wanted to do, and by trying to make things better, he'd actually made it worse.

Looking up, he found Helen observing him with a look of pity in her eyes. She reached out and cupped his cheek. "Kane, you did the wrong thing, but for the right reasons. I know you're worried about becoming your father, but one fight with your mate doesn't mean you're him."

He wasn't so sure of that fact but didn't bother to argue the point. Helen had always had a soft spot for him, and her assessment of his character was more favourable than he knew he deserved. "So, what should I do?"

"Are you looking for another slap on the head?" Helen scolded him. "Hook up that wonderful connection you now have with your mate. Go find her, explain how you feel!" With that, Helen shoved him out the door.

Standing at the edge of the woods, Kane wiped his sweaty palms on his pant legs and shoved his hands into his back pockets. He'd faced a challenge fight to the death with fewer qualms than he had at this moment. Opening up a connection with Elise had him inexplicably nervous. What if Helen was wrong? What if she didn't love him? What if she really hated him for the blood-bond?

"Hey, Kane!" The sound of Julia's voice behind him broke into his thoughts. He turned to observe the athletic blonde jogging down the path. "Are you waiting for Elise?"

He cleared his throat before answering. "Yeah, something like that."

"I'm surprised she hasn't returned yet. I ran into her and Rose over an hour ago and had the impression that they were taking a short walk." Julia leaned against a tree and stretched her leg muscles while talking.

"Really? I wonder why they aren't back yet." He frowned. To the best of his knowledge, Rose wasn't an exercise fanatic and didn't go on long walks. Then again, he didn't know the girl very well; she never drew attention to herself and it was only recently, since she'd been dating Daniel, that he'd taken much notice of her.

"Yeah, it's sort of strange, isn't it? And you know what else? Rose was acting odd. I mean, she's always quiet, but..." Julia paused and then shrugged. "I don't know. Something was off. When Elise asked me to join them, Rose had this weird look on her face. I think she was relieved that I couldn't go with them." She bent down to tighten her shoelaces. "At the time, I didn't think that much about it, except that maybe Rose wasn't feeling well, but now that they aren't back... Well, I suppose Rose could have gotten sick along the way. That would explain why they're so late."

Kane narrowed his eyes as he considered the fact. "Do you know where they were going?"

"Umm...they were headed towards the lake, but I'm sure they didn't actually go that far, since it's still out of bounds." Julia stood and bounced up and down a few times, while efficiently readjusting her ponytail that had started to loosen.

"Thanks, Julia. I think I'll head out and meet them. They're probably on their way home by now, anyway."

"Sounds like a plan. I'll see you later." Julia gave a nod and continued her daily jog.

Once she was on her way, Kane leaned his back against a tree and tilted his head towards the sky. He opened his mind, searching for Elise. As his senses expanded—searching and reaching—his instincts were telling him something was off, but he wasn't sure what. Hoping his inner wolf was wrong, he focused in on Elise and felt his heart lurch. Waves of pain and fear washed over him. She was in danger! Cursing himself for not seeking her out sooner, he shifted into wolf form and raced through the woods, following a call that only his heart and soul could hear.

Chapter 33

Elise stared at the carbon copy of her mate, unsure of what to say. The strength of his muscles was evident by how the material of his clothing stretched tautly over his body. Dark, faintly damp hair hung shaggily over his forehead and there was the faintest curve to his nose as if it had been broken at one point. His mouth was firm and set in a straight, unyielding line. It was amazing that the man could look so much like Kane at first glance yet exude such a different aura. Kane was strong and caring, while Ryne was...dangerous? A part of her mind acknowledged that the rocky, uninviting atmosphere of the ravine seemed to suit him, and she found herself reassured to know that, by Marla's admission, he was not the psycho rogue wolf that she'd been led to believe. However, he was still an unknown quantity and needed to be treated with caution.

Clearing her throat, she gave the lamest greeting possible. "Hi!"

There was no response. Instead, the man's gaze seemed to be assessing her, taking in her appearance from head to toe. She felt inexplicably self-conscious, aware that she was far from looking her best. Her clothes were dirty and torn, scratches and smeared blood stained her hands and probably her face as well. She resisted the urge to finger comb her hair and straighten her jacket, instead forcing herself to meet his gaze. Showing weakness was not an option, despite her vulnerable position.

When he spoke, his voice was deep, similar to Kane's, but harder and lacking the caring quality that she had come to expect from her mate. "Did you kill her?"

"Kill who?" It wasn't what she'd been expecting him to say.

"Rose." He gestured with his head towards the dead woman's body. "Did you kill her?"

"No! Of course not! I was running, and she was chasing me and then she jumped, and we sort of rolled down and..." Her voice trailed off as his blue eyes narrowed and a growl rumbled in his chest.

"I don't know if I should believe you or not. Rose was part of my pack and she wouldn't hurt anyone."

"It was all an accident!" She hastened to reassure him, while thinking that here was another person Rose had managed to fool. "I broke my leg during the fall ..."

He leaned forward and touched her leg as if to check the veracity of her claim. She bit back a cry of pain. Immediately he withdrew his hand, but instead of moving away, came closer and sniffed her. A puzzled frown appeared. "Kane's?"

She nodded. "Kane is my mate."

A smirk appeared. "He works fast. He wasn't even seeing anyone when I left."

"We've only been together three weeks. It was an arranged union. My father is Alpha of the territory to the west of here."

"I wondered if a political pairing would be needed on that front." He was silent for a moment, and then stuck out his hand. "I'm Ryne, Kane's half brother."

"Elise." Her small hand was engulfed in his and comforting warmth came over her. It wasn't the same tingling awareness that she got from Kane, but still it was...nice.

"Care to tell me what happened here?" He sat down and looked at her expectantly.

"I will, but could you possibly help me first?" She wanted to get away before Marla returned.

"No. Tell me your story and then I'll decide." Ryne folded his arms and seemed prepared to wait as long as necessary.

Damn. She wanted to get away but didn't dare push too much. He looked like he was used to getting his own way and right now Ryne was her only hope. Giving an exasperated huff, she launched into a much-edited version of what was happening.

"Do you know about the oil company wanting the land and offering lots of money?" He nodded, so she continued. "Apparently, Marla is trying to force Kane into selling out and she thinks if I'm out of the way, she'll be able to get Kane to listen to her." She paused to gauge his reaction.

Ryne snorted and shook his head. "Typical of the bitch."

Silently, she agreed, but kept her comments to herself. "Marla and Rose were planning to kill me, so when I got a chance, I ran. Rose tackled me, and we rolled down the ravine. She died in the fall and now Marla's gone off to get some stuff so that she can kill me by herself. I've been trying to get away, but, as you can see, I haven't made it very far." She carefully avoided mentioning how Marla had been using Ryne as a scapegoat. Remembering that Ryne had been described as hot-headed and impulsive, she thought she'd avoid getting him all worked up.

"Rose was in on this plan?" He sounded sceptical.

"I was surprised too, but she had a gun pointed at me."

"Humph, it's always the quiet ones you have to watch." Ryne rubbed his chin and appeared lost in thought.

The silence stretched between them and she began to wonder if he even remembered she was there. "Umm... Can I ask you a question?" He looked at her with raised brows. "Did you... I mean, a couple of weeks ago, were you over at Marla's?" She shrank under his gaze, cursing herself for asking the question even as the words left her mouth. Hopefully, it wouldn't set him off.

"Yeah. I was there."

"Oh." She answered in a small voice, averting her eyes. The man beside her had threatened and attacked Marla. While she had no love for the woman, she wasn't comfortable around a man who would hit a female. What if she made him angry? Would he strike out at her too?

"And I hit her...once. I know that's what you want to ask." Ryne made the statement blandly as he scanned the woods around them. "Do you want to know why?"

"Well, I suppose. If you want to tell me, that is." She wondered what possible reason he could give.

"Before the challenge—you know about that?" She nodded. "Well, Marla and I were an item. Originally, she was Kane's girl and around him she would put on this helpless female act, playing up to his need to be the protector, but when Kane wasn't looking, she showed me her true colours. She was the 'bad' girl with a bit of an attitude and I found that appealing for some reason, so I worked hard to steal her away from him. I didn't feel guilty about it, since I knew she was playing him along and he'd never really be happy with her. In a way, I was rescuing him from his own blind stupidity. It was only later that I found out she was stringing me along, too.

"Marla's a master manipulator and without even realizing it, she had me eating out of her hand. She knew my weaknesses and played on them; got me to challenge Kane because of some cock and bull story about him sabotaging Zack's truck. Damn, I can't believe I was such an idiot." He ran his hands through his hair and shook his head in obvious self-disgust. "Anyway, long story short, Kane won. I was embarrassed and left the area. Marla refused to come with me, of course, and that was when I realized that, like Kane, I never really knew her. I'd only seen the image she wanted me to see.

"Unfortunately, the depths of my stupidity hadn't been reached yet. Before I left, I gave her all my photographs to sell with the promise that she'd forward the money to me."

"I've seen one of your pictures. You're quite talented."

Ryne gave her a half smile. "Thanks. I was going to use the proceeds to establish a new pack. Imagine my surprise when I called Bastian's Gallery and found that all but one of my works had been sold, even though, surprisingly enough, there was no money in my account. It turns out she'd kept it all.

"So I came back to town looking for my money and she laughed, saying she'd already spent it and there was no way I'd ever get it back from her. To top it all off, there was also this sports car that I owned—I only used it once in a while—and I'd left it with her to sell. Rather than taking it to a proper dealership where there'd be a fast turnover, she had it sitting at some out of the way garage where it will probably never sell, because she wanted to still have use of it.

"All my money, my heart, even my status with the pack— she took it all from me. Everything I had was gone and she just laughed in my face. I grabbed her by the arms and shook her. She spat in my face and I lost it; I slapped her. It's not something I'm proud of, but I won't hide it either."

She was quiet for a moment, then reached out her hand and squeezed his shoulder. "I'm sorry she did that to you. If it makes you feel any better, you're not her only victim. She's driven a major wedge between Kane and me. I was foolish enough to listen to her too."

Ryne looked over at her and gave a sad smile. "She's a real piece of work, isn't she?"

Nodding, she gave a quick smile back. "And now she wants to kill me."

"Right. Not that I want you dead or anything, but why didn't she kill you when you first fell down here? What did she have to go and get?"

She hadn't really wanted to tell Ryne that Marla had basically been assassinating his character but couldn't think of an alternative and she refused to lie any more. "She went to get some of your clothes that you'd left behind. She's been using them so that your scent was at the scene of some of the bad stuff that's been going on around here."

Ryne stiffened. "What kind of bad stuff?"

"Well, oil purposely dumped in the water, traps have been set, Thomas was shot, and now she wants you blamed for my death and probably Rose's too."

"Damn!" Ryne surged up from the spot he'd been sitting and began to angrily pace back and forth in front of her. "She is such a bitch! I imagine my name is mud within the pack and they're trying to hunt me down now, aren't they? Why the fuck is she doing this to me? What kind of twisted revenge does she want? Just because I lost the challenge, she dumps me and screws up my whole life! Wait until I get my hands on her."

"Ryne, calm down!" She snapped the order at him, hoping to keep him from flying off the handle. "If it's any help, she's not getting revenge on you personally. She's trying to convince Kane it's too dangerous to stay here and that he needs to sell out. After that, she's planning on stealing the money from his bank account. You're being used as a scapegoat to keep suspicion away from her."

Ryne growled and looked around, angry emotion blazing from his eyes.

Worried that he'd charge off and leave her, she pleaded with him. "Please, Ryne! I know you're mad at Marla, but I need you to help me right now. I can't get back to the Alpha house on my own and I'd prefer not to be here when Marla returns. I'll explain everything to Kane and then the two of you can go after her together." She wasn't exactly sure Kane would believe her, but she'd cross that bridge when she got there.

Finally, Ryne stopped his pacing and took a deep breath, visibly trying to calm himself. He clenched and loosened his fists several times before finally turning to face her. The rage he was feeling was evident in the stormy blue of his eyes, and she forced herself to swallow the fear that rose up inside her. Ryne wasn't mad at her, she reminded herself.

"All right. I'll take you to the Alpha house, but then I'm coming back here to find her, regardless of what Kane says."

The Mating

Carefully, Ryne eased his arms under her and picked her up trying not to jostle her leg more than necessary. Each step he took made her wince however and she sought a way to keep her mind off the pain. Picking a question that had been floating around in her mind, she began a conversation.

"So, if you weren't planning on ever coming back, why are you here today?"

"I was trying to track down Marla one last time in an attempt to get my money back. If she wouldn't give it to me, I was going to tell her that I'd approach the gallery and complain. They wouldn't likely give me any money either, but I was hoping the threat of losing her job would make her cough up some of the cash she owes me. She hasn't been back to her apartment in days, so I figured she was staying here. I caught her scent by the road and was following it when I found you."

As she listened, she placed an arm around his shoulder to help steady herself. She could feel the muscles rippling underneath his shirt and his breath came in soft puffs, dancing across her face. Slowly the warmth of his body was seeping into hers, blocking out the chill of the gently falling snow and she relaxed in his arms. The male scent of him was so like Kane's. It wrapped itself around her and she laid her head against his body, the sound of his heart beating barely distinguishable, yet still comforting.

She wished Kane were here. He and Ryne were so alike except for their eyes; she could almost imagine it *was* Kane carrying her. She brushed her nose against Ryne's neck and rubbed his back before allowing her fingers to wander up to his neck, playing with the strands of hair that tumbled over his collar. Mmm... Kane...

Ryne's pace faltered and then he came to a stop.

Immediately, she snapped out of the daydream she'd fallen into. Ryne was her brother-in-law, for heaven's sake! Mortified, she pushed herself away from him, totally forgetting that he was holding her some five feet off the ground.

Nearly dropping her as she struggled, Ryne tightened his grip and she cried out as pain shot through her body from where his fingers had squeezed her broken limb.

A deep growl suddenly reverberated through the trees, causing them both to freeze as a large black wolf burst into sight surrounded by a swirl of white snowflakes.

Chapter 34

"Kane!" She ceased her struggles against Ryne and stared at her mate. He snarled and lowered his head, lips drawn back to reveal an impressive set of teeth. Slowly he stalked towards them, the fur on his back rising. With surprise, she realized that the door to his mind had been opened to her and she had some idea of what he was thinking and feeling. It was still hard to interpret, but she knew he was incredibly angry. She hastened to offer reassurance, trying to project her thoughts while speaking. "I'm all right. Ryne was carrying me because of my leg. He accidentally squeezed it but didn't mean me any harm."

Her efforts had some effect, since Kane stopped in his tracks, but he still didn't back down.

Ryne kept his eyes locked on Kane and a low rumble emitted from his chest. She felt his muscles tensing around her and her head snapped to look at the man holding her. What was he doing?

"Ryne!" She gasped at his audacity. Anxious to move away from Ryne in order to keep the peace, she tried to step back as soon as her feet touched the ground, while still sending good thoughts Kane's way. Unfortunately, she discovered she wasn't that good at doing two things at once. Forgetting to balance her weight on one leg, her injured limb gave way. With a cry, she automatically grabbed onto the nearest object that could provide some stability. Unfortunately, it was Ryne's arm and that was enough to send Kane over the edge.

What happened next was a blur of movement. She pushed herself away from Ryne and gave a sideways hop, shifting her grip to a nearby tree trunk. Kane leapt towards his half brother and Ryne jumped back, phasing into his wolf form even as he moved. In the blink of an eye, the two males were engaged in combat, growling and biting each other, while she clung to a tree trunk, watching in horror as the situation dissolved into a primitive battle.

It was a terrifying sight, yet some ancient part of her thrilled at the idea of the powerful males fighting over her. Her heart was pounding, blood rushed through her body, raising her temperature and stimulating her desire. Shaking her head, she tried to suppress the erotic feelings inside her and clear her thinking. She wasn't some animal waiting to mate the strongest male! This was barbaric and she had to stop it. Frantically, she looked around for something that could be used to separate the two, but of course there was nothing to be found. Returning her gaze to the scene in front of her, she stood transfixed.

Snarls filled the air as teeth flashed and claws slashed. The two were equally matched, with first one and then the other seeming to be ahead. Ryne grabbed Kane's back leg, but Kane whipped around and grabbed his brother's neck. Rolling over Ryne freed himself and regained his footing, then charged his opponent again. Kane yipped in pain as teeth slashed his side, but he pulled away and swiped his claws across Ryne's face, narrowly missing his eye. Blood was freely streaming from their wounds and their fur was matted with dirt and saliva. Around them, the trampled snow was stained with a combination of mud and blood. Drawing back, they circled each other panting heavily, each looking for an opening that would allow them to get past the other's guard.

"Stop it!" She knew she had to get through to them. The thoughts coming at her from Kane were frighteningly violent and primitive. Had his wolf taken over completely? Had he lost touch with his human side? Did either of them even understand what she was saying?

"Listen! You both have to listen to me! Please! There's no need for this." She projected her thoughts towards Kane but had no idea if he was sensing her. There was no break in his movement as he slowly circled Ryne, his gaze locked on those of his opponent. His step never faltered, his ear didn't even twitch in her direction. Knowing it was useless, she still felt compelled to try again, since there was little else she could do. "Kane! Ryne isn't trying to take me away from you and he isn't the bad guy in all of this! I know what's going on. It's all M—"

Mid-sentence, she stopped speaking. So intent was she on the fight in front of her that she hadn't noticed anyone approaching, until a cold blade pressed against her throat.

"Hello, Elise." Marla whispered into her ear.

A wave of icy fear washed over her and Kane suddenly froze, his head swinging her way. Ryne, obviously not knowing what was going on, lunged at Kane who neatly sidestepped, allowing Ryne to overshoot his mark and fall heavily to the ground. Ryne leapt up and twirled around, only to stop dead in his tracks as he finally noticed the new arrival.

"My, my! Look at you two. All bloody and dirty. Tsk, tsk. Is that any way for loving brothers to behave, fighting over a little bitch?" Marla mocked the pair of black wolves that faced her.

Kane's eyes reflected his confusion, disbelief, and then rapid assimilation of the situation as it dawned on him that Marla had a knife to Elise's neck, and was the source of his mate's fear. He took a step towards her, growling, only to stop when Marla spoke.

"I wouldn't come any closer Kane, darling. I might get nervous and flinch. This knife is extremely sharp, and the slightest pressure could break the skin."

Kane shifted into human form, while Ryne's wolf snarled.

Marla laughed. "Temper, temper, Ryne. Remember all of the trouble it's caused you already."

"What are you up to, Marla?" Kane's voice was cold, his face stony.

"Just trying to convince you to sell the land, so I can get my hands on the money it will generate."

"Sell the land?" Kane's voice was incredulous. "Is that what this is all about?"

"Well, it's certainly not about getting you back—not that it wouldn't be a nice side benefit—but really, good-looking men are a dime a dozen once you have money."

As she spoke, Kane was slowly stepping to the left and Marla turned to keep him in sight, seeming not to realize that Ryne was inching his way to the right. Elise said nothing, silently watching the two brothers instinctively work as a unit, one providing the distraction while the other circled their prey.

"So how is hurting Elise going to get me to sell the land?" Kane inquired blandly.

"You sign the papers from Northern Oil and I set her free, unharmed." Marla explained.

"I don't have them here." Kane's gaze darted in Ryne's direction.

She snorted derisively. "Of course not. I'm no fool. Elise is staying with me until the papers are in the hands of Northern Oil's lawyers. I have friends there who will let me know when it happens. Then you'll deposit the money into my bank account. Once that's taken care of, Elise will be free to go."

Kane rubbed his chin thoughtfully as if considering the situation.

Elise observed him carefully, widening her eyes as a feeling—just the inkling of an idea—began to form in her head. She focused herself as best as she could, pushing through her own feelings of panic to find what Kane was trying to communicate to her. It was a jumble and she strained to make sense of it, finally grasping a repeated thread; I love you. Be ready.

He loved her? Oh my gosh! Her heart leapt inside her chest. What a time to find out, when there was no chance of savouring the sweet words. She had to be ready, but ready for what? What was Kane going to do? How would he signal her when Ryne was going to attack? Her gaze flew to his face hoping for a hint, but it remained impassive. She wished she could see Marla's face to get some indication of what the woman might be thinking, but from her position with the knife against her throat, it wasn't possible.

Marla sighed impatiently. "Hurry up, Kane. Just agree. You know there's no other way out of this. Oh, and Ryne?" Elise felt Marla move behind her. "Quit trying to sneak up behind me or I'll blow your brains out sooner rather than later. I have a gun and I'm ambidextrous, so it won't be a problem using my other hand to shoot." There was the distinctive click of a gun, followed by a frustrated whine from Ryne. Trust Marla to have two weapons on her.

Elise saw the muscle in Kane's jaw flex, but his voice revealed nothing. "Well..." Kane drawled the word out. "The problem is, Marla, I have to consider the needs of the whole pack, rather than what I might personally want."

"Don't give me all of that 'for the good of the pack' crap. This is what you need to deal with right here and now." Marla's voice had gone from mocking to hard and exasperated. She pressed the point of the knife into Elise's neck causing her to whimper as warm liquid slowly trickled down her neck and between her breasts.

Kane narrowed his eyes and they began to glow eerily. His body was shaking almost imperceptibly. Elise sensed how hard he was trying to maintain control of his human side, when the wolf within was crying out to be released and allowed to seek revenge.

"You really shouldn't have done that, Marla." Kane's voice was so cold and deadly that Elise shivered.

Marla possibly sensed she'd gone too far. She backed up a step, trying to drag Elise with her, but of course Elise couldn't keep her balance on one leg without the tree to hold onto. She stumbled backwards into Marla, who flinched, causing the knife to dig deeper into her flesh. Her cry and Marla's shout blended together as Elise reached up to push the knife away.

Her body lurched to the left and Marla's went to the right. As she hit the ground, two black blurs launched themselves toward their mutual enemy.

In rapid succession, two shots rang out, signalling the beginning of a terrifying symphony of screams, snarls, and whimpers of pain. Elise pulled herself upright and saw one black wolf was down, a puddle of red spilling onto the snow-covered ground. The remaining wolf, though bleeding heavily, had Marla by the leg. While badly injured, the woman wasn't giving up. She was kicking and trying to pull herself away. Her arm was stretching towards the gun that had fallen to the ground.

"Hey!" A voice shouted from some distance away. Elise swung her head towards the sound and saw Bryan a few hundred yards away, running in their direction. Help was coming, but would it be in time? She turned her attention back towards the fight.

Horrified, Elise saw that Marla's hand had reached the gun... She was wrapping her fingers around the handle... Lifting the weapon... Now, she was bending her arm towards her unsuspecting attacker...

Elise tried to get up. She had to do something. Bryan was still too far away. Frantically, she dragged herself towards the combatants using her arms. Her hand hit against something cold and hard, half buried in the snow... It was the knife that moments before had been pressed to her own throat! Grabbing it, she used all of her remaining energy to get to her feet and as a blinding pain shot up her leg, she threw herself forward on top of Marla.

"No!"

As the world went black, Elise was aware of three things. The gun had discharged. A warm, sticky substance was oozing over her body and the forest was suddenly incredibly quiet.

Chapter 35

Elise awoke, sensing she wasn't in her own room. The surface beneath her was too firm, the sheet covering her was too scratchy. She felt...numb...as if she was drifting on a cloud. Did that mean she was dead? She opened her eyes a crack to check, wincing as the bright light assaulted her pupils. A large expanse of white greeted her through the veil of her lashes. Hmm... No, definitely not dead unless the afterlife had a crack in the ceiling plaster. And she certainly wasn't at home. Her bed wasn't this uncomfortable. The infirmary? Possibly. Licking her lips, she tried to swallow. Her mouth was dry, and a bad chemical taste was assaulting her tongue. She needed water. Maybe beside the bed? Starting to turn her head, she frowned as something pulled at the skin on her throat. Carefully lifting her hand, she felt the gauze that was there and tried to recall what had happened.

A slight rustling sound drew her attention and she cautiously turned to see Kane sleeping in a chair beside her. Dark circles under his eyes gave them a bruised look and stubble darkened his jaw line. A wave of love and warmth washed over her as she viewed his beloved features. She scanned down his powerful body only to stop when she noticed that his shirt was unbuttoned, revealing bandages wrapped around his chest.

The events of the past twenty-four hours came rushing back to her. As she relived those last few moments, tears pricked at the back of her eyes and she blinked rapidly to keep them at bay. So much had happened; arguing with Kane and then blood-bonding, Ryne and Kane fighting, Marla. Just the woman's name caused a shiver to run through her.

Ambivalence filled her over the woman's fate. She hated what Marla had done, pitting the brothers against each other, killing Zack, trying to ruin Kane's relationship with her... Yet, no matter how she felt about the woman, her own part in Marla's demise was hard to take.

It wasn't in her nature to react violently, but she knew if the situation arose again, she'd do whatever was needed in order to protect her mate. She'd come so close to losing him. Watching the steady rise and fall of Kane's chest comforted her; knowing he was still alive and by her side. Soon her breathing was in time with his own; steady and deep as she drifted off to sleep.

Sometime later, fingers gently brushing her forehead drew her from her rest. Kane was leaning over her, softly calling her name. She blinked at him sleepily and curved her lips into a smile. "Hi!"

"Hi yourself." His voice was deep and raspy as if he, too, had just woken up, and indeed that was how he looked. His dark hair was falling in his eyes and he still hadn't shaved. She reached up to caress his stubbled jaw and he pressed a kiss to her palm. "How are you feeling?"

"Okay," she automatically answered. "A bit stiff and sore." She tried to shift herself up into a sitting position and was surprised to feel a sense of heaviness coming from her leg. Looking down, she saw a cast around her lower limb.

Kane followed the direction of her gaze with his eyes and he answered her unspoken question. "You had surgery. Your leg was a real mess and it took some work to get it set properly. Nadia was swearing a blue streak when she saw it. Something about idiots that try to walk on a broken leg and the fact that she isn't a miracle worker." He chuckled at the memory and she winced, imagining the expression on the nurse practitioner's face. "Your leg will be fine, but unfortunately, even with our rapid healing abilities, you'll be stuck in a cast for some time."

Grimacing, she eased herself back against the pillows. Well, at least she was alive. "How's Ryne?"

"He's fine. They removed the bullet and stitched him up. He's resting at the Alpha house right now. In a few days, he'll be as good as new."

She reached for Kane's hand and laced her fingers with his. "And you?"

"I'm good, now that I know you're okay." He stared at her as if memorizing her features then leaned down to give her a slow, warm kiss. She opened to him and revelled in the sense of closeness she now had with him. Everything he was thinking and feeling came rushing at her and all of it was good and comforting, enveloping her in the warmth of his love. He pulled away and she traced his lips with her finger.

"I was so scared." She admitted in a whisper.

"I know. I was, too. But it's all over now. Marla's gone and so is Rose, though I still can't believe she was involved in this."

"I can't either. I wonder why she did it?"

Kane shrugged. "We'll never know. I've talked to her parents. They aren't sure either but wonder if being involved with Marla and her scheme gave Rose a feeling of importance because someone was paying attention to her. It was also a chance to show off how clever she was; that's something we never gave her enough credit for, I guess. Rose was so quiet, no one ever really noticed her. She was just...there. Maybe we're all at fault for ignoring her."

She nodded slowly. "And what about Daniel? I thought he and Rose were starting to become a pair."

"He feels bad and thinks he should have known something was going on, but really, it was a new relationship. The whole thing started before he was even in the picture."

"It will still take him a while to get over this."

"Possibly. We've talked and he's thinking of making a new start."

"A new start? Where?"

315

"With Ryne."

"Ryne is still leaving? Even though his name has been cleared?"

Kane nodded. "I've asked him to stay and told him he could be co-Beta with John—there's certainly enough work around here—but he's not interested and I can see his point."

Biting her lip, she hesitated to ask the next question. She knew she could find out the answer by probing Kane's mind, but felt he needed to say the actual words. "Umm... How do you feel about what happened to Marla?"

His jaw tightened. "It's all my fault. I should have believed what you told me—what everyone tried to tell me over the years—but I guess I didn't want to hear it. In some ways, Marla was like my little sister when we were growing up. Later, I thought there was something else, but it was familiarity and a misplaced sense of responsibility. I know I should be sad that she's gone, but I'm not. The Marla I thought I knew never really existed."

She wanted to ask more questions, but Nadia arrived and shooed Kane outside while she delivered medication, checked Elise's leg, and fixed the dressing on her neck. Nadia was efficient, but in Elise's opinion, had no bedside manner. She endured the woman's fussing by watching Kane through the window. He was talking to someone, she just couldn't see who. From the look on his face, he wasn't pleased.

Hitching herself up in the bed, she earned a scolding from Nadia, but gained a better view of the activity outside. Kane was talking...to Bryan! Uh-oh! And he looked upset. This couldn't be good. She had been sure that since she and Kane now had their mental connection, the rivalry between the two would cease. Apparently, she was wrong. She considered eavesdropping on the conversation but that would be rude. Even though they now had a special bond between them, she believed each of them still deserved some privacy.

After a few more verbal exchanges, Bryan left and Kane stood watching him go, shaking his head. Kane rubbed his neck, staring at the sky and exhaling gustily before turning to re-enter the infirmary. She braced herself for what she might hear. Without even trying, she could sense Kane's mental disquiet. Deciding to grab the proverbial bull by the horns, she broached the subject as soon as he was near.

"I saw you were talking to Bryan. What's wrong?"

Kane glanced towards the window, obviously realizing she'd had a perfect view of their exchange. "You mean you don't already know?" He quirked an eyebrow at her.

"No, I don't already know. Just because we're blood-bonded doesn't mean I'll be constantly tiptoeing through your head." She picked at the blanket covering her and glanced up at him through her lashes.

Sitting down beside the bed, Kane stilled her agitated fingers and gently rubbed his thumb back and forth over her hand. "I know you won't. I was only teasing. And don't worry; I'll try to give you some space, too."

She squeezed his hand, but then lifted her brows in inquiry. "So, you and Bryan?"

"Oh. Bryan. Well, he had some disturbing news. After the...er...fight was over, I carried you here and Bryan helped Ryne. We left the bodies there, planning to return for them later."

She nodded. She'd regained consciousness for that part.

Kane looked away for a moment before speaking. "They've retrieved Rose's body, but..." He paused and then met her eye. "Marla's body is gone."

"What?" She sat bolt upright, then grimaced as her body protested. She paid it no mind however, too shocked at this news. "But she's dead! I know I missed her with the knife, but I landed on her arm—the one with the gun. It bent back against her stomach so that it was pointed directly at her when it went off. I felt her body jerk and suddenly go limp beneath mine..." She gulped as the horror of the moment returned; feeling the kickback of the gun against her stomach, the hot stickiness of blood seeping into her clothing.

"You're right. She did shoot herself, but no one ever checked that she was dead. I was too worried about you, as was Bryan. We assumed..." Kane frowned. "I suppose she must have dragged herself off, but I don't know how far she could have crawled. Bryan says Ryne's having a fit and is determined to head out right now to see if there's still a trail to follow."

"Surely he's in no condition for that?"

"Of course not, but my brother's more than a bit hard-headed and impulsive. I've told Bryan to go out in the morning with a few of my patrols and see what they can find. In the meantime, he's supposed to be trying to talk some sense into his Alpha." Kane snorted. "If Ryne heads out now, he'll probably rip out his stitches and then Nadia will really be on his case. She hates having her handiwork messed up."

She snuck a peak at the stern woman sitting at the far end of the room and figured that the threat of Nadia being upset should be enough to deter anyone.

A week later, Elise was home and sitting in the front room, her leg almost healed. Many times during the past few days, she'd thanked her genetics for the recuperative properties that Lycans possessed. She couldn't imagine how normal humans endured an extended period of time lugging a cast around.

For once Kane wasn't with her, having rarely left her side since their ordeal. However, a meeting with the pack's lawyers had required his presence, and he'd been forced to go into town. She didn't mind. It was nice to have some time to herself. Snow was falling softly outside, and she stared at the scene, letting her mind drift. Tall snow encrusted pines lined one side of the property, casting interesting shadows across the blanket of white fluff. Individual crystals twinkled like diamonds, while lazy snowflakes slowly floated down, only to disappear and lose their identity in the pristine drifts that covered the landscape.

The Mating

It was a beautiful territory to live in and she smiled, reminiscing how only a short while ago she'd thought her life was over when she came here. Now, she couldn't begin to imagine living anywhere else.

Ryne popped into her mind, no doubt due to the fact that he was leaving tomorrow. No sign of Marla had been found much to everyone's frustration, but Ryne vowed to keep an eye out for her and would warn any pack he might come in contact with, as he searched for a new home. Both Bryan and Daniel were accompanying him and she wondered how the three would fare.

She'd miss Bryan of course, but knew their lives were heading down separate paths. Daniel had been very quiet lately; hopefully a new environment would help him come around. And Ryne... She smiled when she thought of him. He was so like Kane, but with a very strange sense of humour. The man was also rough around the edges, at times making her blush with some of his comments. It was all meant in fun however, and she wished she could have longer to get to know her brother-in-law. Still, once he settled somewhere, they'd be able to visit occasionally.

As if he'd known her thoughts, Ryne appeared in the doorway. He was dressed all in black, exuding the same air of confidence and power that Kane did. "Hey, Elise. What are you up to?"

"Nothing much. Just enjoying some quiet time."

"Mind if I join you?"

She patted the spot beside her and he wandered in, his stride fluid and predatory. She loved Kane with her whole heart, but it didn't stop her from admiring the pure male beauty of the man approaching her. With his slightly too long black hair, and piercing blue eyes, broad chest and long legs, the man personified sex appeal. She couldn't stop the smile that appeared on her lips when he sat down beside her.

"You look happy." He commented as he leaned back in the sofa. "What brings that smile to your face?"

Nicky Charles

"You." She laughed at the shocked look on his face. "I was thinking that, next to Kane, you're probably the best looking Lycan I've ever encountered, and here I am with both of you under the same roof."

Quick to regain his composure, Ryne leered at her. "You're lucky that Kane saw you first or I'd be carrying you off with me."

"No, you wouldn't. There's nothing that special about me and you can have your pick of any number of beautiful females. Don't think I haven't noticed how every single girl in the pack has been hanging around here. And you haven't exactly been turning them away, either."

The slightest hint of a flush appeared on Ryne's cheeks and he ducked his head in acknowledgement. "True. But I haven't encouraged any of them. None of them can hold a candle to you."

She folded her arms and gave him a disbelieving look.

"I mean it, Elise. You're special. You have guts. When I think of how you tried to drag yourself through the ravine with a broken leg, and then saved us all from being killed by Marla..." He reached out and brushed a curl from her face, staring deeply into her eyes. "And you're sweet and kind..." His gaze dropped to her mouth and he slowly leaned closer.

A wave of panic washed over her as the attraction built between them. She tried to lean away, but the arm of the couch was preventing her.

"What's going on here?" A rough voice rumbled from the doorway and both turned to see Kane framed in it. He had clenched his hands into fists and was holding them stiffly at his side. His expression was anything but pleased.

"Kane, it's nothing. I was just—" She pushed against Ryne's chest trying to create some space between them. She immediately sent positive thoughts Kane's way in order to reassure him, only to shiver in fear as they bounced off the edge of his mind. Kane was blocking her, and from the look on his face, he was more than a little annoyed.

320

The Mating

"You, I trust." Kane barked the words as he strode into the room. "It's this rogue that I don't."

"What's the matter, Kane? Don't you believe in sharing?" Ryne taunted, getting to his feet and facing his brother.

Oh damn! Her relationship with Kane was finally on solid ground and she didn't want anything to upset it. "Ryne, don't tease him like that! Kane, I don't know why he's behaving this way." Her gaze darted back and forth between the two men.

"Don't you, Elise?" Ryne mocked. "I'm starting a new pack. I need a female and you'd suit me just fine."

Gasping at his boldness, she struggled to her feet and placed herself in between the two, her back firmly pressed to Kane's chest. She could feel it starting to rumble. "But you're his brother; part of the pack. You can't claim a pack member's mate!" She hoped he was joking. There was a glint in his eye, which made her think he simply had a weird and ill-timed sense of humour, but still...

Ryne reached out towards her as if to grab her arm and pull her away from Kane. His gaze was hot, and he seemed intent on having her, no matter what the consequences. Suddenly, he veered his hand off course and flicked the end of her nose. "Gotcha!" He burst out laughing, and then Kane started to chuckle, too.

She looked from one to the other, then put her hands on her hips and scowled. "That was *not* funny!"

"Yes it was." Ryne chuckled. "The look on your face was priceless! I figured life has been pretty quiet around here lately and you needed some excitement."

"Oh you did, did you?" She turned to look at Kane and glowered. "And what's your excuse?"

Kane shrugged and pointed at Ryne. "He made me do it."

"That's right. Two big bad Alphas teaming up and picking on a poor, defenceless female. One who's injured no less! Honestly, if this is how you two behave together, I don't know how this pack ever survived!" She huffed and hobbled out of the room, catching their surprised expressions out of the corner of her eye. Good, she chuckled to herself as she made her way down the hall; let them stew for a while. It serves them right! Making sure her mind was firmly shut to Kane, so he'd have no idea that she wasn't really that upset, she paused outside the kitchen.

Smiling, she reflected how good it felt to be herself again. Ever since she'd mated Kane, her life had been in turmoil and she'd never really known where she stood. She'd been so busy trying to please everyone that she'd lost herself. Joining a new pack had been nerve wracking. Suddenly being a mate—and an Alpha's mate no less—had her stepping into a job that she was ill-prepared to handle. And then, in trying to please Kane, she'd done her best to befriend Marla when she didn't want to and that had certainly ended up a mess! Sighing in relief that it was all behind her now, she pushed the kitchen door open.

Of course, Helen was there as always, preparing the next meal and humming away. She was never happier than when she had an army to feed. Carrie sat in a rocking chair, feeding John Jr. and after greeting everyone, she settled into a nearby chair, watching in envy as the child suckled, his small fist brushing against his mother's breast while he looked up at her with big, blue eyes.

She slowly exhaled, feeling a trifle melancholy. There'd be no baby for her this season.

Looking up, she noticed Helen watching her with knowing eyes that seemed to say 'Don't worry, maybe next time.' She nodded. Possibly it was all for the best. At least now she and Kane had some time together without any danger or drama.

"So," Helen spoke out loud. "Where are the two hooligans?"

"Hooligans?" Elise asked.

"Yes, hooligans. Kane and Ryne."

"Oh, them." Rolling her eyes, Elise explained what had happened.

Helen chuckled. "Reminds me of when they were pups. Those two could come up with some of the most outlandish schemes."

"Yeah, remember when..." Carrie chimed in as she lifted the baby over her shoulder and began to pat his back. Soon all three were laughing as the antics of the two Alphas were related.

"Oh, it's good to have Ryne back." Helen wiped tears of laughter from her face as she leaned against the counter. "He always kept Kane from being too serious."

"And Kane kept Ryne from flying off the handle." Carrie added.

The two men in question chose that minute to enter the kitchen, both looking a little sheepish. Kane spoke first. "Elise, I'm sorry. Our little joke wasn't in the best of taste."

"Yeah, we were teasing. I never thought it might upset you." Ryne added.

Elise tried to look stern but ended up shaking her head and allowing a smile to creep onto her face. "All right. I'll forgive you this time."

Ryne, being the closest, grabbed her and pulled her up into a quick hug, which she returned. Surprisingly, while pulling away, he whispered in her ear. "If you ever get tired of my brother, remember I was only half-joking."

Before she could respond, he passed her over to Kane who enveloped her in a bear hug. Over Kane's shoulder, she saw Ryne watching them with a strange look on his face. When he noticed her, he smiled and winked, then went to invade the cookie jar.

Maybe it isn't such a bad idea that Ryne was leaving after all!

Chapter 36

Ryne had been gone two weeks by the time Elise was totally recovered from her ordeal. The cast had come off the previous week and it had taken another week to get the muscles and joints limbered up again. Now she felt as good as new, and eager to resume a normal life, whatever that might be. She was still planning on working part time at the Grey Goose, but she was also going to help Kane with some of the administrative work in the office. After all, she was the Alpha female and should have some understanding of the ins and outs of the pack's business.

The correct environmental report finally had been obtained and the pack's lawyers were sure the courts would rule in their favour. Once the land was designated as environmentally significant, Northern Oil wouldn't have a leg to stand on. All the water and soil samples had come back clear, and now that Marla wasn't trying to sabotage the pack, Kane had lifted the restrictions on where they were allowed to roam. Everything appeared to be falling nicely into place.

Elise smiled as she reflected on all these things. Standing by the bedroom window, staring out at the peaceful, snow covered landscape, a feeling of contentment welled up inside her. Despite everything that had happened, the pack was united and strong, their land was safe, and Ryne's name had been cleared of all wrong-doing. Most importantly, in her mind at least, she and Kane were still together. Kane had even begun taking her exploring throughout the territory, and she revelled in finally being able to run at his side, his mate both in fact and spirit. He was proudly showing her all his favourite places and explaining his plans to 'christen' several of them once the weather was warmer. Yes, all in all, life was good.

It was approaching midnight, but she hadn't put on the lights, preferring the soothing darkness after the business of the day. They'd celebrated Thanksgiving, the house filled to the rafters with members of the pack. While it had been a fun occasion, quiet was what she now craved.

The door opened behind her and she half turned. Kane stood in the doorway, light from the hallway silhouetting his frame. Once again, she was struck by the power and beauty of her mate. He shut the door blocking the illumination and throwing the room into darkness. Leaving the lights off, he moved unerringly towards her. She waited silently until he stood beside her. As he slid his hands around her waist, she sighed happily and twisted slightly so that she was leaning back against him. He nuzzled her neck, and in response she tilted her head to give him better access.

"Are you tired?" His voice rumbled in her ear, sending shivers down her spine.

"Yeah."

"Oh." He straightened behind her, loosening his grip, disappointment evident in his voice.

She chuckled to herself. Her mate could never get enough of her, not that she was complaining, of course! Turning in the circle of his arms, she slid her hands up his chest, "I'm not *that* tired."

His whole demeanour perked up and he pulled her closer, kissing her tenderly before trailing his lips over her cheeks and brow then down to her ear. "I'm happy to hear that."

"So I noticed." She giggled.

With a growl, Kane walked her backwards to the bed.

Some time later, Kane held her cuddled against his chest, gently playing with her hair by wrapping strands into ringlets then letting them cascade down onto the pillow. Eventually, he whispered into the silence. "Have I told you recently how much I love your hair? The colour is like chocolate and it's so long and silky and..." He buried his nose in it. "It smells like flowers."

"Thanks. It's that new shampoo from the gift set Ryne gave me."

Kane stilled and drew back, staring at her. "Ryne?"

She yawned and stretched. "Uh-huh. You remember. He sent it to me as a late birthday present. It had shampoo and lotions and—"

"Oh. Right." Kane interrupted, sounding slightly miffed. He rolled onto his back. "I still don't think it was an appropriate gift." Disapproval radiated from him and she tried to keep her face expressionless. For all that he and Ryne had been joking that last day, there was still an undercurrent of jealousy between the two males, which she found rather entertaining. Ryne was a great tease and she was sure he'd never do anything to jeopardize her relationship with Kane. At least she hoped so...

"It was very kind of him and I didn't appreciate you trying to throw it out." She rolled onto her side as she scolded him, softening her words by trailing her fingers gently down his chest. Kane just rumbled, neither agreeing nor disagreeing.

After another moment of silence, he sighed. "He called today."

"Really?" She raised herself up on her elbow, looking at him in surprise.

"Yeah. He's headed for Canada. There's this little town in Northern Ontario that apparently has no established pack."

"Wow! That's quite a distance away. We won't be able to see him very often." She settled back down on her pillow and stared thoughtfully at the ceiling.

"Uh-huh." Kane rolled onto his side.

"Kane, that's not very nice." Even without looking, she knew he was smiling.

"What?"

"Sounding so pleased that Ryne will be living far away. He is your brother, after all."

"I know, and I have only the warmest of brotherly feelings for him. I think that, until he gets a mate of his own, we'll get along a lot better if there's some distance between us."

She said nothing, but turned her head towards him, and gave him a doubtful stare.

"Elise?" He looked at her with a pleading, puppy-dog expression in his eyes.

"Yes?"

"I love you."

Her heart melted and she rolled over so that she was on top of him. "I love you, too," she said as she leaned down to kiss him. As he caressed her back with his hands, bringing her into even closer contact with his body, she couldn't help but smile. Who would have thought the mating she had so dreaded would have turned out this way?

Epilogue

Somewhere in Northern Ontario...

Ryne shifted the truck into park and stared at the old farm house. Its clapboard siding was grey and weather-worn, the roof looked like it had seen better days and the porch was on the verge of collapse. Using the interior light of the vehicle, he checked the paper in his hand and then peered at the house number. No mistake. This was the place. He elbowed the man beside him.

"Come on, Bryan, Daniel—wake up. We're here." As the two men groaned and stretched, Ryne stepped out and looked around. He inhaled deeply, appreciating the smell of pine that overlaid the cool, crisp air. A faint smile creased his face as he viewed the land around him, totally ignoring the weed infested lawn, overgrown shrubbery and cracked driveway. All he saw was the wooded land around him. Yep, this was going to be his territory.

Chicago, Illinois, USA...

Far away, in a richly furnished room somewhere on the outskirts of the city, an elderly man was admiring his new acquisition. Standing in front of the fireplace he stared at the large picture of a magnificent black wolf that his man had just hung on the wall above the mantel. The corner of his mouth curled upward and he nodded in satisfaction. His years of searching had finally paid off. This was exactly what he'd been looking for.

~**FIN**~

A Message from Nicky Charles

Hi!

Thank you for taking the time to read my story. I hope you enjoyed it. If so, you might be interested to know it is now available in audio!

The Mating started out as a one-chapter story but response from readers was so positive that I turned it into a novel. The characters in this book have since inspired numerous other tales which are collectively known as The Law of the Lycans series.

~ Nicky

Connect with Nicky Charles

Email me at
nicky.charles@live.ca

Visit my website:
http://www.nickycharles.com

Follow me on Facebook:
https://www.facebook.com/NickyCharles/

Books by Nicky Charles

Forever In Time

Law of the Lycans series

The Mating
The Keeping
The Finding
Bonded
Betrayed: Days of the Rogue
Betrayed: Book 2 – The Road to Redemption
For the Good of All
Deceit can be Deadly
Kane: I am Alpha
Veil of Lies

Hearts & Halos Series
(Written with Jan Gordon)
In the Cards
Untried Heart

CPSIA information can be obtained
at www.ICGtesting.com
Printed in the USA
BVHW062303131021
618892BV00020B/1173